THE MYSTERY AT THE OLD RANCHO

KIM

D0950659

SURFSIDE GIRLS: THE MYSTERY AT THE OLD RANCHO © 2019 Kim Dwinell.

ISBN: 978-1-60309-447-4   22 21 20 19   1 2 3 4

Published by Top Shelf Productions, PO Box 1282, Marietta, GA 30061-1282, USA. Top Shelf Productions is an imprint of IDW Publishing, a division of Idea and Design Works, LLC. Offices: 2765 Truxtun Road, San Diego, CA 92106. Top Shelf Productions®, the Top Shelf logo, Idea and Design Works®, and the IDW logo are registered trademarks of Idea and Design Works, LLC. All Rights Reserved. With the exception of small excerpts of artwork used for review purposes, none of the contents of this publication may be reprinted without the permission of IDW Publishing. IDW Publishing does not read or accept unsolicited submissions of ideas, stories, or artwork.

Editor-in-Chief: Chris Staros.
Edited by Chris Staros and Zac Boone.
Designed by Gilberto Lazcano.
Surfside Girls Logo design by Chris Ross.
Visit our online catalog at www.topshelfcomix.com.

Printed in Korea.

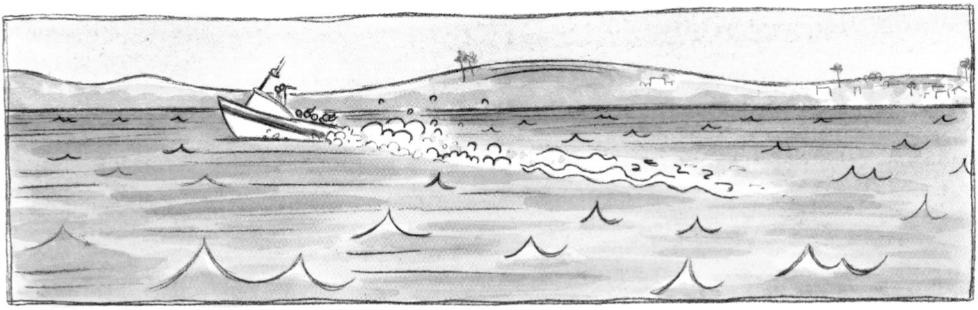

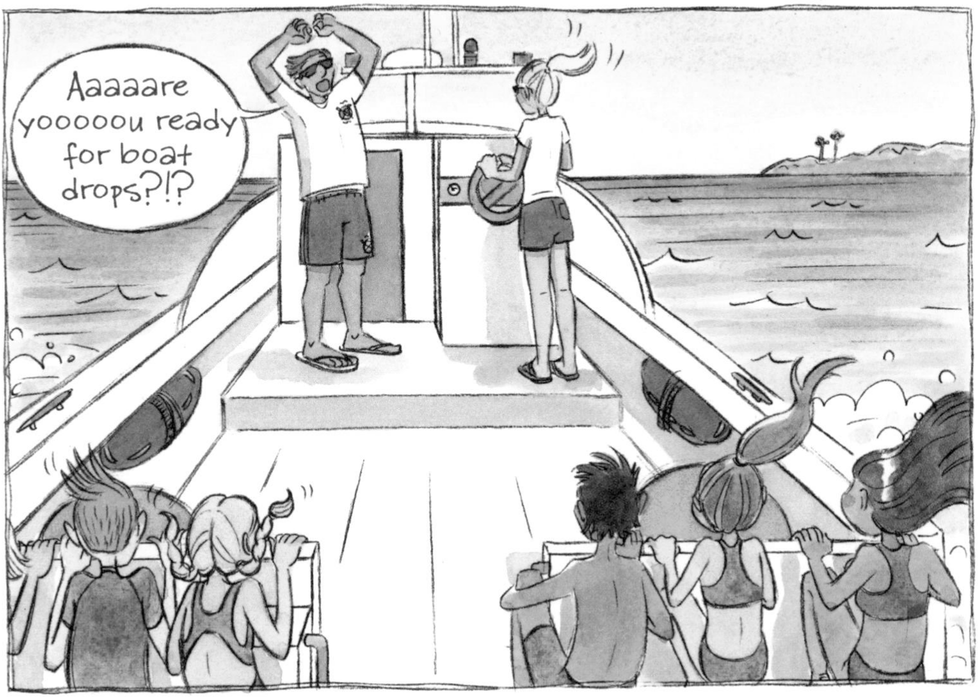

Aaaaare yoooooou ready for boat drops?!?

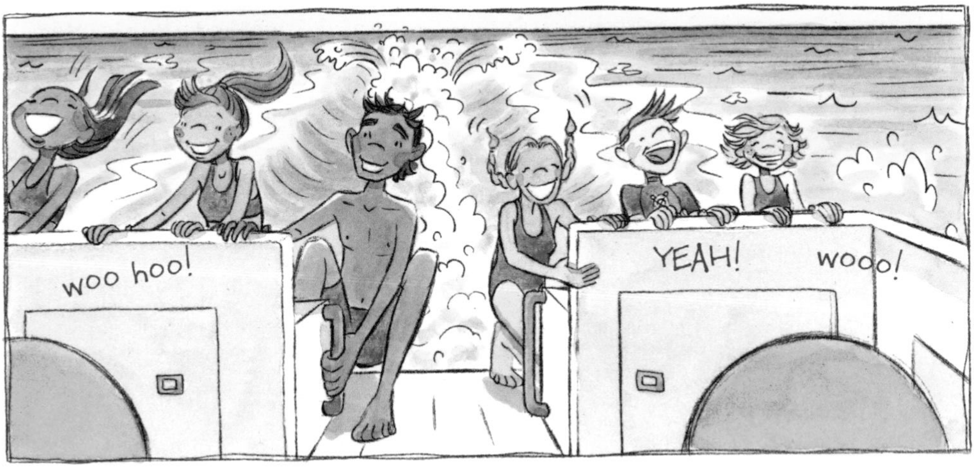

woo hoo!
YEAH!
wooo!

First up...
GO!

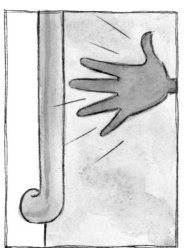

wooo!

You're up, Sam.

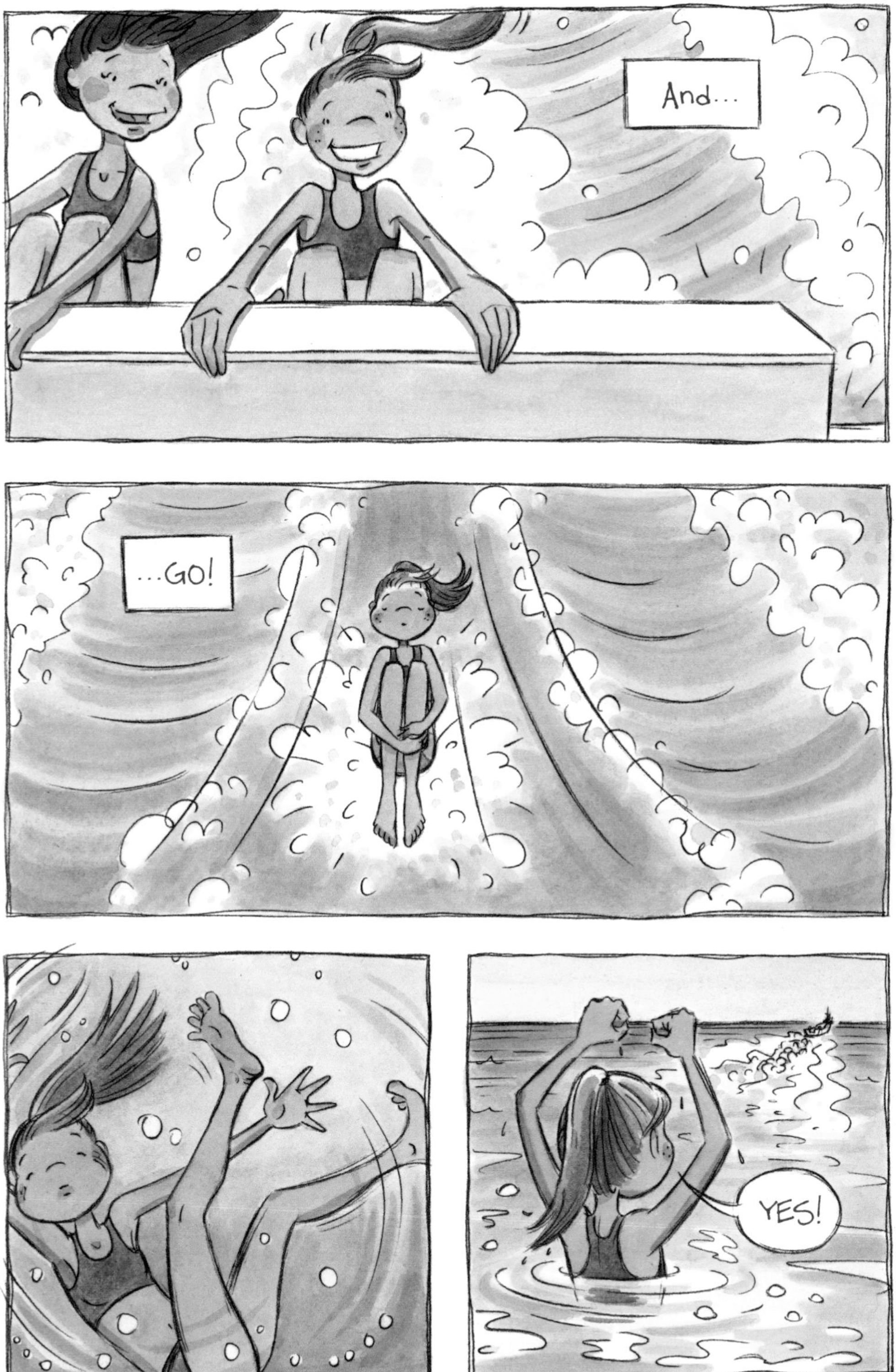
And...
...GO!
YES!

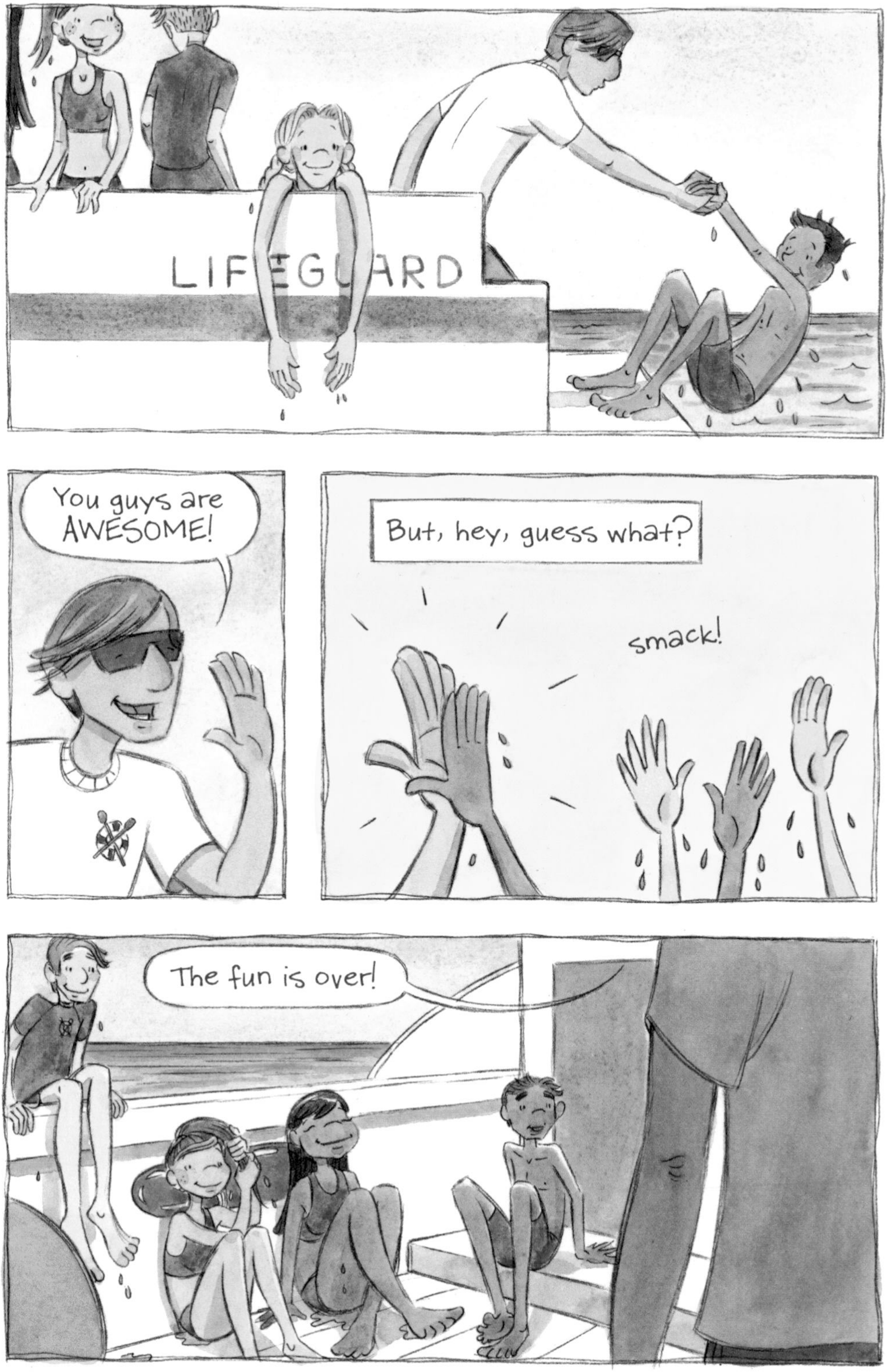
LIFEGUARD
You guys are AWESOME!
But, hey, guess what?
smack!
The fun is over!

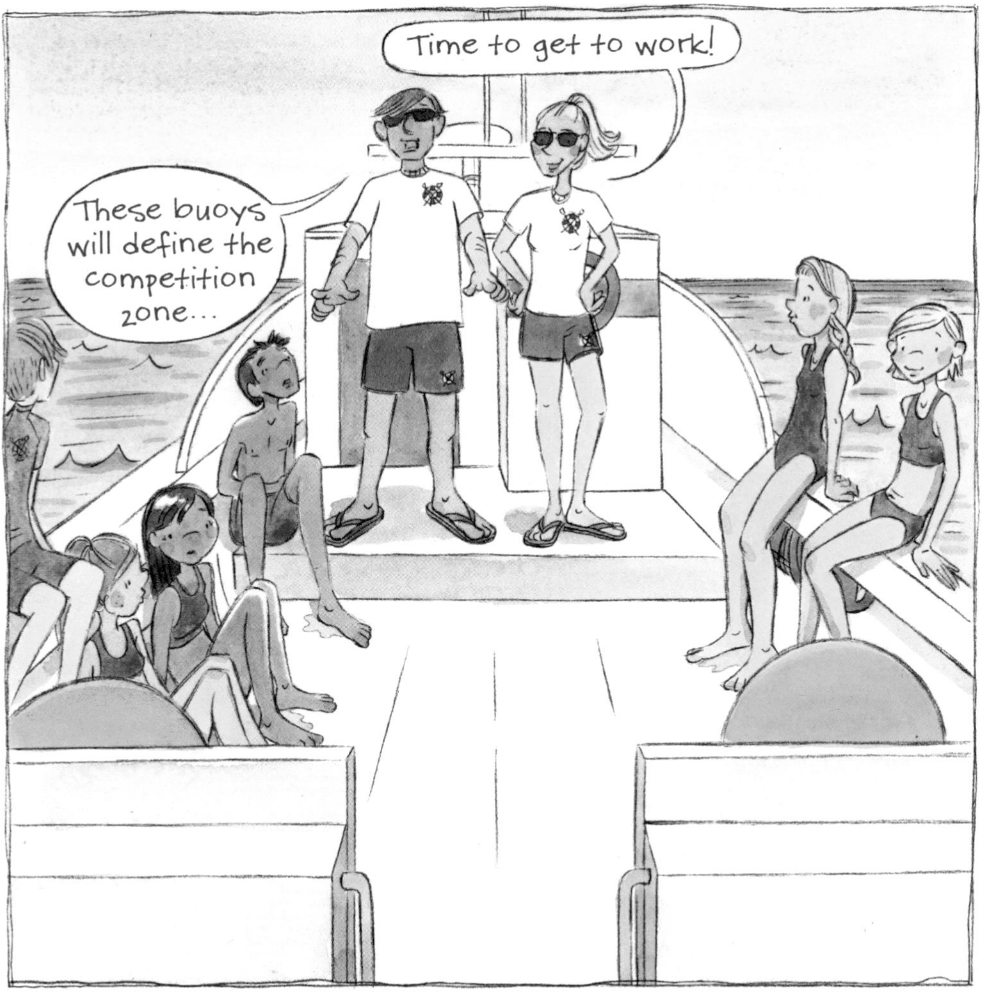
Time to get to work!
These buoys will define the competition zone...
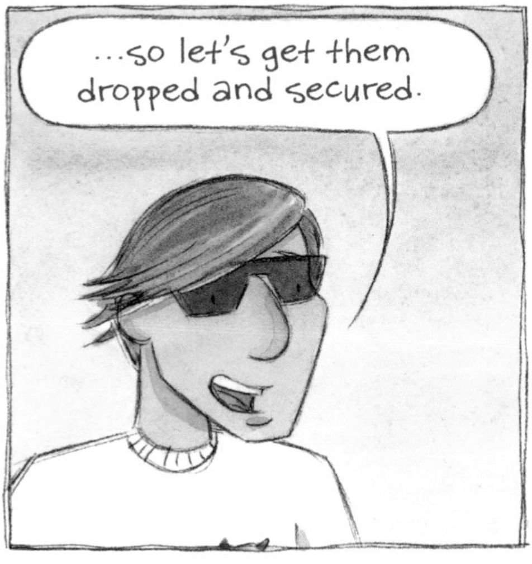
...so let's get them dropped and secured.
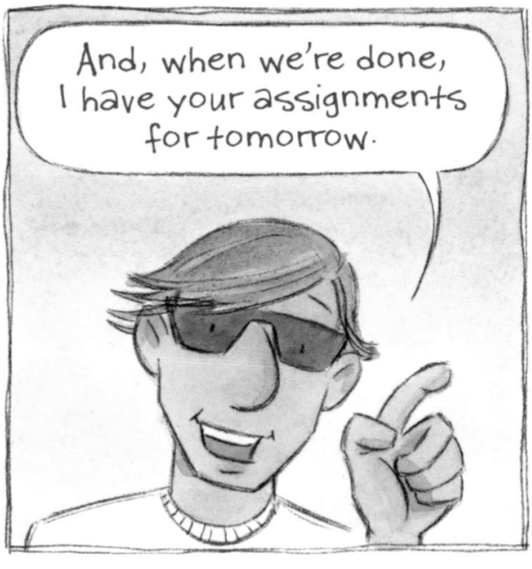
And, when we're done, I have your assignments for tomorrow.

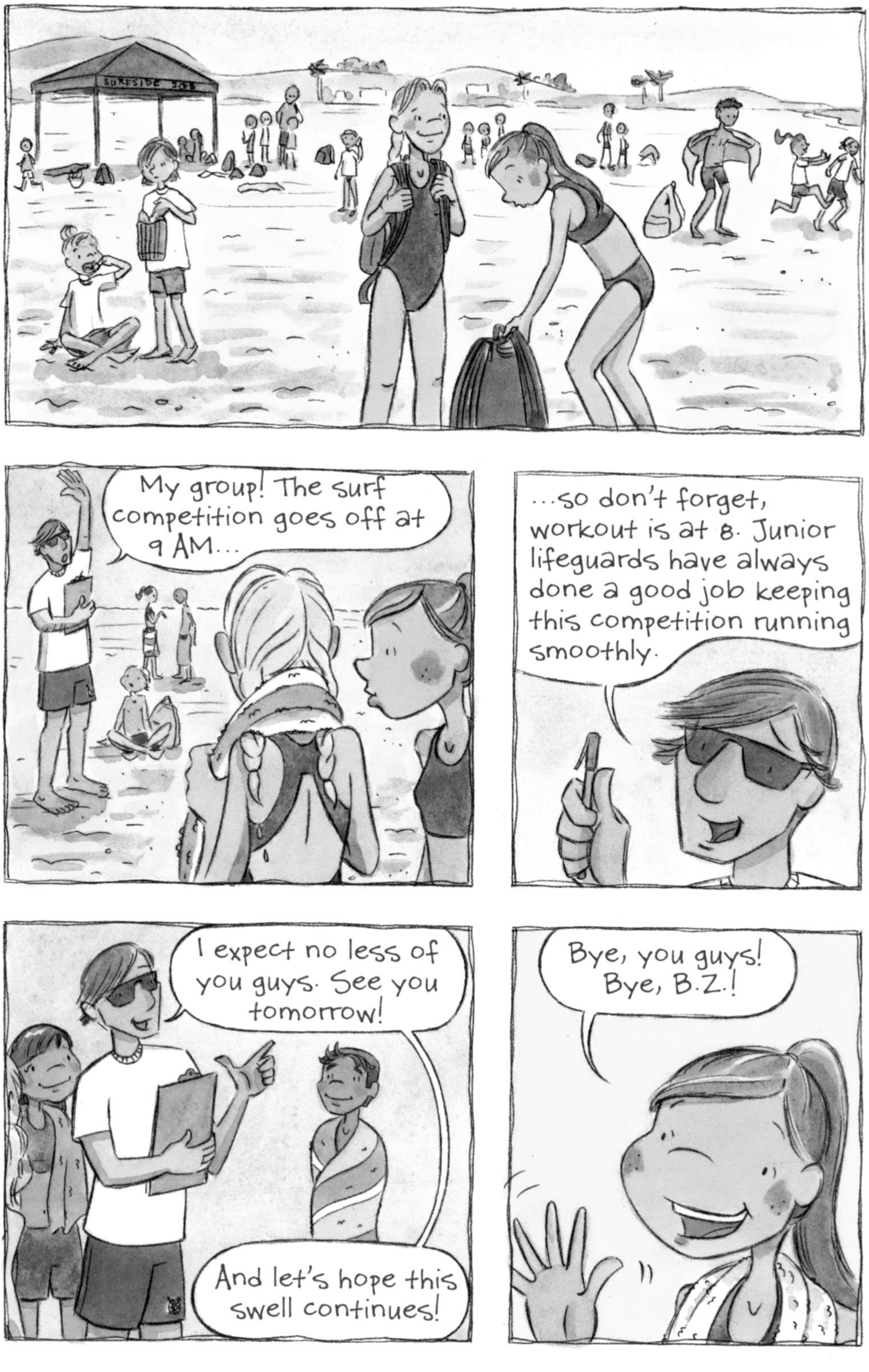
SURFSIDE JGS
My group! The surf competition goes off at 9 AM...
...so don't forget, workout is at 8. Junior lifeguards have always done a good job keeping this competition running smoothly.
I expect no less of you guys. See you tomorrow!
And let's hope this swell continues!
Bye, you guys! Bye, B.Z.!

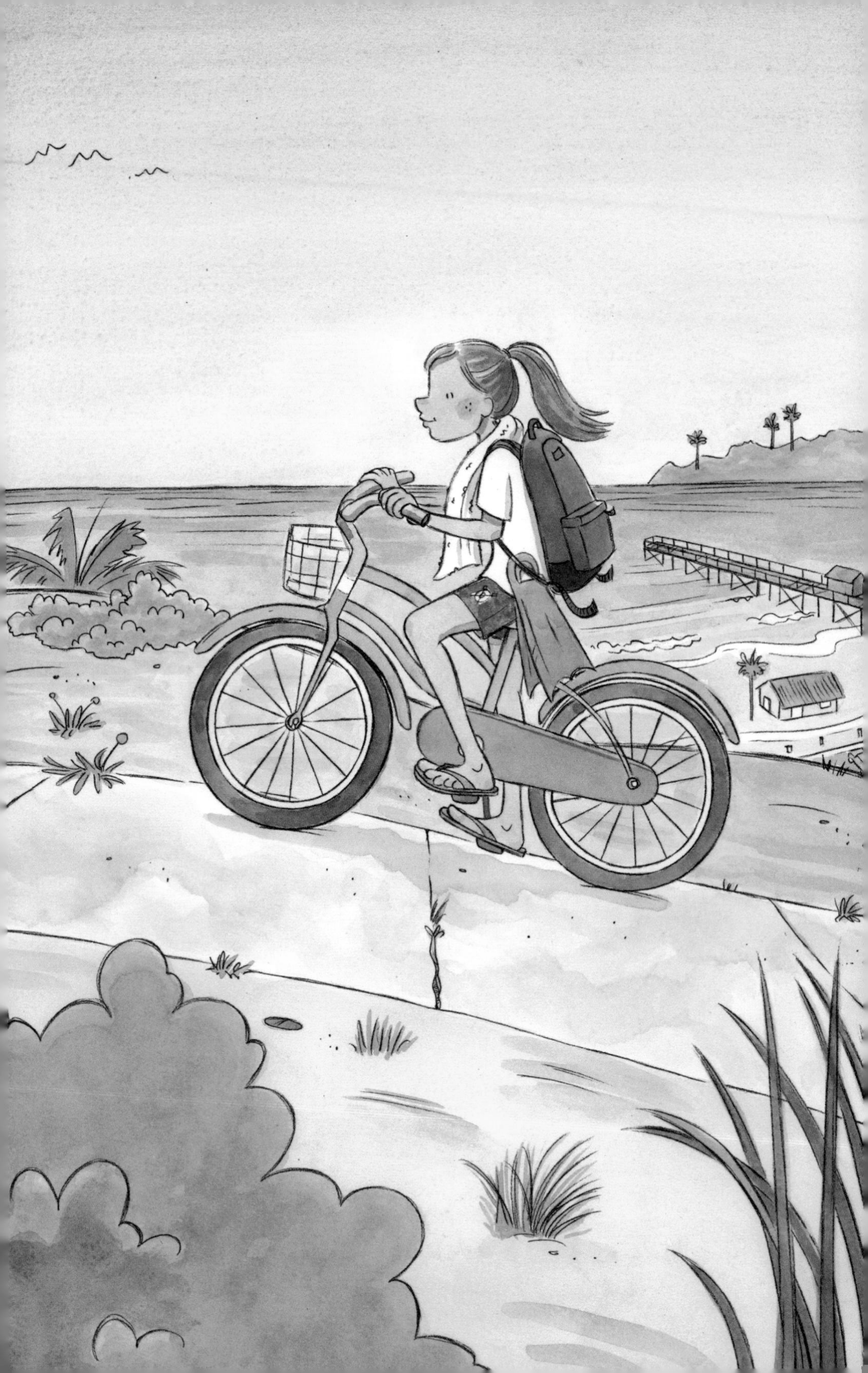

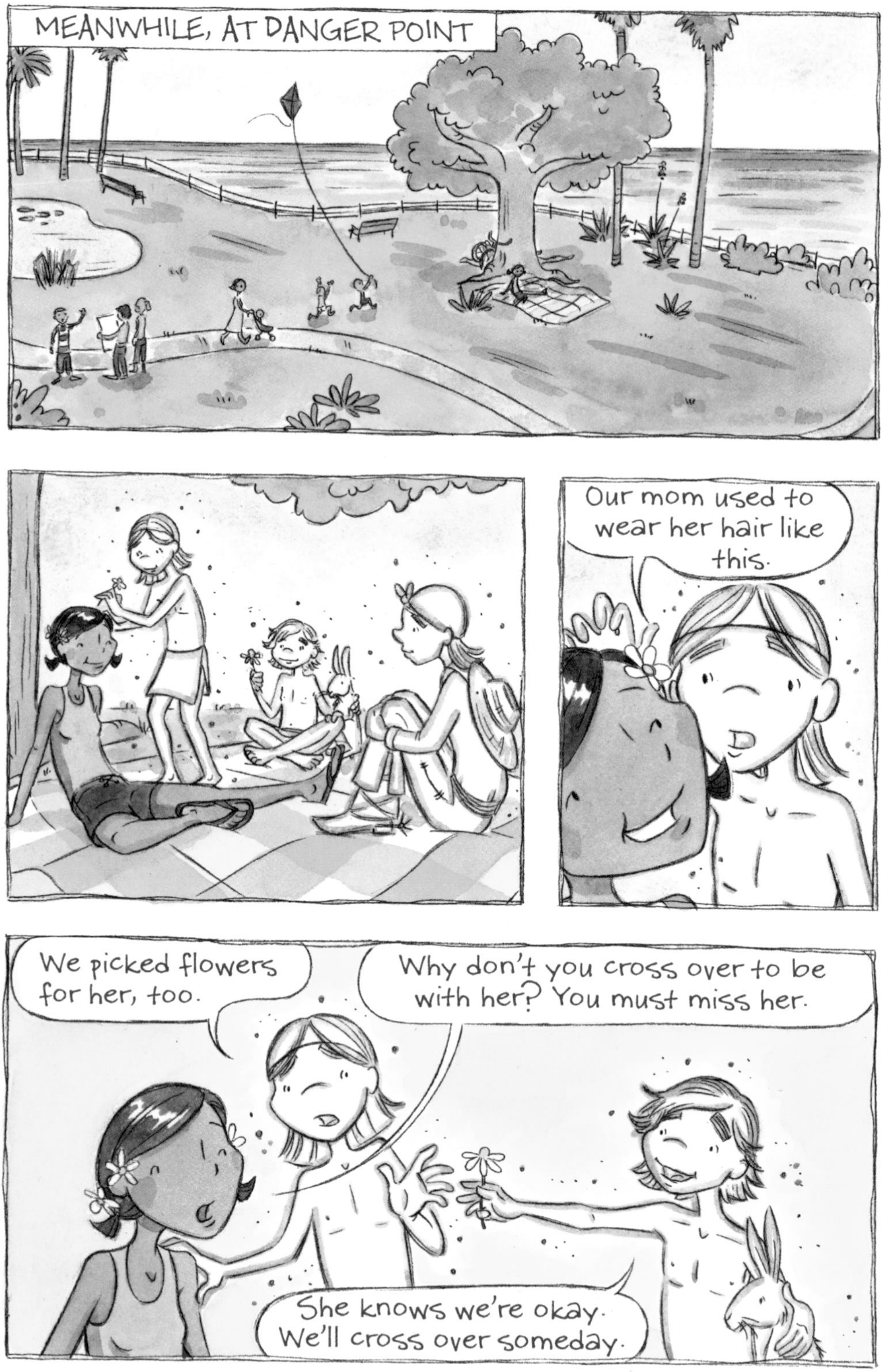
MEANWHILE, AT DANGER POINT
Our mom used to wear her hair like this.
We picked flowers for her, too.
Why don't you cross over to be with her? You must miss her.
She knows we're okay. We'll cross over someday.

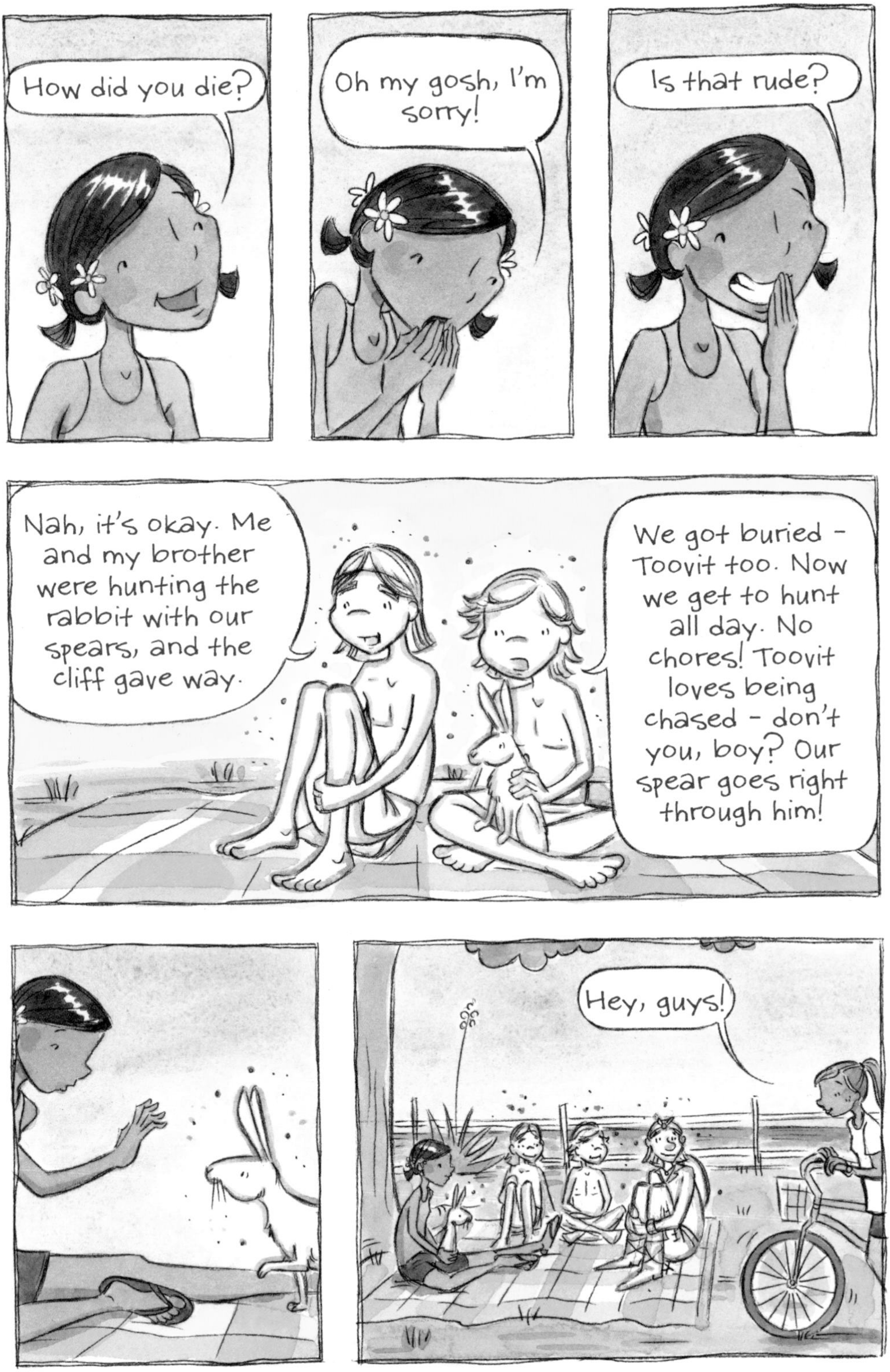
How did you die?
Oh my gosh, I'm sorry!
Is that rude?
Nah, it's okay. Me and my brother were hunting the rabbit with our spears, and the cliff gave way.
We got buried - Toovit too. Now we get to hunt all day. No chores! Toovit loves being chased - don't you, boy? Our spear goes right through him!
Hey, guys!

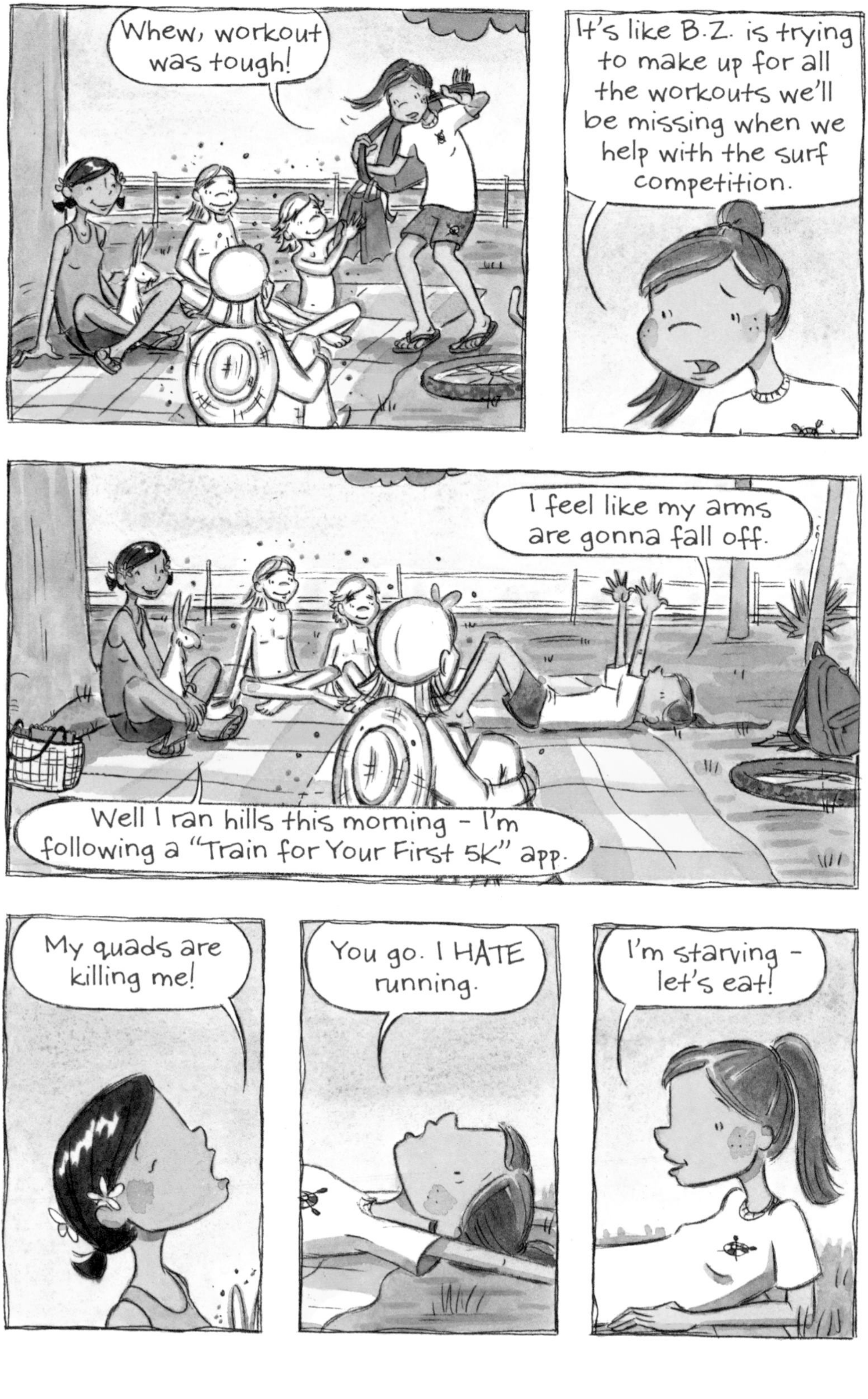
Whew, workout was tough!
It's like B.Z. is trying to make up for all the workouts we'll be missing when we help with the surf competition.
I feel like my arms are gonna fall off.
Well I ran hills this morning – I'm following a "Train for Your First 5K" app.
My quads are killing me!
You go. I HATE running.
I'm starving – let's eat!

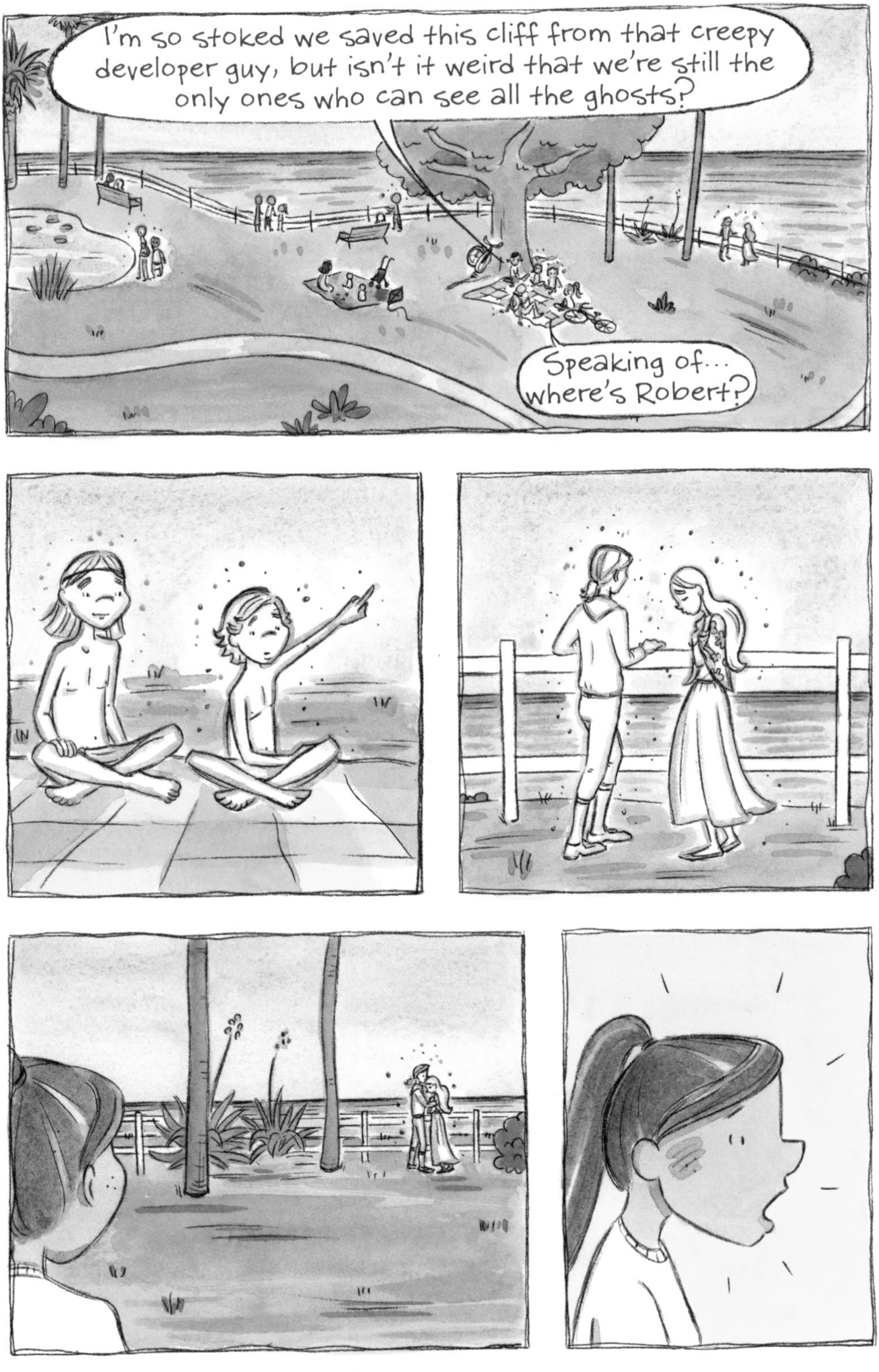
I'm so stoked we saved this cliff from that creepy developer guy, but isn't it weird that we're still the only ones who can see all the ghosts?
Speaking of... where's Robert?

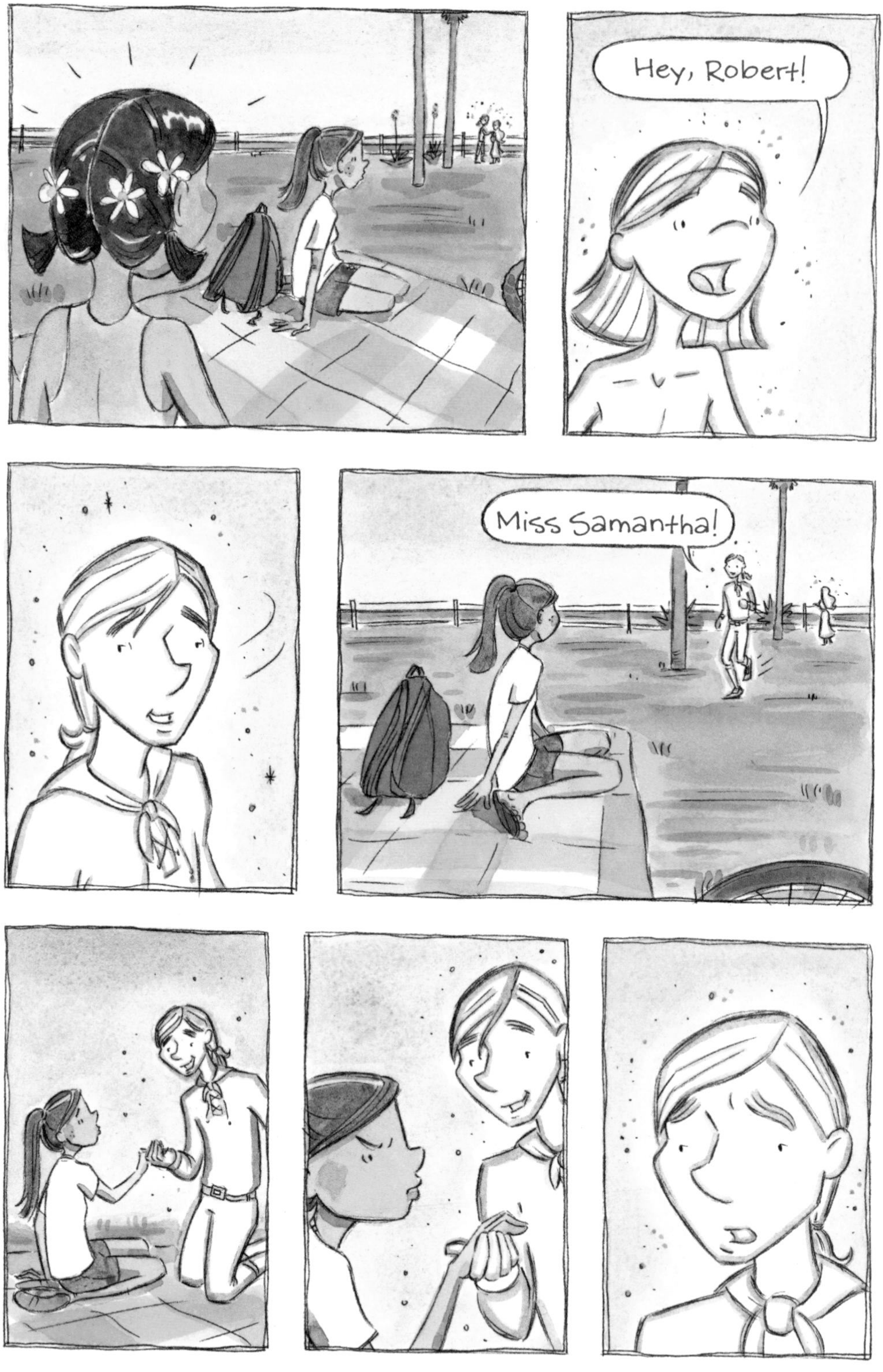
Hey, Robert!
Miss Samantha!

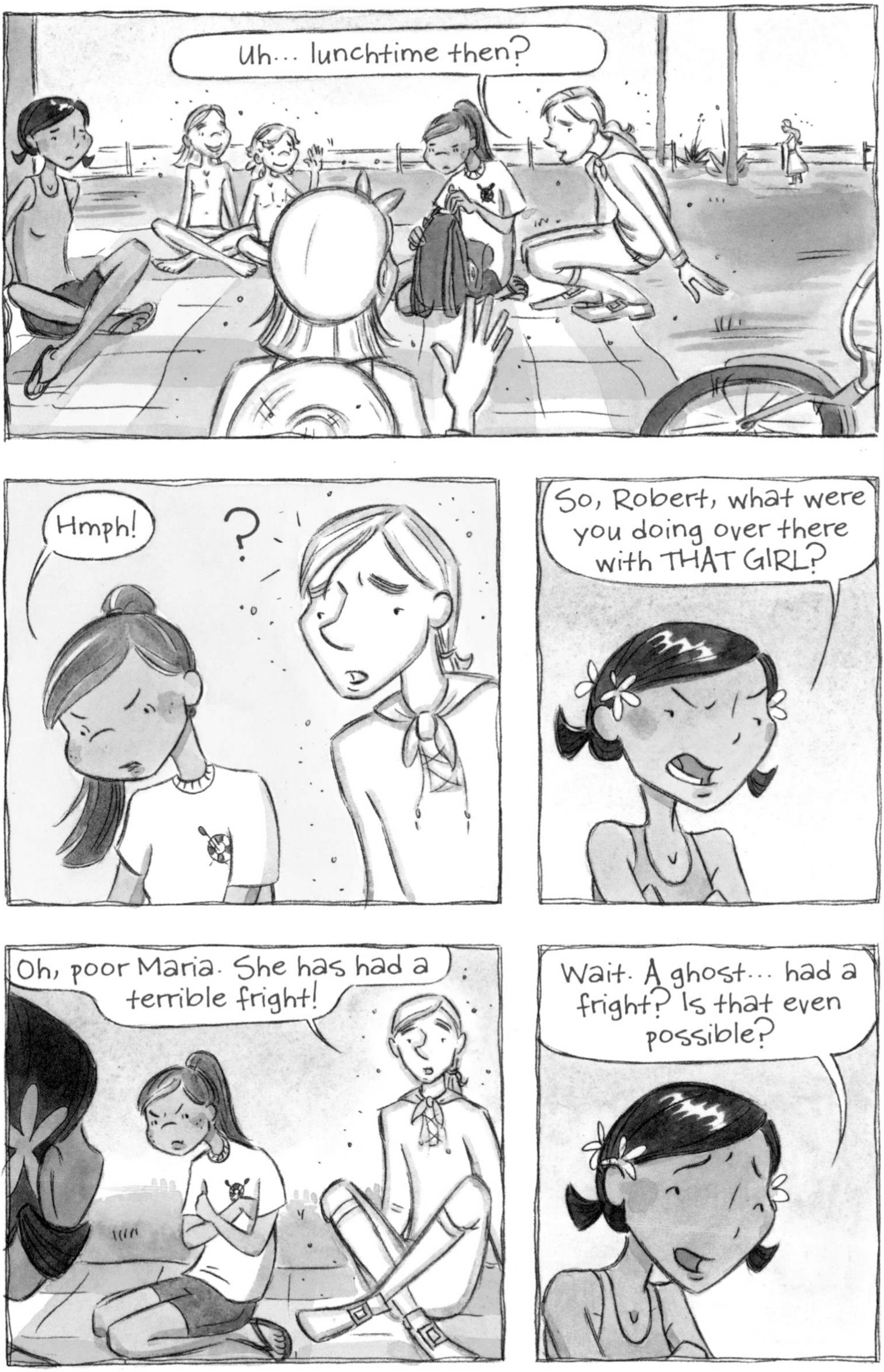
Uh... lunchtime then?
Hmph!
?
So, Robert, what were you doing over there with THAT GIRL?
Oh, poor Maria. She has had a terrible fright!
Wait. A ghost... had a fright? Is that even possible?

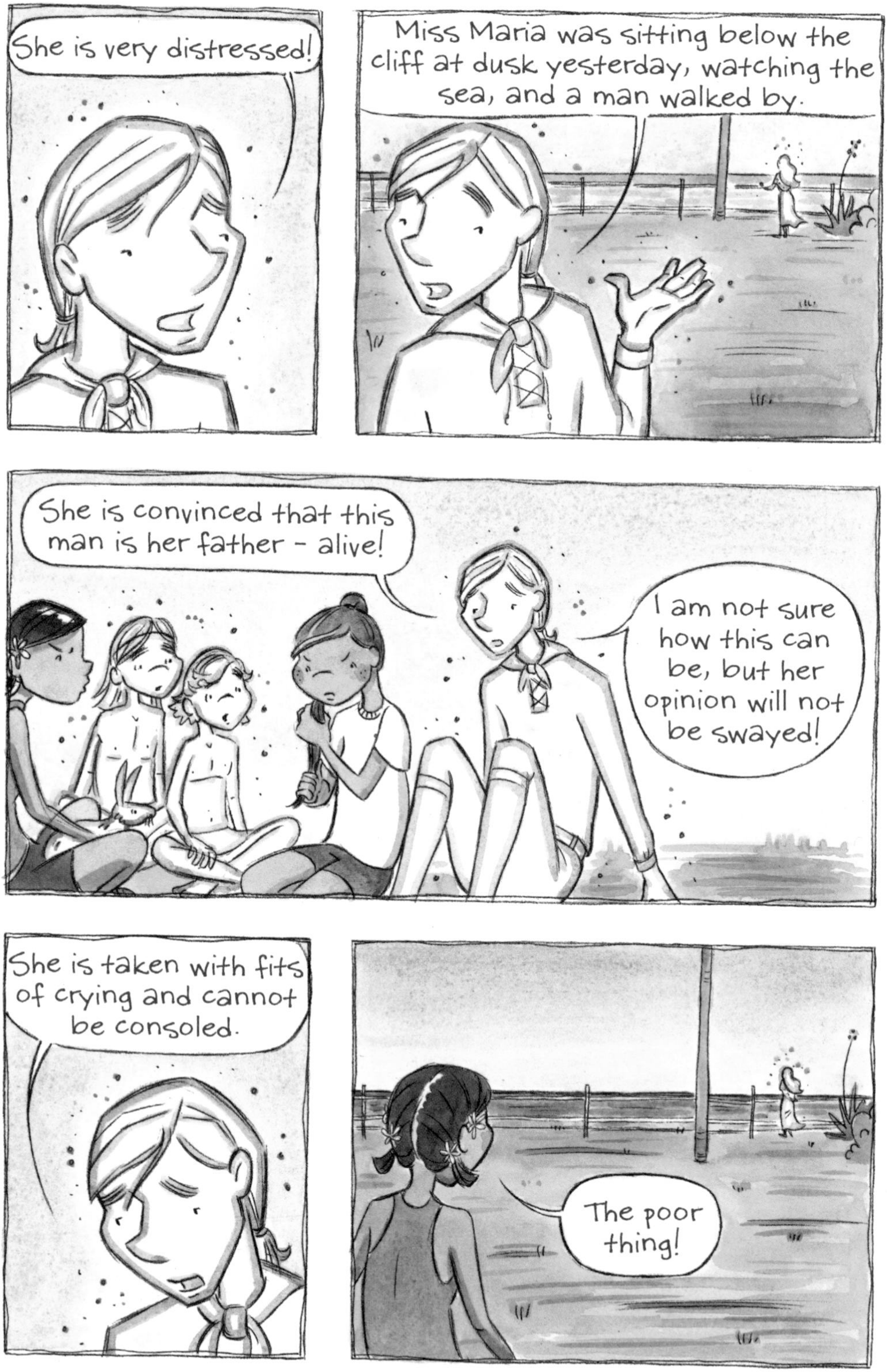
She is very distressed!
Miss Maria was sitting below the cliff at dusk yesterday, watching the sea, and a man walked by.
She is convinced that this man is her father - alive!
I am not sure how this can be, but her opinion will not be swayed!
She is taken with fits of crying and cannot be consoled.
The poor thing!

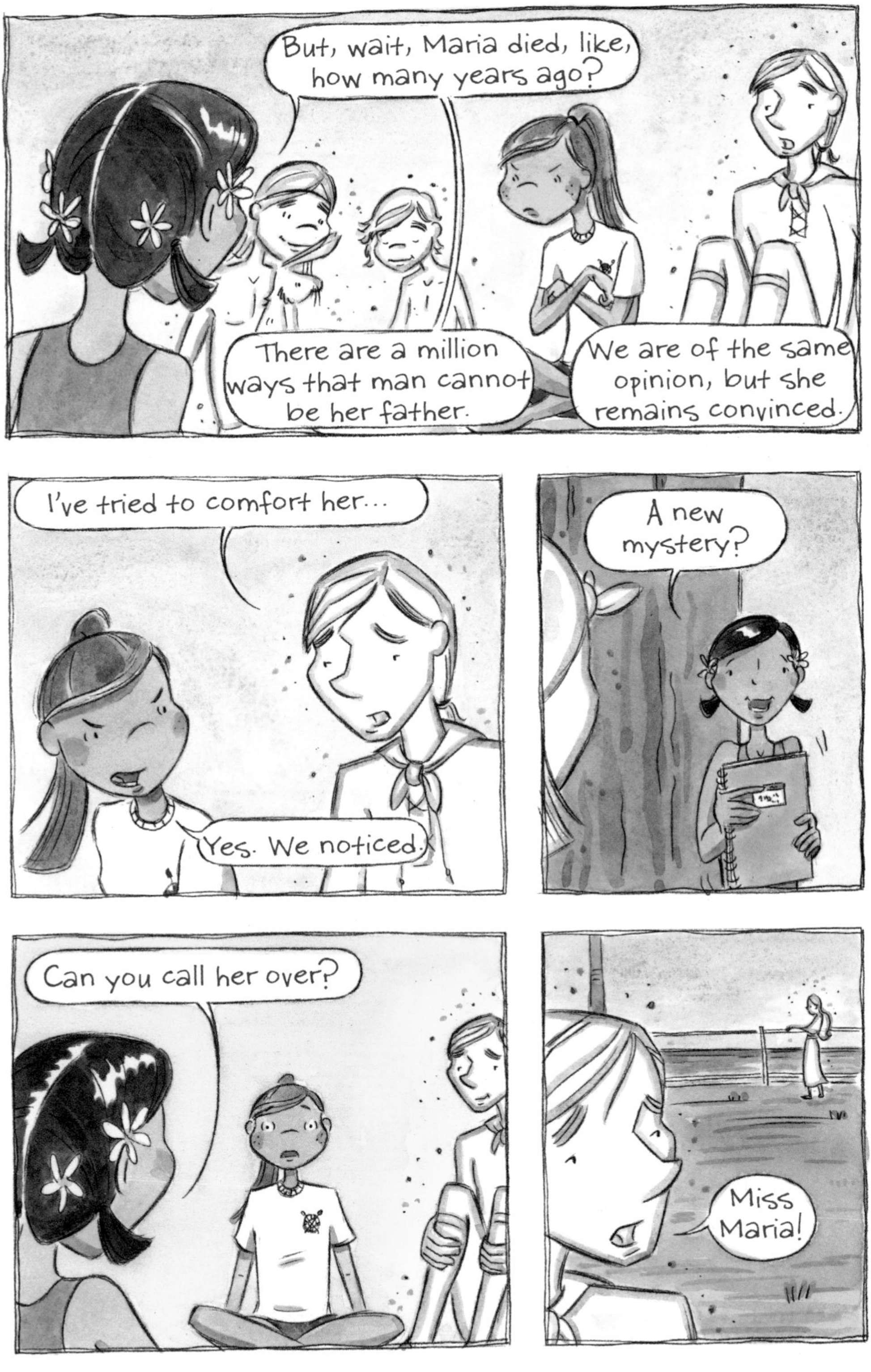

But, wait, Maria died, like, how many years ago?
There are a million ways that man cannot be her father.
We are of the same opinion, but she remains convinced.
I've tried to comfort her...
Yes. We noticed.
A new mystery?
Can you call her over?
Miss Maria!

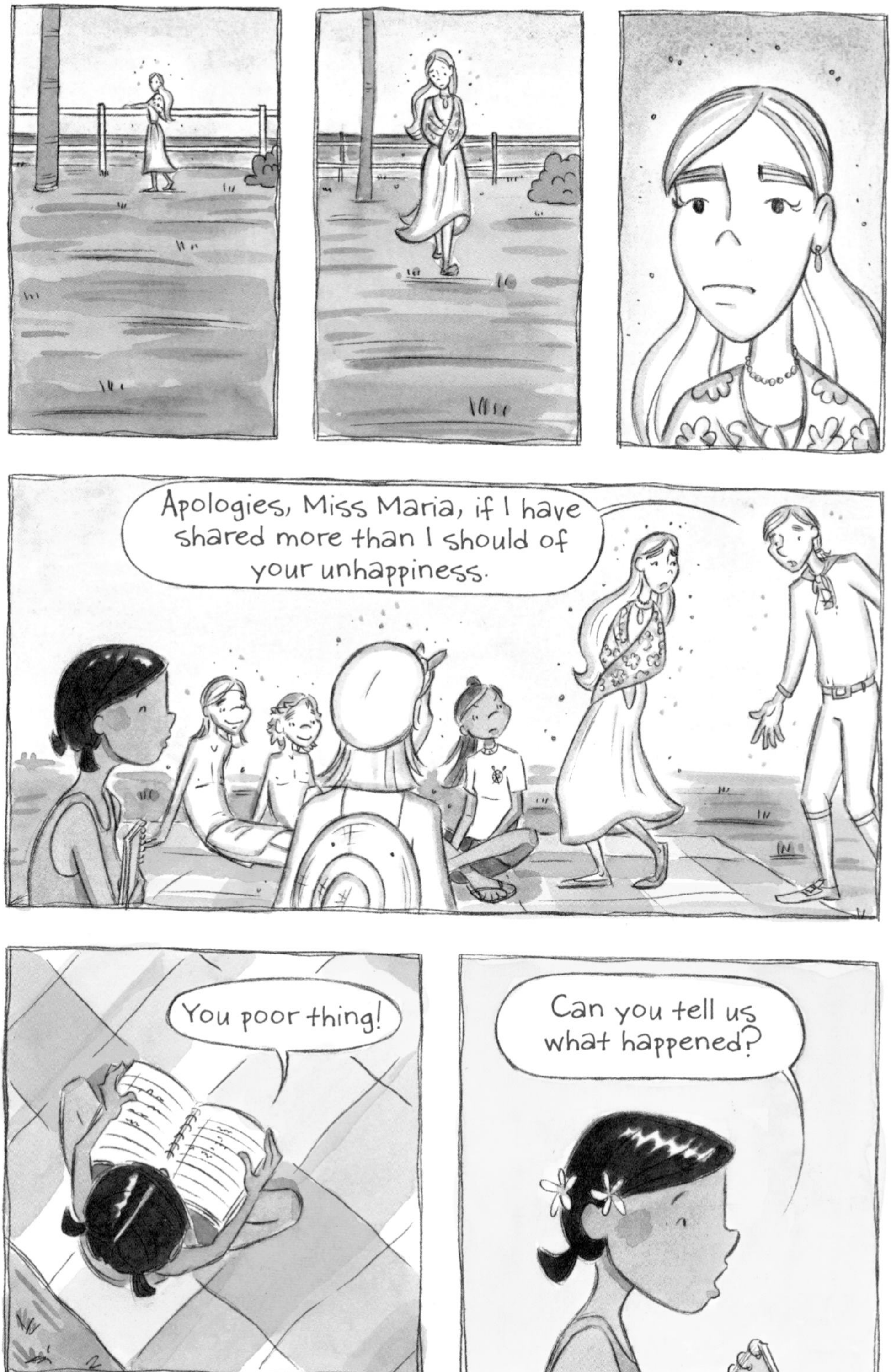
Apologies, Miss Maria, if I have shared more than I should of your unhappiness.
You poor thing!
Can you tell us what happened?

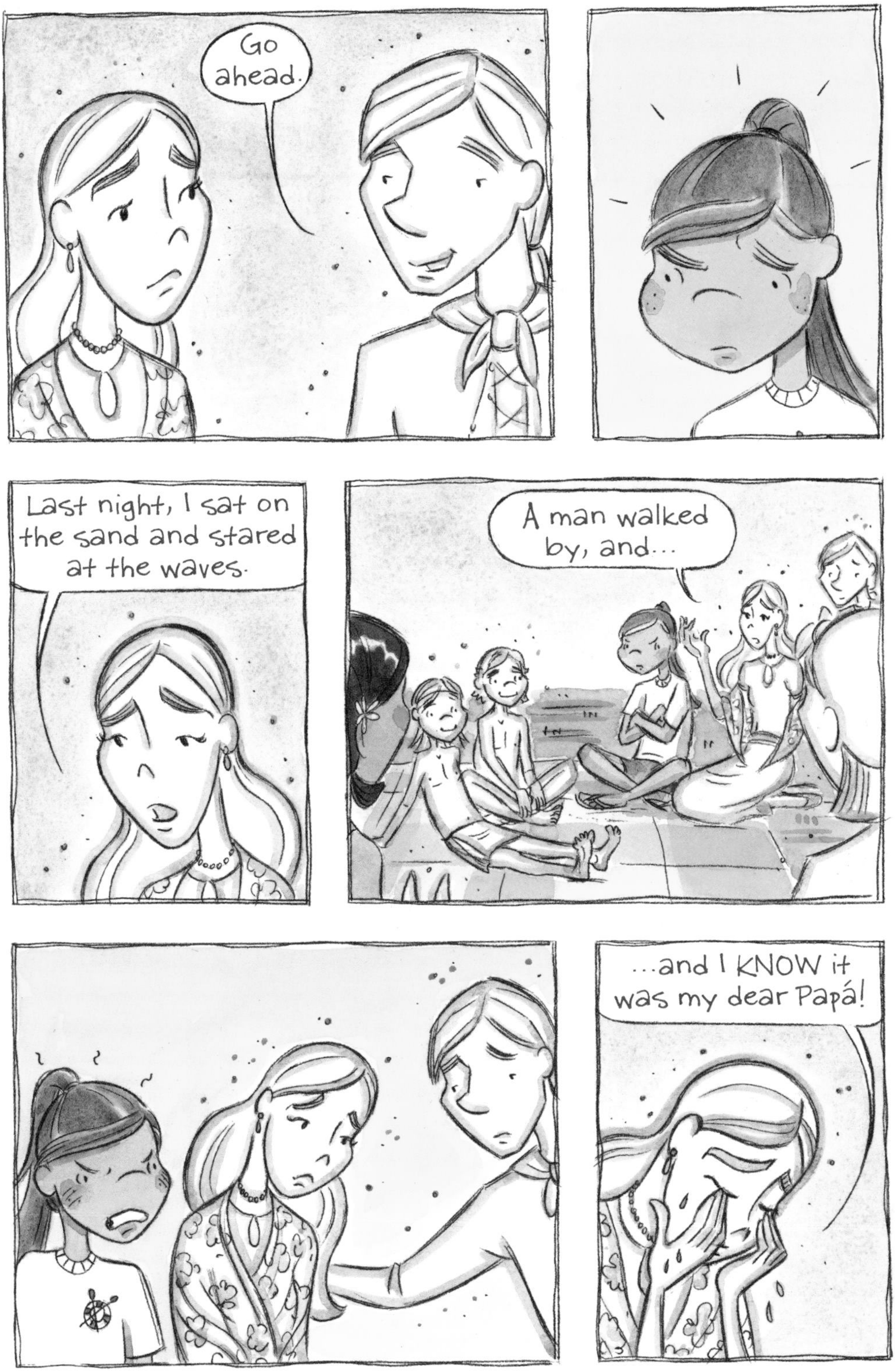
Go ahead.
Last night, I sat on the sand and stared at the waves.
A man walked by, and...
...and I KNOW it was my dear Papá!

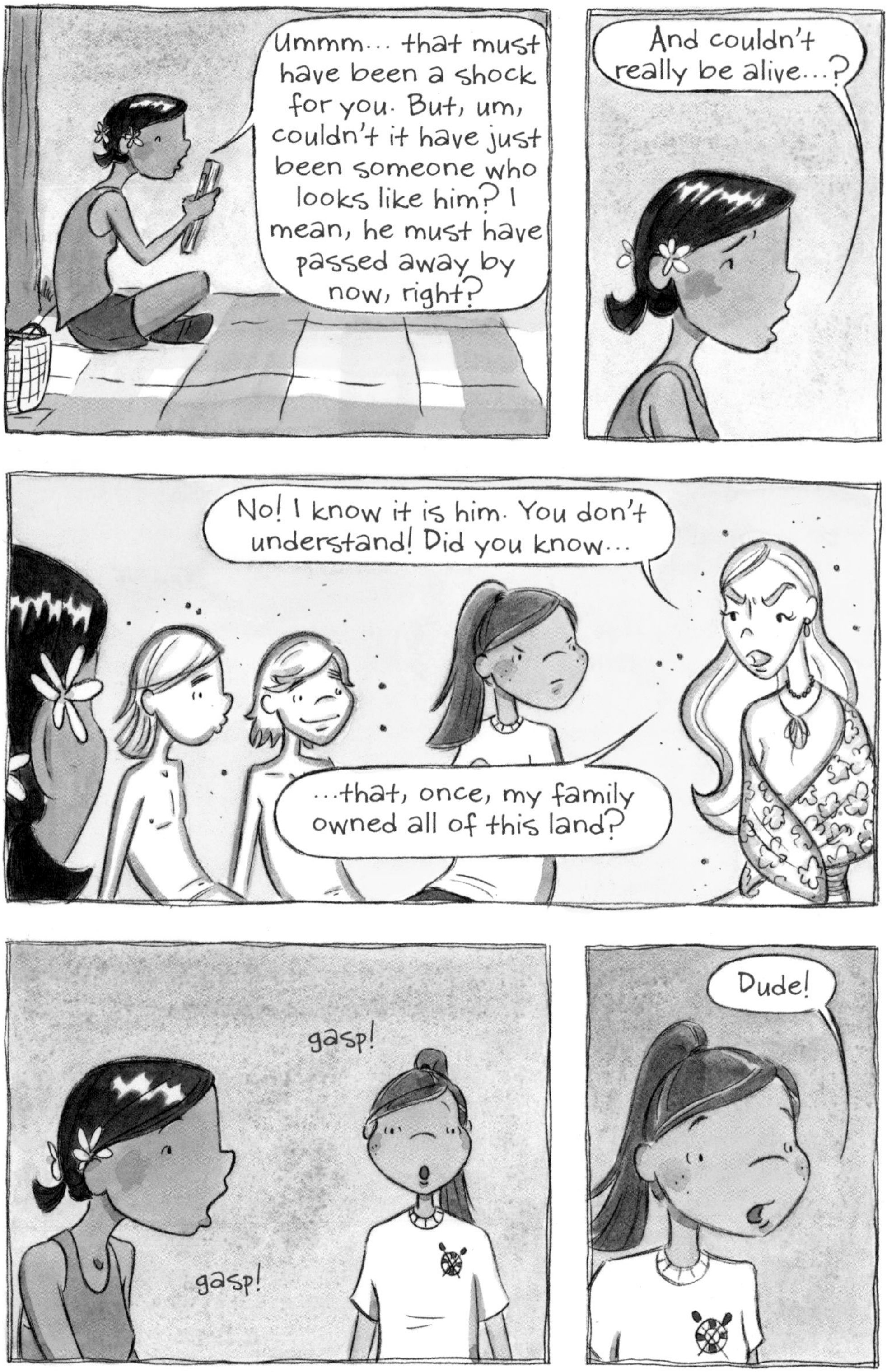
Ummm... that must have been a shock for you. But, um, couldn't it have just been someone who looks like him? I mean, he must have passed away by now, right?
And couldn't really be alive...?
No! I know it is him. You don't understand! Did you know...
...that, once, my family owned all of this land?
gasp!
gasp!
Dude!

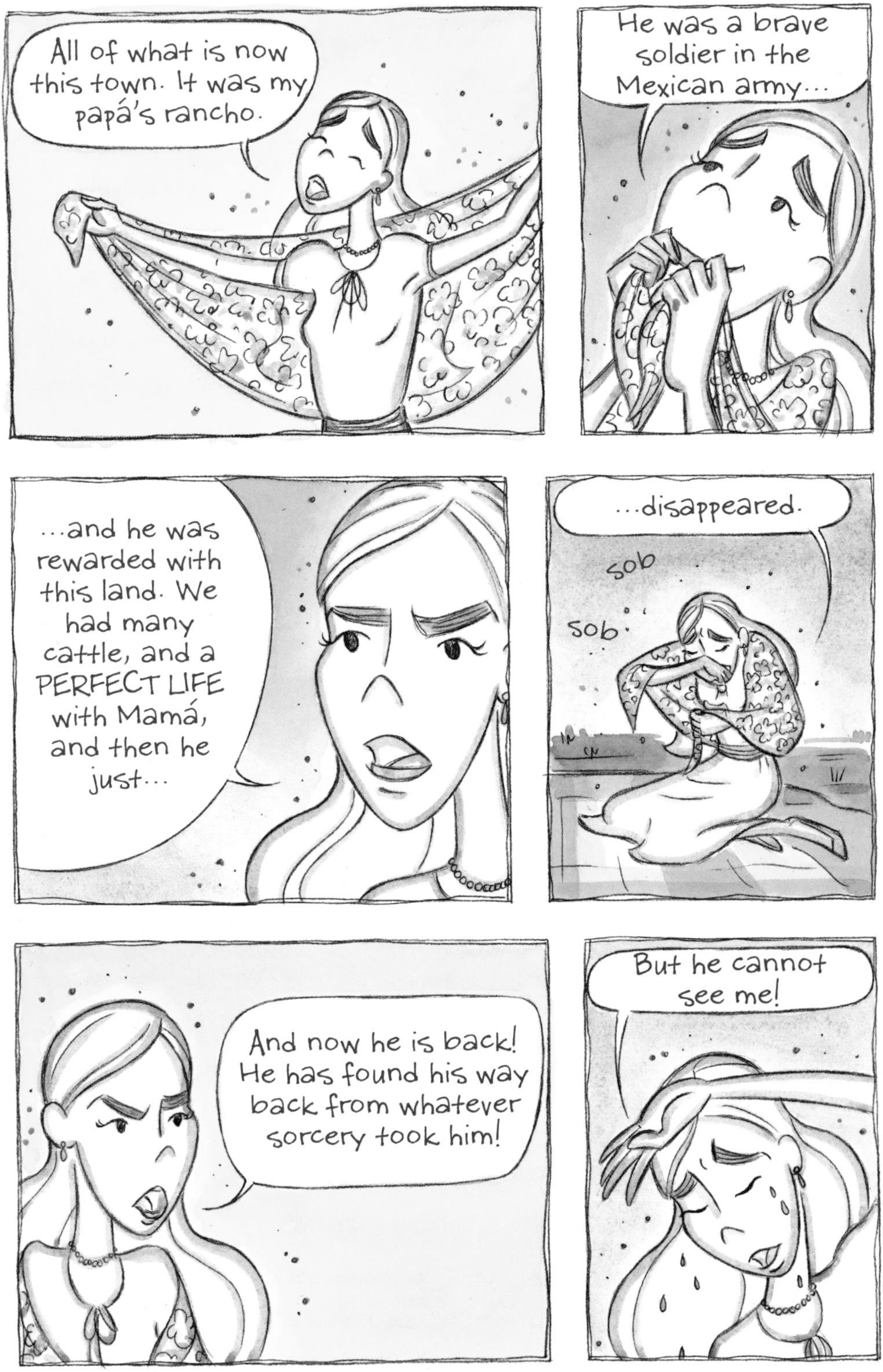
All of what is now this town. It was my papá's rancho.
He was a brave soldier in the Mexican army...
...and he was rewarded with this land. We had many cattle, and a PERFECT LIFE with Mamá, and then he just...
...disappeared.
sob
sob
And now he is back! He has found his way back from whatever sorcery took him!
But he cannot see me!

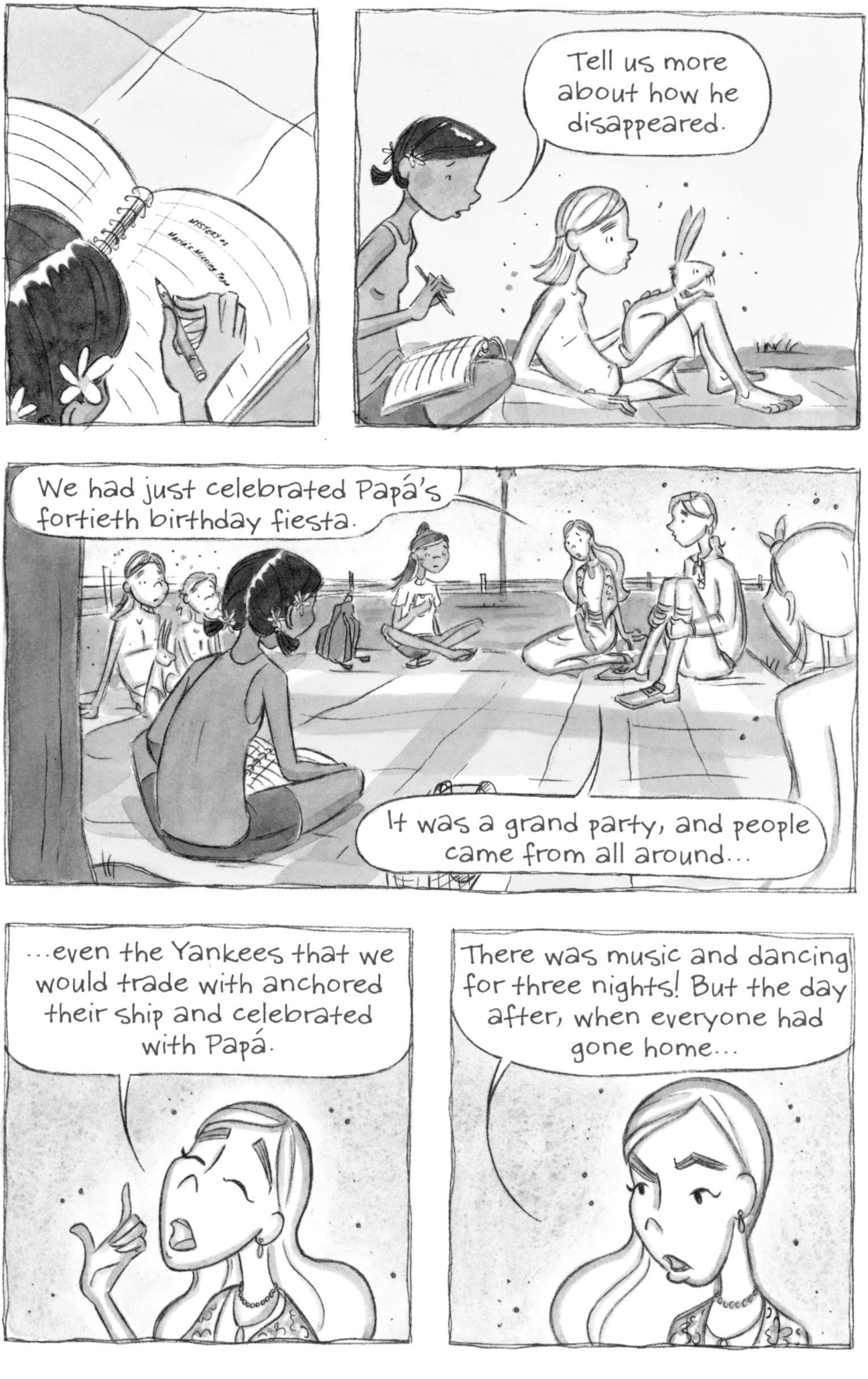
MYSTERY #1
María's Missing Papa
Tell us more about how he disappeared.
We had just celebrated Papá's fortieth birthday fiesta.
It was a grand party, and people came from all around...
...even the Yankees that we would trade with anchored their ship and celebrated with Papá.
There was music and dancing for three nights! But the day after, when everyone had gone home...

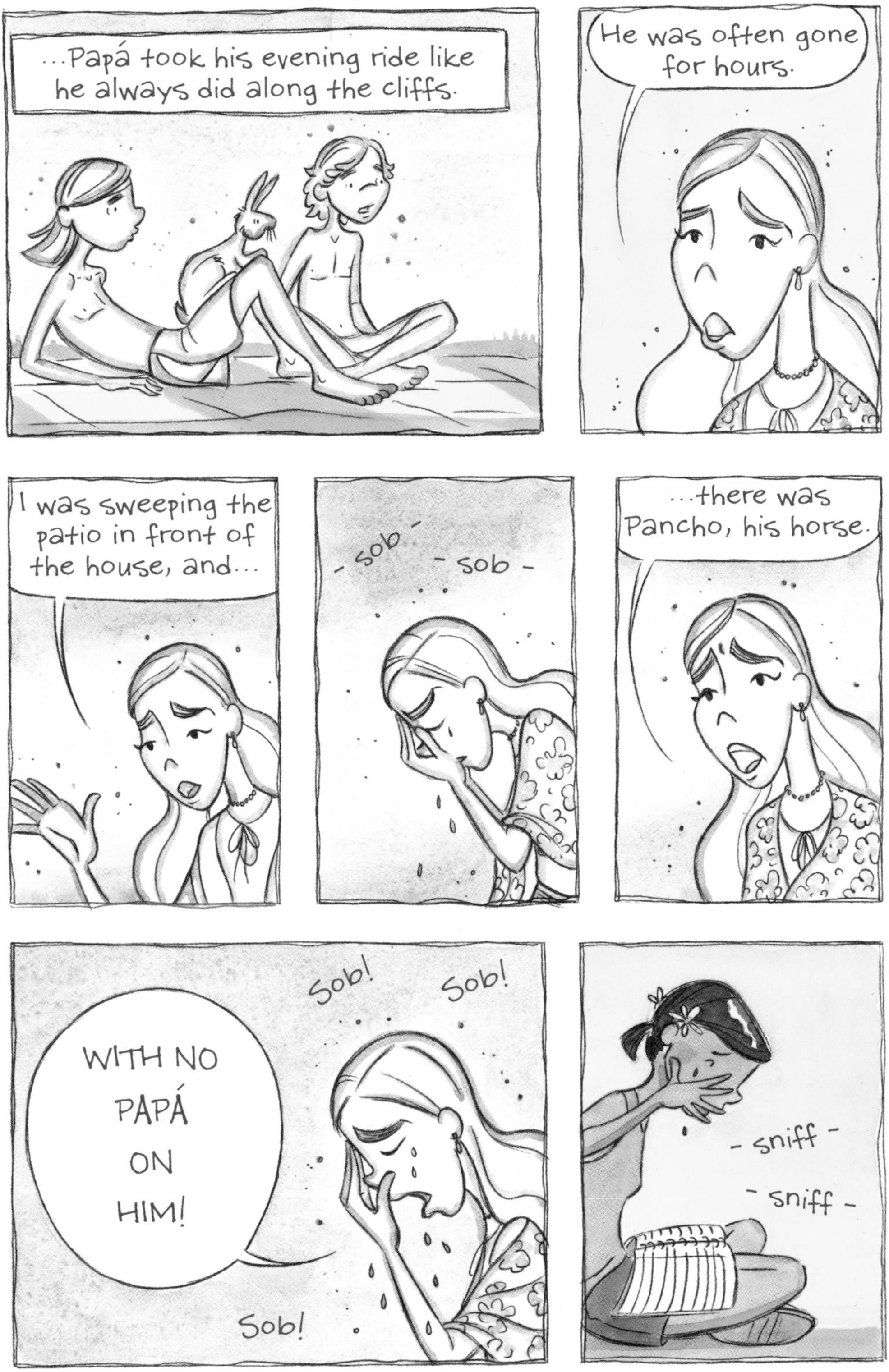
...Papá took his evening ride like he always did along the cliffs.
He was often gone for hours.
I was sweeping the patio in front of the house, and...
- sob -
- sob -
...there was Pancho, his horse.
WITH NO PAPÁ ON HIM!
Sob!
Sob!
Sob!
- sniff -
- sniff -

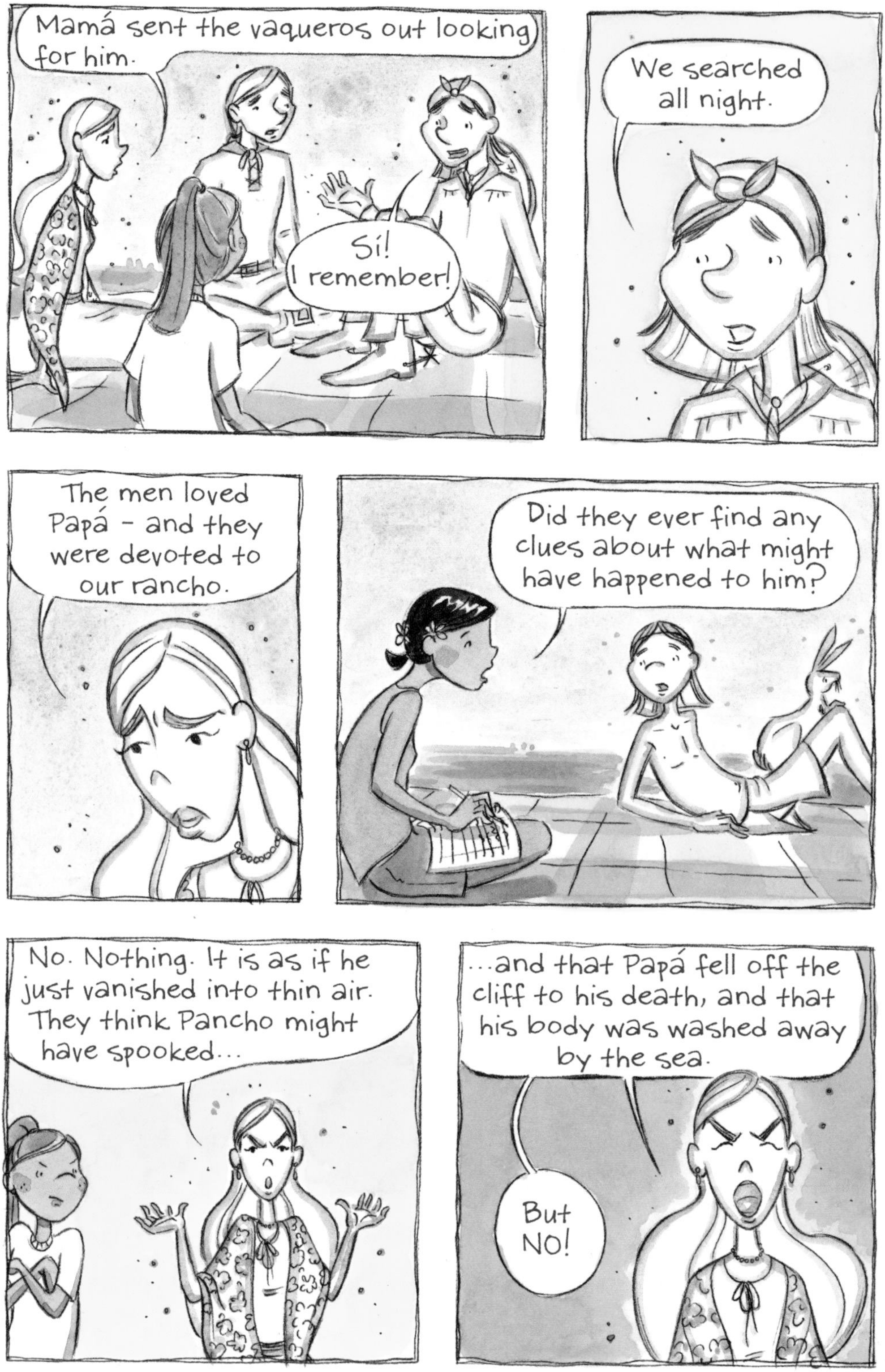
Mamá sent the vaqueros out looking for him.
Sí! I remember!
We searched all night.
The men loved Papá - and they were devoted to our rancho.
Did they ever find any clues about what might have happened to him?
No. Nothing. It is as if he just vanished into thin air. They think Pancho might have spooked...
...and that Papá fell off the cliff to his death, and that his body was washed away by the sea.
But NO!

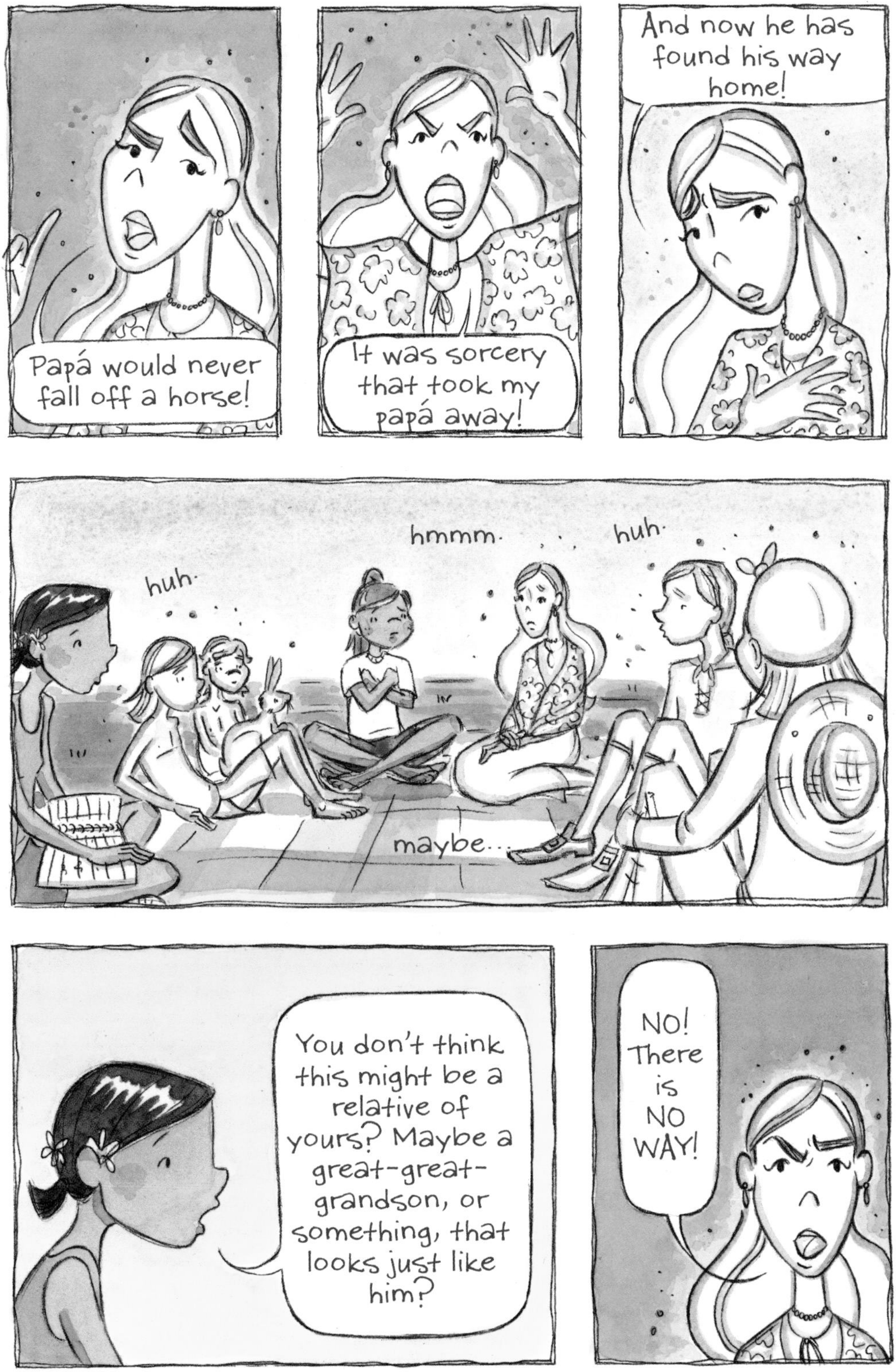
Papá would never fall off a horse!
It was sorcery that took my papá away!
And now he has found his way home!
huh.
hmmm.
huh.
maybe...
You don't think this might be a relative of yours? Maybe a great-great-grandson, or something, that looks just like him?
NO! There is NO WAY!

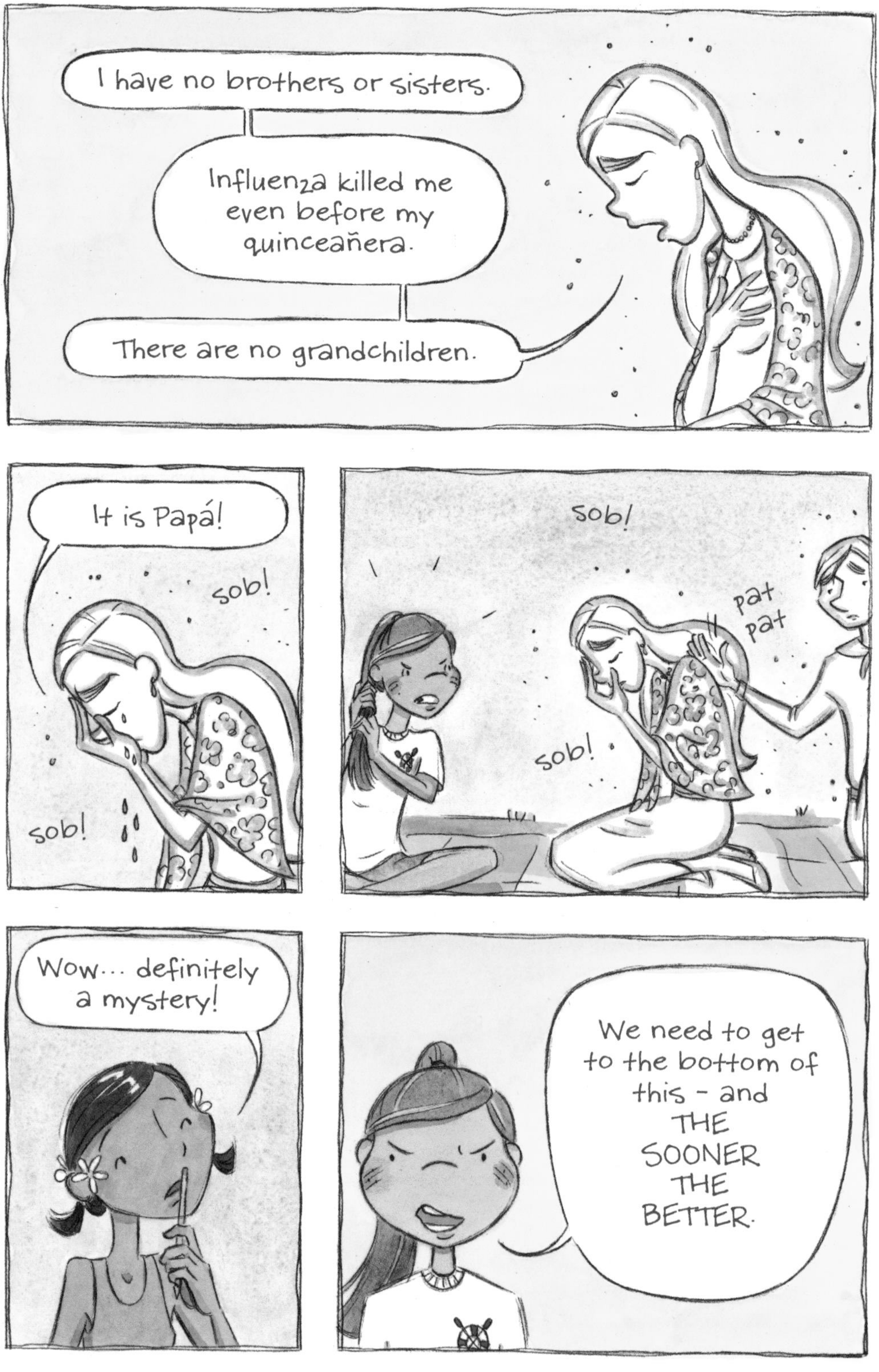
I have no brothers or sisters.
Influenza killed me even before my quinceañera.
There are no grandchildren.
It is Papá!
sob!
sob!
sob!
pat pat
sob!
Wow... definitely a mystery!
We need to get to the bottom of this - and THE SOONER THE BETTER.

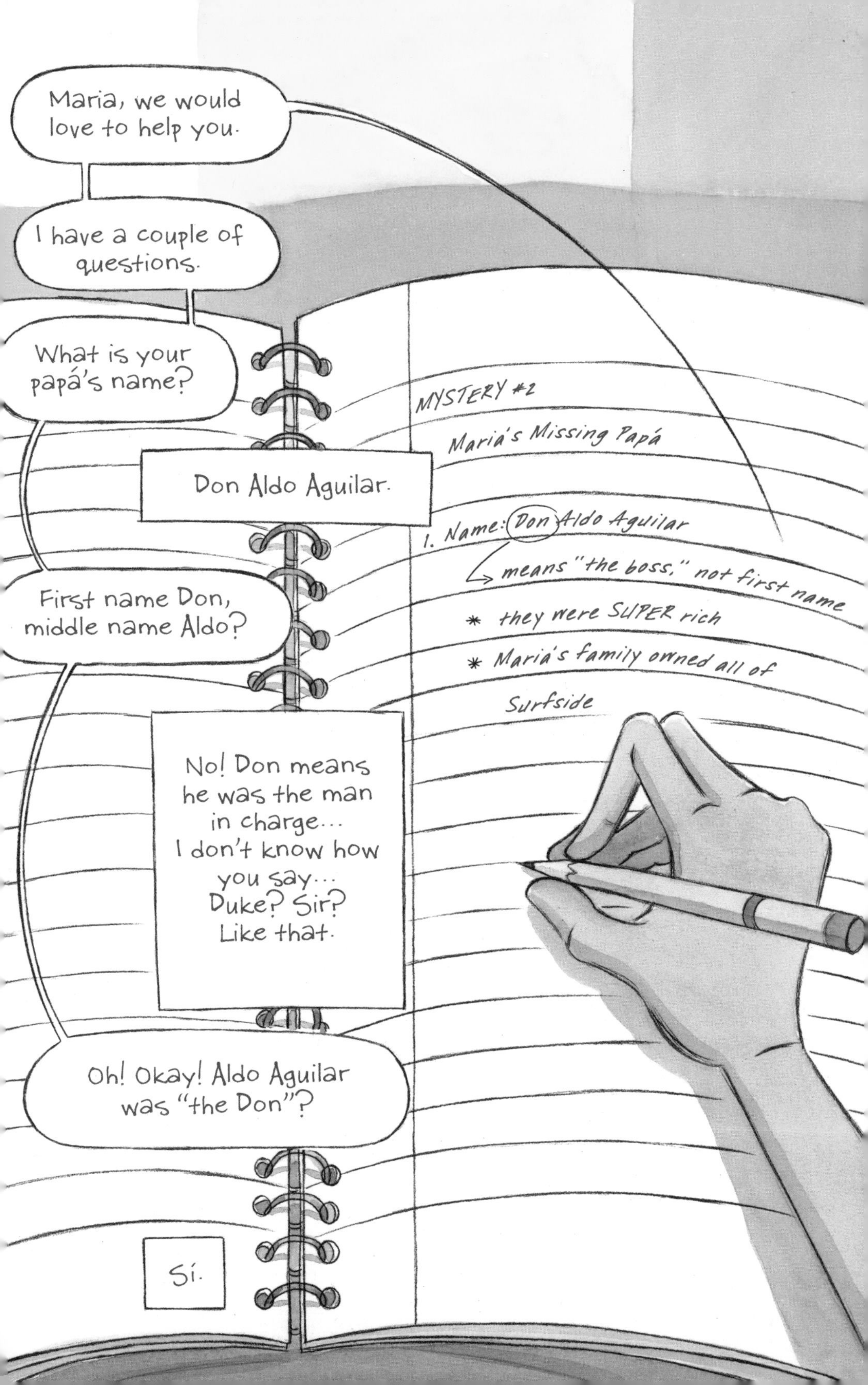
Maria, we would love to help you.
I have a couple of questions.
What is your papá's name?
Don Aldo Aguilar.
MYSTERY #2
Maria's Missing Papá
1. Name: Don Aldo Aguilar
means "the boss," not first name
* they were SUPER rich
* Maria's family owned all of Surfside
First name Don, middle name Aldo?
No! Don means he was the man in charge... I don't know how you say... Duke? Sir? Like that.
Oh! Okay! Aldo Aguilar was "the Don"?
Sí.

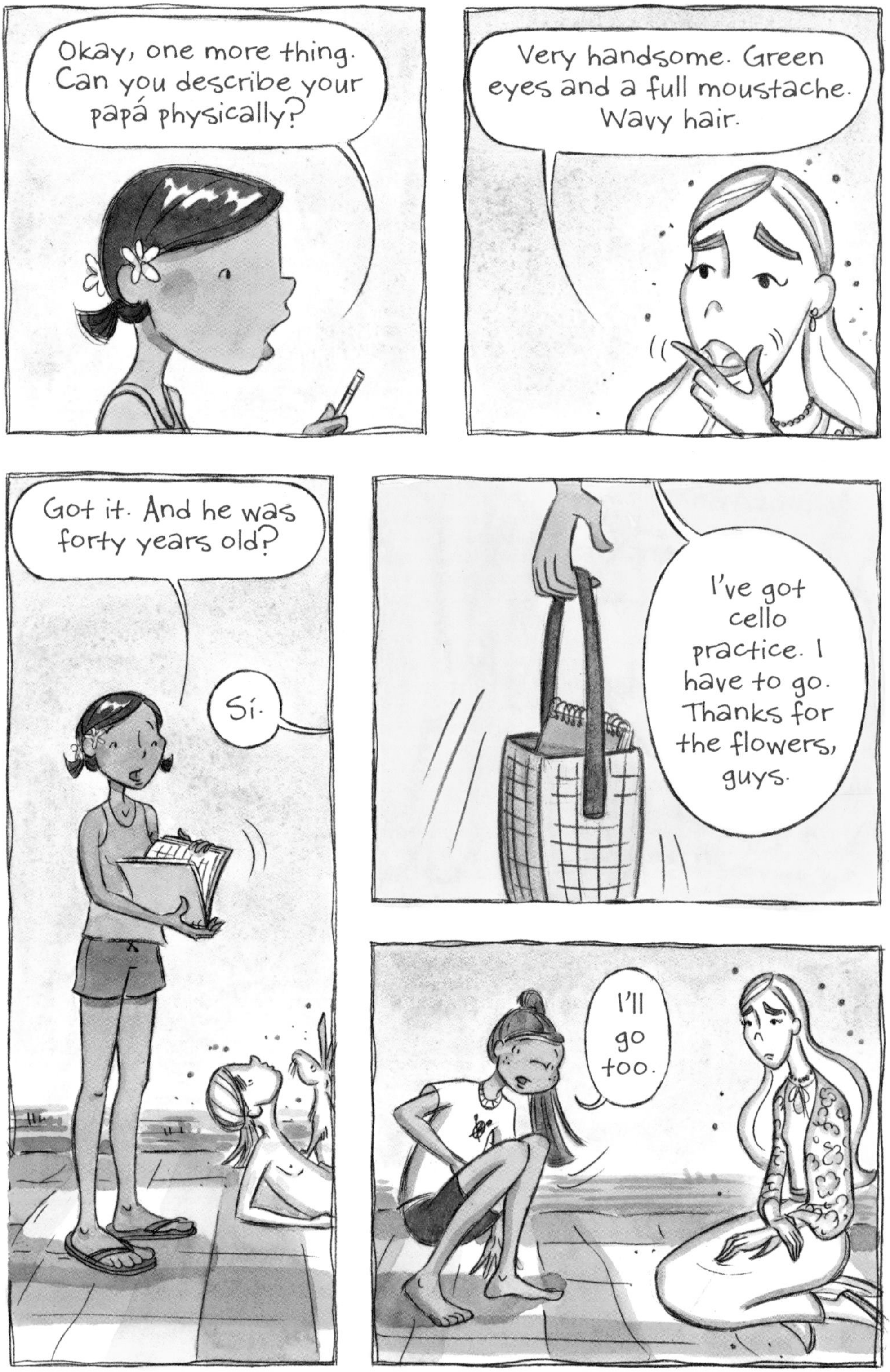
Okay, one more thing. Can you describe your papá physically?
Very handsome. Green eyes and a full moustache. Wavy hair.
Got it. And he was forty years old?
Sí.
I've got cello practice. I have to go. Thanks for the flowers, guys.
I'll go too.

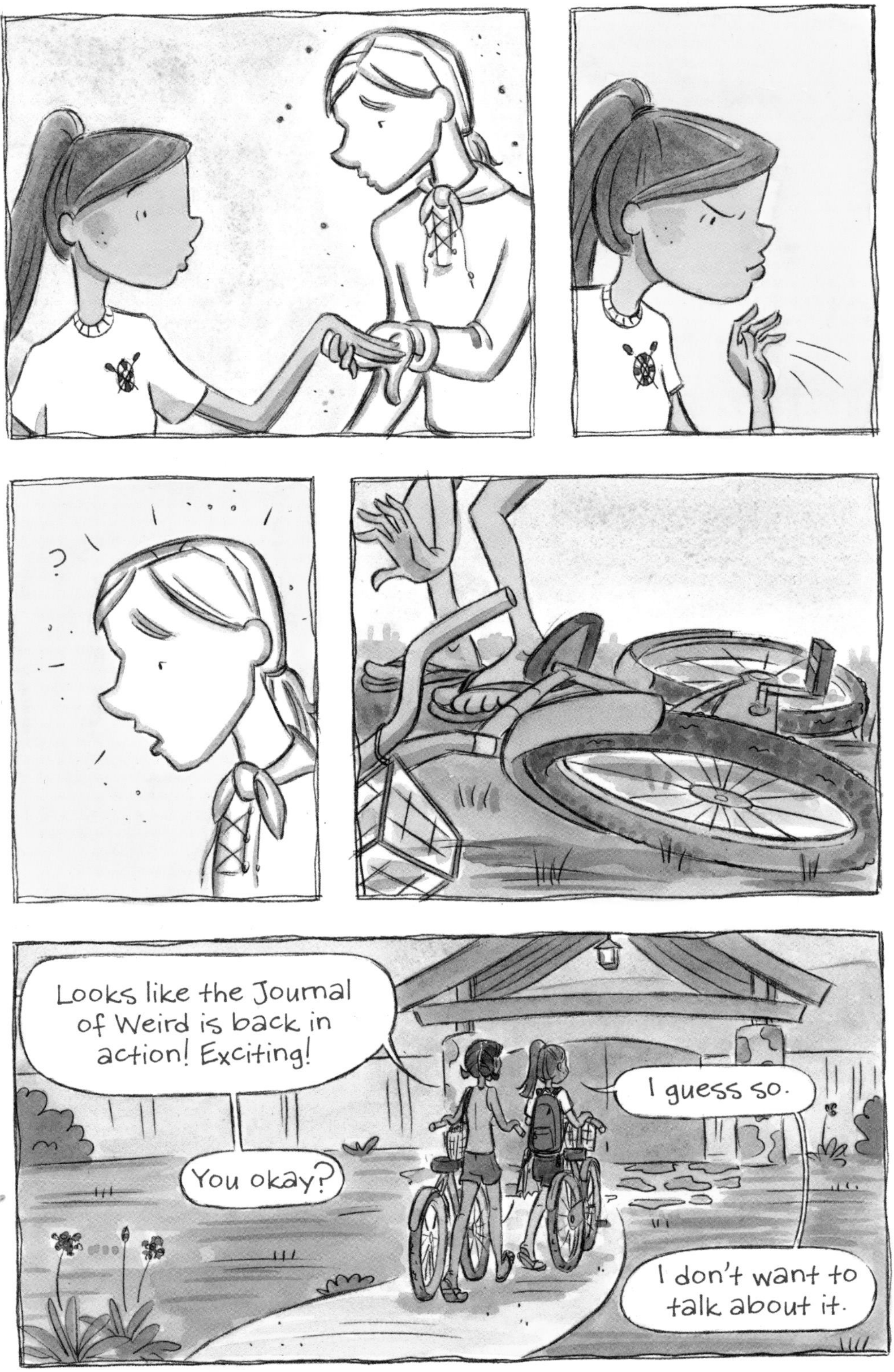

Looks like the Journal of Weird is back in action! Exciting!
You okay?
I guess so.
I don't want to talk about it.

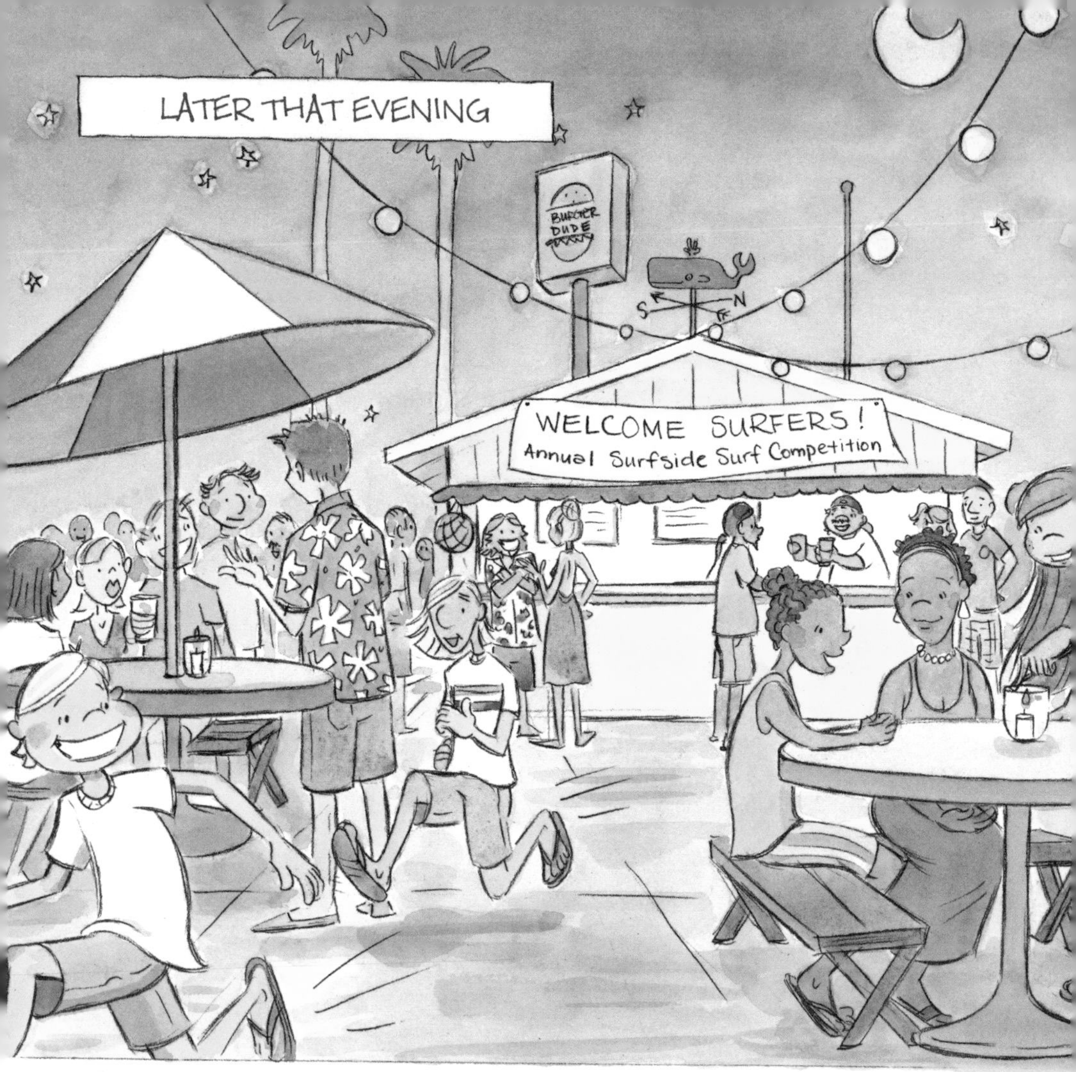
LATER THAT EVENING
BURGER DUDE
S
N
WELCOME SURFERS!
Annual Surfside Surf Competition

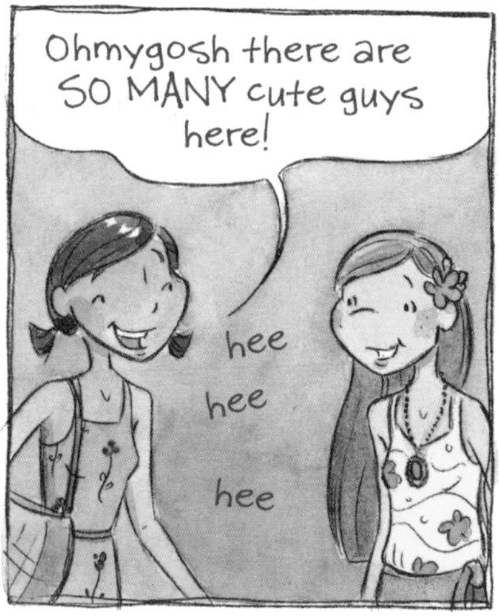
Ohmygosh there are SO MANY cute guys here!
hee
hee
hee

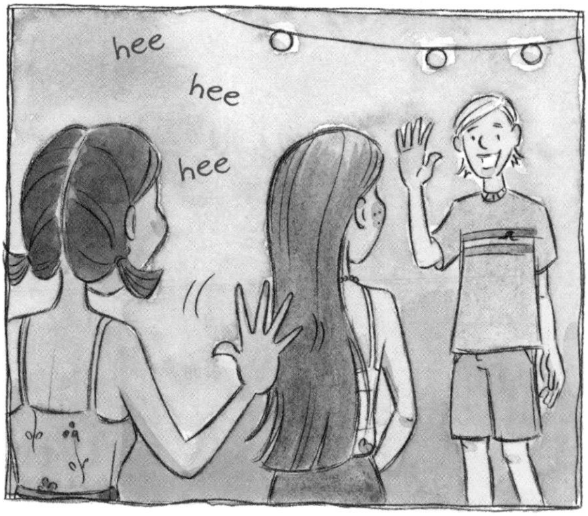
hee
hee
hee

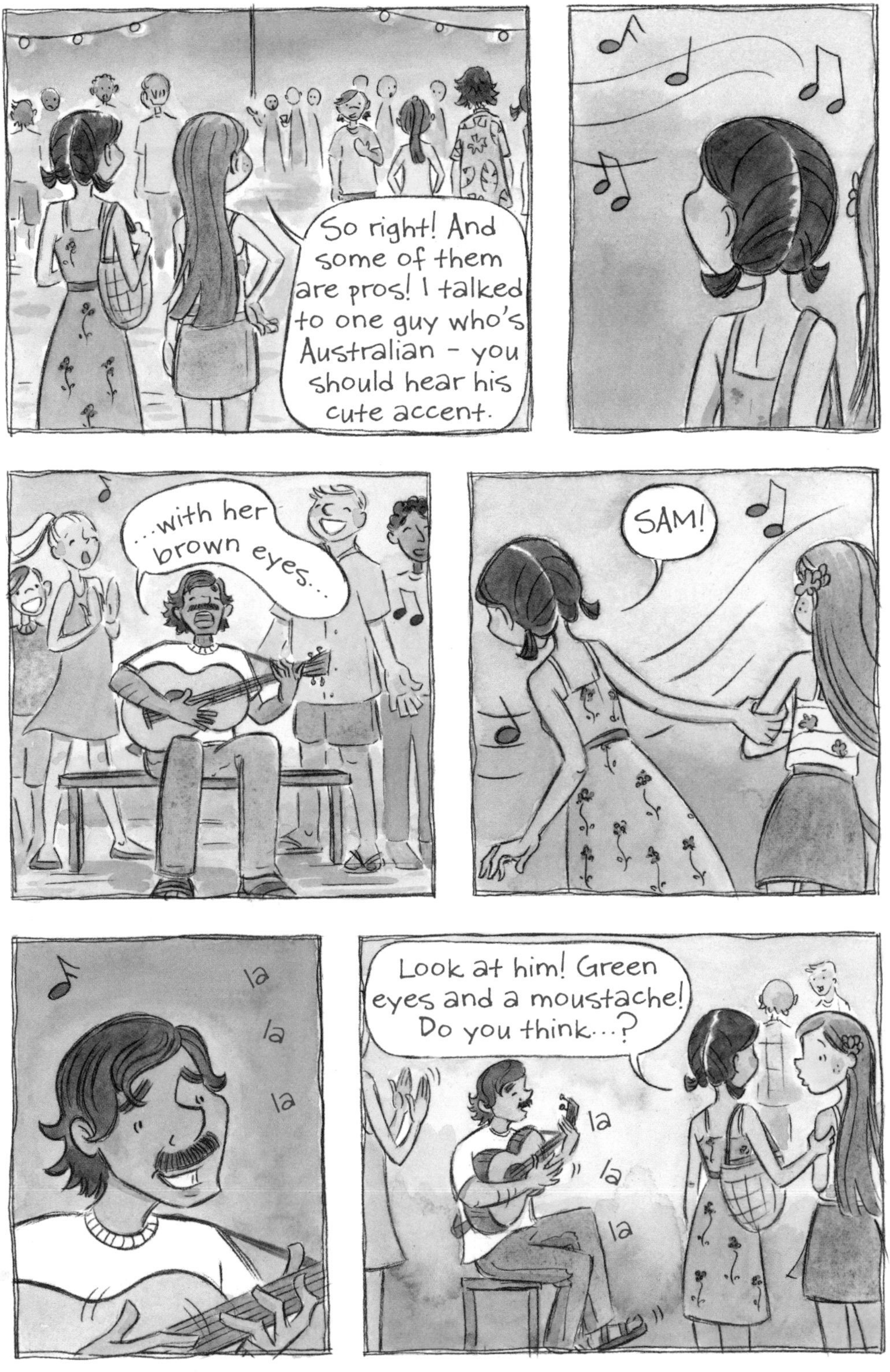
So right! And some of them are pros! I talked to one guy who's Australian - you should hear his cute accent.
...with her brown eyes...
SAM!
la
la
la
Look at him! Green eyes and a moustache! Do you think...?
la
la
la

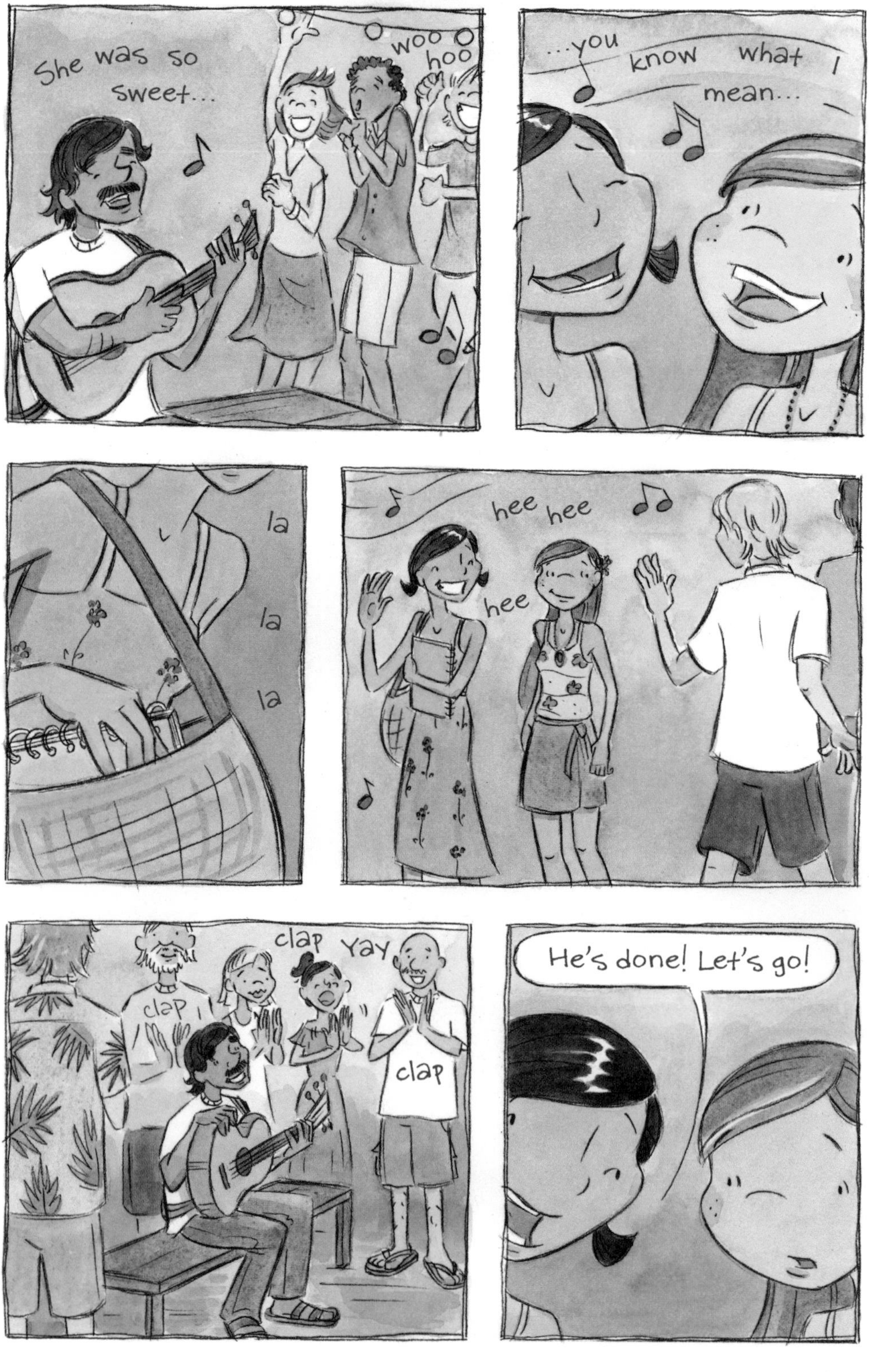
She was so sweet...
woo hoo
...you know what I mean...
la
la
la
hee hee
hee
clap
clap
Yay
clap
He's done! Let's go!

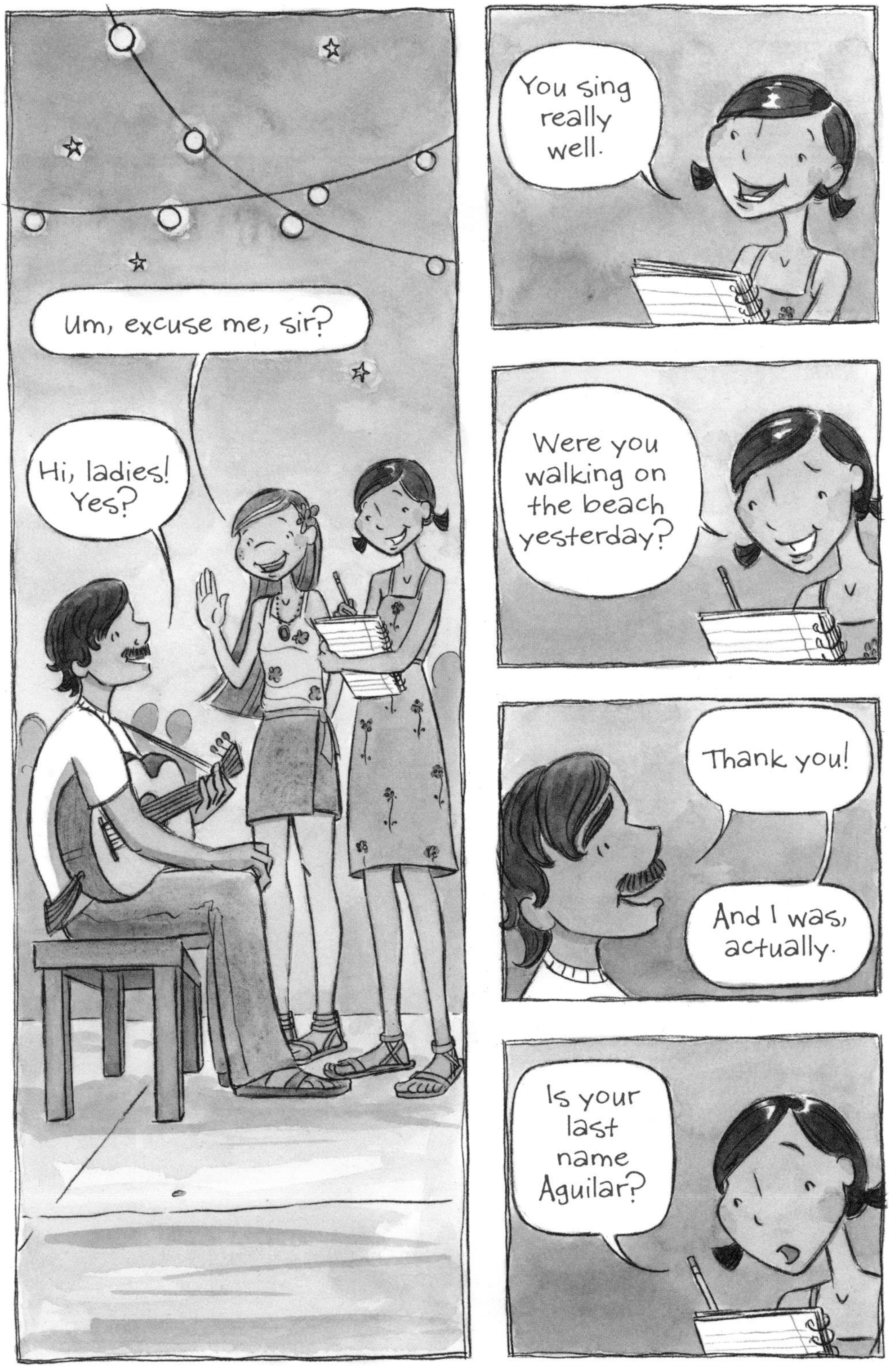
Um, excuse me, sir?
Hi, ladies! Yes?
You sing really well.
Were you walking on the beach yesterday?
Thank you!
And I was, actually.
Is your last name Aguilar?

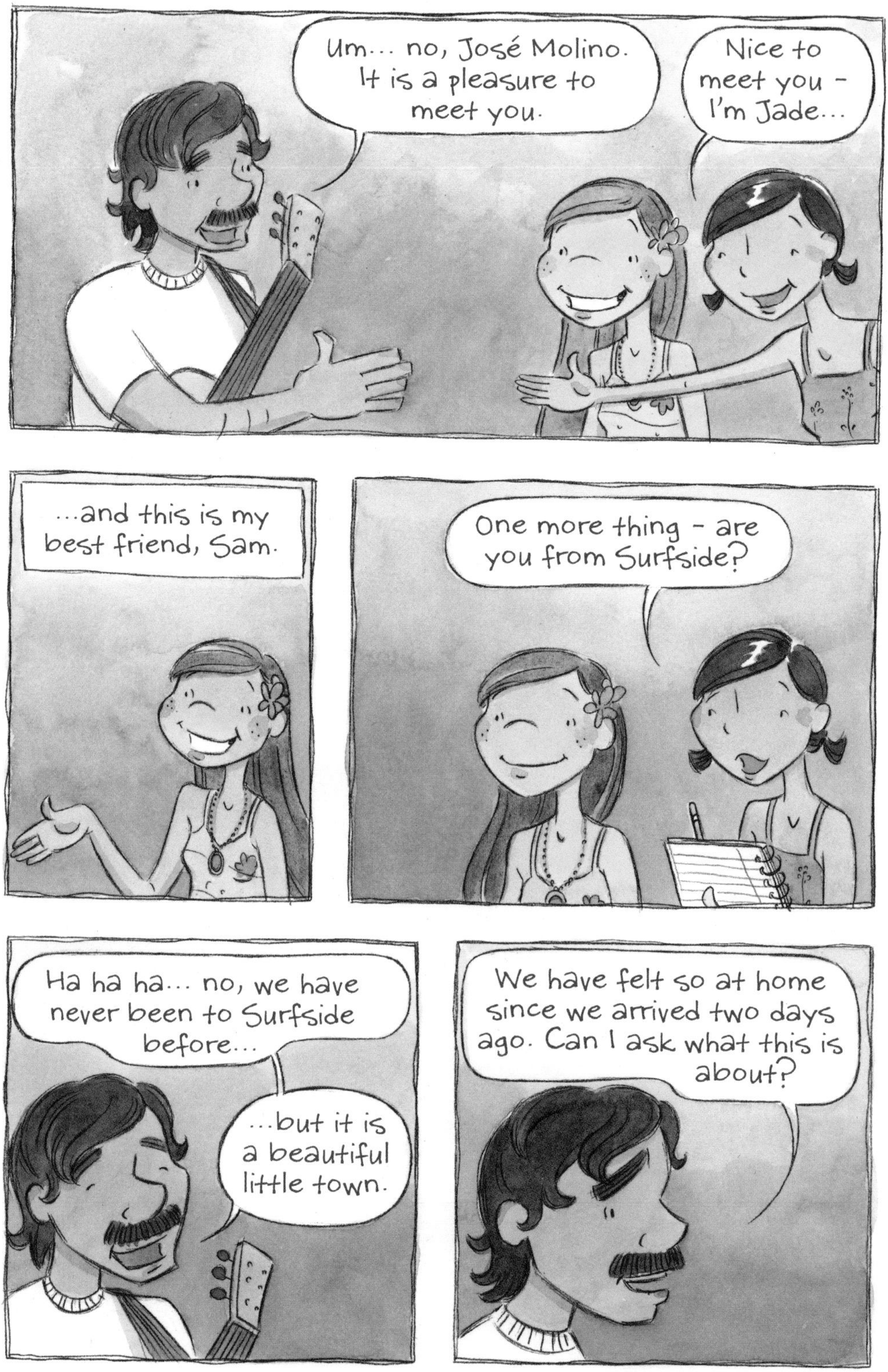
Um... no, José Molino. It is a pleasure to meet you.
Nice to meet you - I'm Jade...
...and this is my best friend, Sam.
One more thing - are you from Surfside?
Ha ha ha... no, we have never been to Surfside before...
...but it is a beautiful little town.
We have felt so at home since we arrived two days ago. Can I ask what this is about?

Oh, just curious. "We"?

Myself and my son, Diego. We are here for the surf competition tomorrow.

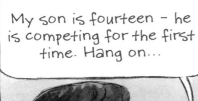

My son is fourteen – he is competing for the first time. Hang on...

Diego!

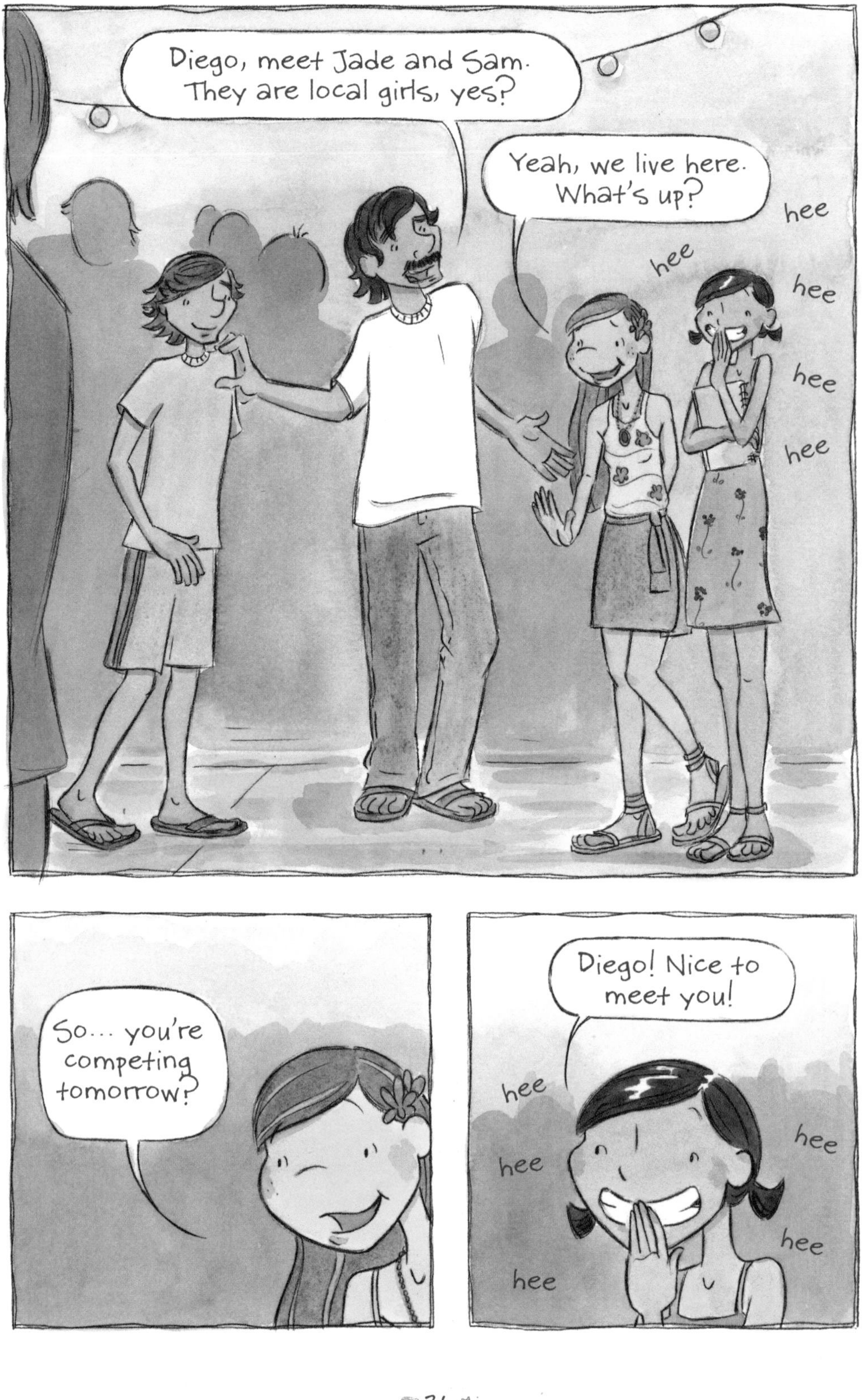
Diego, meet Jade and Sam. They are local girls, yes?
Yeah, we live here. What's up?
hee
hee
hee
hee
hee
hee
So... you're competing tomorrow?
Diego! Nice to meet you!
hee
hee
hee
hee
hee

Yeah, this is my first competition.

I'm totally nervous.

My junior lifeguard group is helping work the competition tomorrow.

I'm handing out singlets. I'll make sure you get a lucky one!

I'll be watching. I'll cheer for you!

Wow, cool! I don't know anyone else.

I think these girls will bring you good luck...

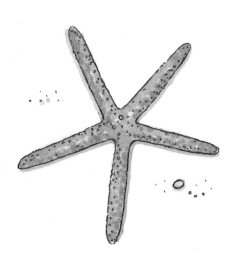

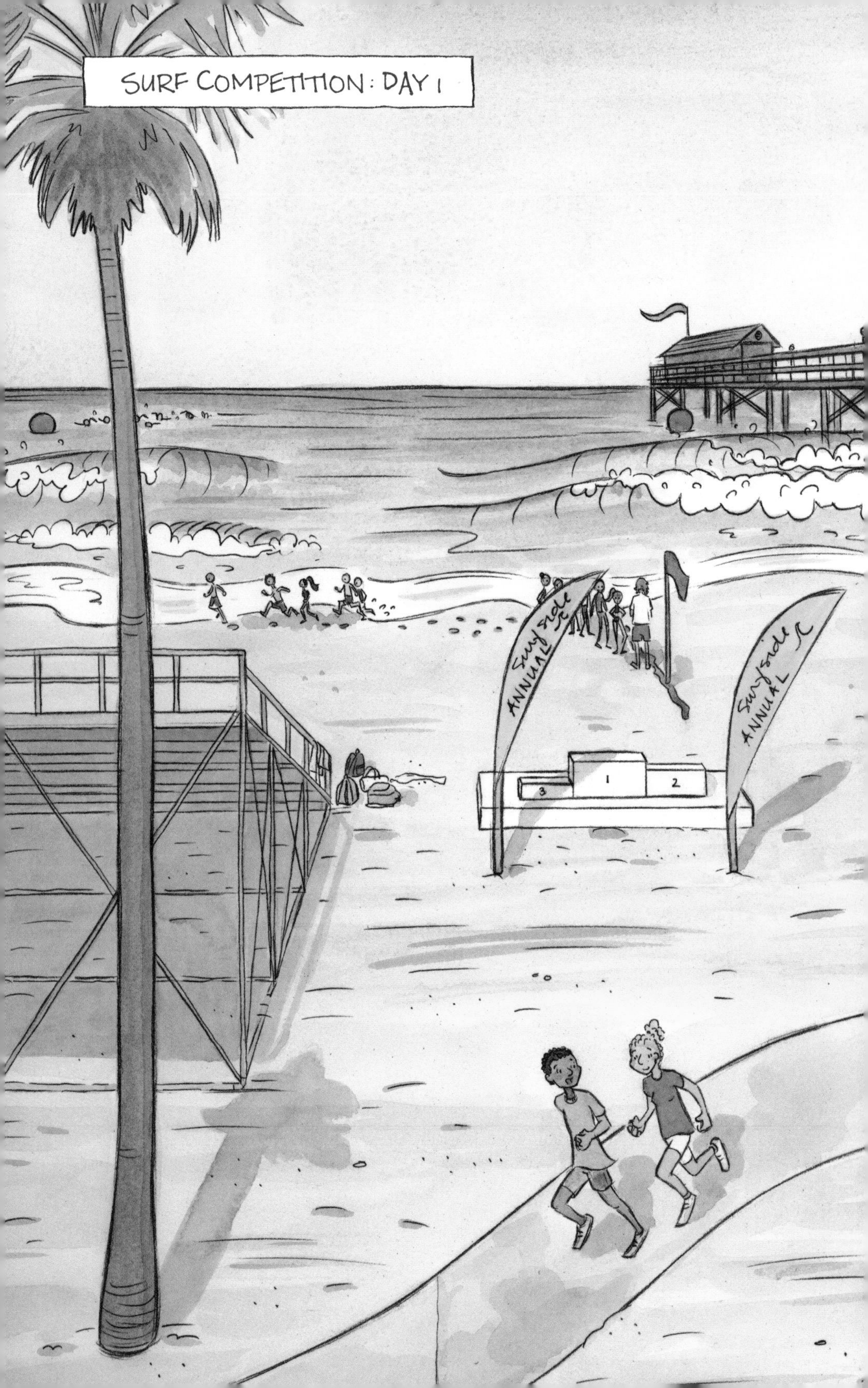
SURF COMPETITION: DAY 1
Surfside ANNUAL
1
2
3
Surfside ANNUAL

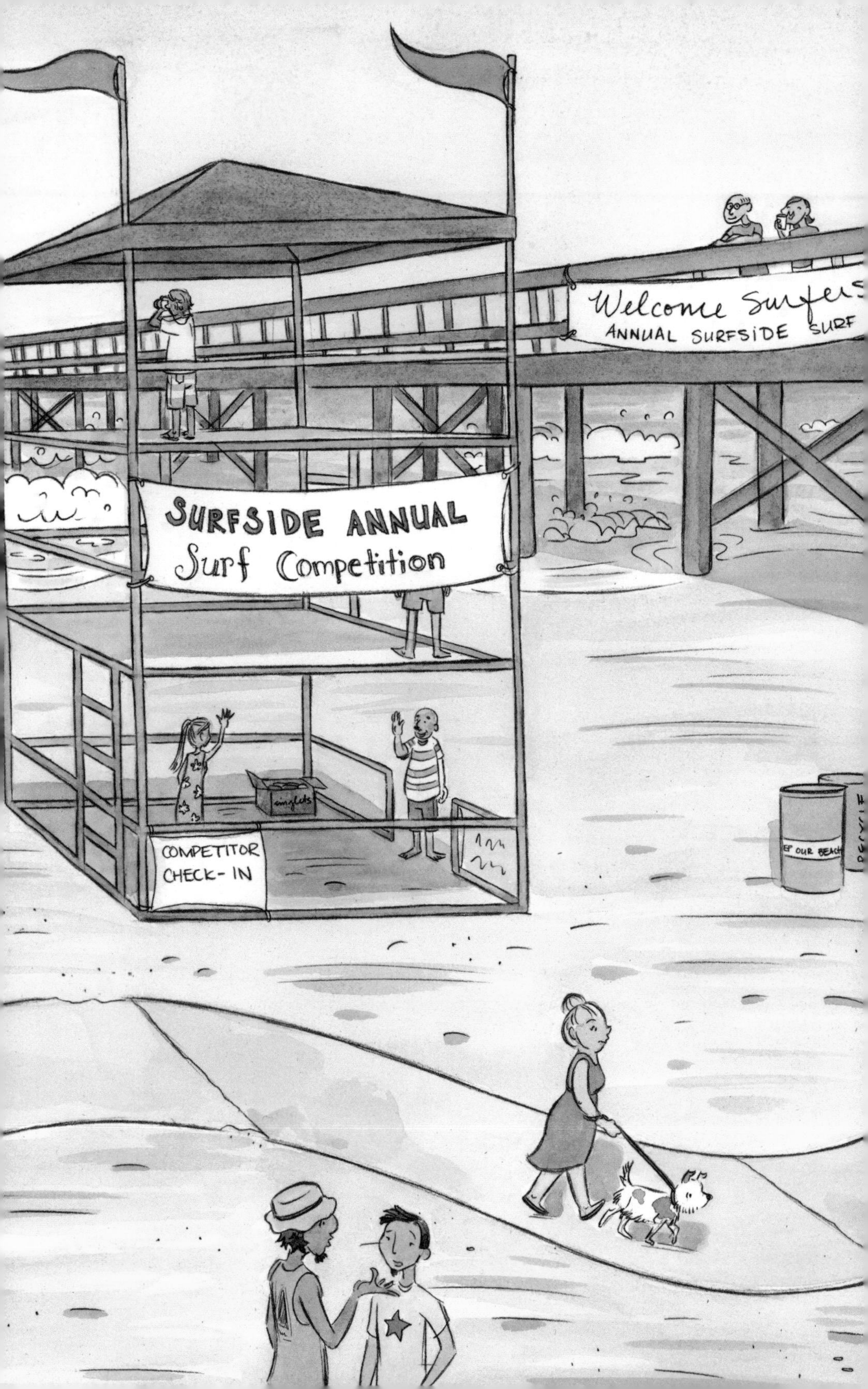

SURFSIDE ANNUAL
Surf Competition
Welcome
ANNUAL SURFSIDE SURF
COMPETITOR CHECK-IN

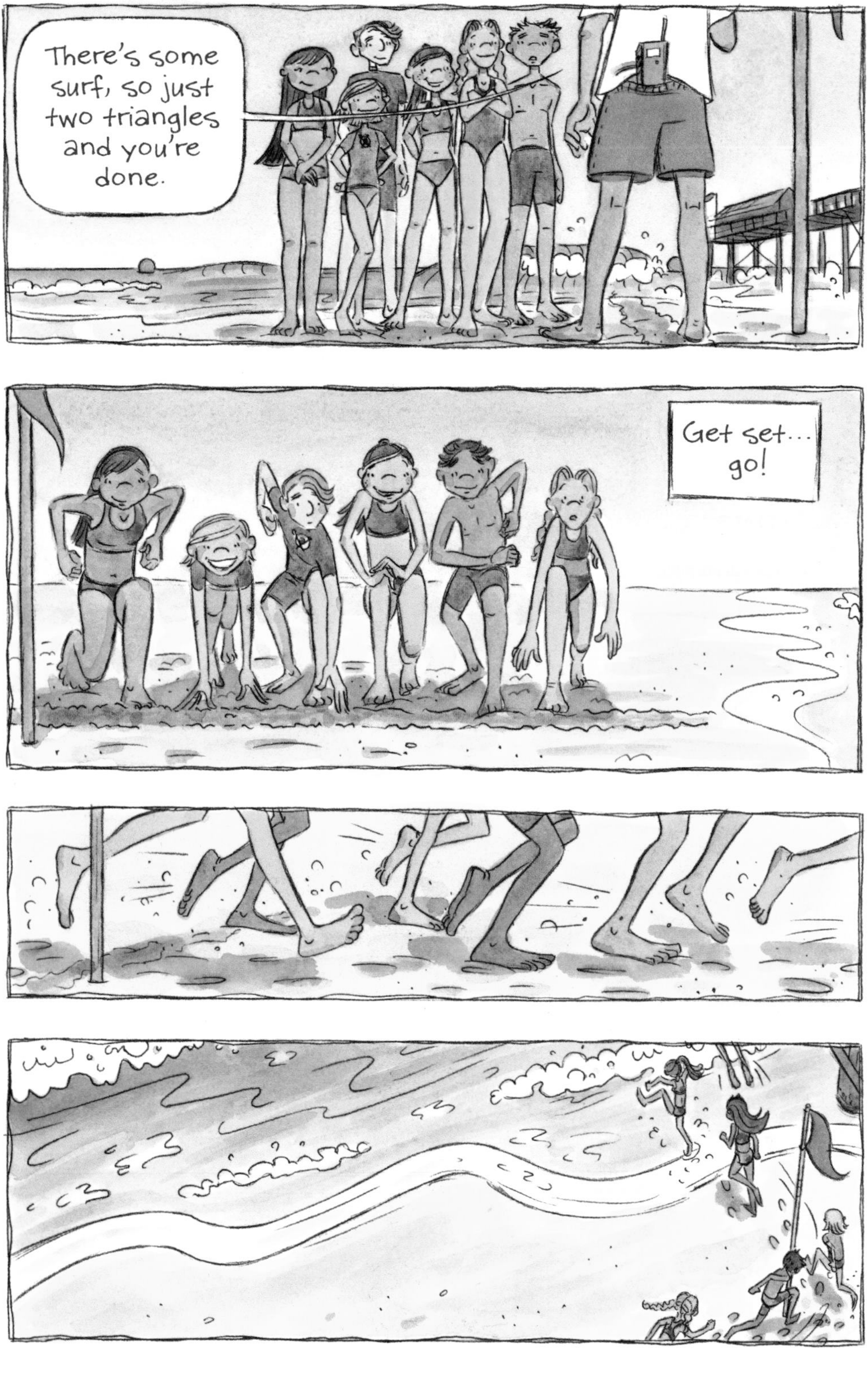
There's some surf, so just two triangles and you're done.
Get set... go!

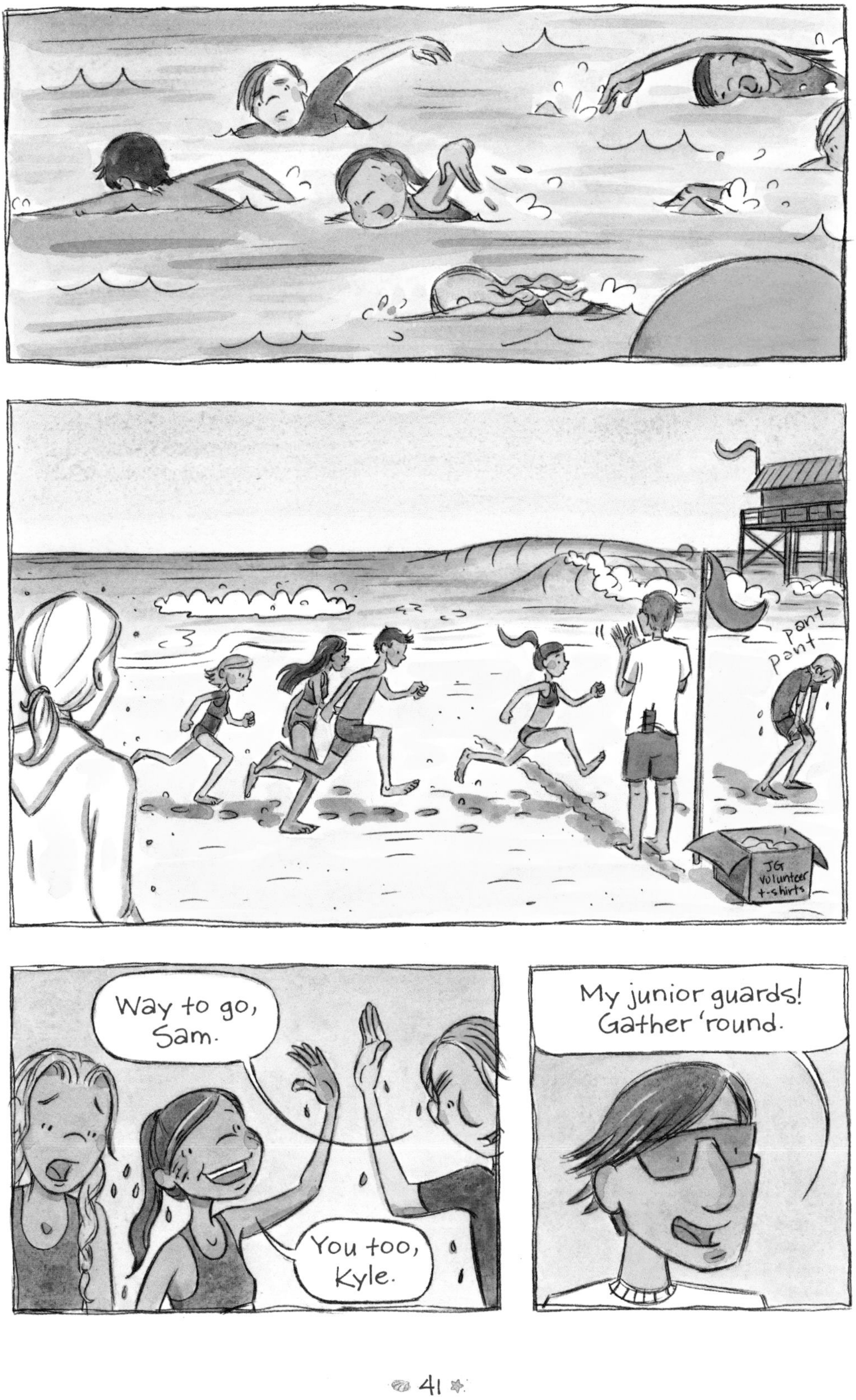
pant
pant
JG volunteer t-shirts
Way to go, Sam.
You too, Kyle.
My junior guards! Gather 'round.

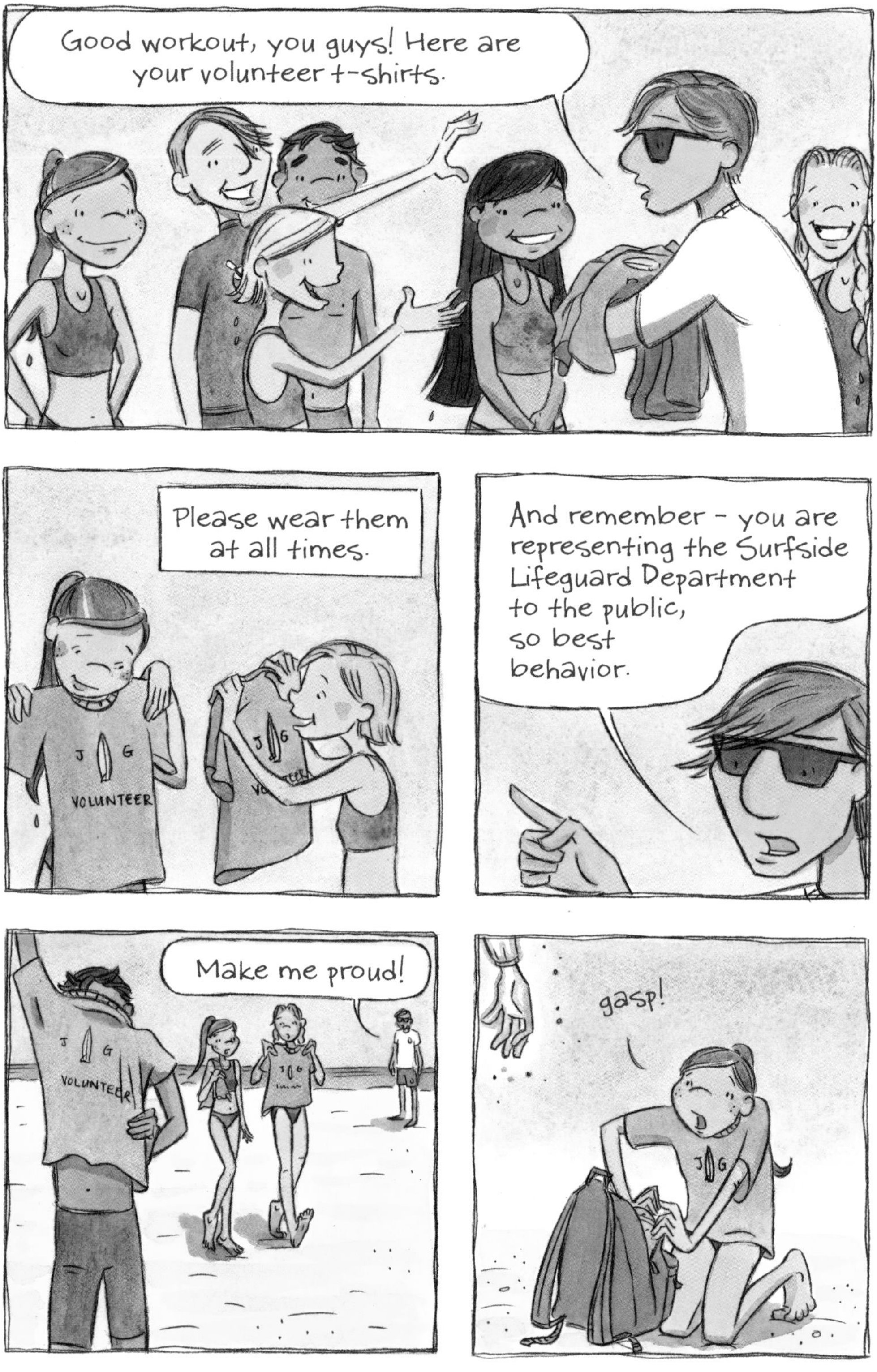

Good workout, you guys! Here are your volunteer t-shirts.
Please wear them at all times.
And remember - you are representing the Surfside Lifeguard Department to the public, so best behavior.
J G
VOLUNTEER
Make me proud!
gasp!

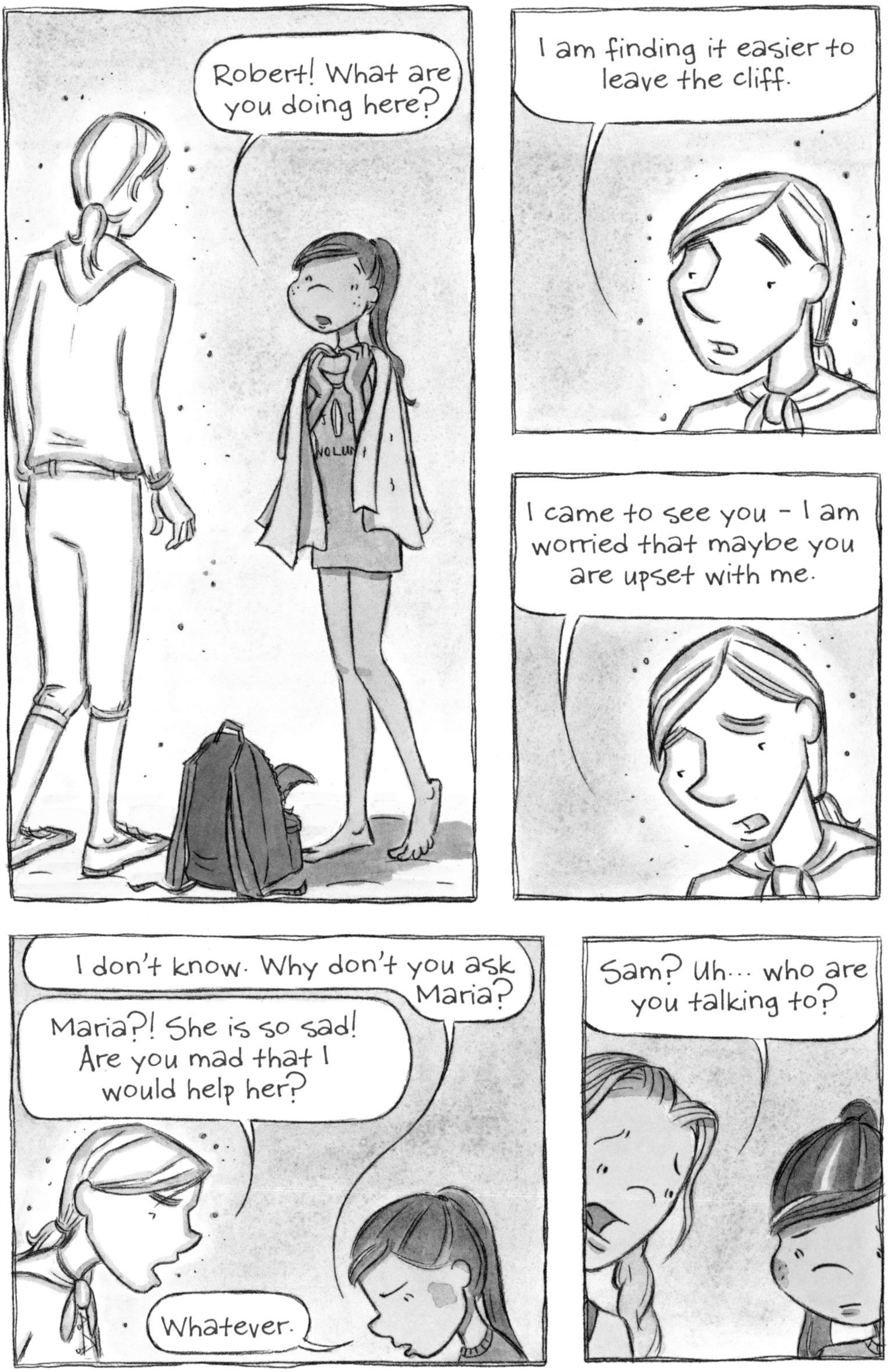
Robert! What are you doing here?
I am finding it easier to leave the cliff.
I came to see you - I am worried that maybe you are upset with me.
I don't know. Why don't you ask Maria?
Maria?! She is so sad! Are you mad that I would help her?
Whatever.
Sam? Uh... who are you talking to?

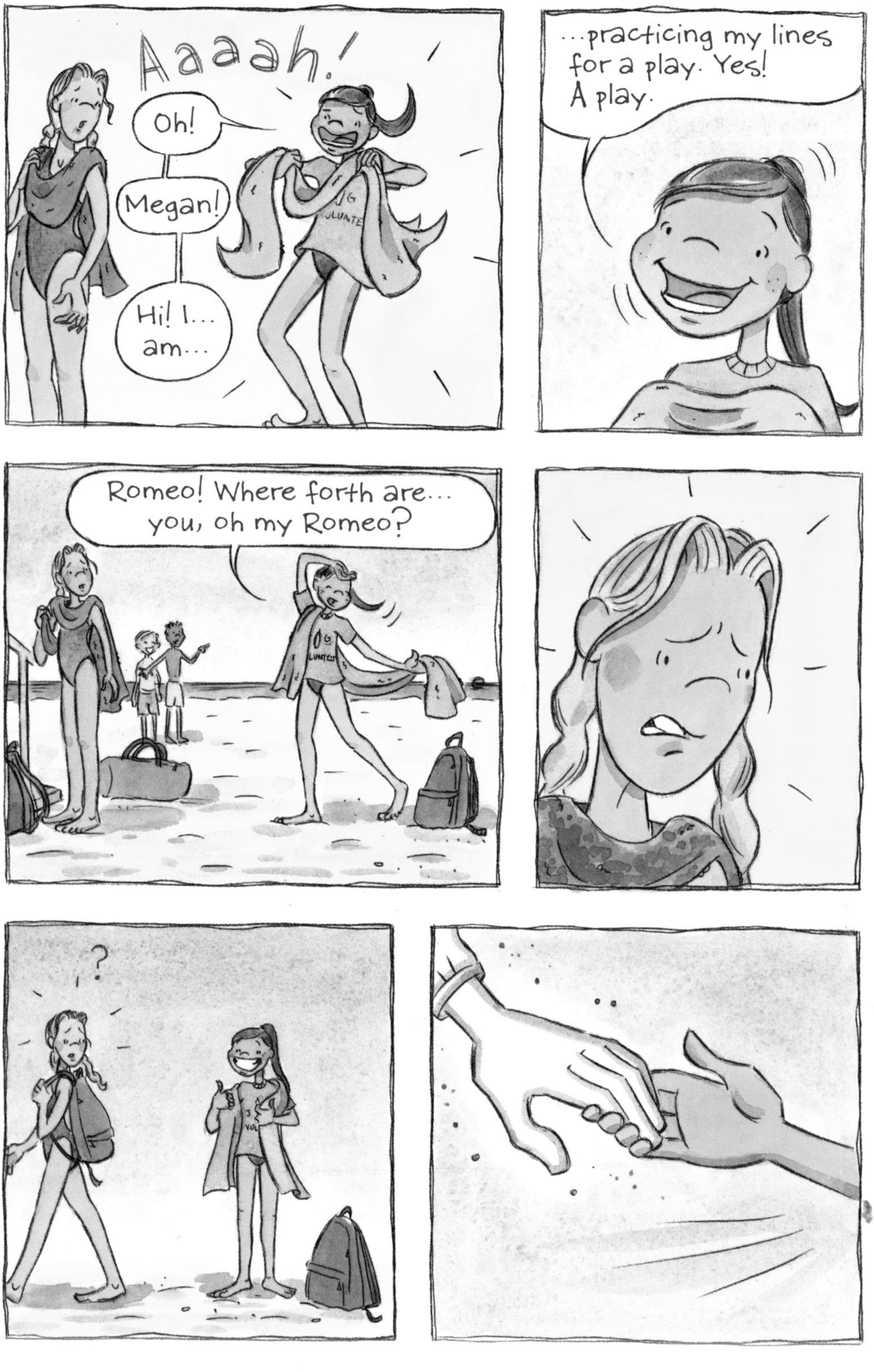
Aaaah!
Oh!
Megan!
Hi! I... am...
...practicing my lines for a play. Yes! A play.
Romeo! Where forth are... you, oh my Romeo?
?

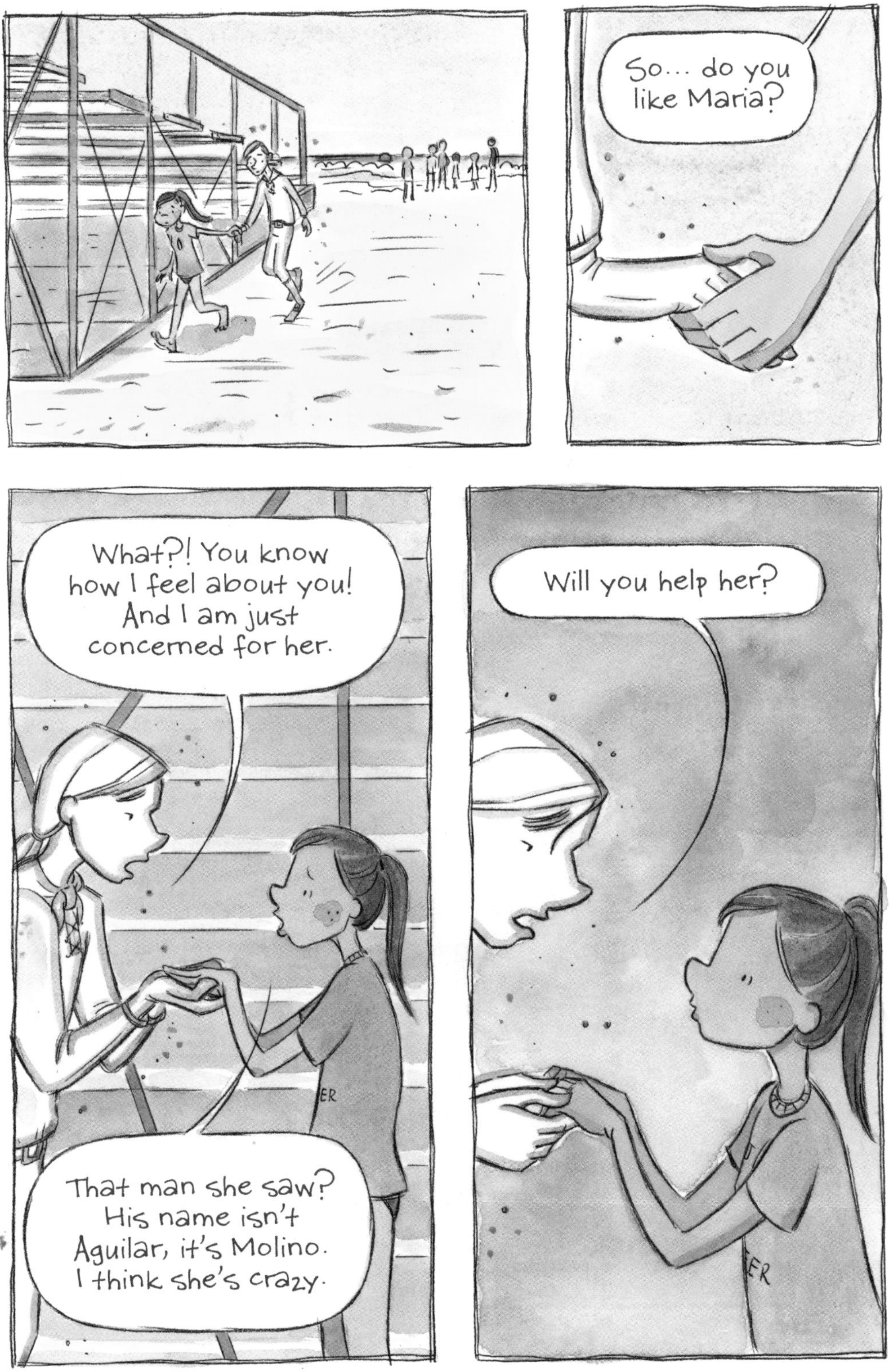
So... do you like Maria?
What?! You know how I feel about you! And I am just concerned for her.
That man she saw? His name isn't Aguilar, it's Molino. I think she's crazy.
Will you help her?

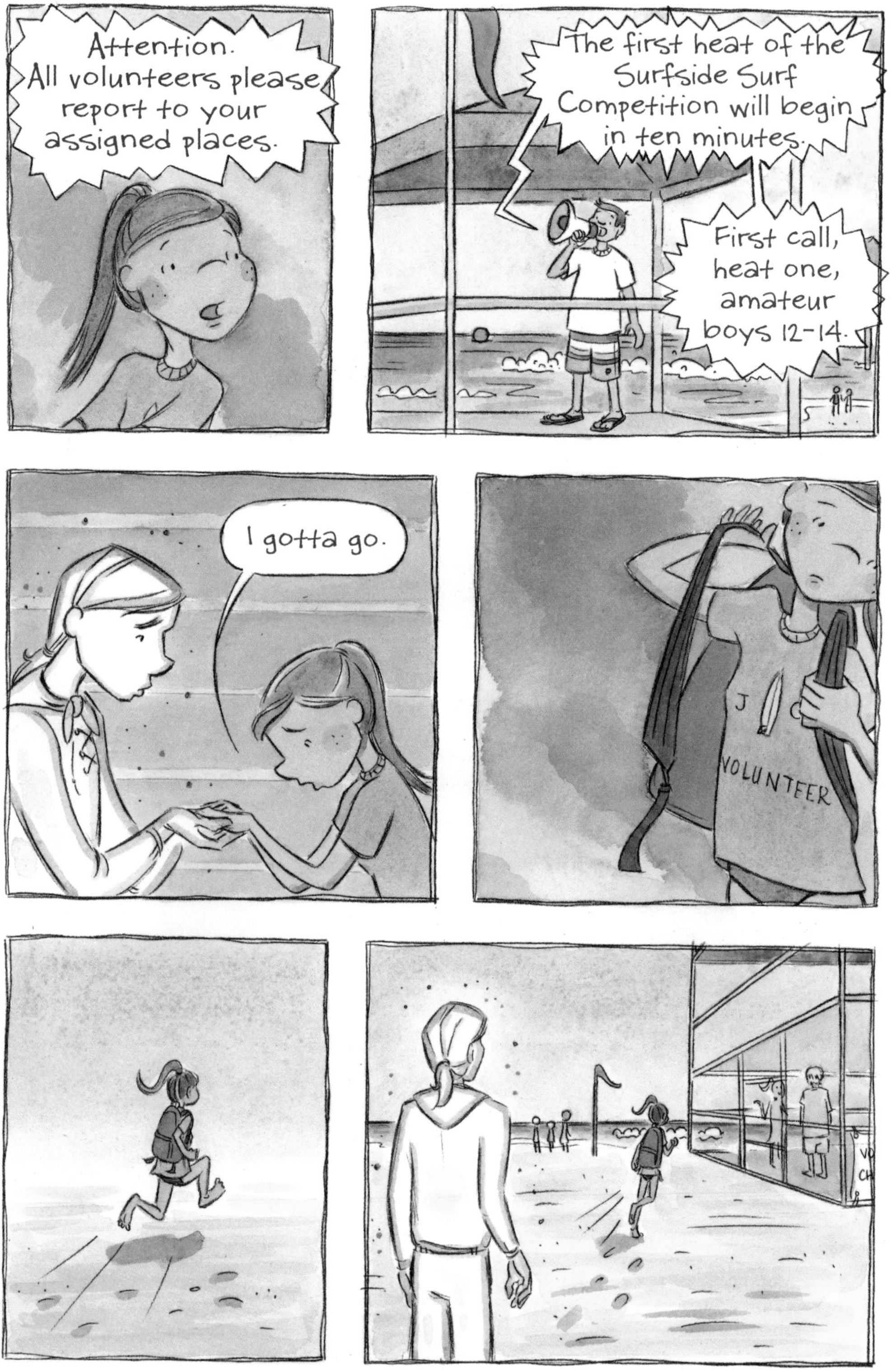
Attention.
All volunteers please report to your assigned places.
The first heat of the Surfside Surf Competition will begin in ten minutes.
First call, heat one, amateur boys 12-14.
I gotta go.
VOLUNTEER

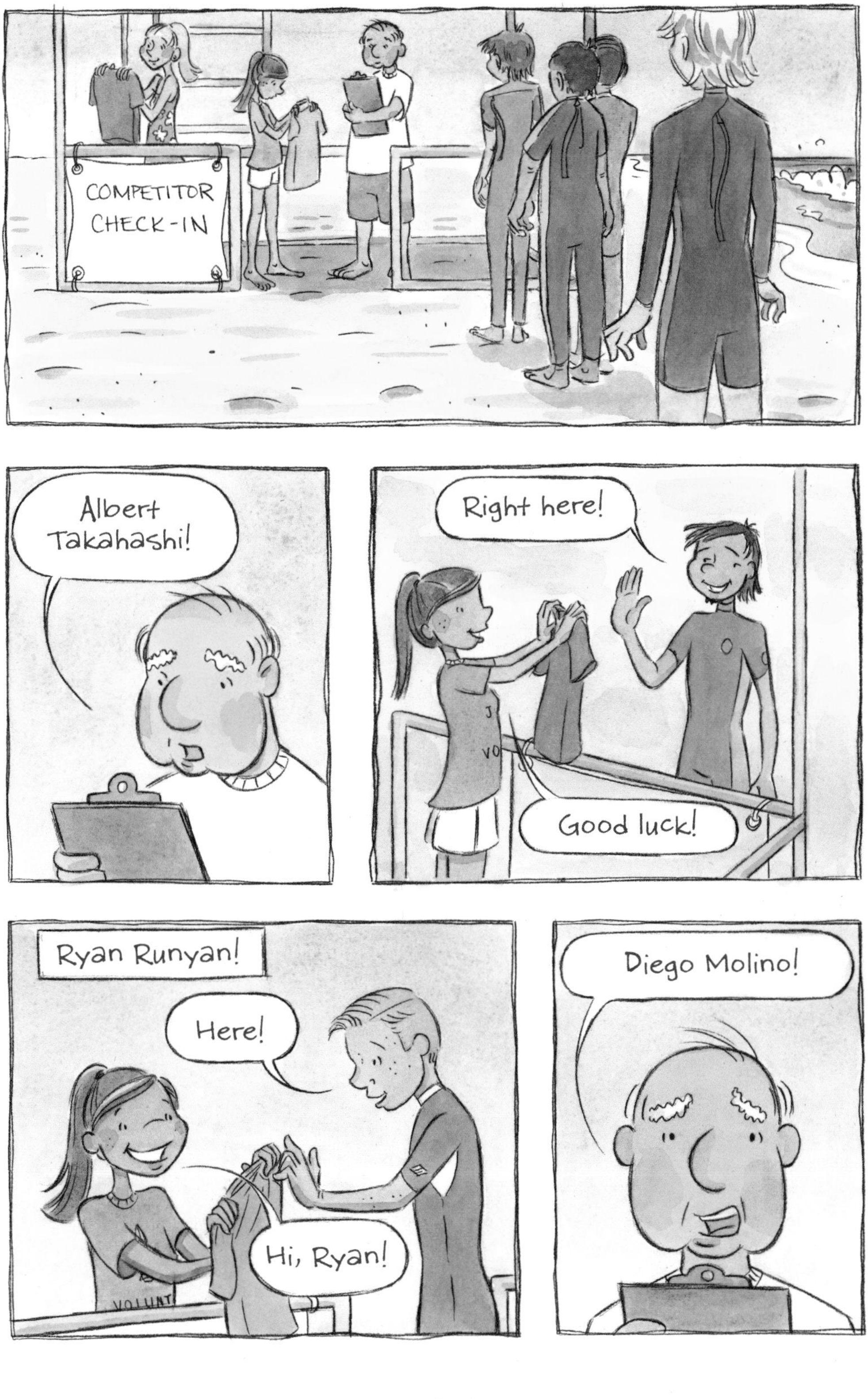
COMPETITOR
CHECK-IN
Albert Takahashi!
Right here!
Good luck!
Ryan Runyan!
Here!
Hi, Ryan!
Diego Molino!

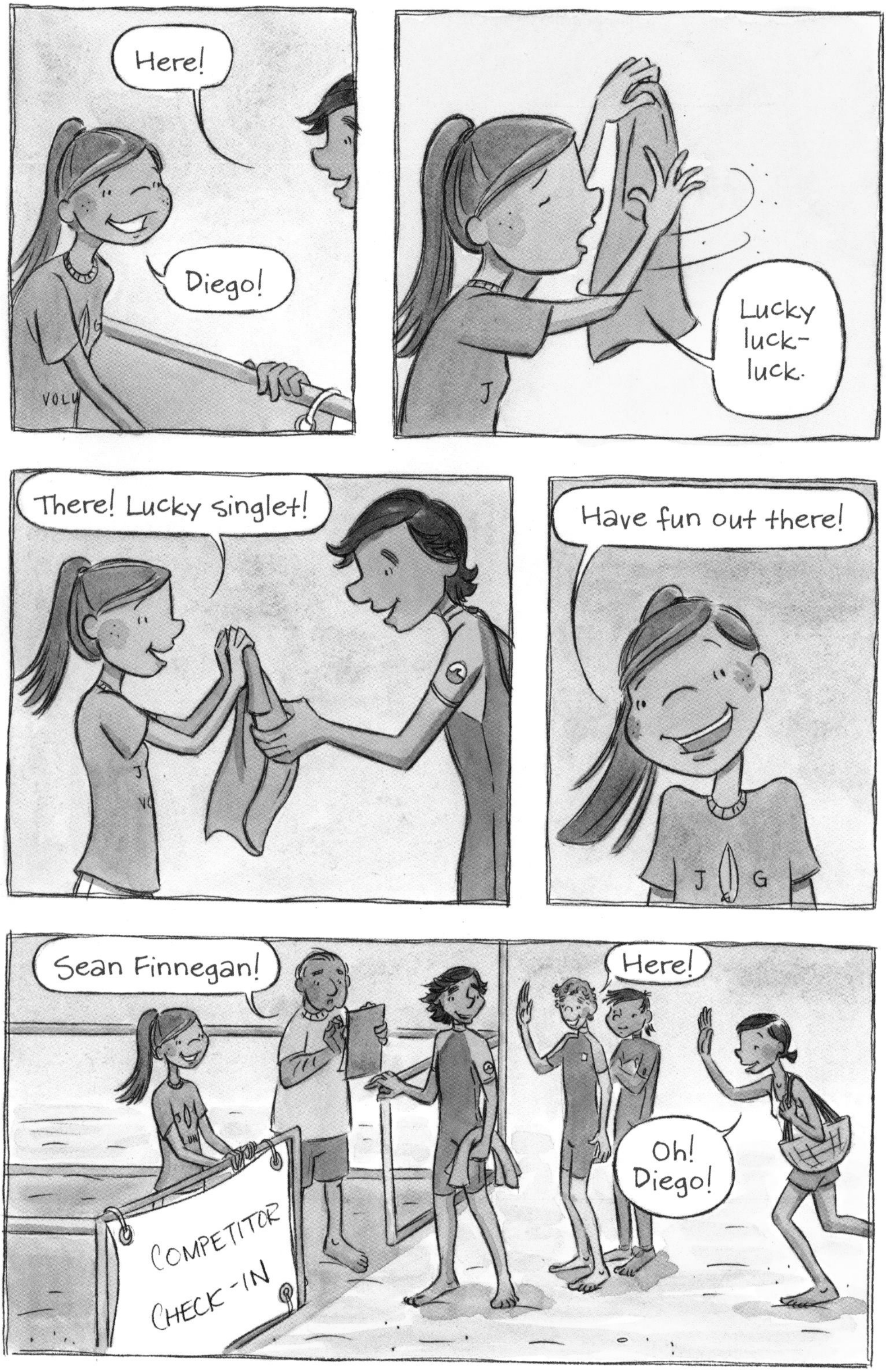
Here!
Diego!
Lucky luck-luck.
There! Lucky singlet!
Have fun out there!
Sean Finnegan!
COMPETITOR CHECK-IN
Here!
Oh! Diego!

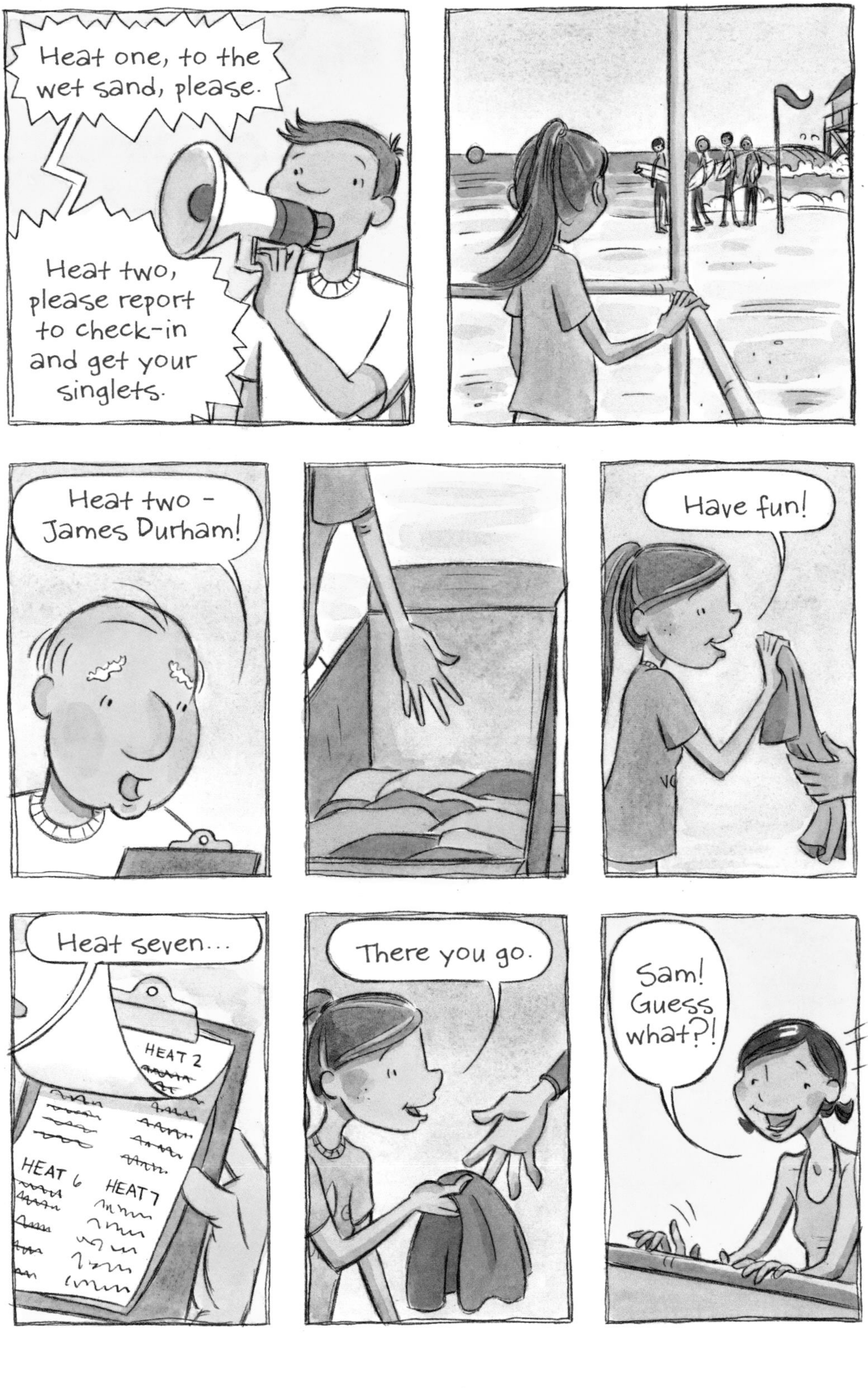
Heat one, to the wet sand, please.
Heat two, please report to check-in and get your singlets.
Heat two - James Durham!
Have fun!
Heat seven...
HEAT 2
HEAT 6
HEAT 7
There you go.
Sam! Guess what?!

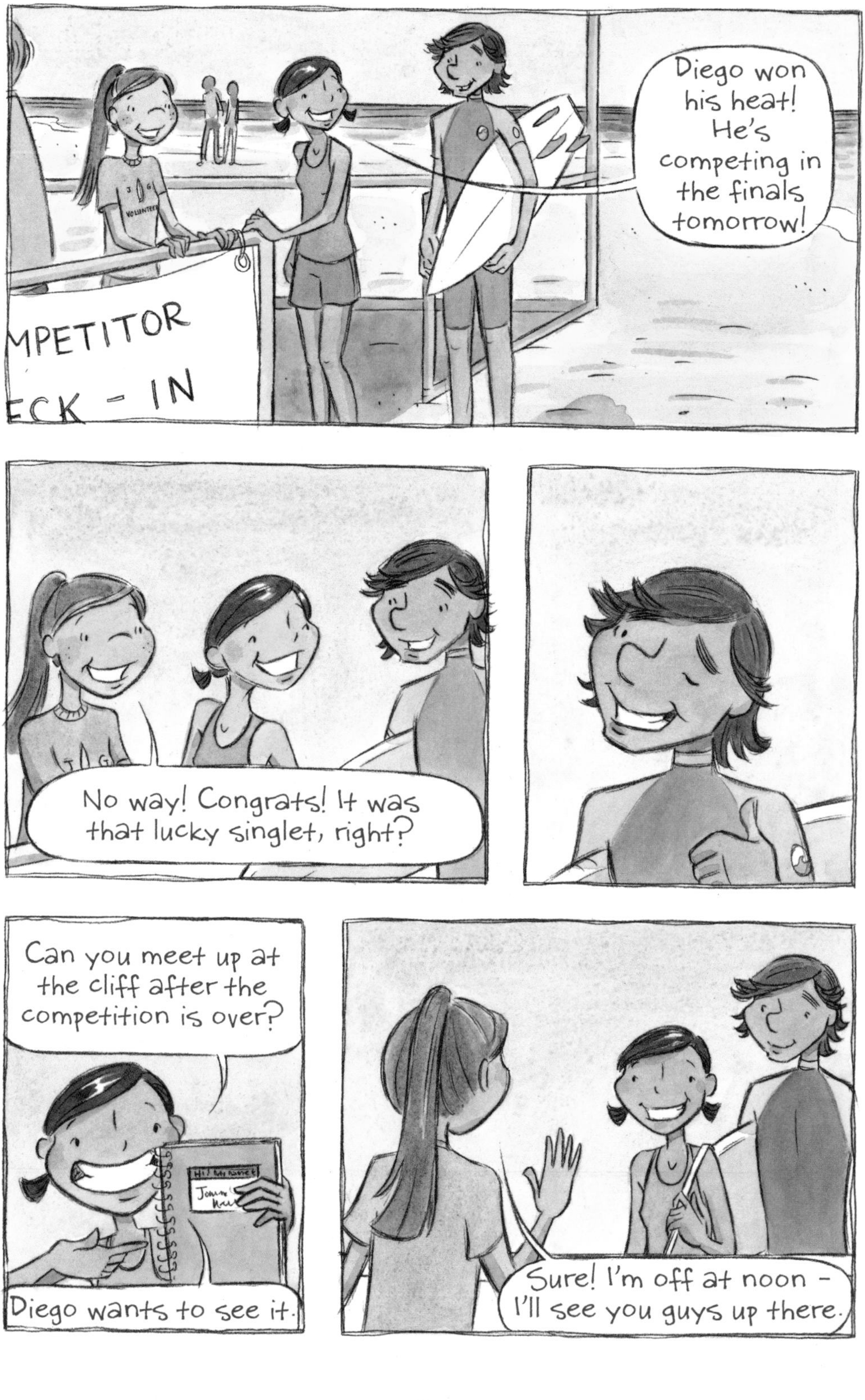
MPETITOR
ECK - IN
Diego won his heat! He's competing in the finals tomorrow!
No way! Congrats! It was that lucky singlet, right?
Can you meet up at the cliff after the competition is over?
Diego wants to see it.
Sure! I'm off at noon - I'll see you guys up there.

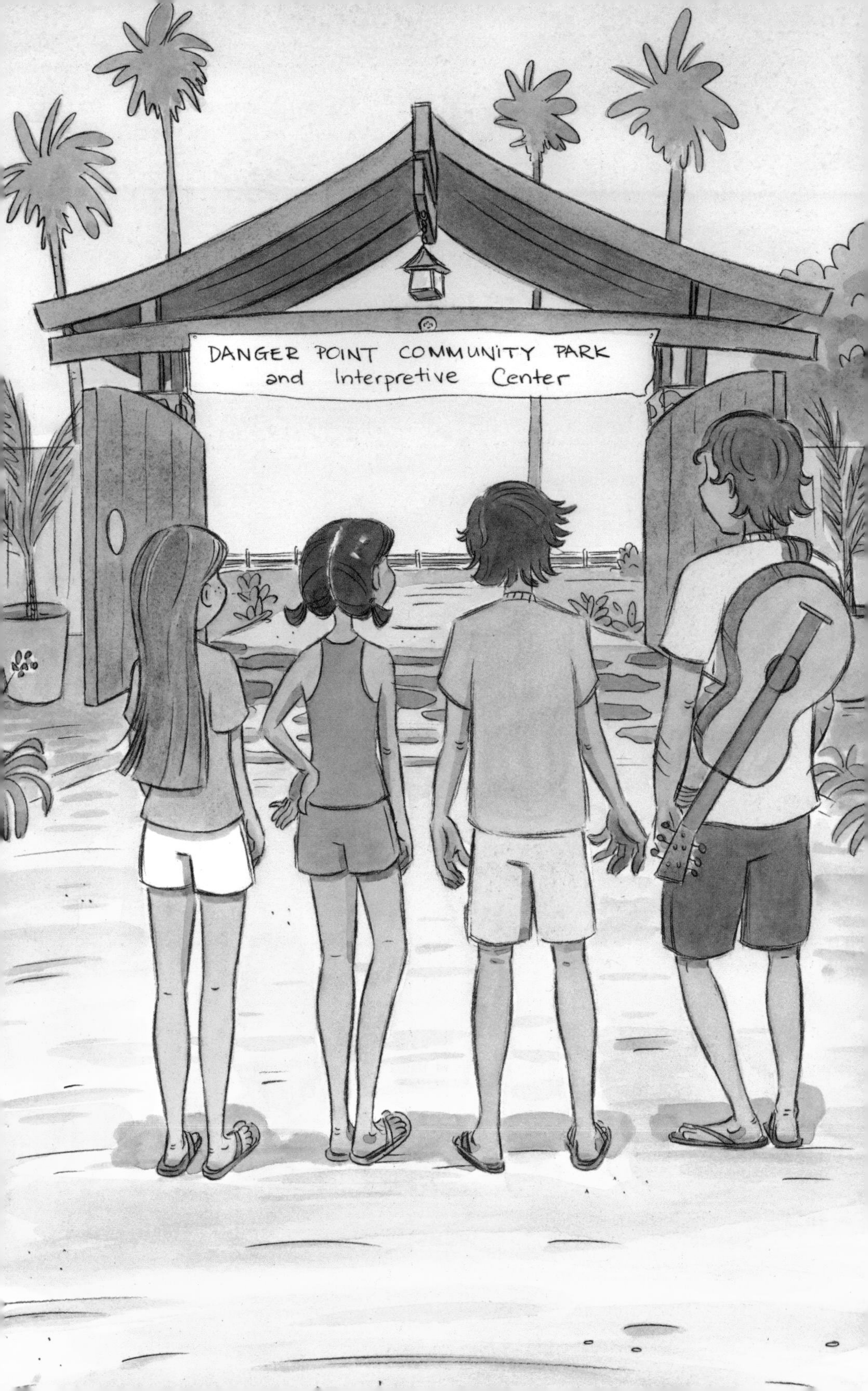
DANGER POINT COMMUNITY PARK
and Interpretive Center

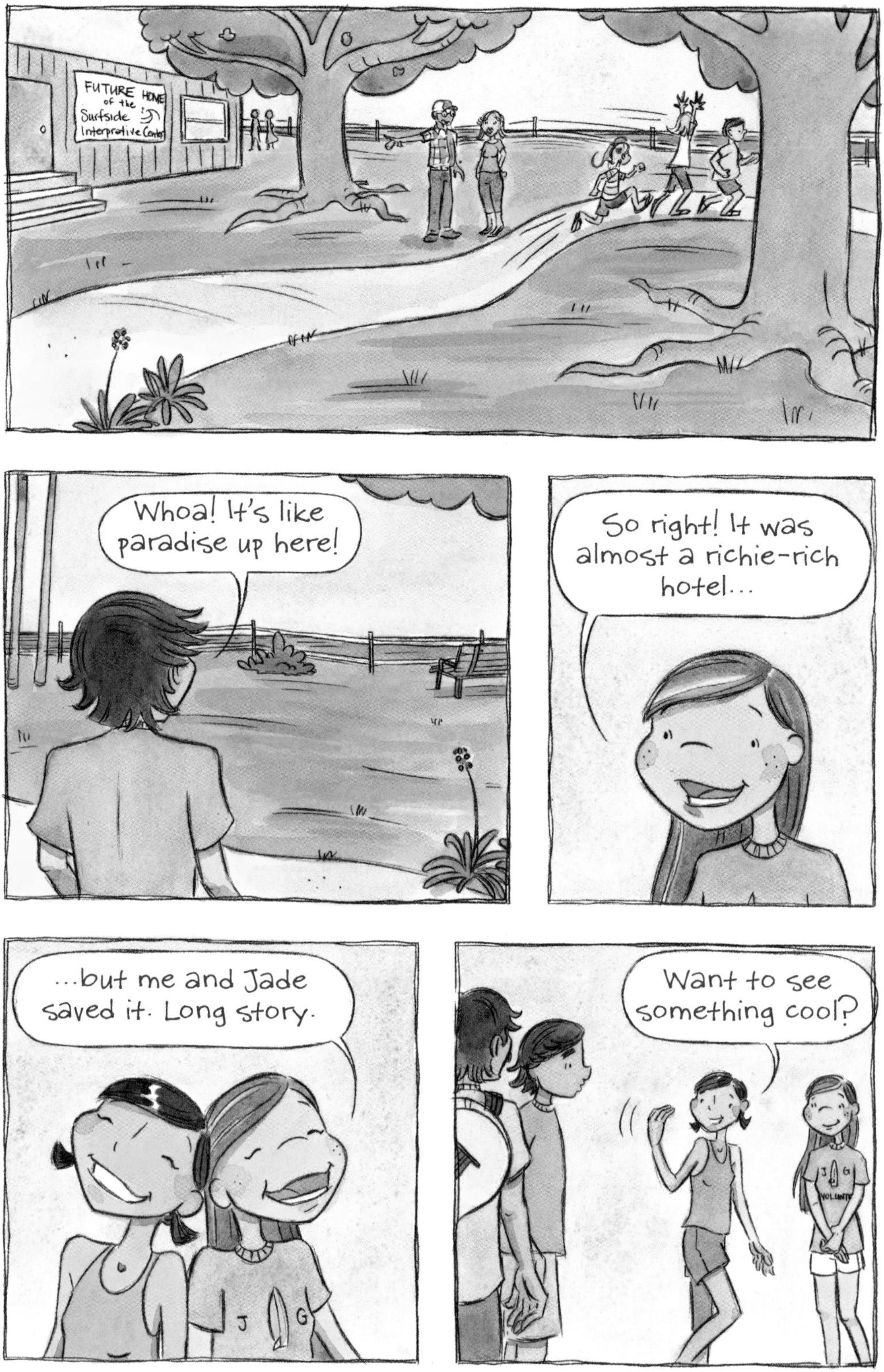
FUTURE HOME of the Surfside Interpretive Center
Whoa! It's like paradise up here!
So right! It was almost a richie-rich hotel...
...but me and Jade saved it. Long story.
Want to see something cool?

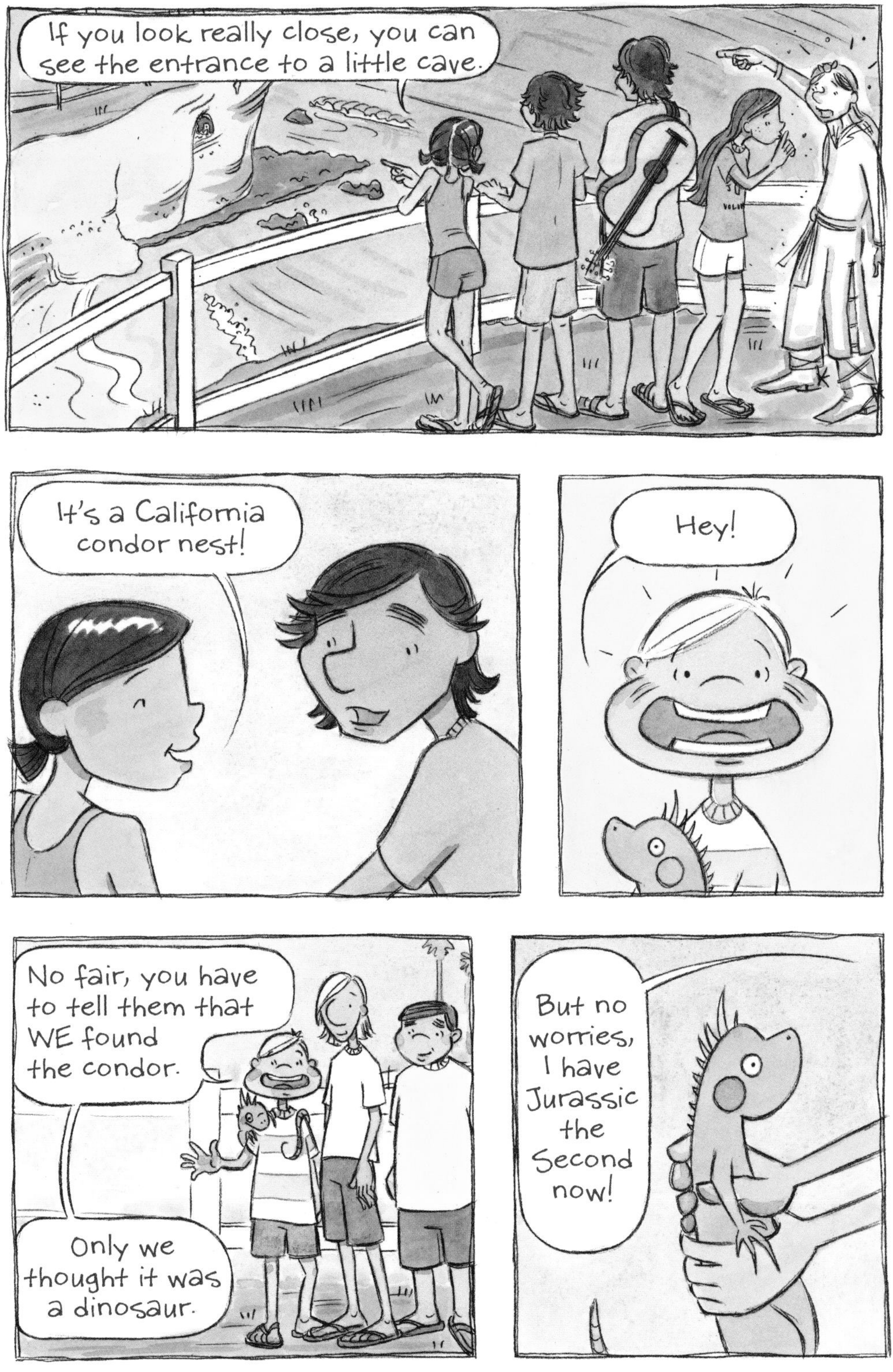
If you look really close, you can see the entrance to a little cave.
It's a California condor nest!
Hey!
No fair, you have to tell them that WE found the condor.
Only we thought it was a dinosaur.
But no worries, I have Jurassic the Second now!

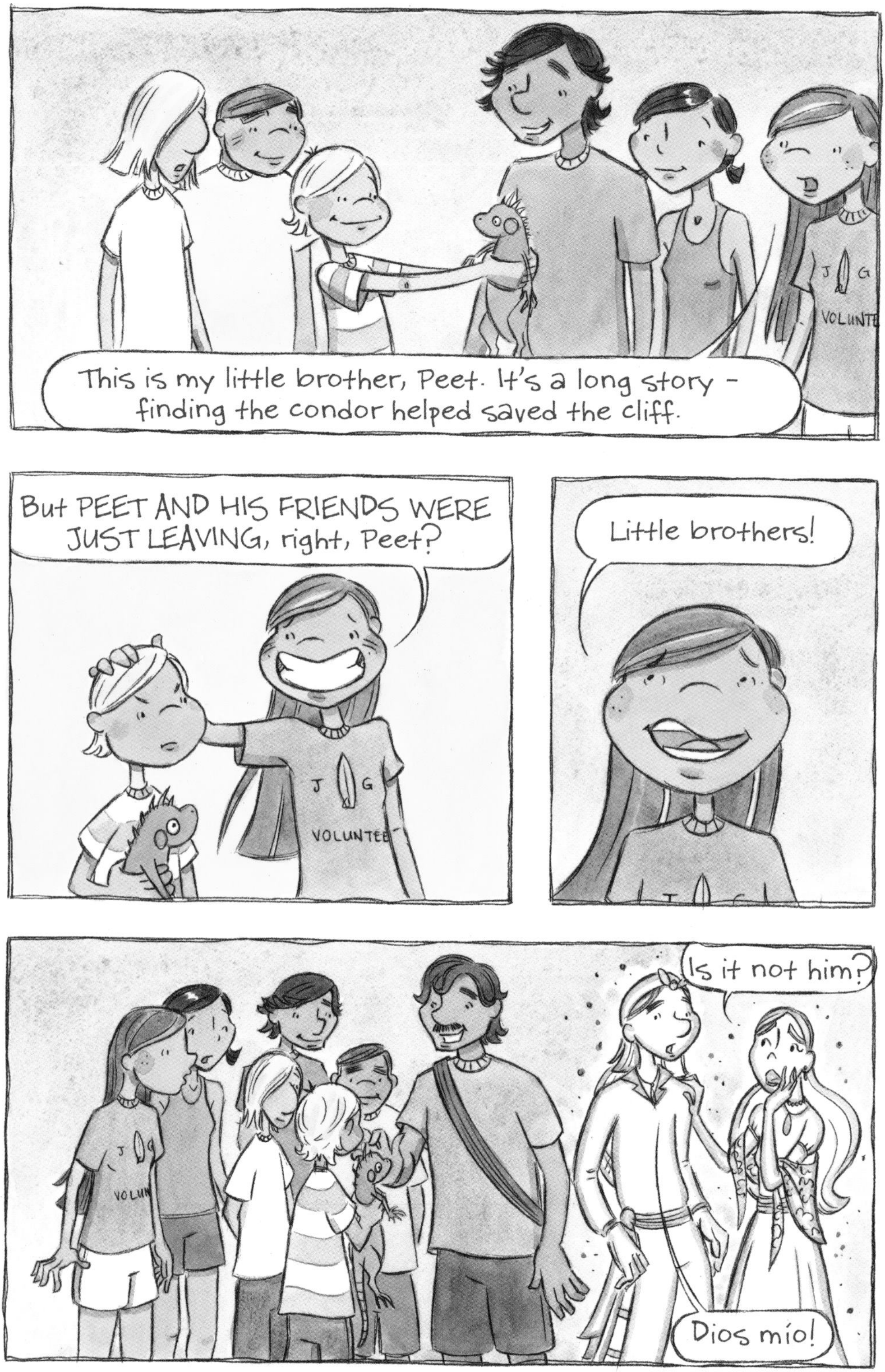
This is my little brother, Peet. It's a long story - finding the condor helped saved the cliff.
But PEET AND HIS FRIENDS WERE JUST LEAVING, right, Peet?
Little brothers!
Is it not him?
Dios mío!

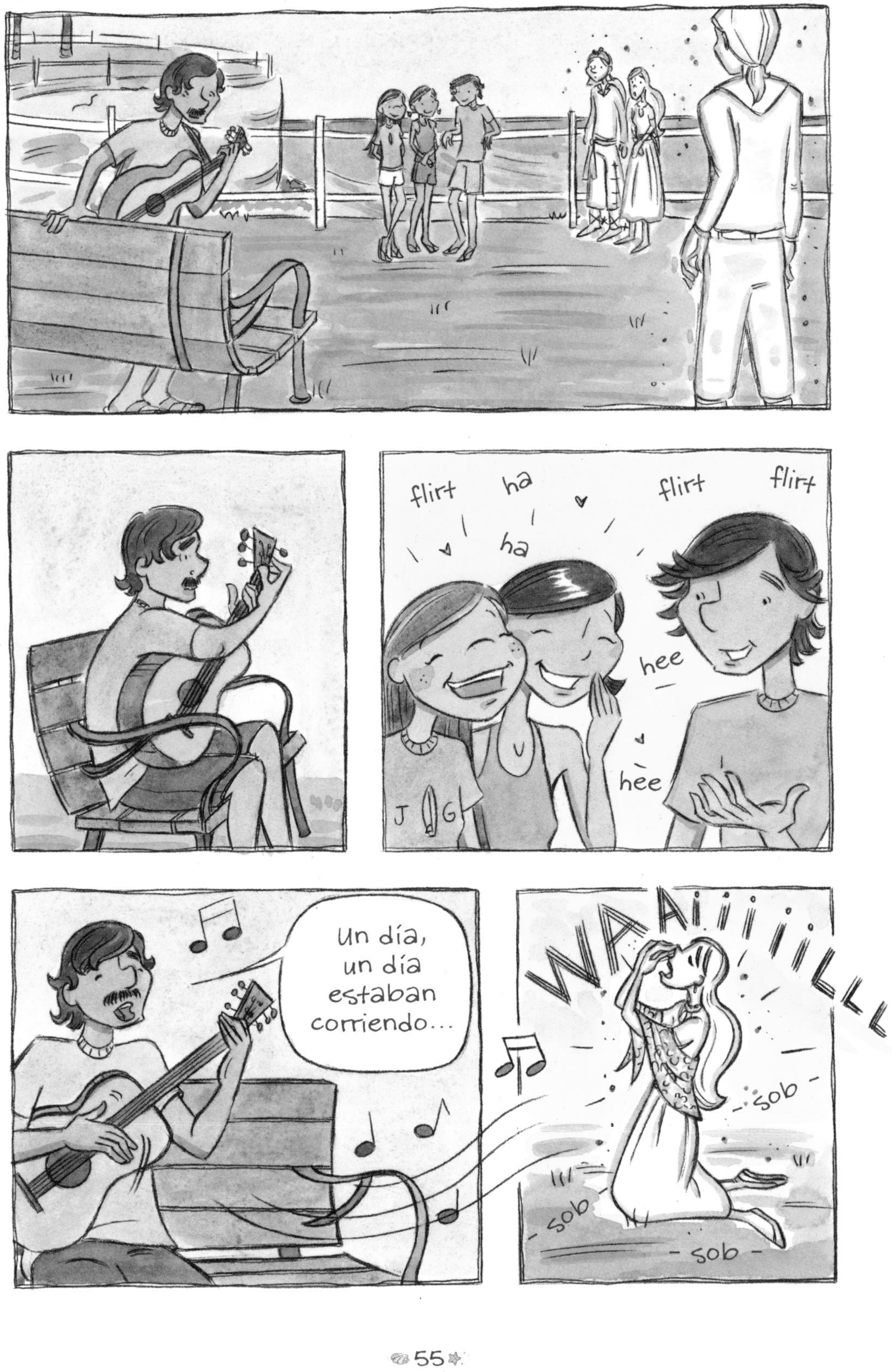
flirt
ha
ha
flirt
flirt
hee
hee
J G
Un día, un día estaban corriendo...
WAAiiiiLLL
sob
sob
sob

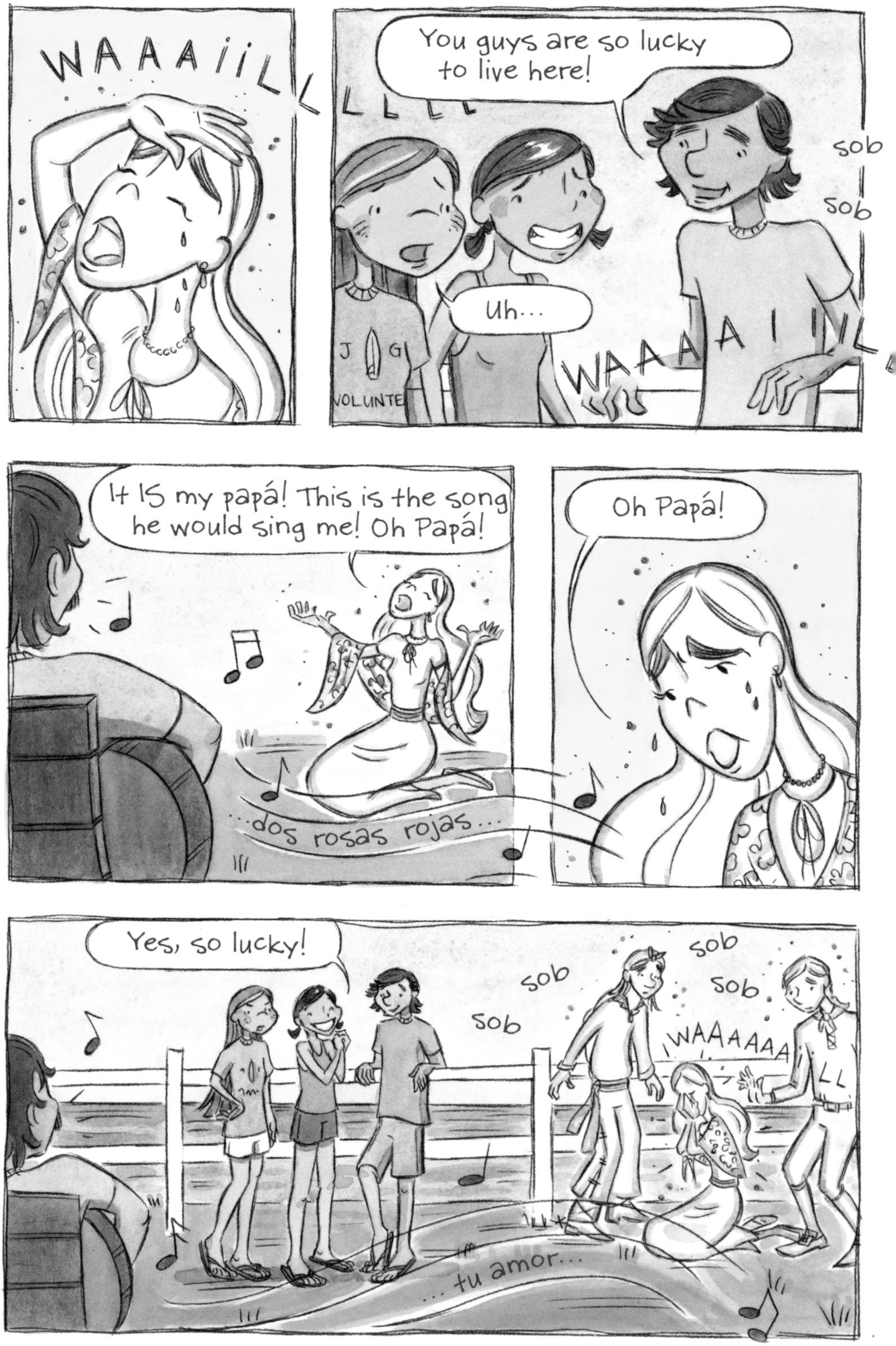
WAAAiiLLLLLL
You guys are so lucky to live here!
sob
sob
Uh...
WAAAAIIL
VOLUNTE
It IS my papá! This is the song he would sing me! Oh Papá!
...dos rosas rojas...
Oh Papá!
Yes, so lucky!
sob
sob
sob
sob
WAAAAAA
LL
...tu amor...

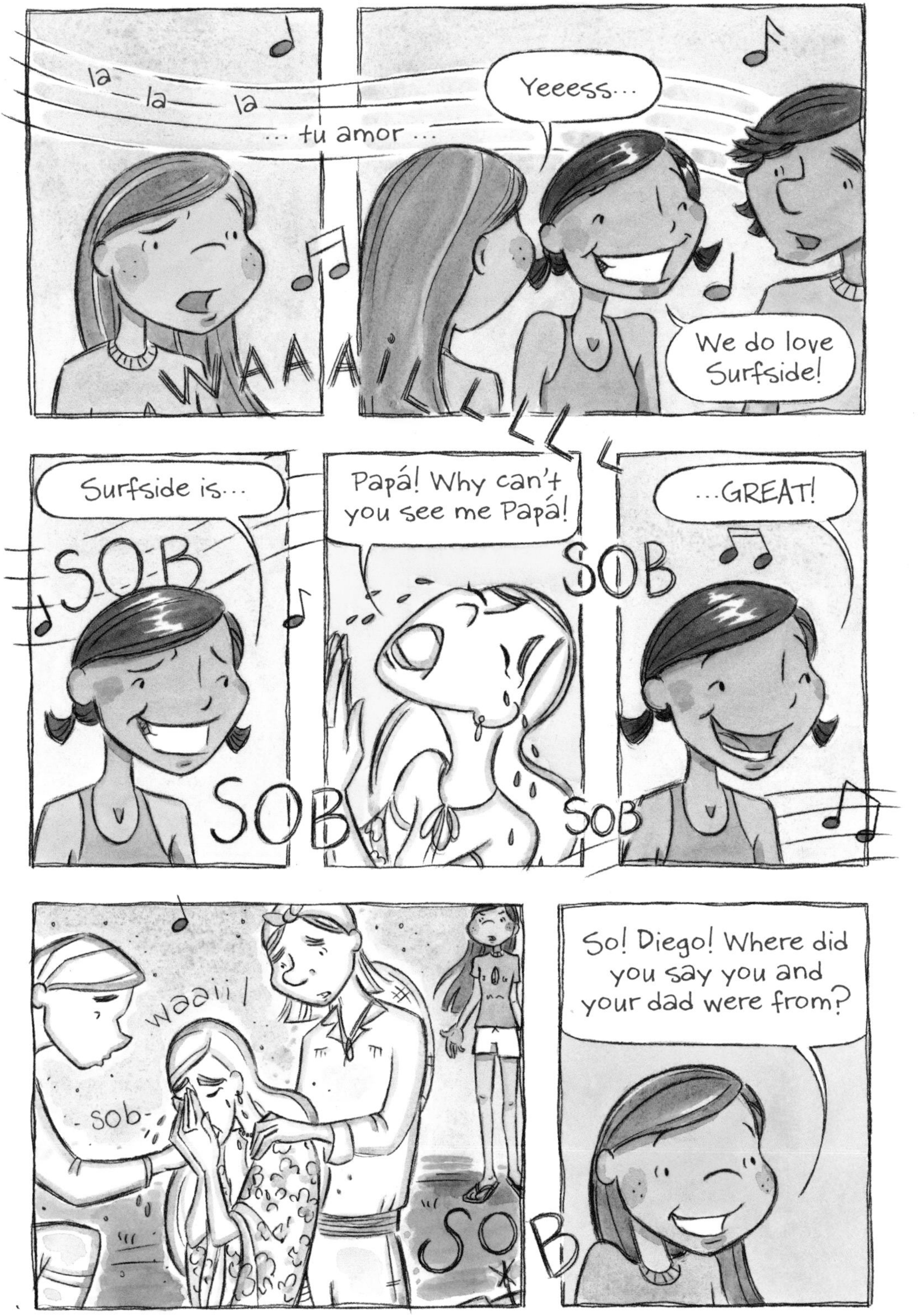
la
la
la
... tu amor ...
Yeeess...
We do love Surfside!
WAAAILLLLL
Surfside is...
SOB
SOB
Papá! Why can't you see me Papá!
SOB
SOB
...GREAT!
waaiil
sob
SOB
So! Diego! Where did you say you and your dad were from?

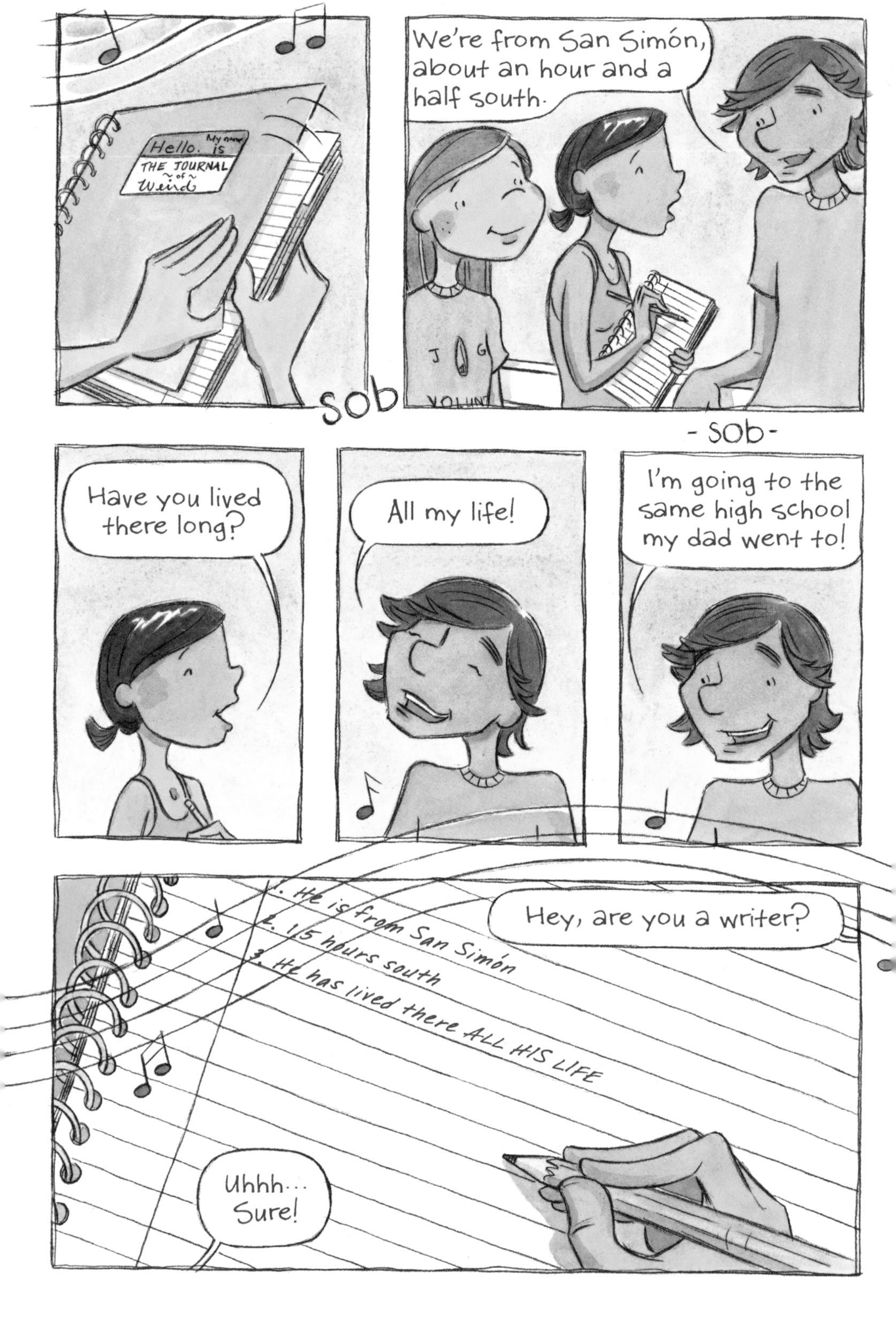
Hello. My name is THE JOURNAL ~of~ Weird
We're from San Simón, about an hour and a half south.
sob
- sob -
Have you lived there long?
All my life!
I'm going to the same high school my dad went to!
1. He is from San Simón
2. 1.5 hours south
3. He has lived there ALL HIS LIFE
Hey, are you a writer?
Uhhh... Sure!

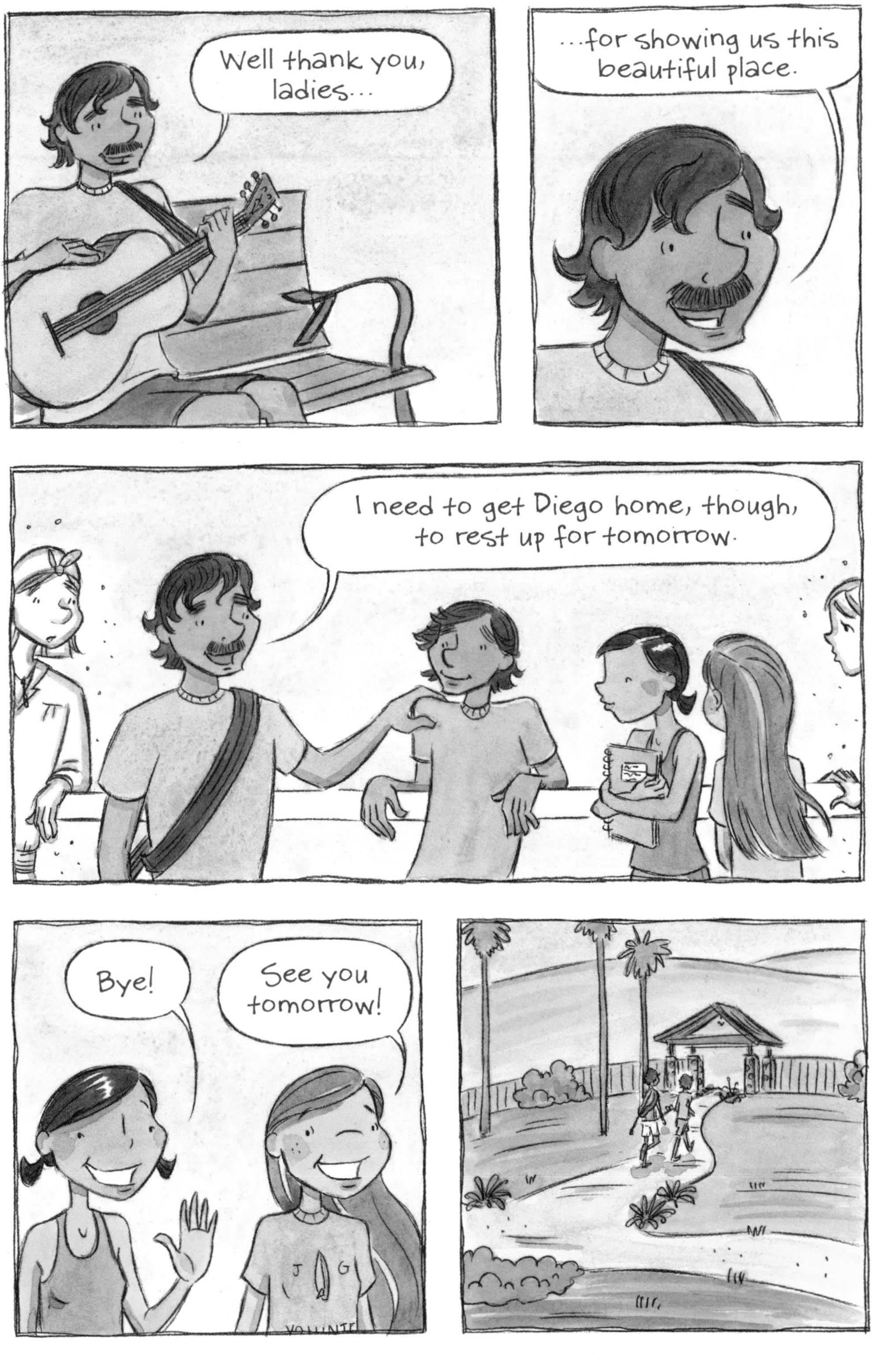
Well thank you, ladies...
...for showing us this beautiful place.
I need to get Diego home, though, to rest up for tomorrow.
Bye!
See you tomorrow!

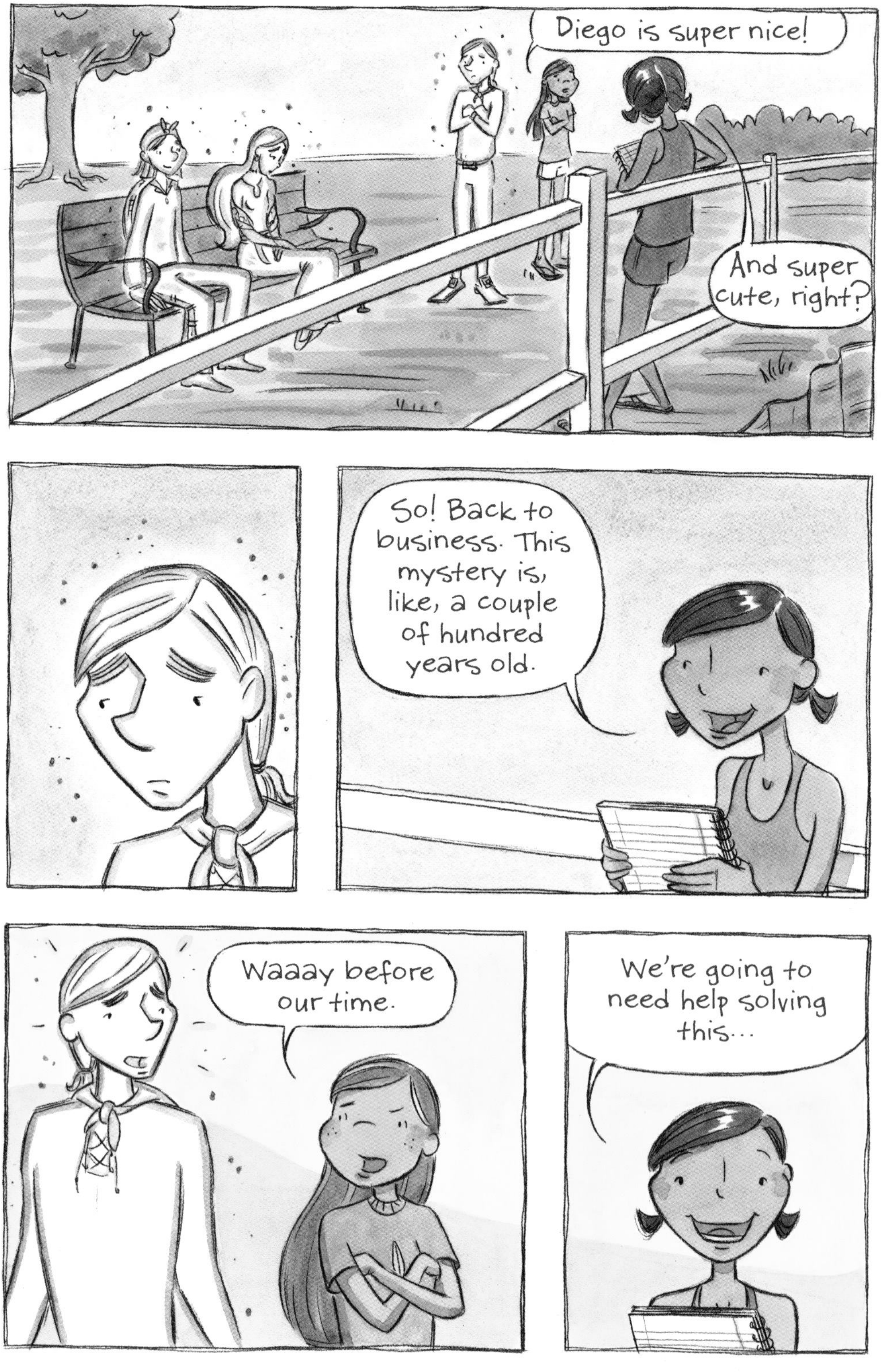
Diego is super nice!
And super cute, right?
So! Back to business. This mystery is, like, a couple of hundred years old.
Waaay before our time.
We're going to need help solving this...

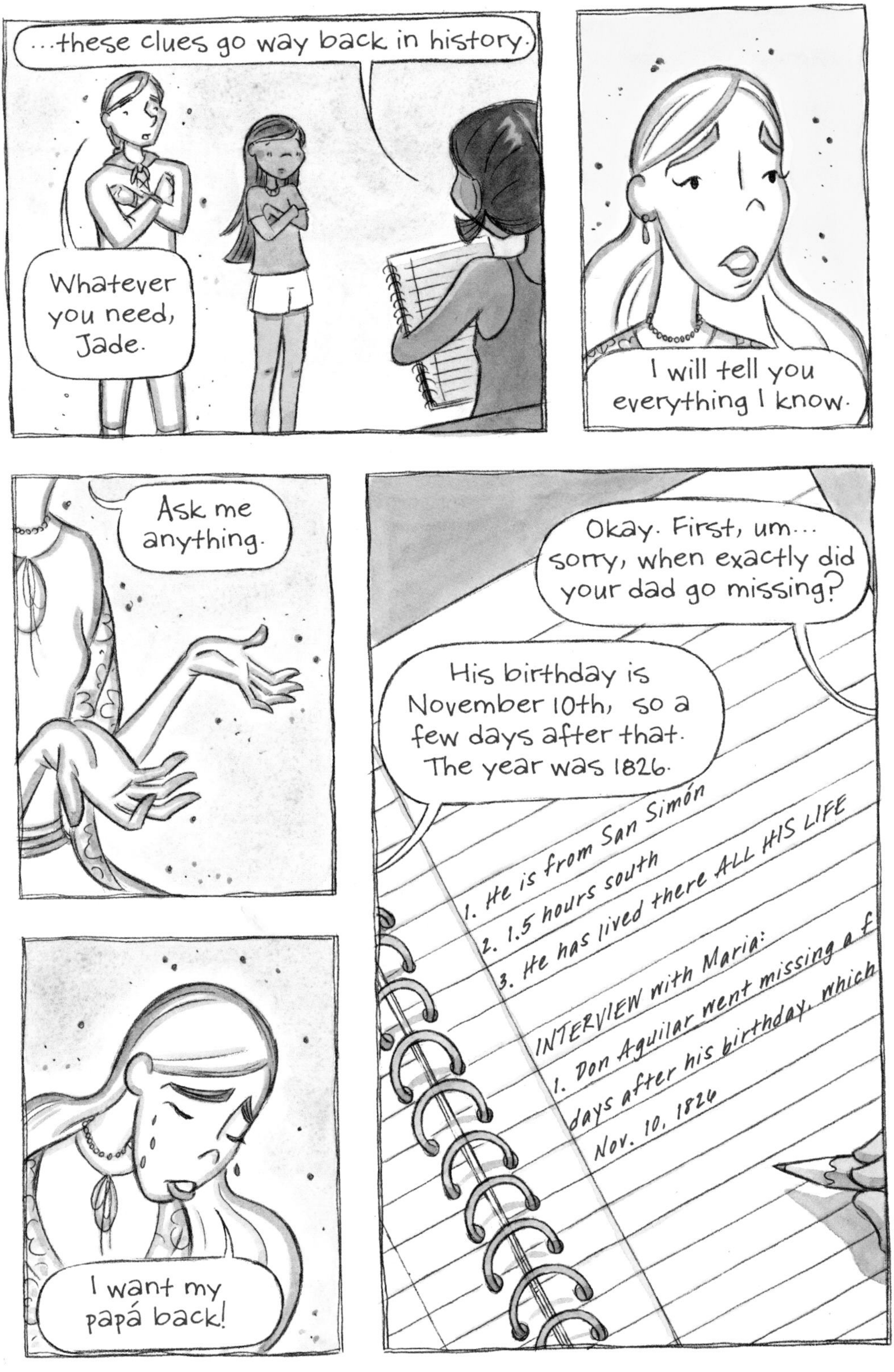
...these clues go way back in history.
Whatever you need, Jade.
I will tell you everything I know.
Ask me anything.
I want my papá back!
Okay. First, um... sorry, when exactly did your dad go missing?
His birthday is November 10th, so a few days after that. The year was 1826.
1. He is from San Simón
2. 1.5 hours south
3. He has lived there ALL HIS LIFE
INTERVIEW with Maria:
1. Don Aguilar went missing a f
days after his birthday, which
Nov. 10, 1826

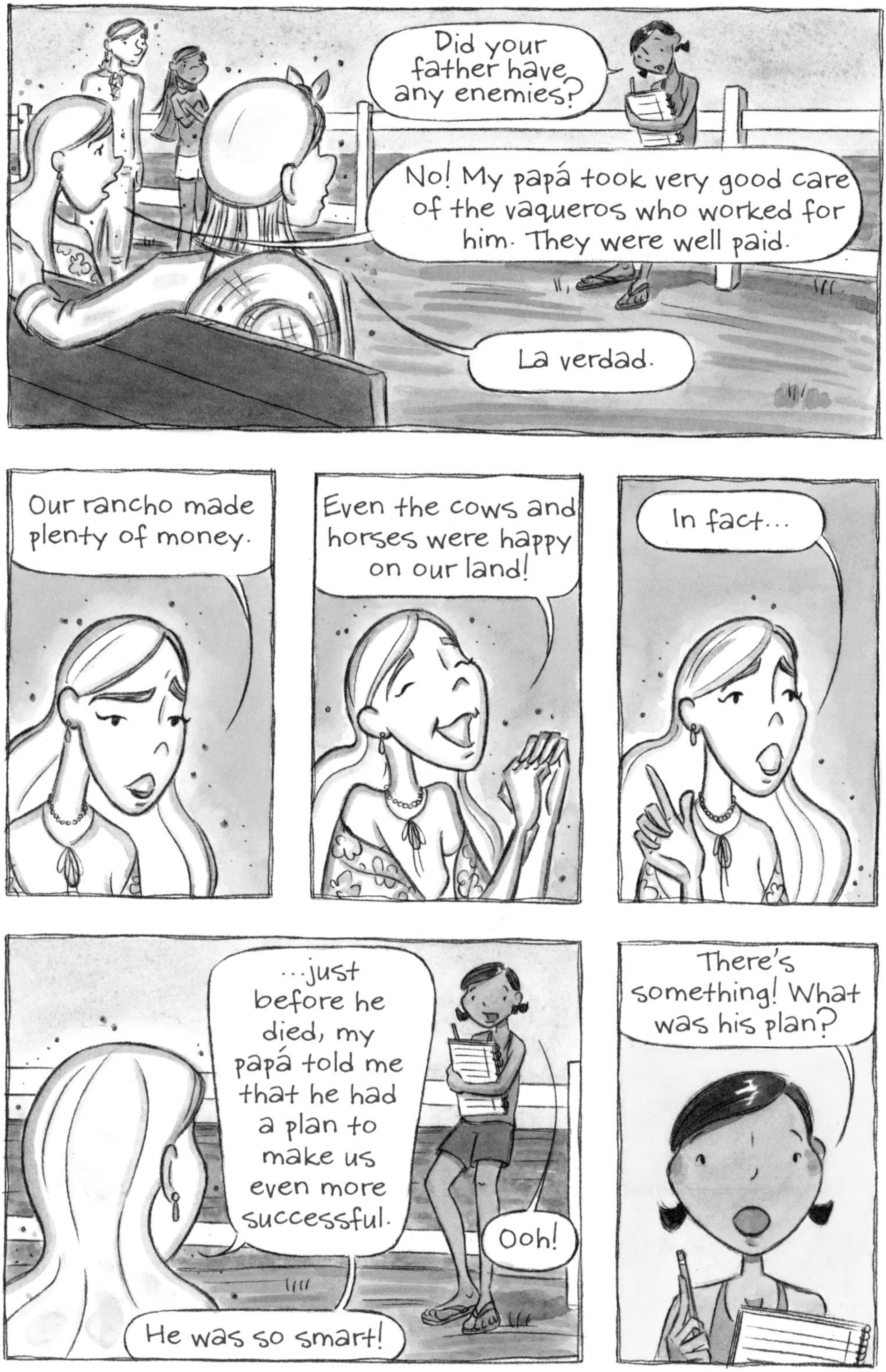
Did your father have any enemies?
No! My papá took very good care of the vaqueros who worked for him. They were well paid.
La verdad.
Our rancho made plenty of money.
Even the cows and horses were happy on our land!
In fact...
...just before he died, my papá told me that he had a plan to make us even more successful.
Ooh!
He was so smart!
There's something! What was his plan?

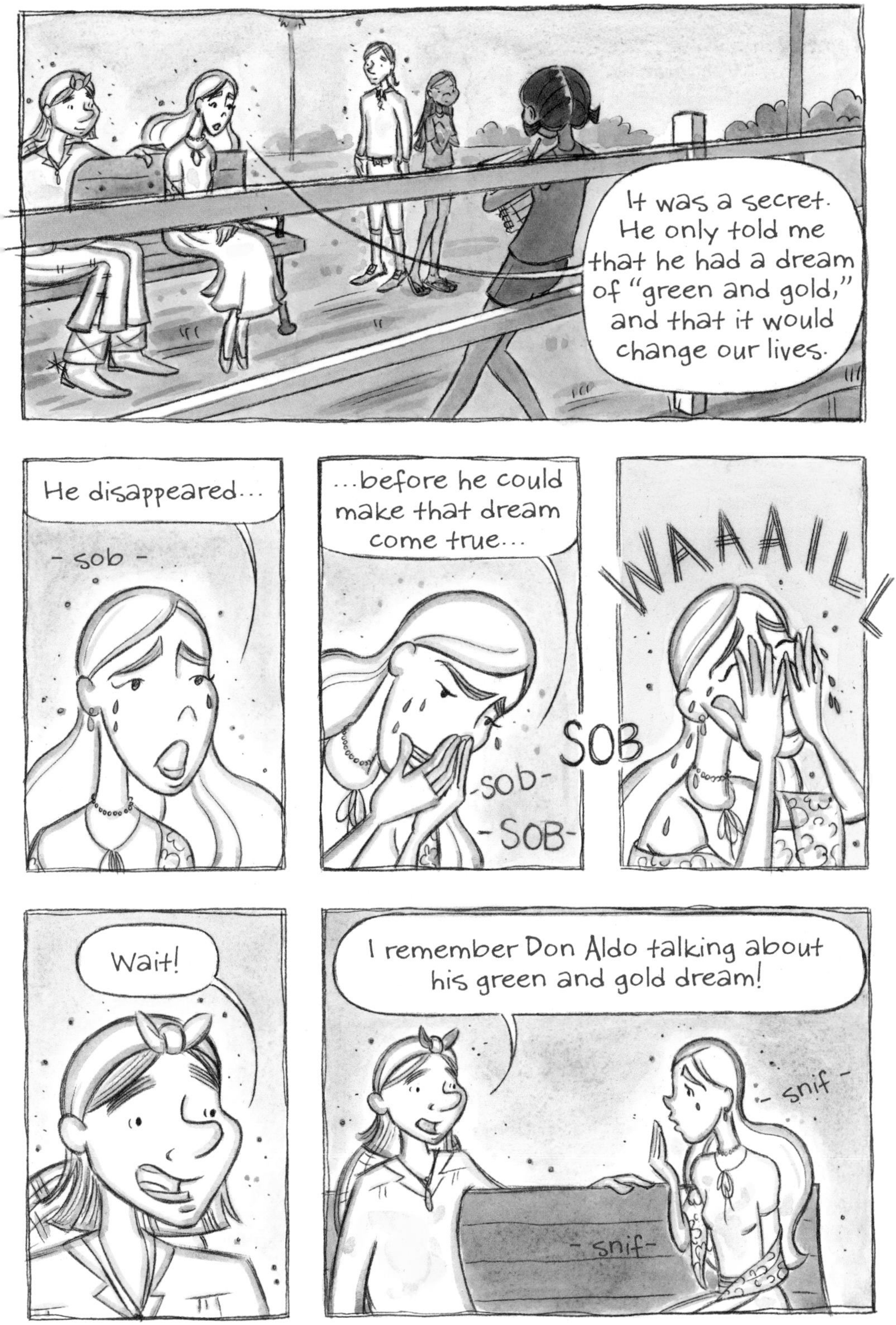
It was a secret. He only told me that he had a dream of "green and gold," and that it would change our lives.
He disappeared...
- sob -
...before he could make that dream come true...
-sob-
-SOB-
SOB
WAAAIL
Wait!
I remember Don Aldo talking about his green and gold dream!
- snif -
- snif-

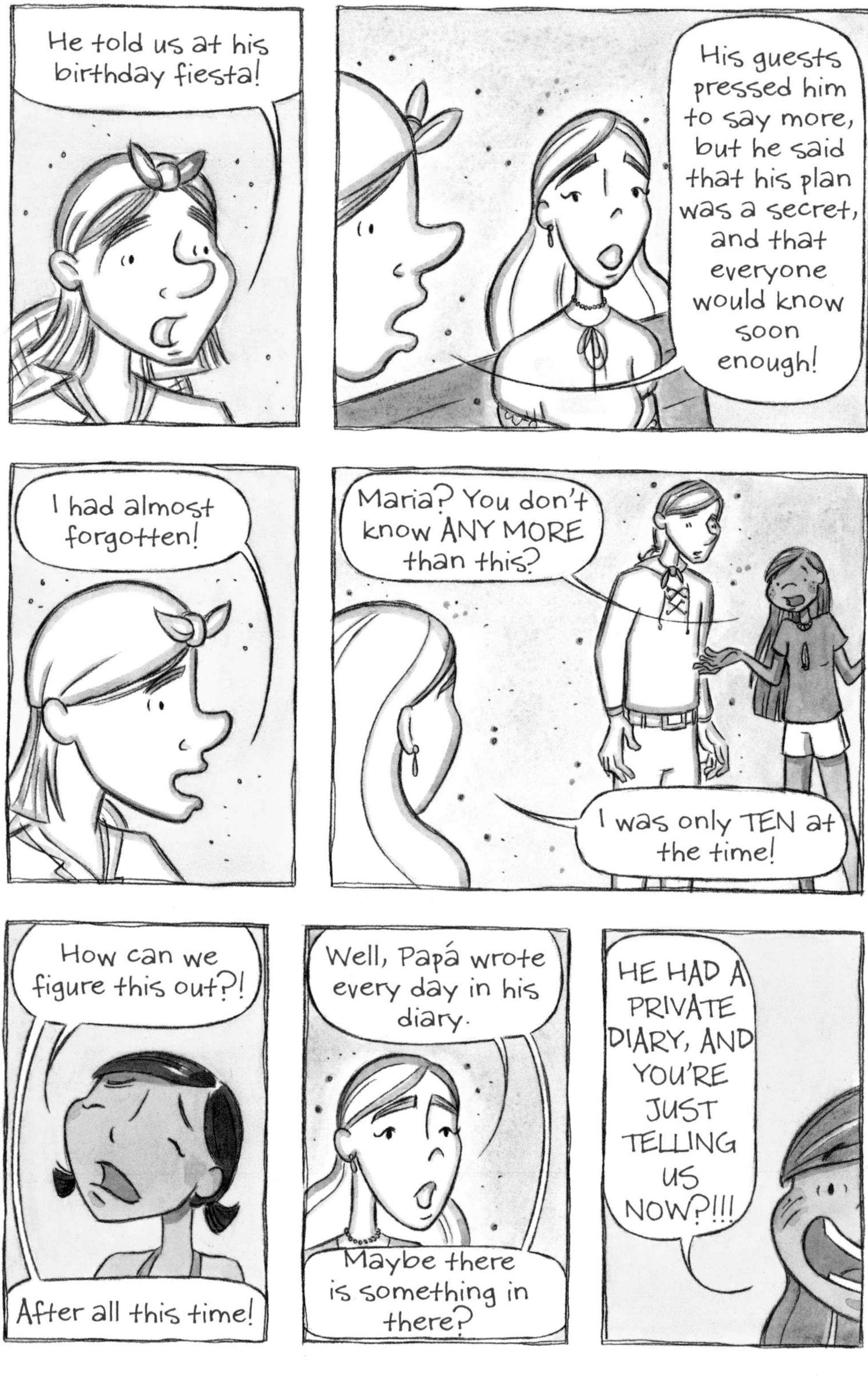
He told us at his birthday fiesta!
His guests pressed him to say more, but he said that his plan was a secret, and that everyone would know soon enough!
I had almost forgotten!
Maria? You don't know ANY MORE than this?
I was only TEN at the time!
How can we figure this out?!
After all this time!
Well, Papá wrote every day in his diary.
Maybe there is something in there?
HE HAD A PRIVATE DIARY, AND YOU'RE JUST TELLING US NOW?!!!

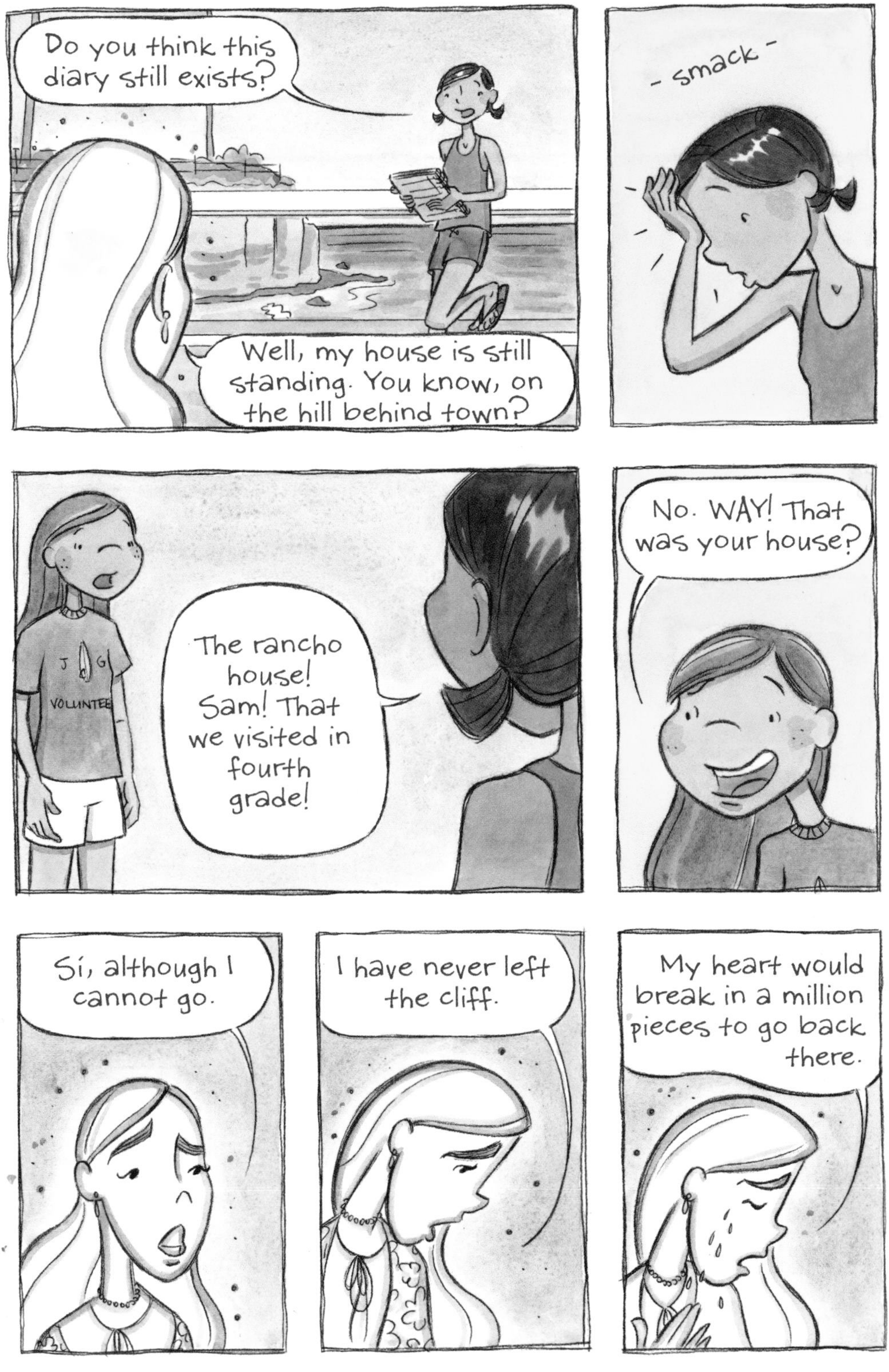
Do you think this diary still exists?
Well, my house is still standing. You know, on the hill behind town?
- smack -
JG
VOLUNTEE
The rancho house! Sam! That we visited in fourth grade!
No. WAY! That was your house?
Sí, although I cannot go.
I have never left the cliff.
My heart would break in a million pieces to go back there.

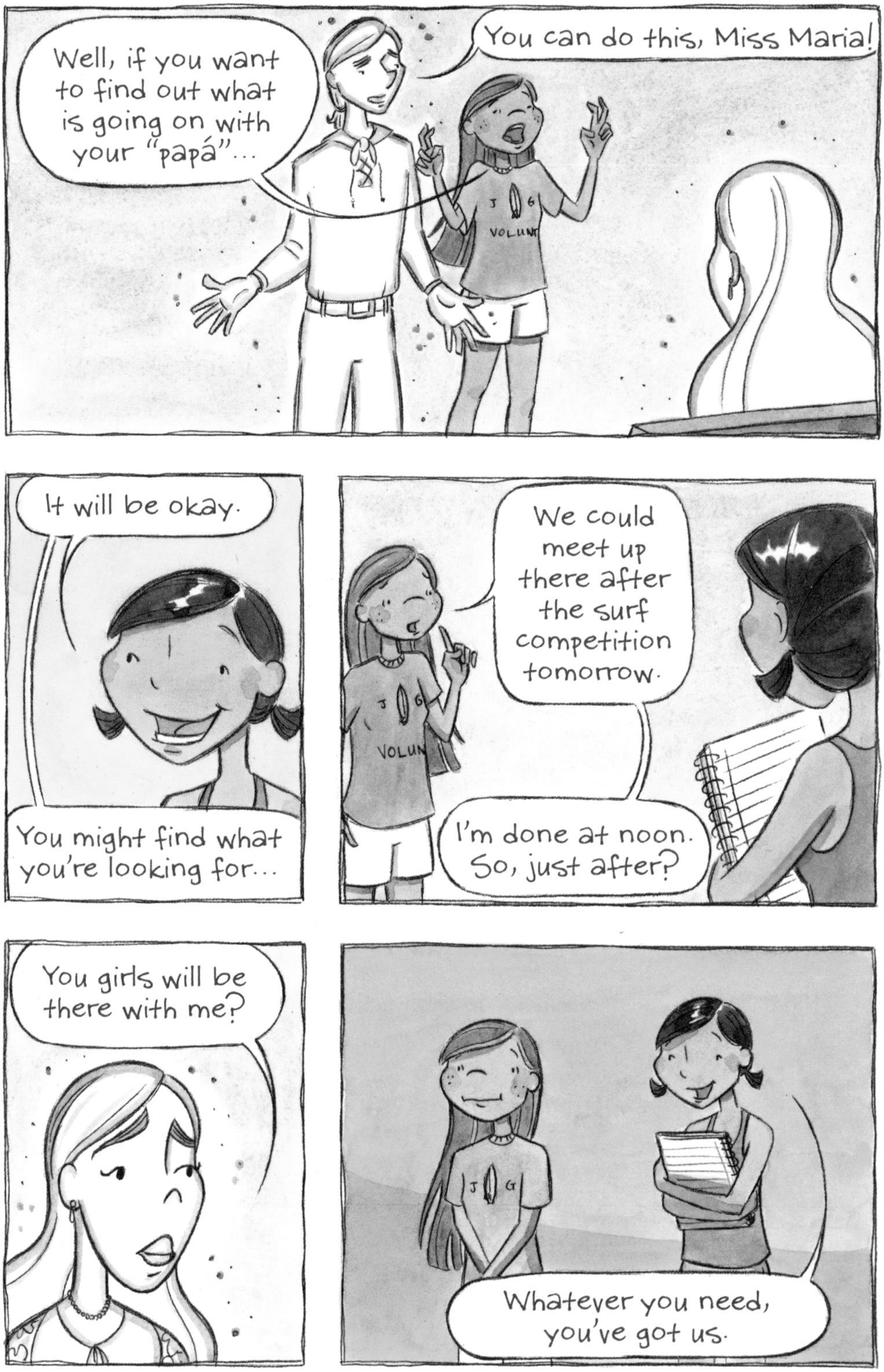
Well, if you want to find out what is going on with your "papá"...
You can do this, Miss Maria!
JG
VOLUN
It will be okay.
You might find what you're looking for...
We could meet up there after the surf competition tomorrow.
JG
VOLUN
I'm done at noon. So, just after?
You girls will be there with me?
JG
Whatever you need, you've got us.

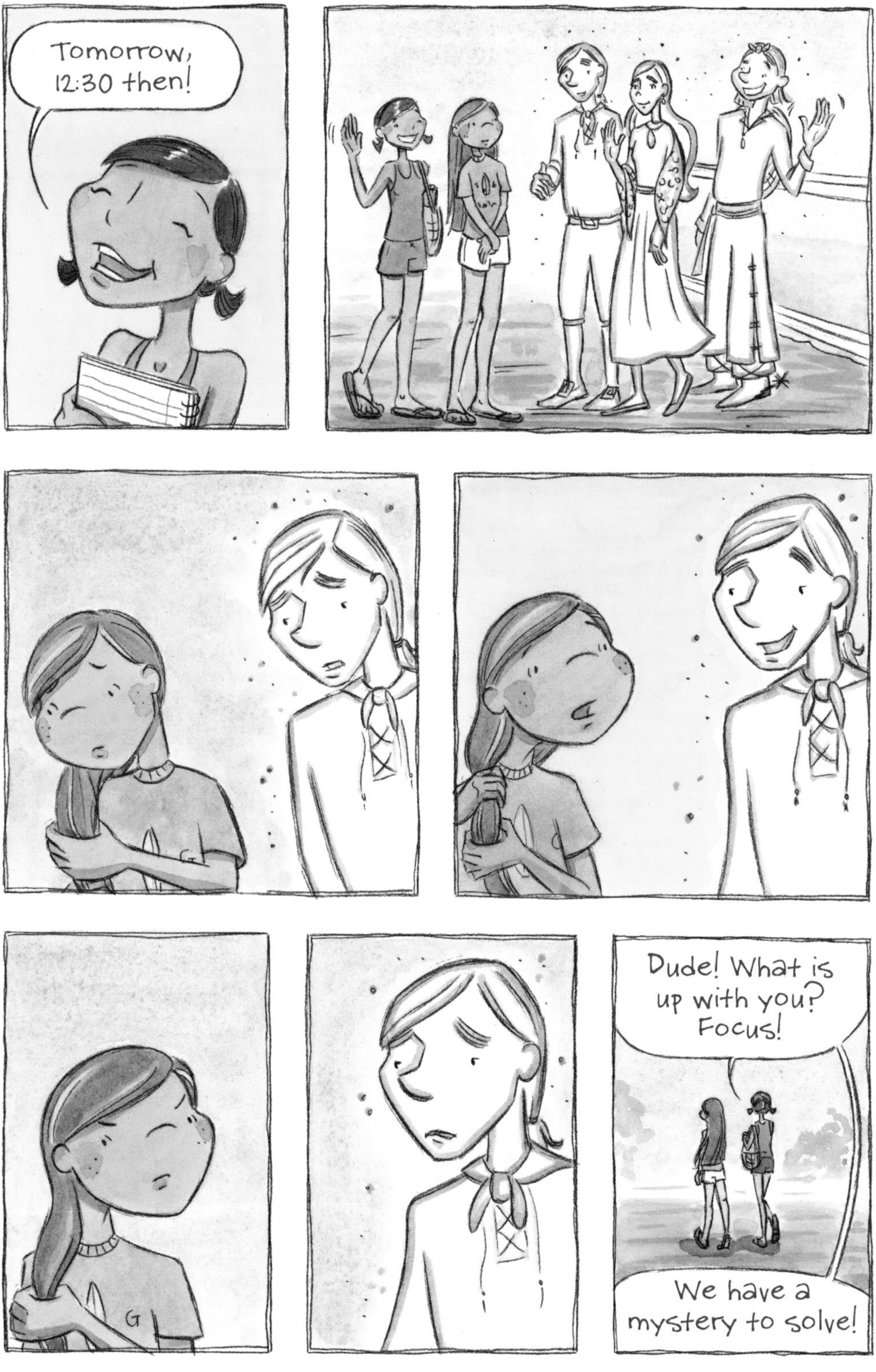
Tomorrow, 12:30 then!
Dude! What is up with you? Focus!
We have a mystery to solve!

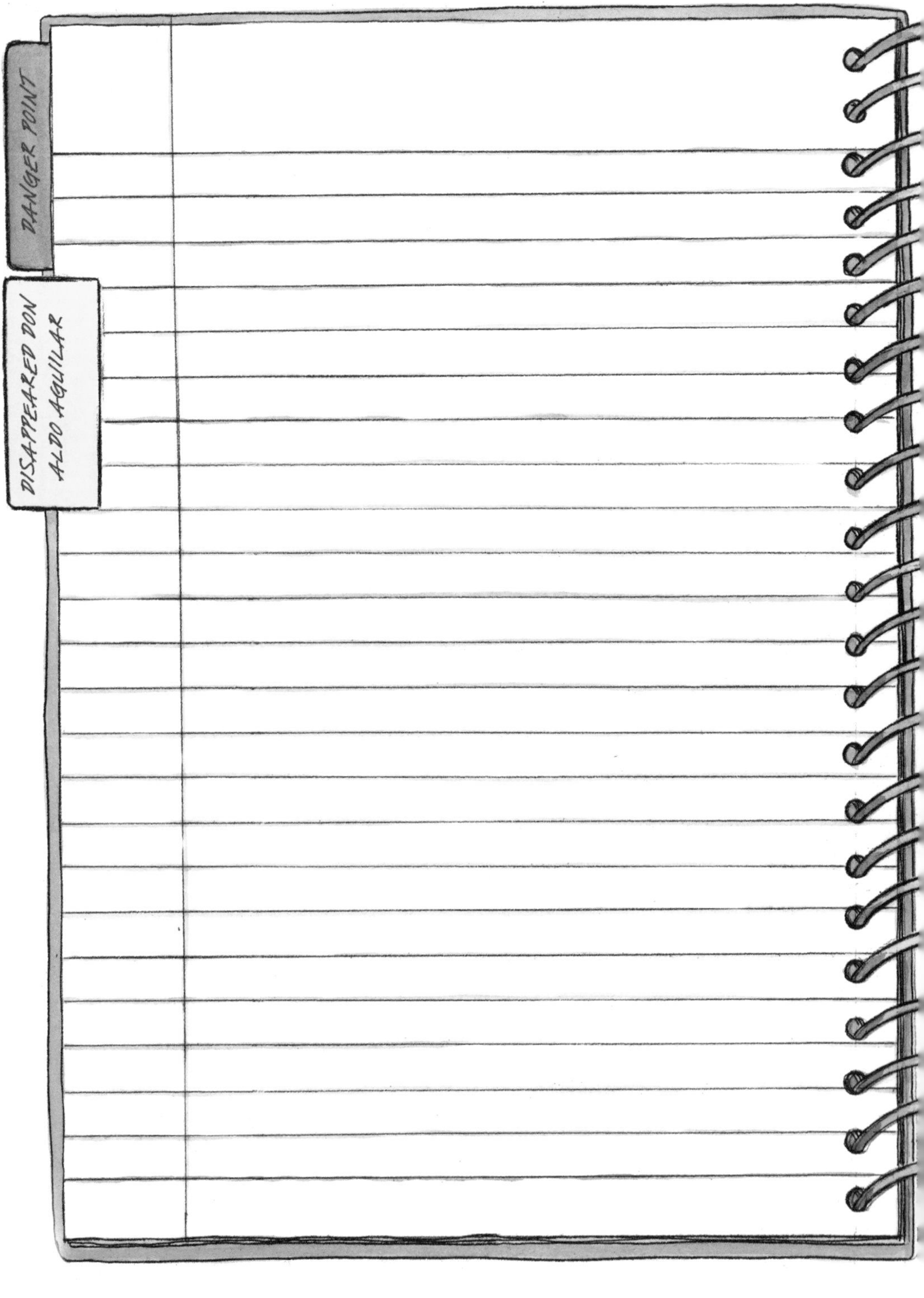
DANGER POINT
DISAPPEARED DON ALDO AGUILAR

☆ Don Aldo had a SECRET PLAN to make the rancho more
successful!!!

* Ignacio confirms existence of this plan

* He had a "dream of green and gold"

▽

What could this mean?

* Don Aldo disappeared before he could realize his dream

(NOTE TO SELF: Maria gets HYSTERICAL!)

* Ignacio remembers that Don Aldo mentioned that he had
a secret plan at his birthday party

Who was there? Would they try to rob Don Aldo?

☆ DON ALDO HAD A SECRET DIARY!!!

* Maria remembers him writing in it

* Where is this diary?

PS Sam is
acting
SUPER WEIRD

▽ OMG

☆ IN THE RANCHO HOUSE:

* Maria lived in the old rancho house

* Is the diary still there?

* Field trip!

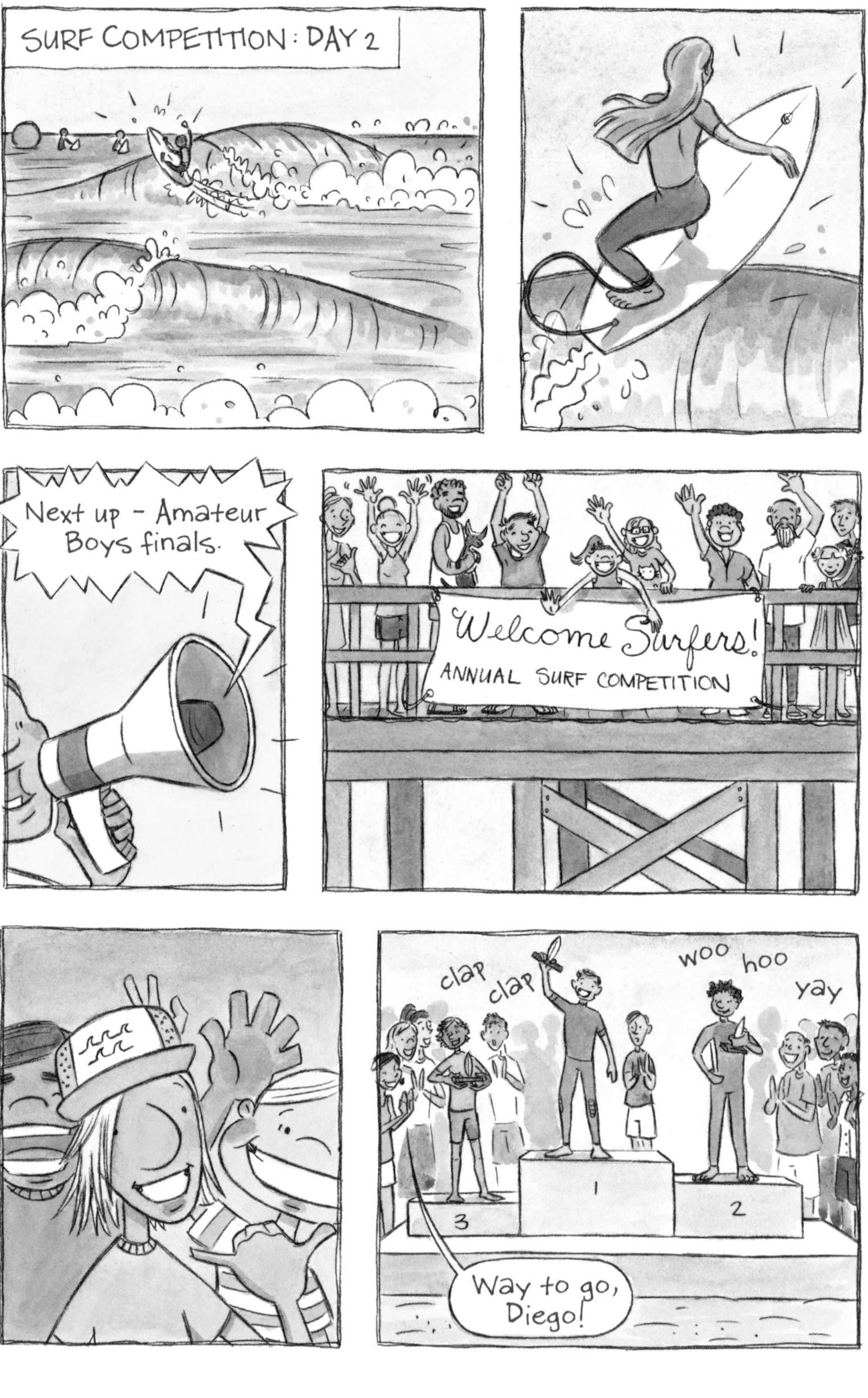
SURF COMPETITION: DAY 2
Next up - Amateur Boys finals.
Welcome Surfers!
ANNUAL SURF COMPETITION
clap
clap
woo
hoo
yay
1
2
3
Way to go, Diego!

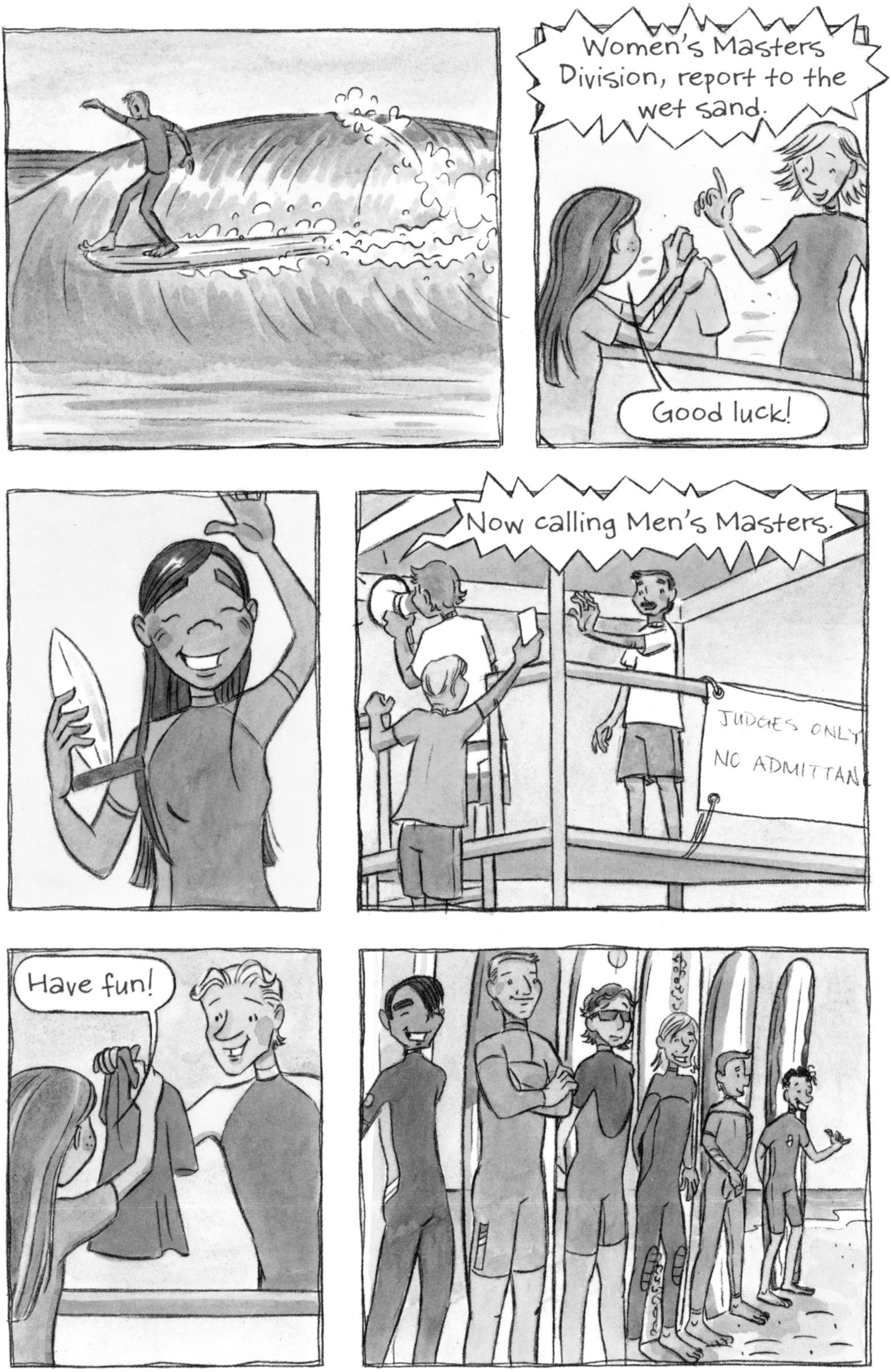
Women's Masters Division, report to the wet sand.
Good luck!
Now calling Men's Masters.
JUDGES ONLY
NO ADMITTAN
Have fun!

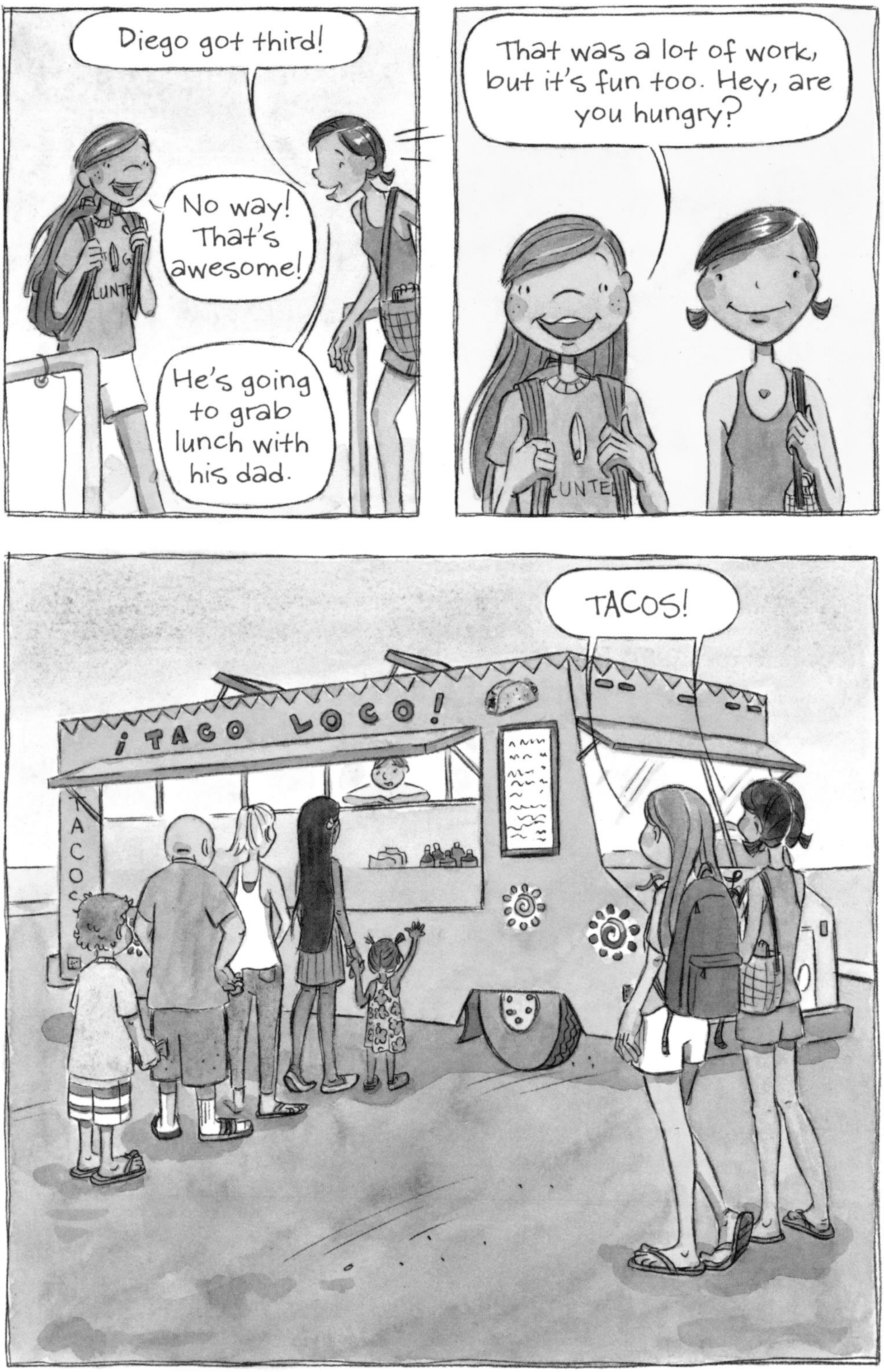

Diego got third!
No way! That's awesome!
He's going to grab lunch with his dad.
That was a lot of work, but it's fun too. Hey, are you hungry?
¡TACO LOCO!
TACOS!

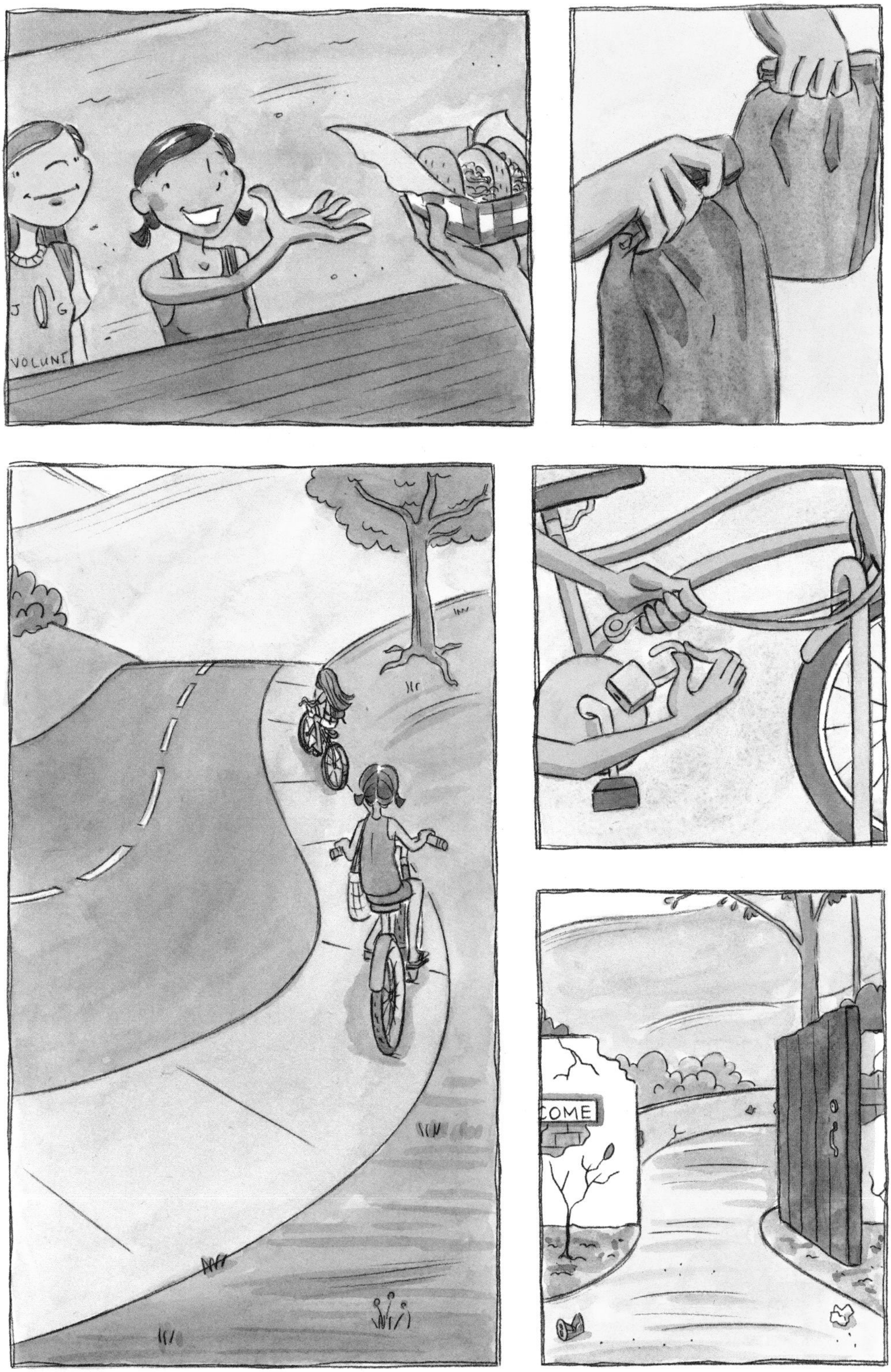
VOLUNT
COME

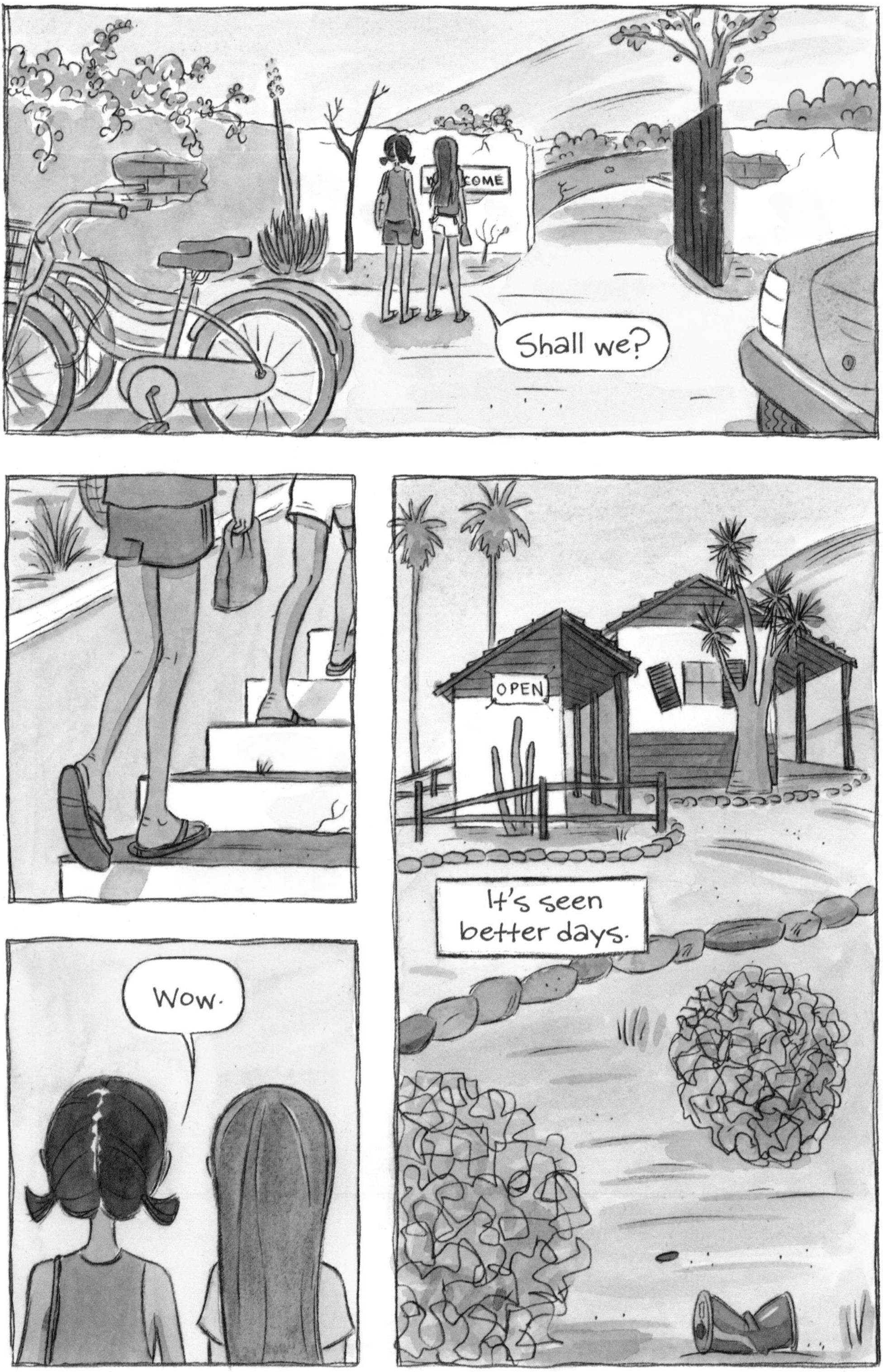
Shall we?
OPEN
It's seen better days.
Wow.

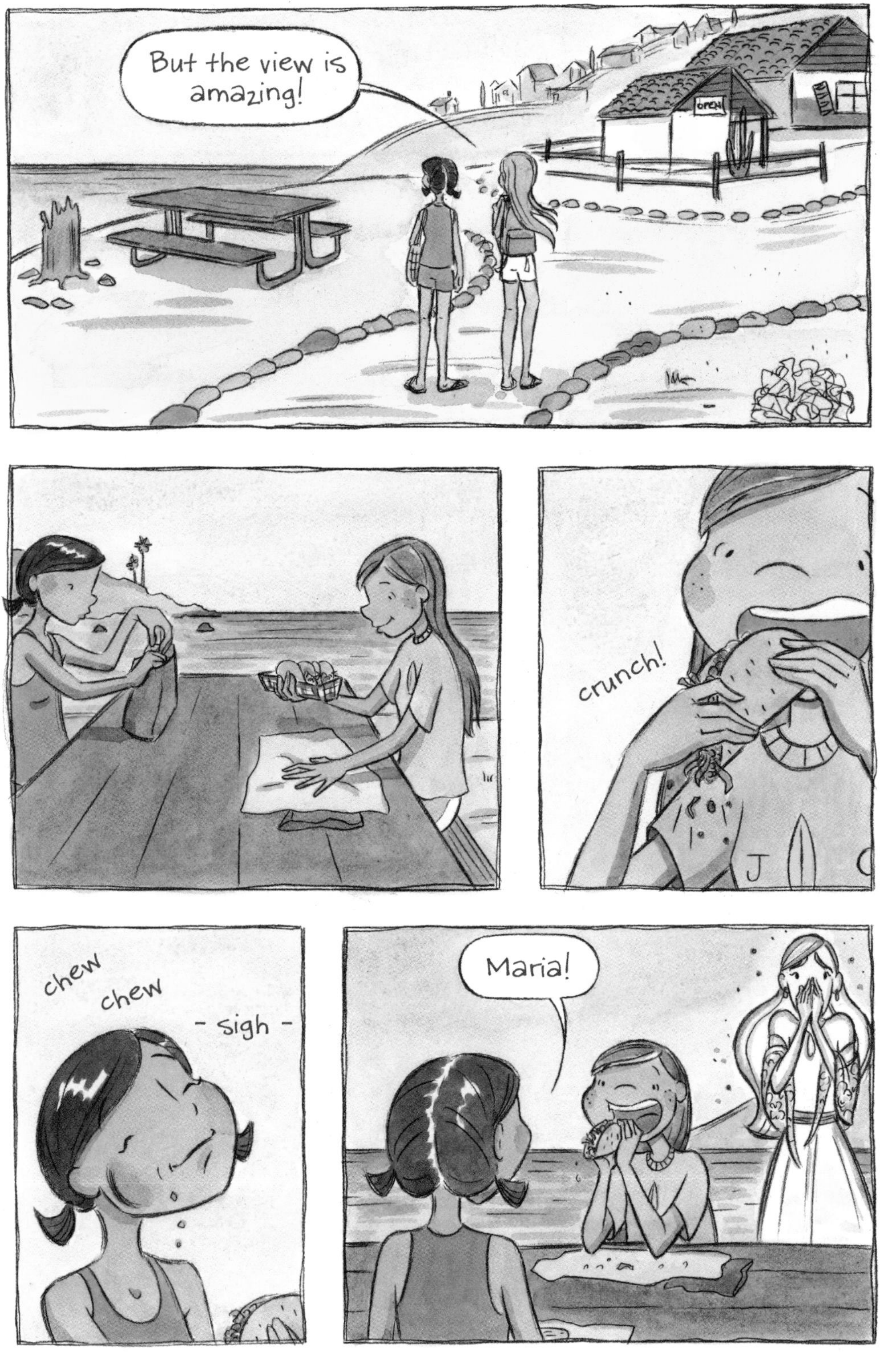
But the view is amazing!
OPEN
crunch!
chew
chew
- sigh -
Maria!

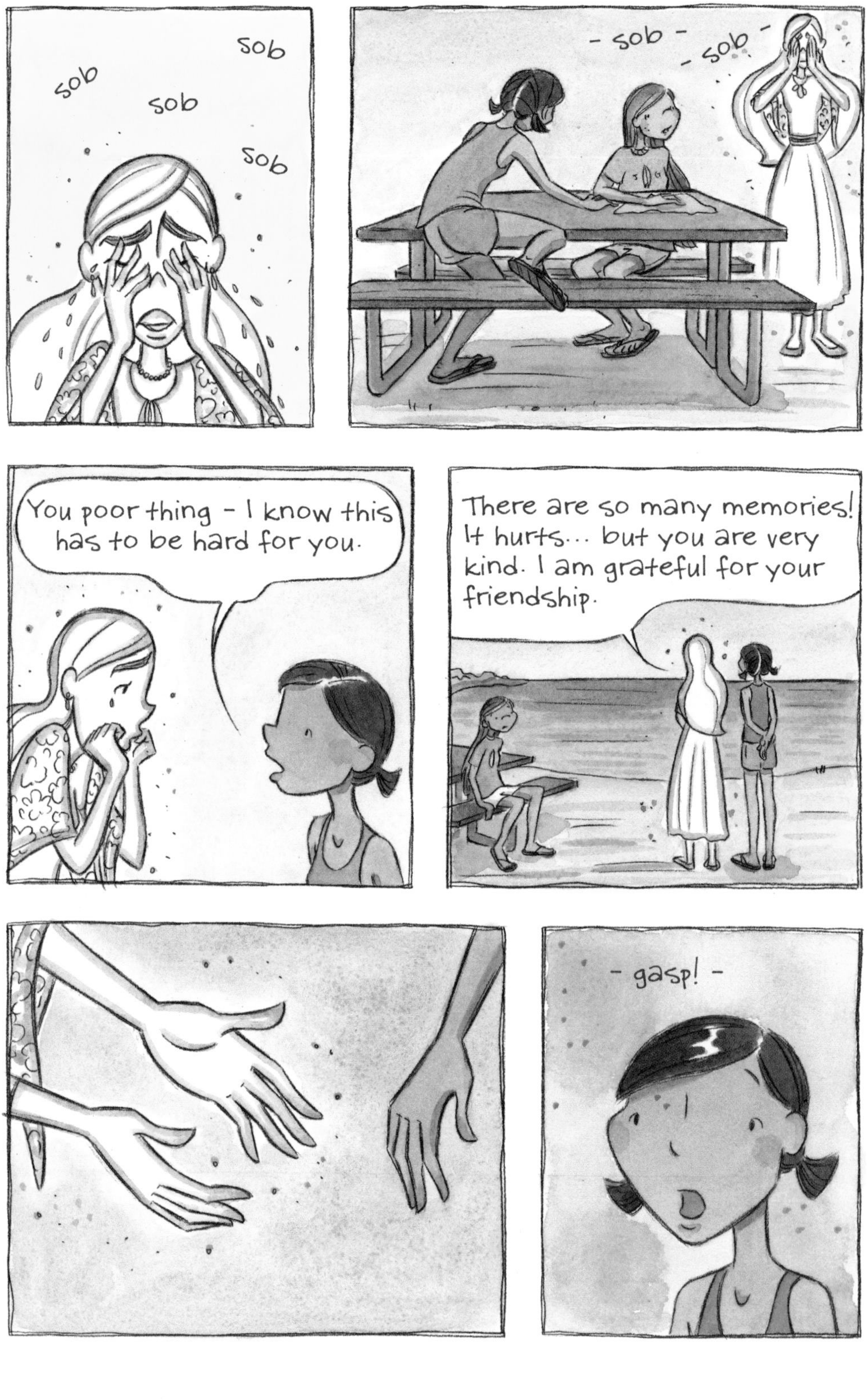
sob
sob
sob
sob
- sob -
- sob -
You poor thing - I know this has to be hard for you.
There are so many memories! It hurts... but you are very kind. I am grateful for your friendship.
- gasp! -

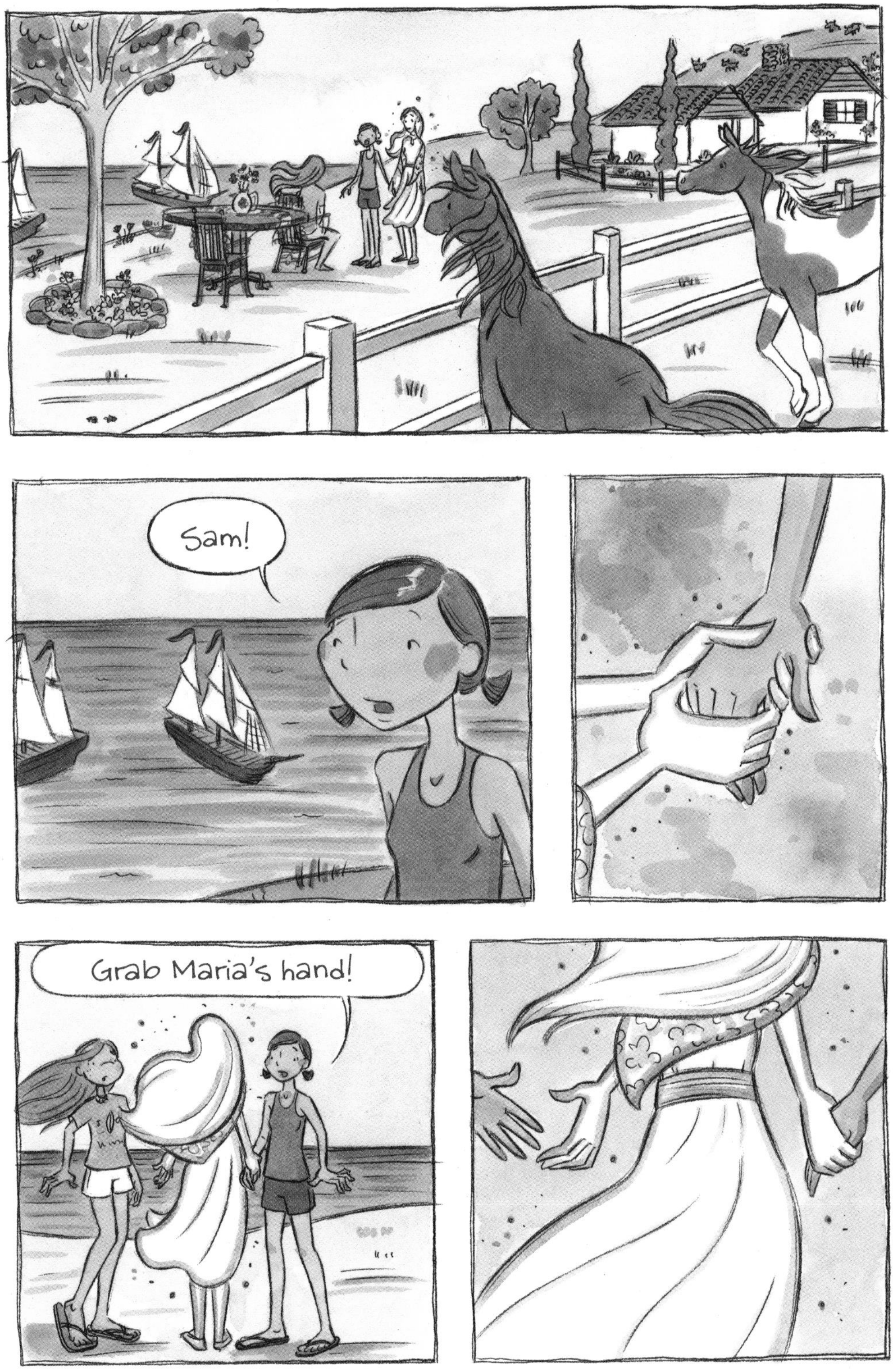
Sam!
Grab Maria's hand!

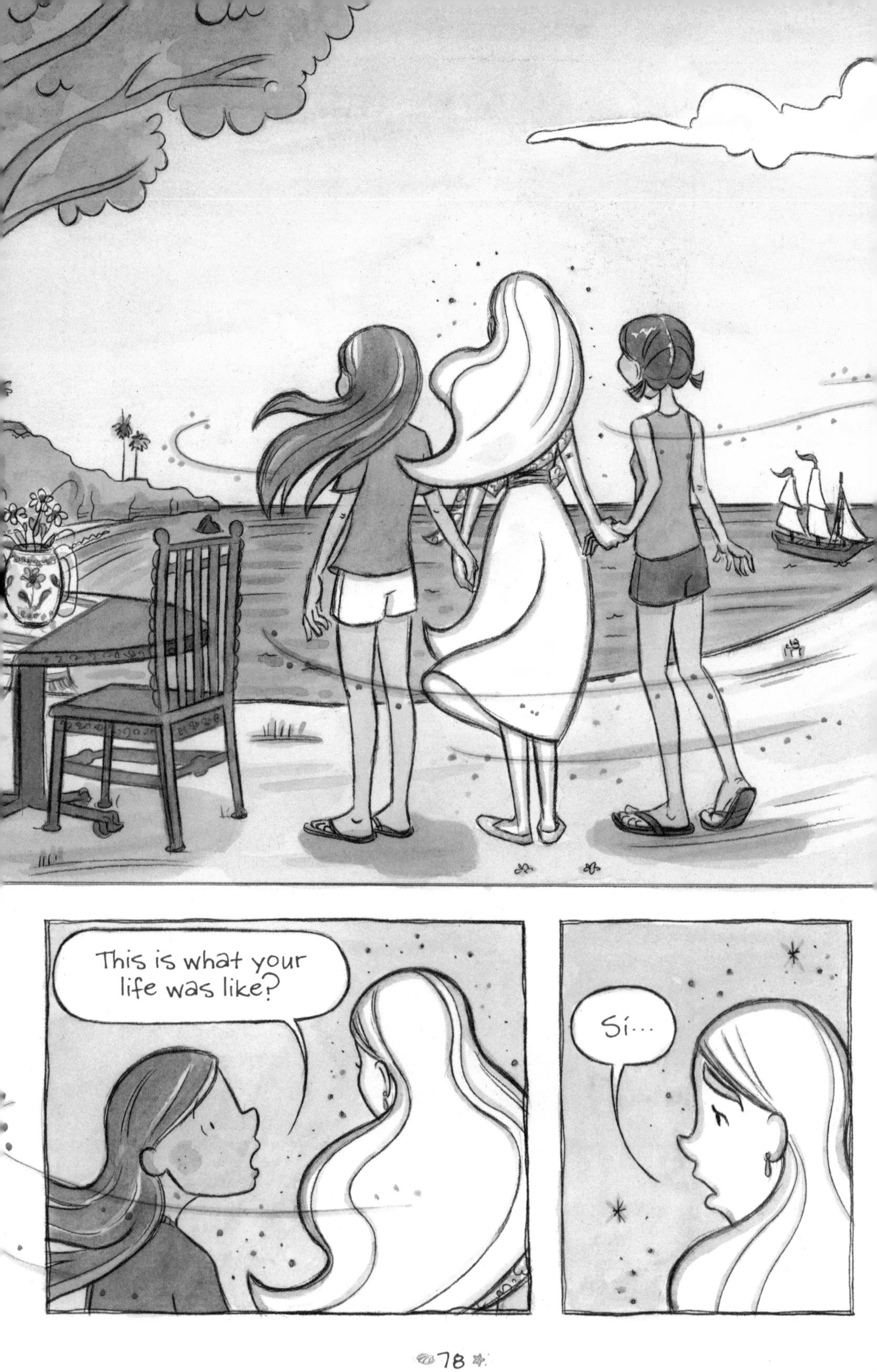
This is what your life was like?
Sí...

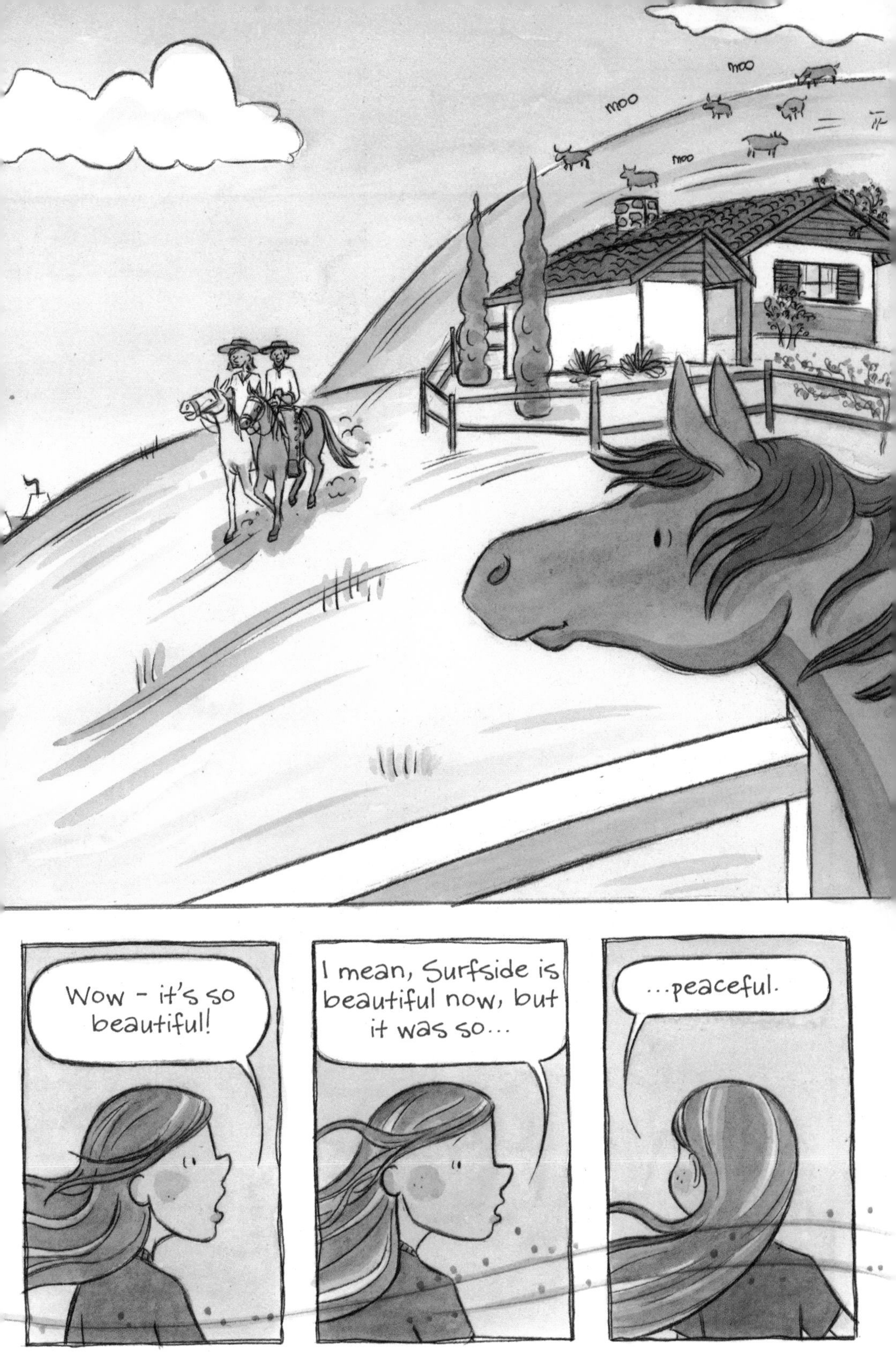
moo
moo
moo
Wow - it's so beautiful!
I mean, Surfside is beautiful now, but it was so...
...peaceful.

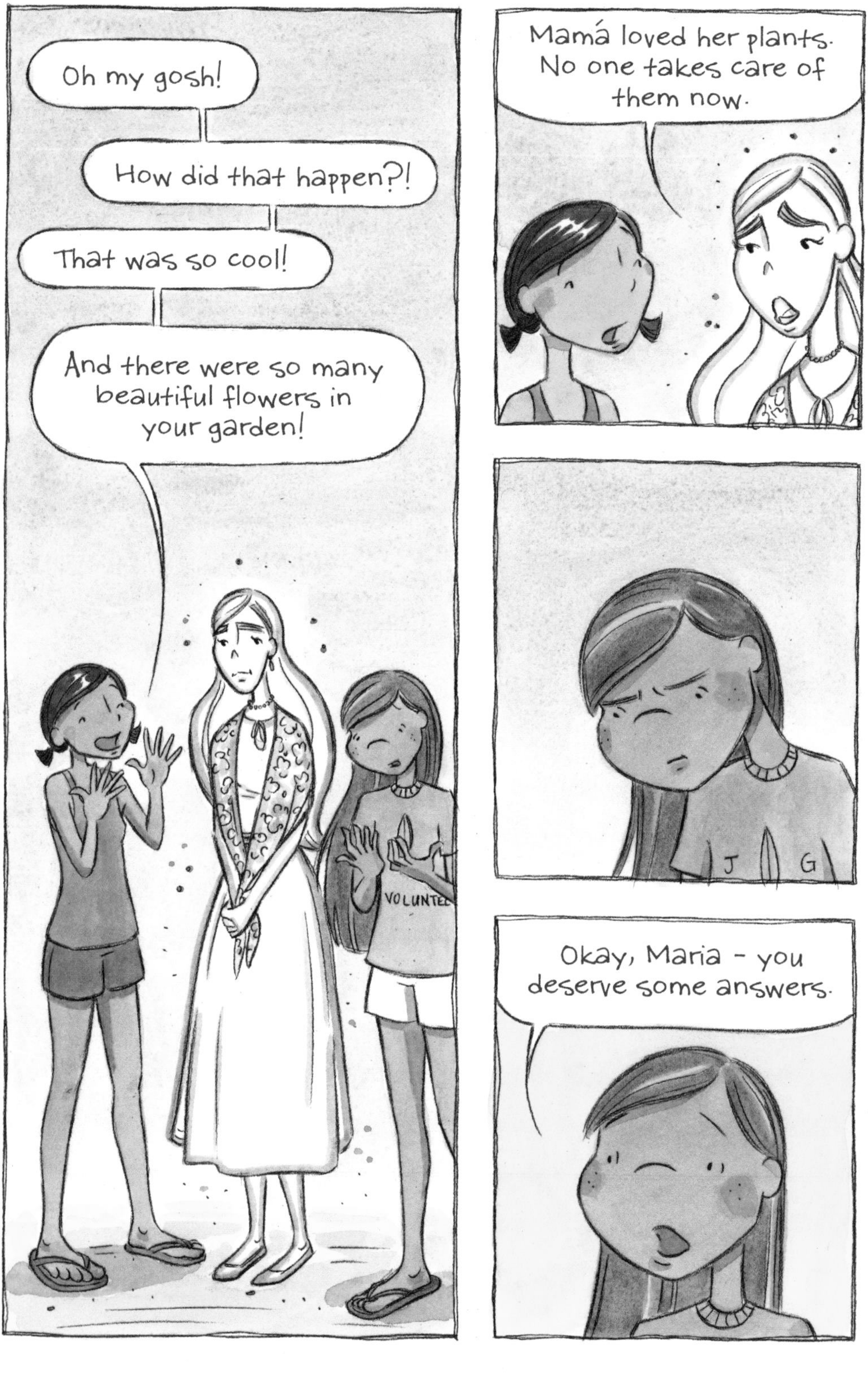
Oh my gosh!
How did that happen?!
That was so cool!
And there were so many beautiful flowers in your garden!
VOLUNTE
Mamá loved her plants. No one takes care of them now.
J G
Okay, Maria - you deserve some answers.

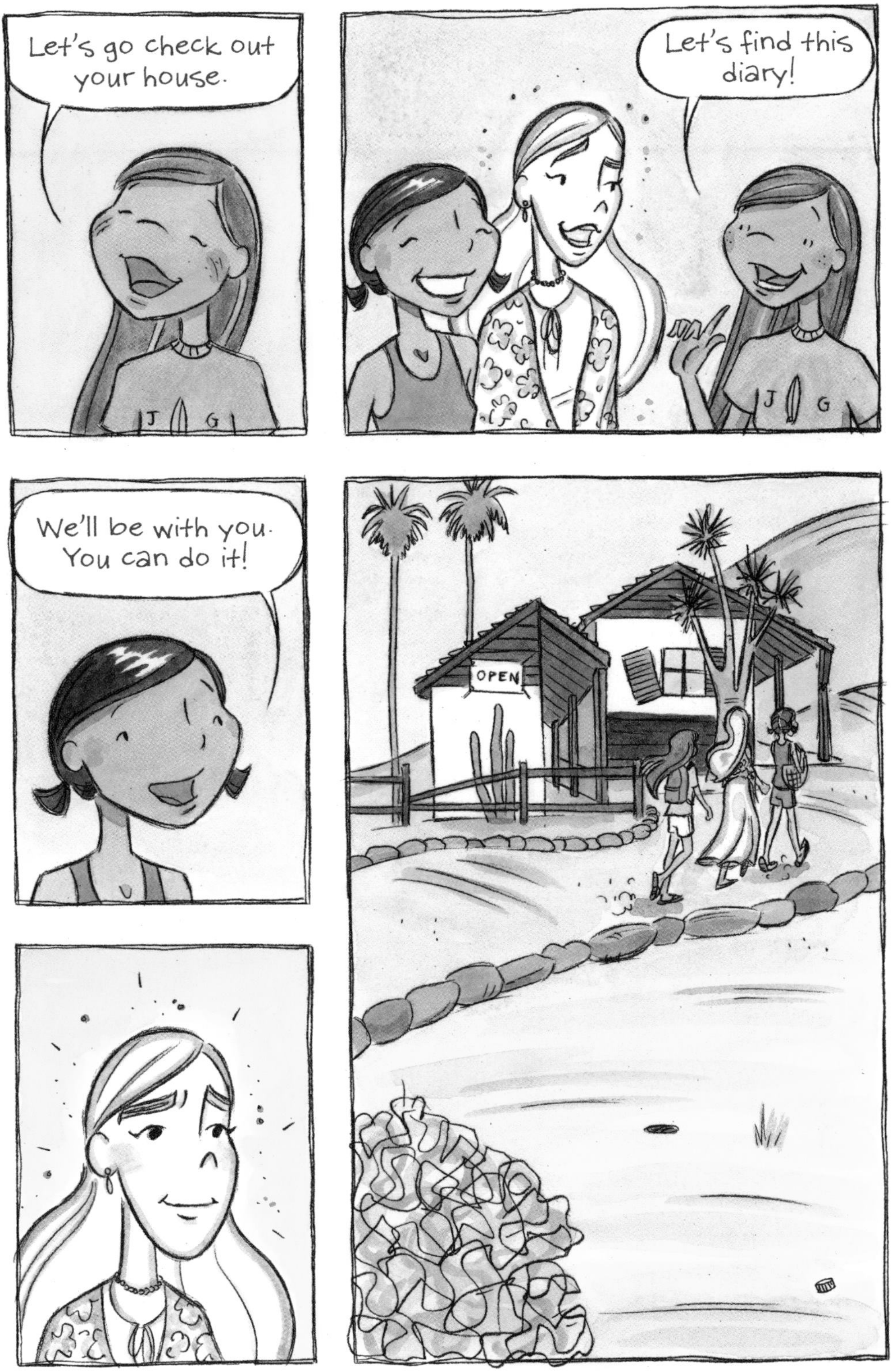

Let's go check out your house.
Let's find this diary!
We'll be with you. You can do it!
OPEN

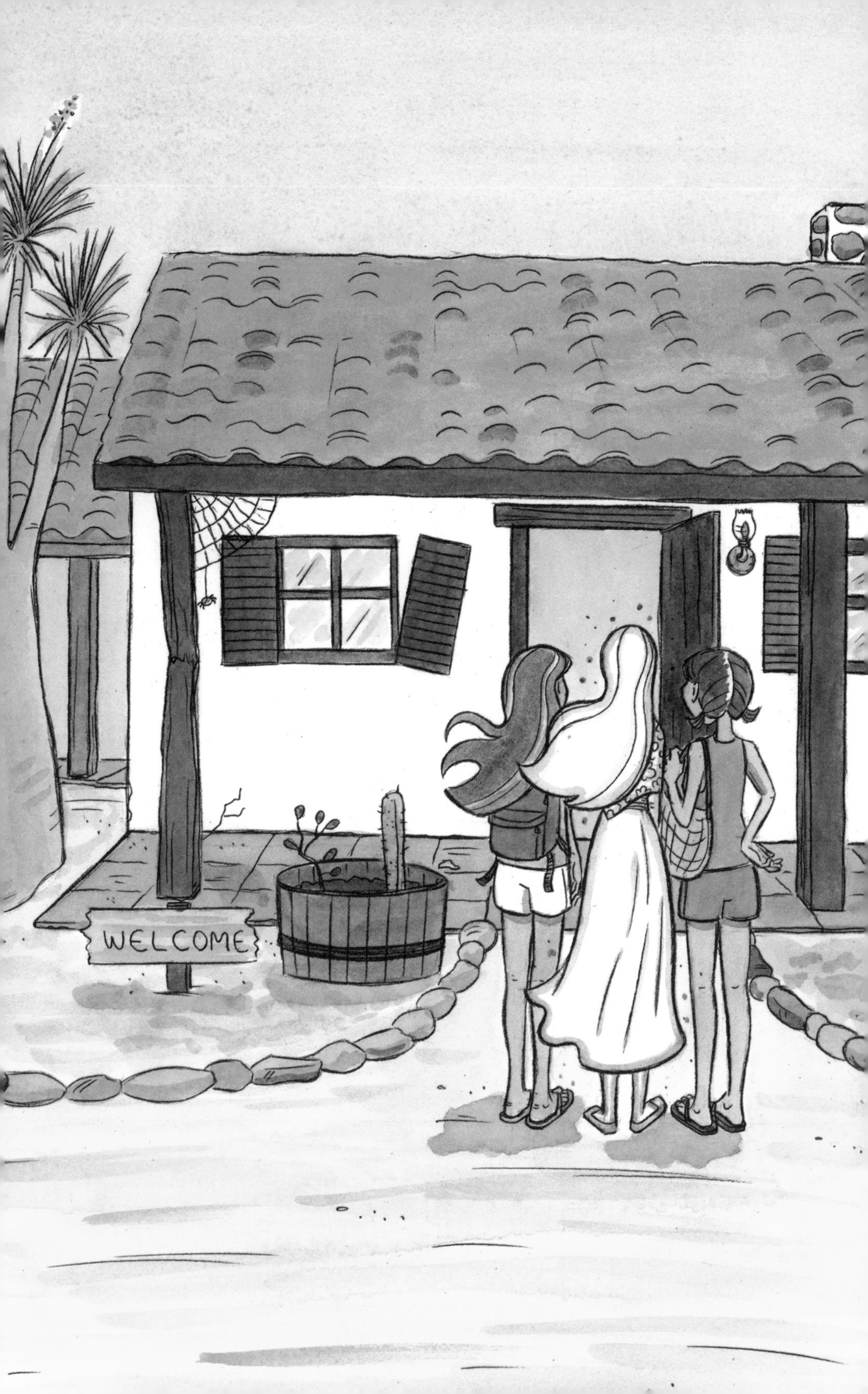
WELCOME

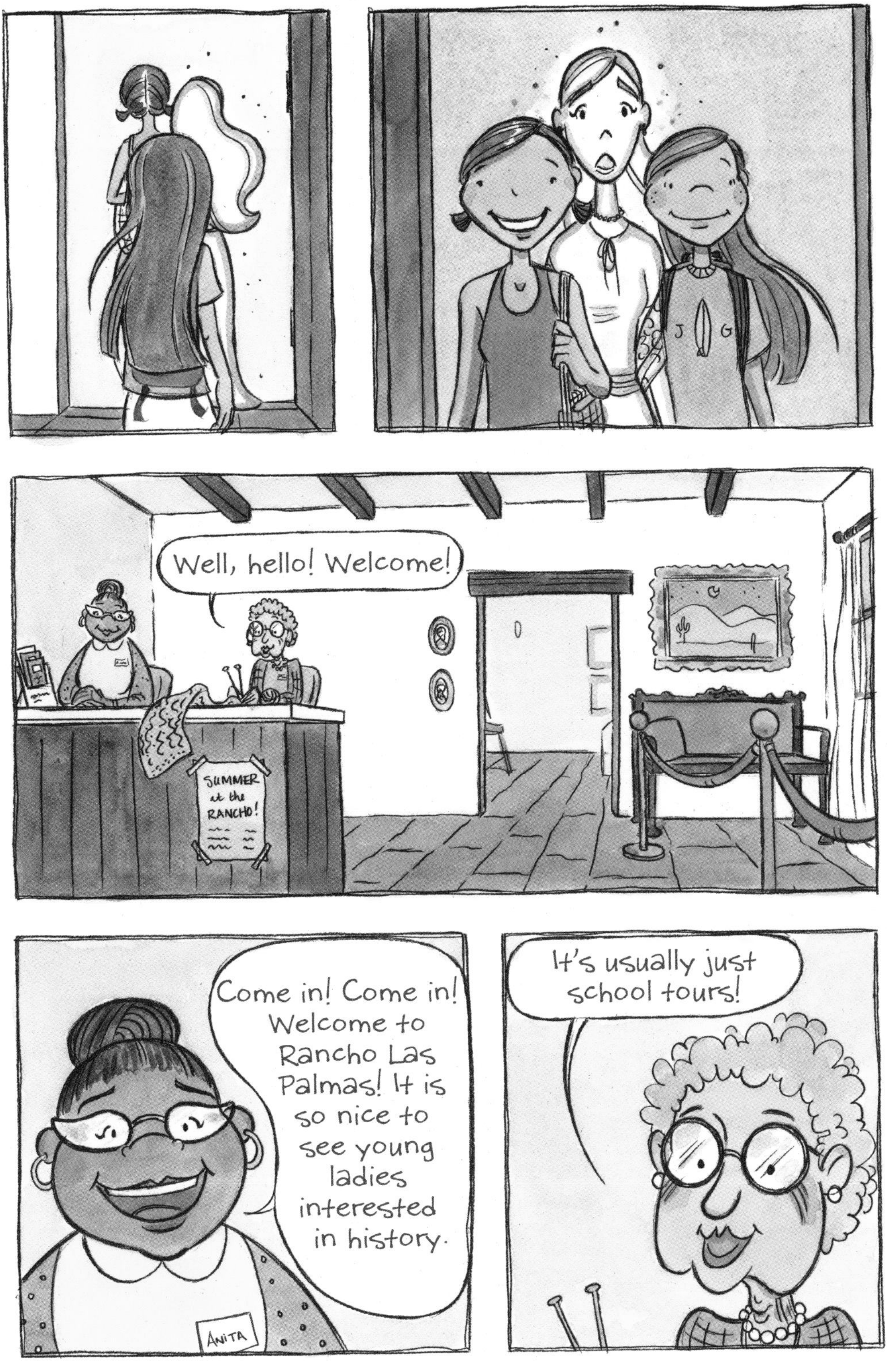
Well, hello! Welcome!
SUMMER at the RANCHO!
Come in! Come in! Welcome to Rancho Las Palmas! It is so nice to see young ladies interested in history.
ANITA
It's usually just school tours!

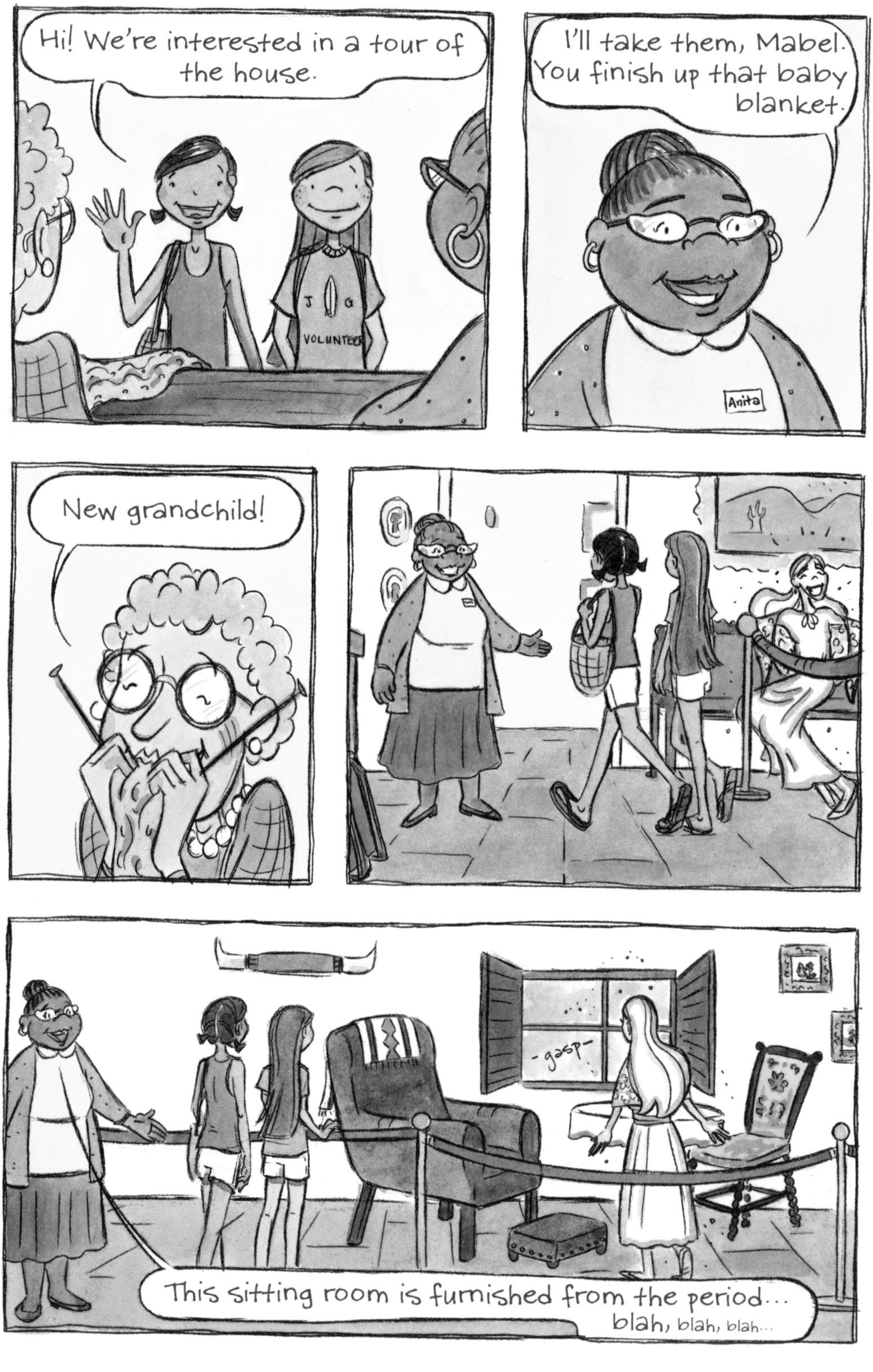
Hi! We're interested in a tour of the house.
J G
VOLUNTEER
I'll take them, Mabel. You finish up that baby blanket.
Anita
New grandchild!
-gasp-
This sitting room is furnished from the period... blah, blah, blah...

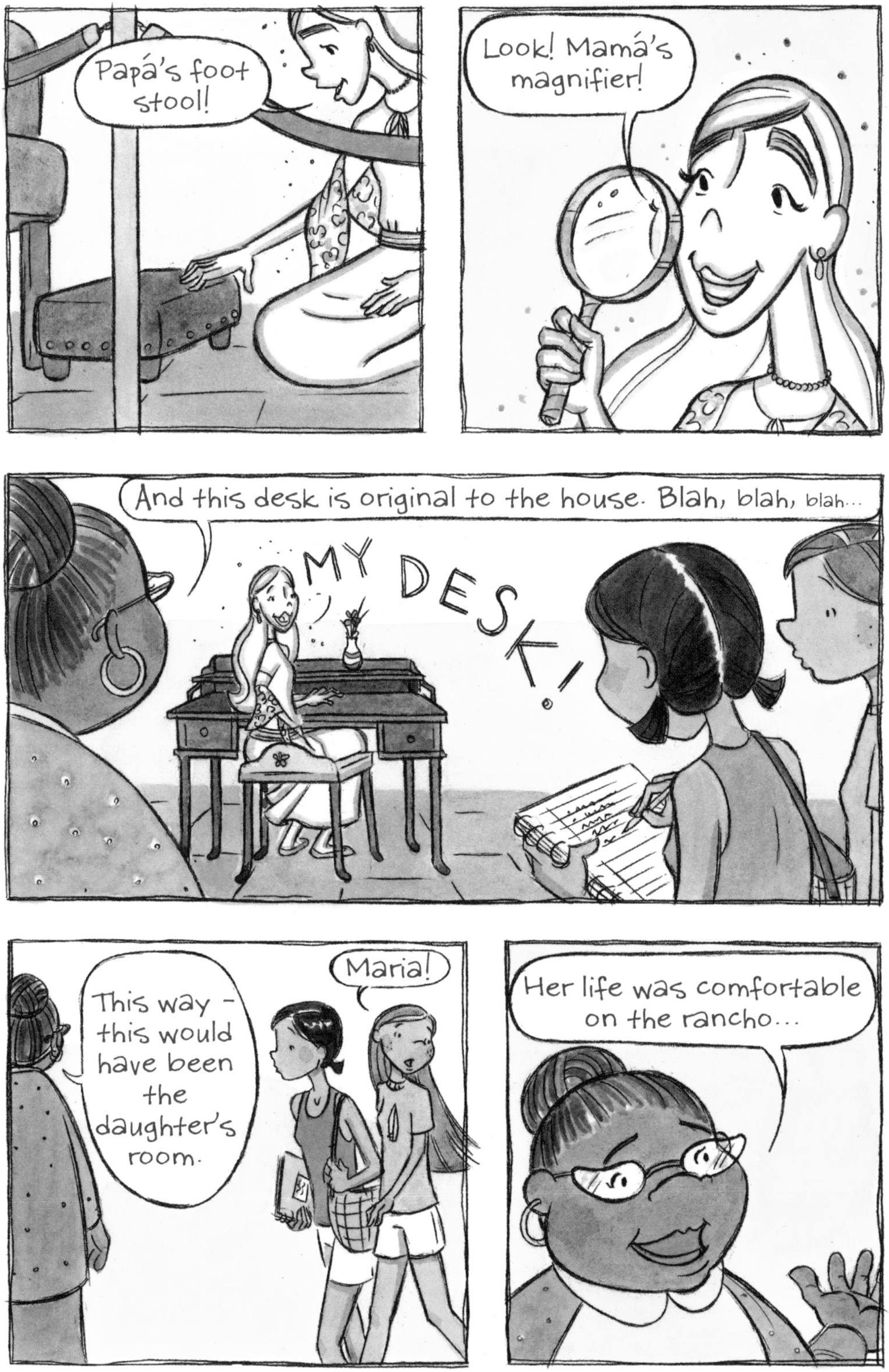
Papá's foot stool!
Look! Mamá's magnifier!
And this desk is original to the house. Blah, blah, blah...
MY DESK!
This way - this would have been the daughter's room.
Maria!
Her life was comfortable on the rancho...

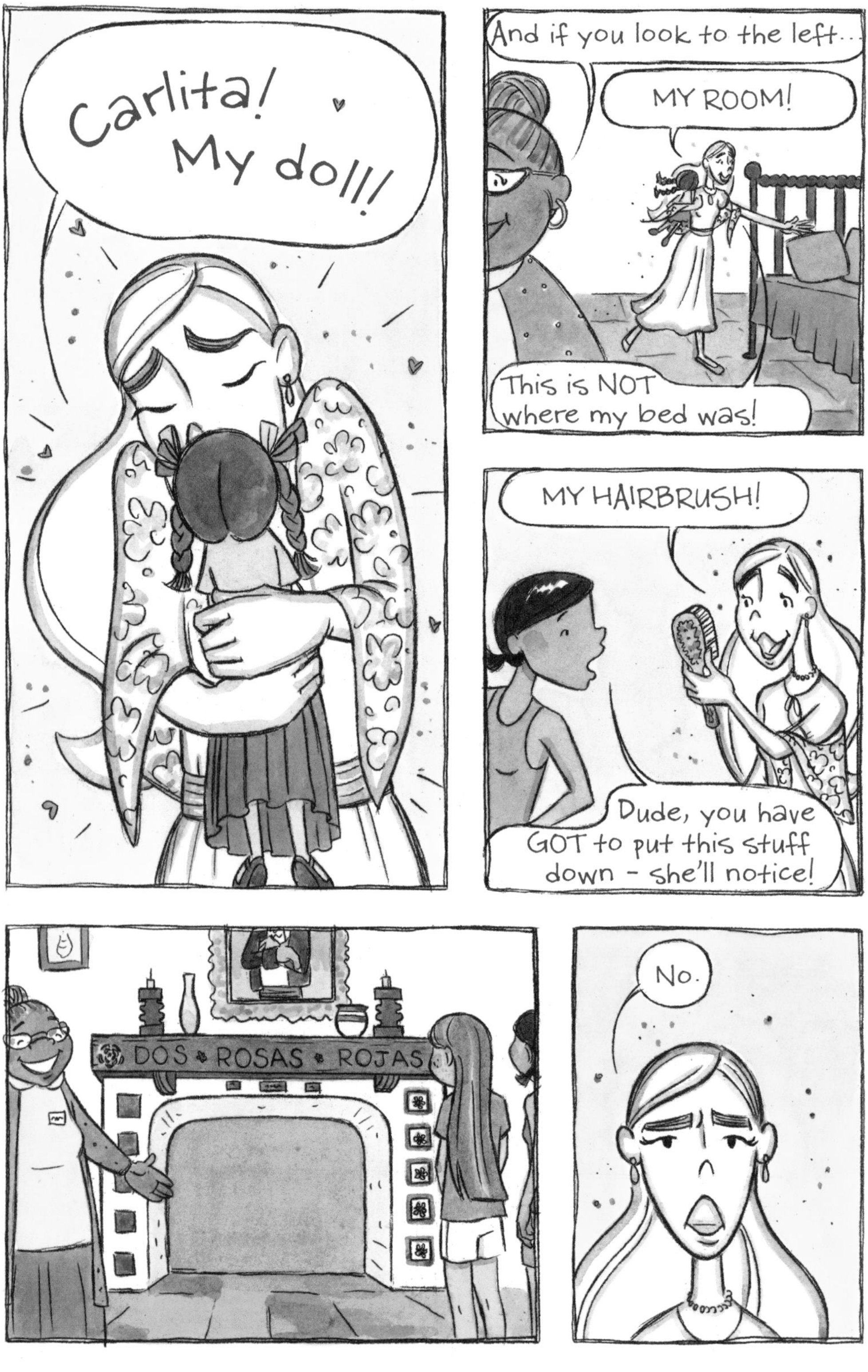
Carlita! My doll!
And if you look to the left...
MY ROOM!
This is NOT where my bed was!
MY HAIRBRUSH!
Dude, you have GOT to put this stuff down - she'll notice!
DOS ROSAS ROJAS
No.

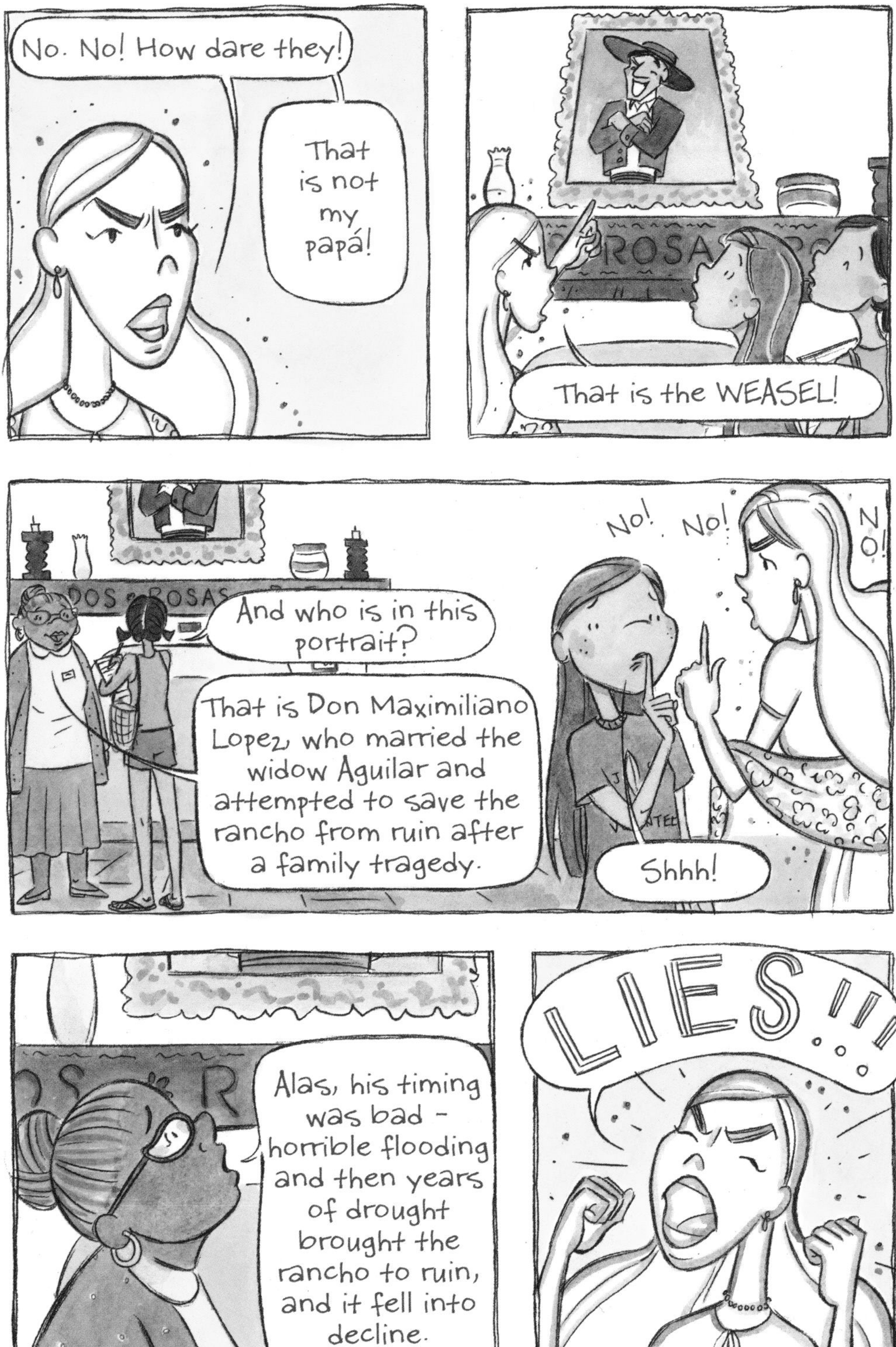
No. No! How dare they!
That is not my papá!
That is the WEASEL!
ROSAS
DOS ROSAS
And who is in this portrait?
That is Don Maximiliano Lopez, who married the widow Aguilar and attempted to save the rancho from ruin after a family tragedy.
No! No! NO!
Shhh!
Alas, his timing was bad - horrible flooding and then years of drought brought the rancho to ruin, and it fell into decline.
LIES!!!...

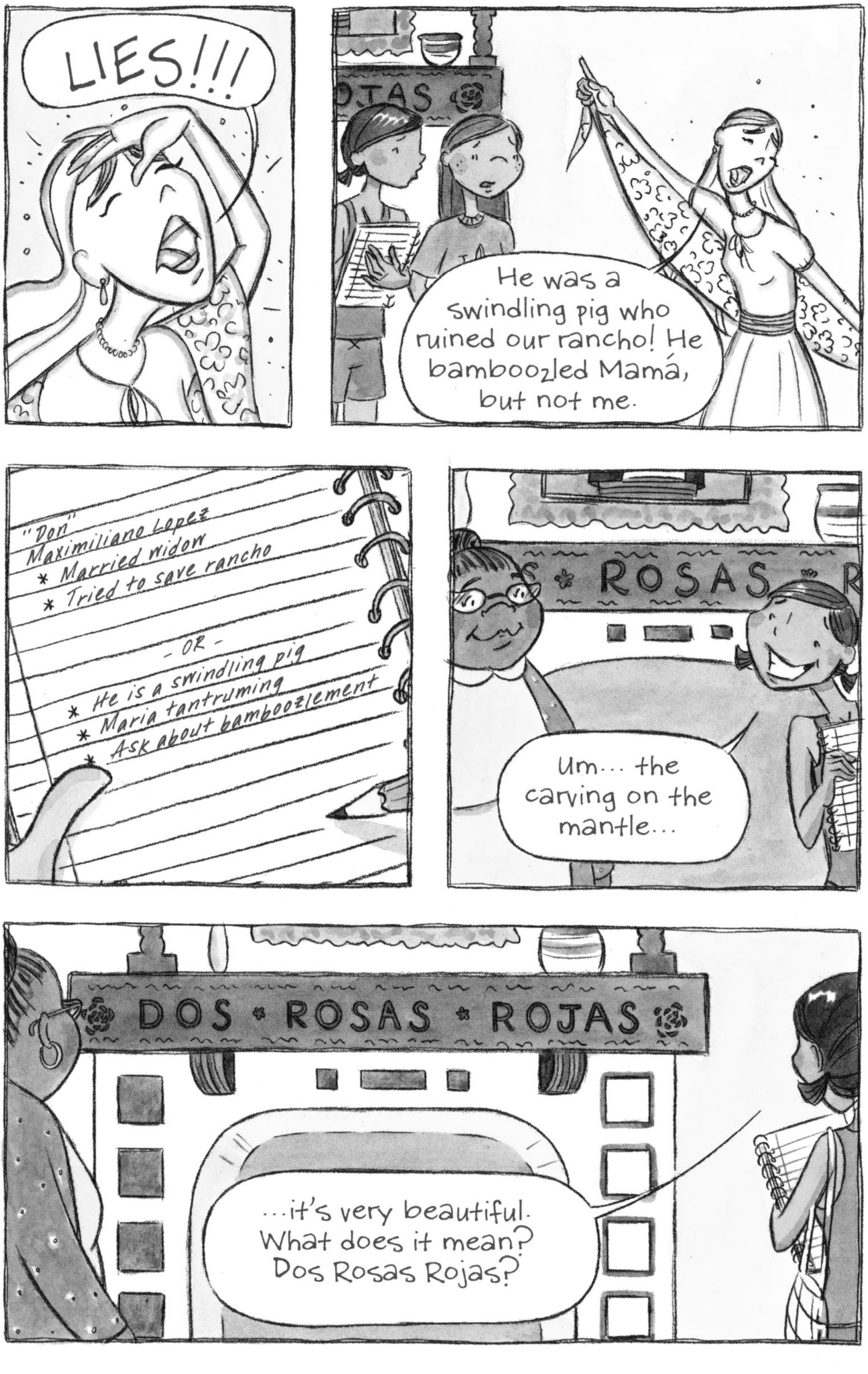
LIES!!!
He was a swindling pig who ruined our rancho! He bamboozled Mamá, but not me.
"Don" Maximiliano Lopez
* Married widow
* Tried to save rancho
- OR -
* He is a swindling pig
* Maria tantruming
* Ask about bamboozlement
Um... the carving on the mantle...
DOS ROSAS ROJAS
...it's very beautiful. What does it mean? Dos Rosas Rojas?

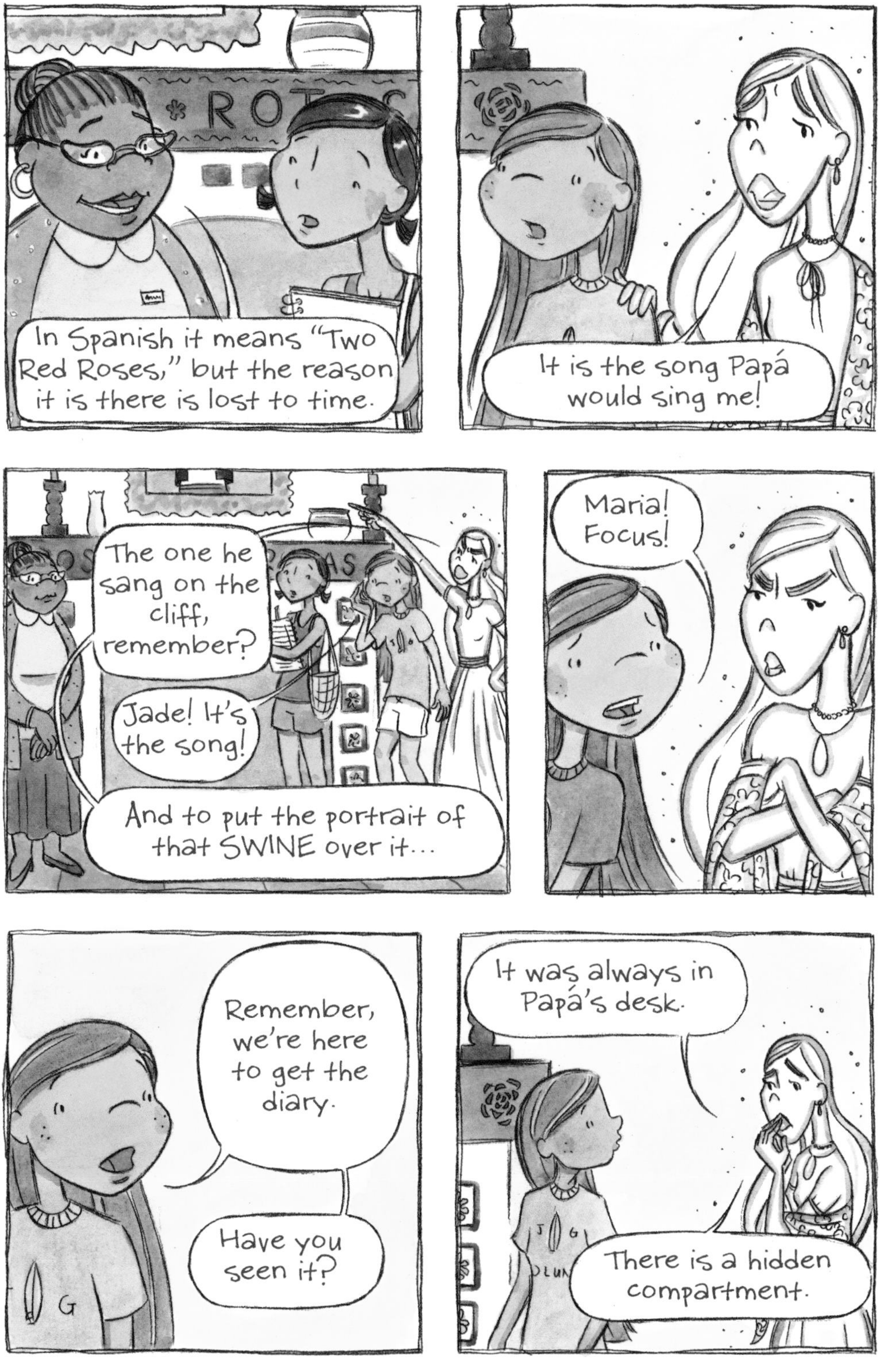
In Spanish it means "Two Red Roses," but the reason it is there is lost to time.
It is the song Papá would sing me!
The one he sang on the cliff, remember?
Jade! It's the song!
And to put the portrait of that SWINE over it...
Maria! Focus!
Remember, we're here to get the diary.
Have you seen it?
It was always in Papá's desk.
There is a hidden compartment.

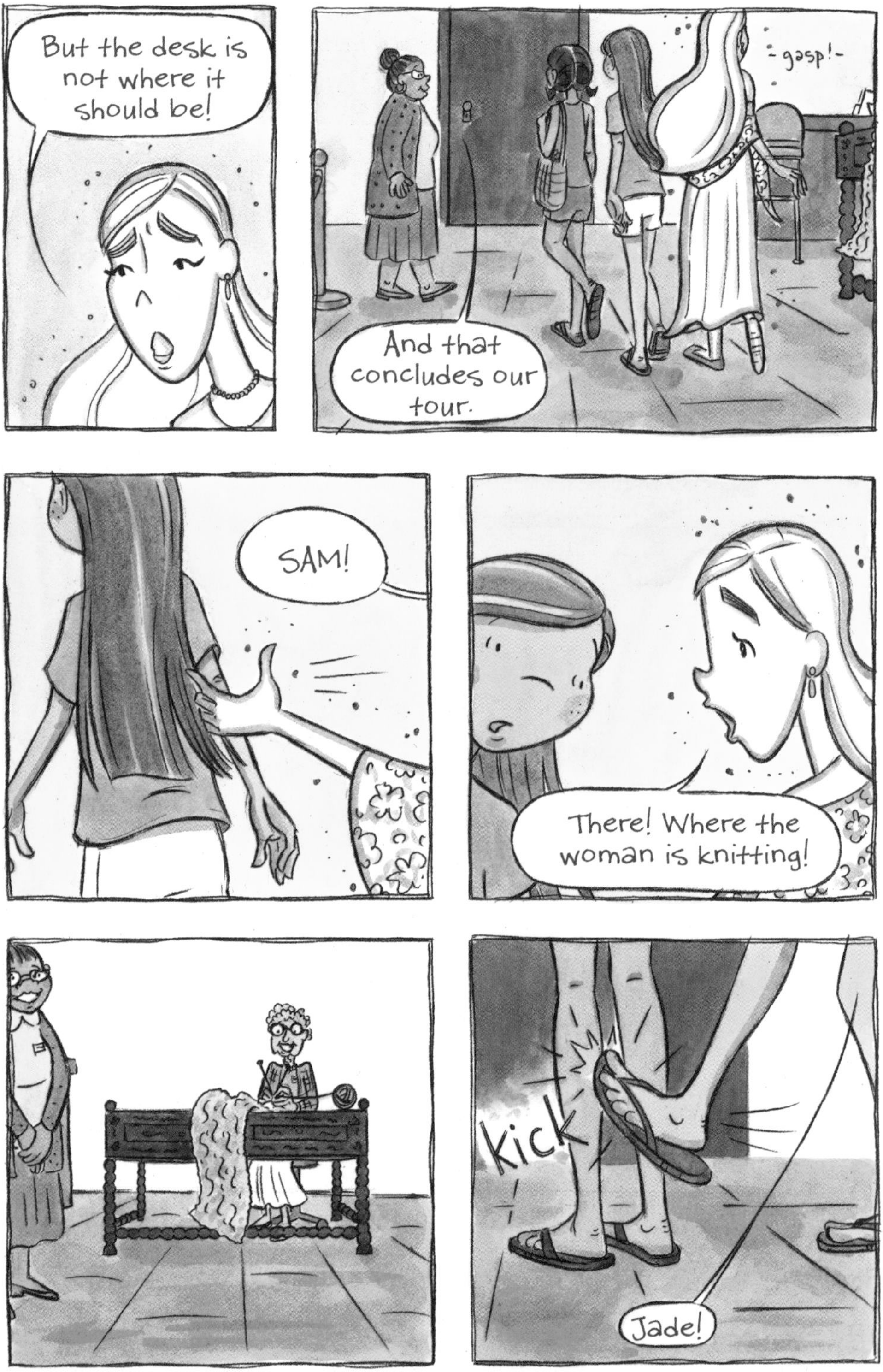
But the desk is not where it should be!
-gasp!-
And that concludes our tour.
SAM!
There! Where the woman is knitting!
kick
Jade!

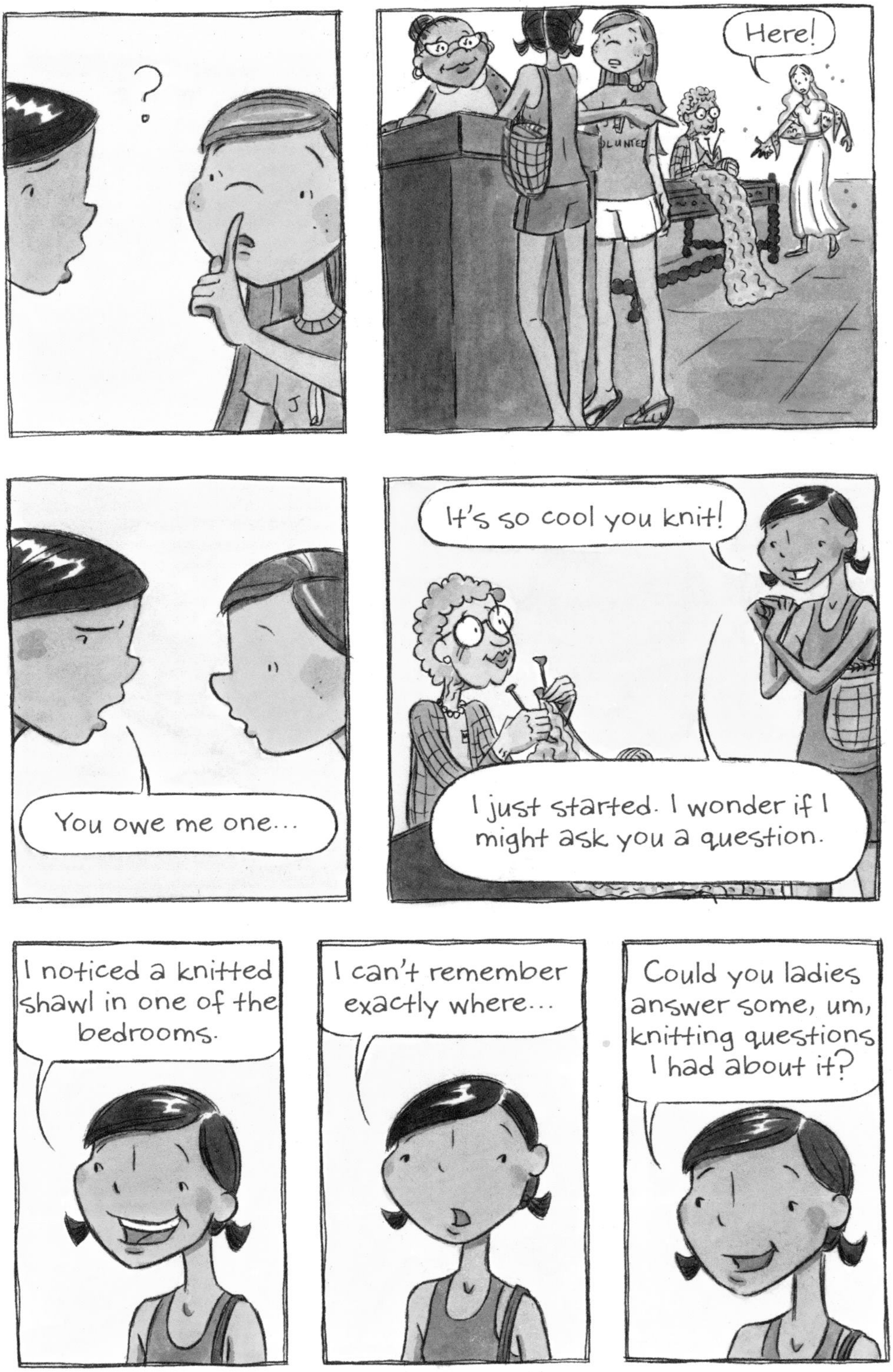
?
Here!
You owe me one...
It's so cool you knit!
I just started. I wonder if I might ask you a question.
I noticed a knitted shawl in one of the bedrooms.
I can't remember exactly where...
Could you ladies answer some, um, knitting questions I had about it?

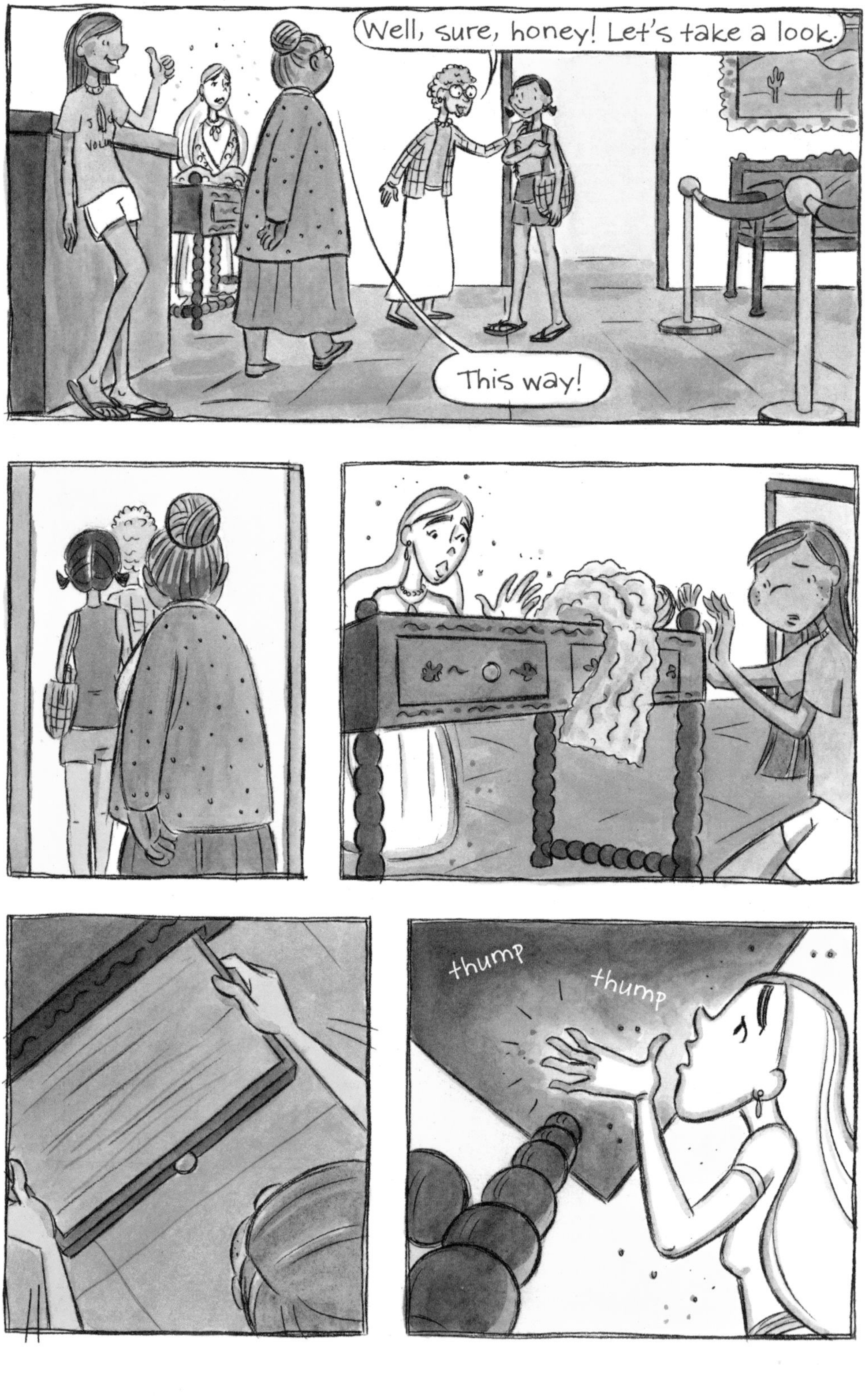
Well, sure, honey! Let's take a look.
This way!
thump
thump

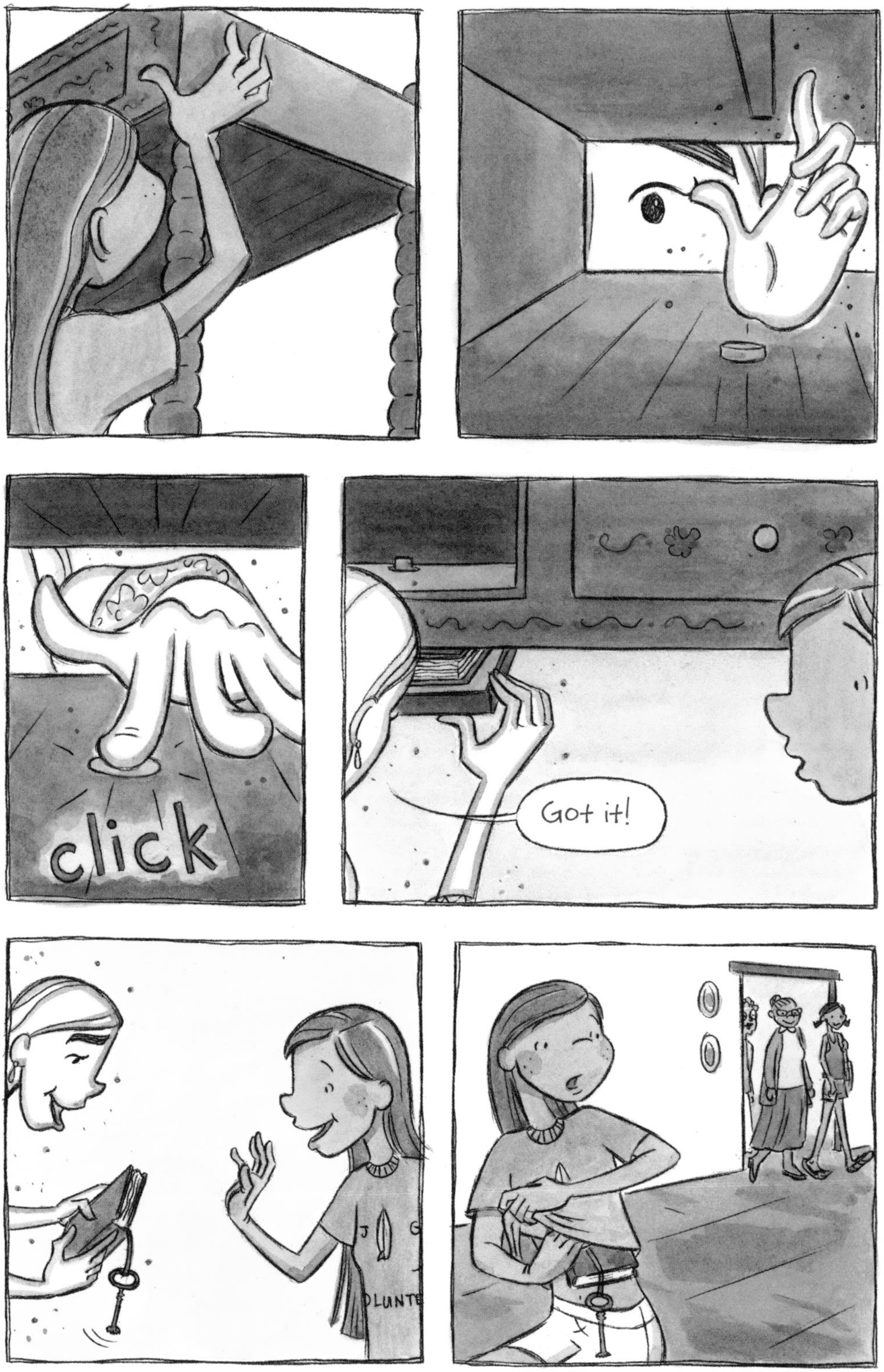
click
Got it!
J G
OLUNTE

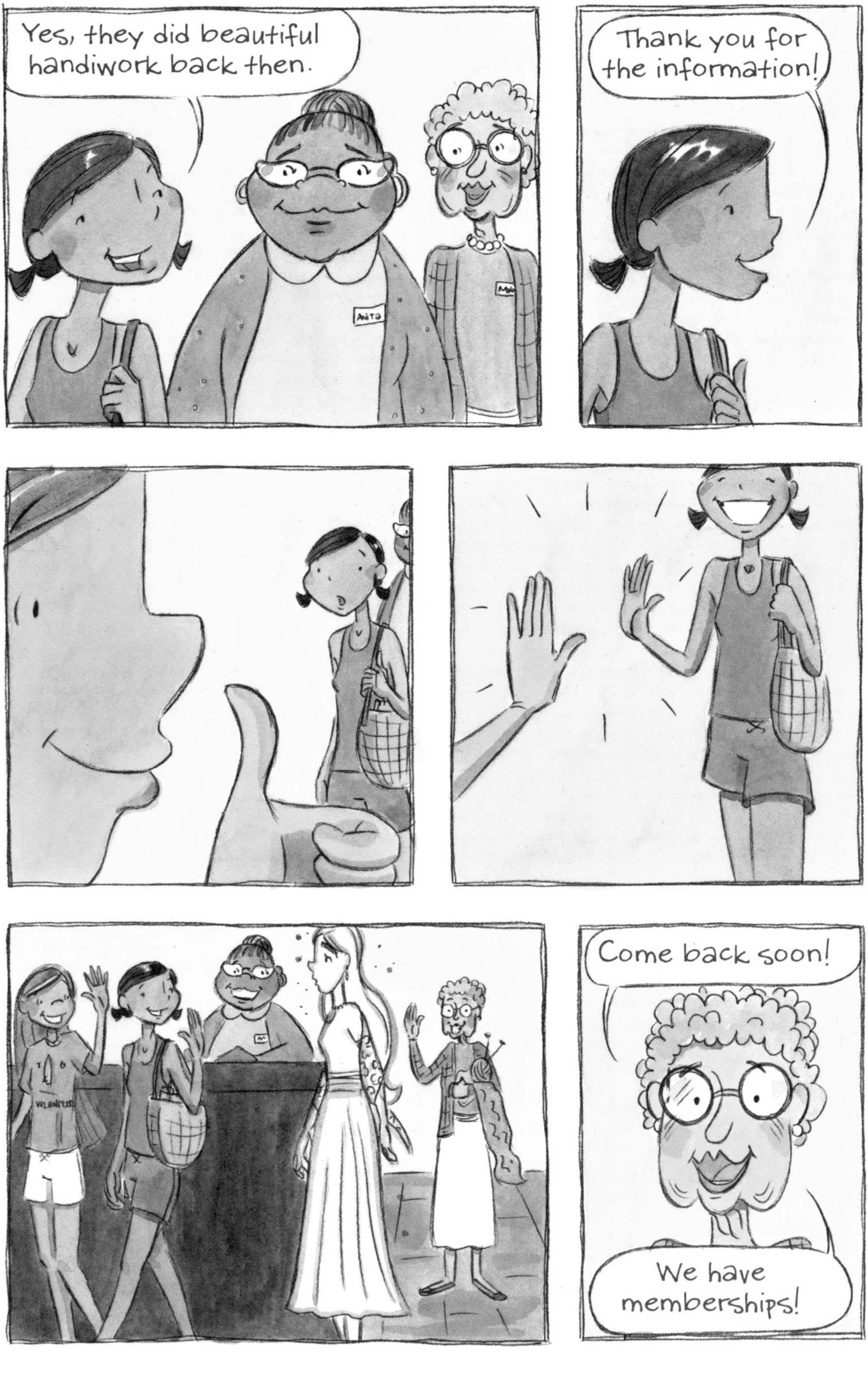

Yes, they did beautiful handiwork back then.
Thank you for the information!
Come back soon!
We have memberships!

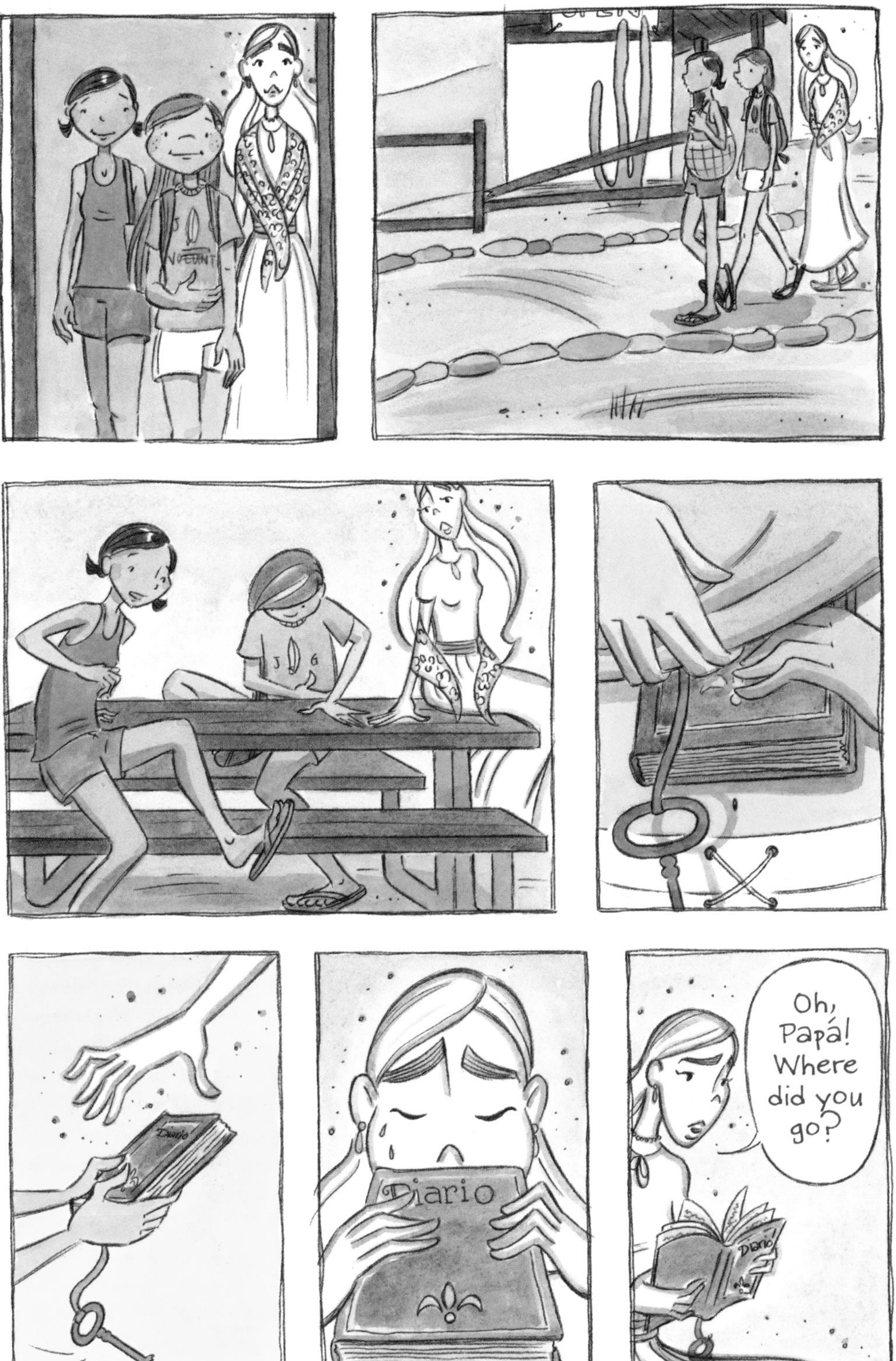
Diario
Diario
Oh, Papá! Where did you go?
Diario

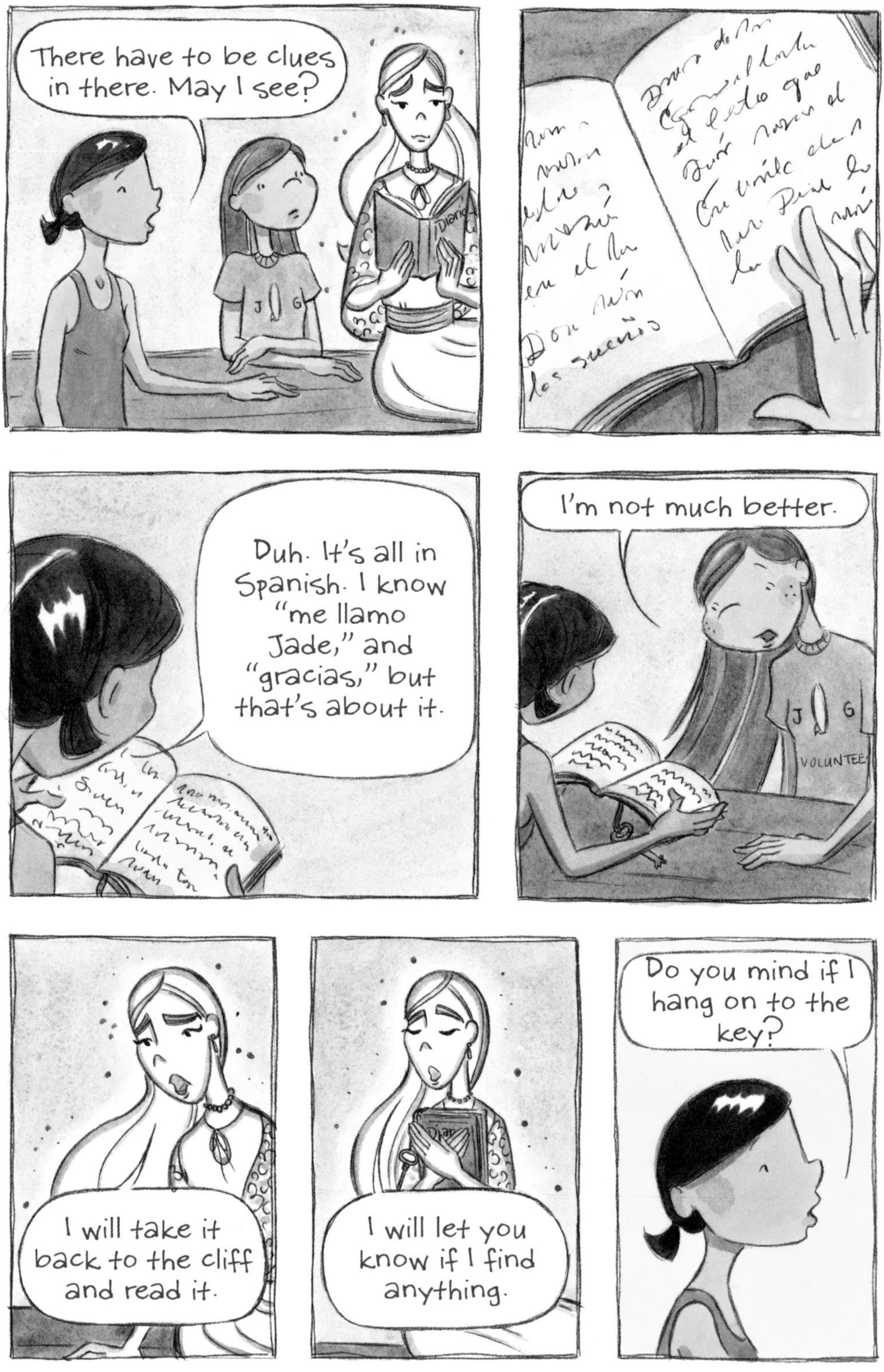
There have to be clues in there. May I see?
Duh. It's all in Spanish. I know "me llamo Jade," and "gracias," but that's about it.
I'm not much better.
I will take it back to the cliff and read it.
I will let you know if I find anything.
Do you mind if I hang on to the key?

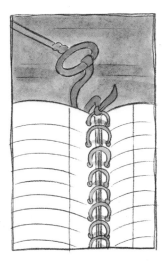

Maria, wait... I have a question.

What did you mean when you said Maximiliano bamboozled your mom?

Papá was a good man. He treated people and animals kindly.

After he disappeared, Maximiliano started bringing Mamá gifts.

But after they were married, there were no more gifts.

He fed the cattle less and less and wouldn't buy medicine when they were sick. And he started to yell at Mamá if she bought a new dress.

So he was a bad dude?

Sí. A bad dude.

I will see you later on the cliff.

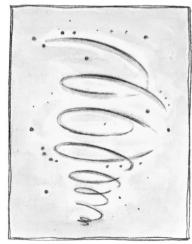

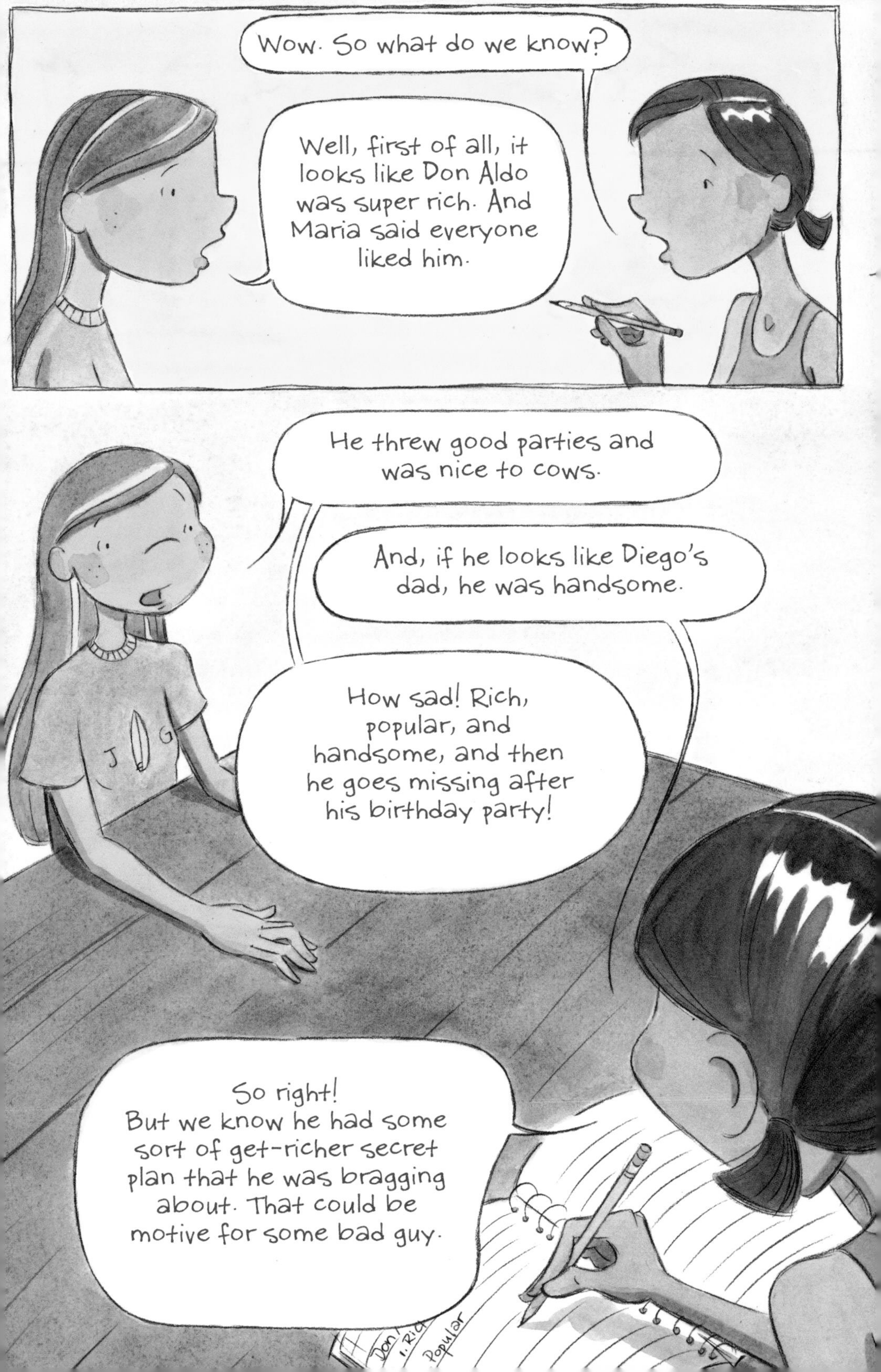
Wow. So what do we know?
Well, first of all, it looks like Don Aldo was super rich. And Maria said everyone liked him.
He threw good parties and was nice to cows.
And, if he looks like Diego's dad, he was handsome.
How sad! Rich, popular, and handsome, and then he goes missing after his birthday party!
So right! But we know he had some sort of get-richer secret plan that he was bragging about. That could be motive for some bad guy.

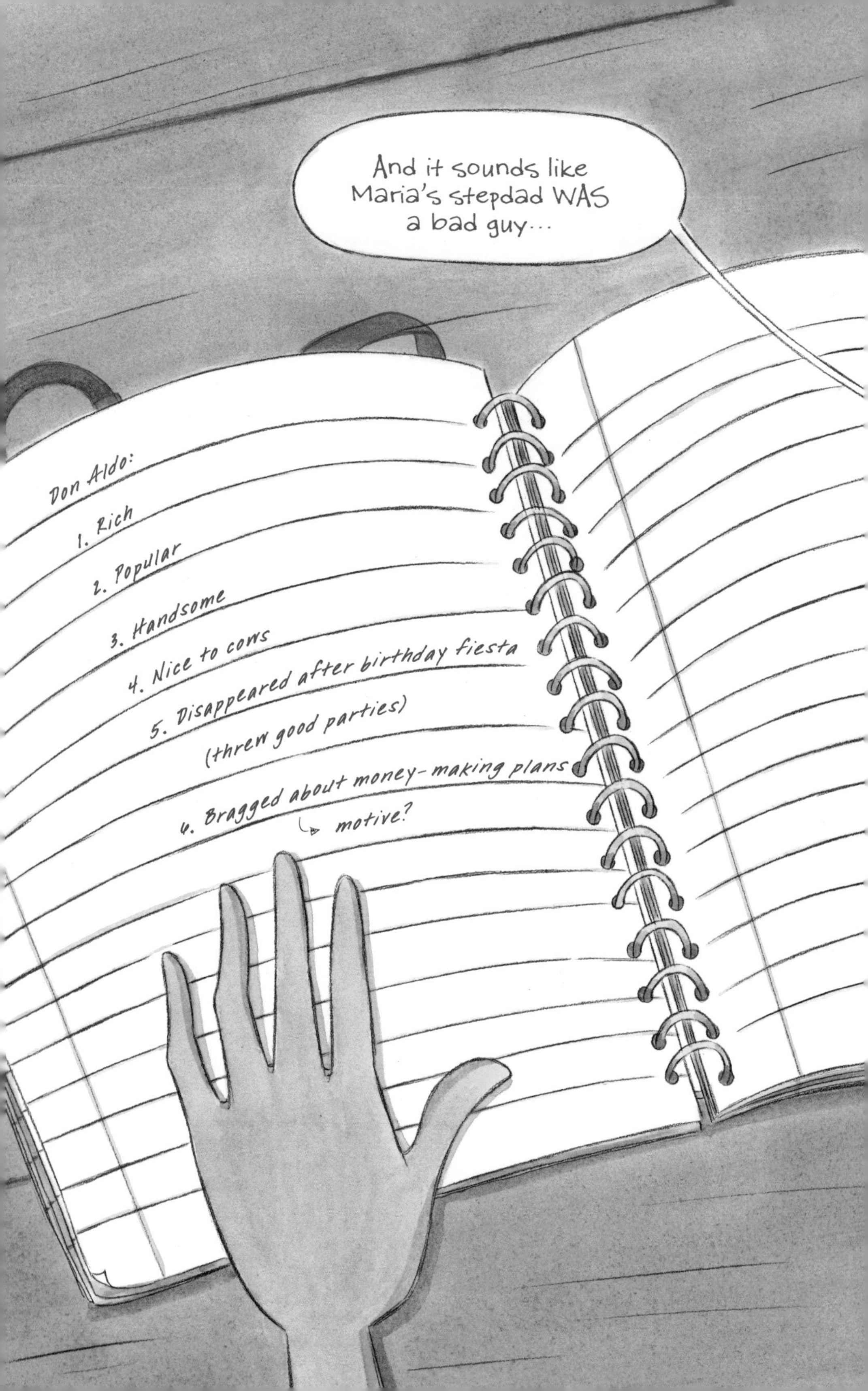
And it sounds like Maria's stepdad WAS a bad guy...
Don Aldo:
1. Rich
2. Popular
3. Handsome
4. Nice to cows
5. Disappeared after birthday fiesta
(threw good parties)
6. Bragged about money-making plans
motive?

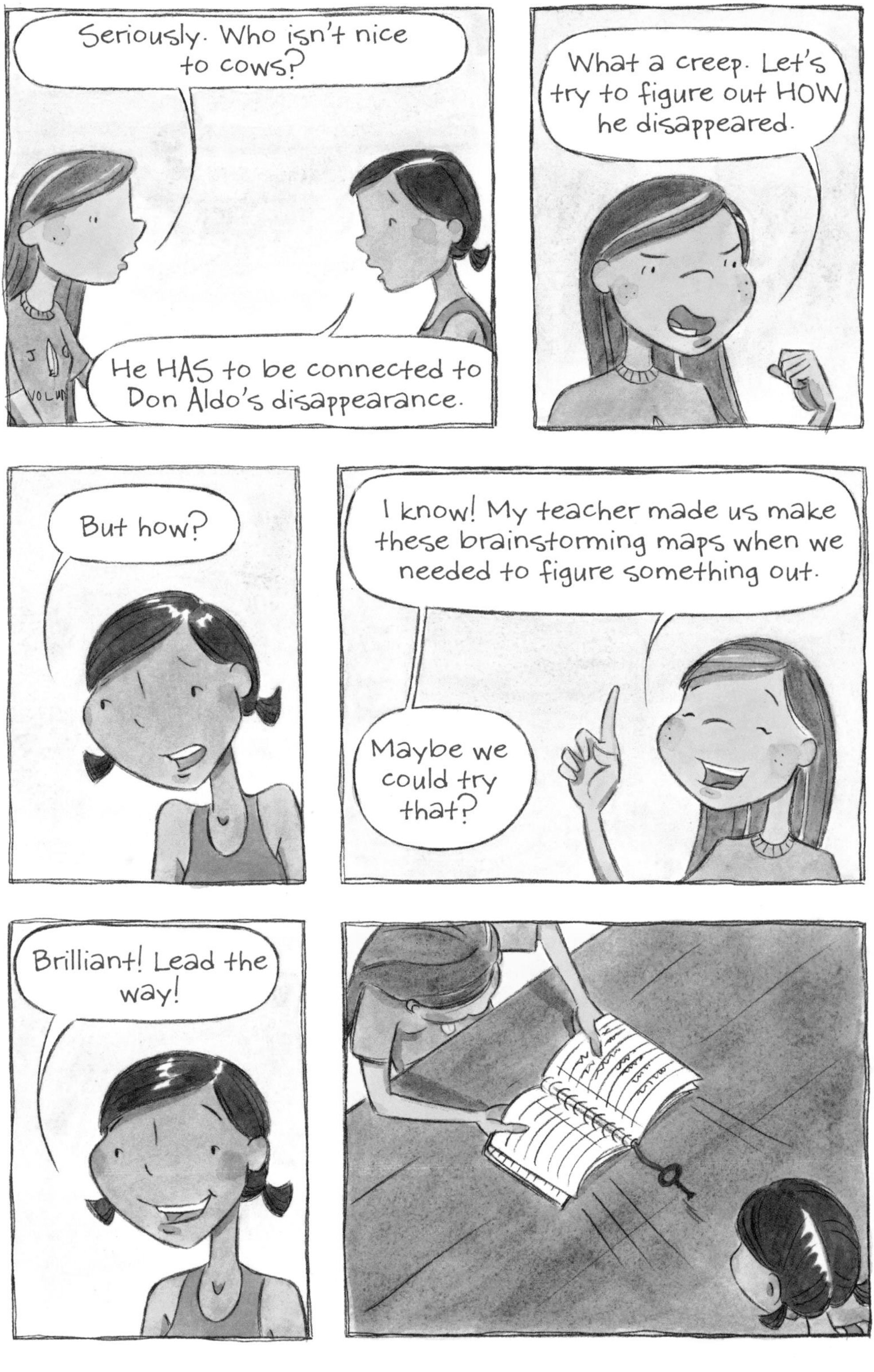
Seriously. Who isn't nice to cows?
He HAS to be connected to Don Aldo's disappearance.
What a creep. Let's try to figure out HOW he disappeared.
But how?
I know! My teacher made us make these brainstorming maps when we needed to figure something out.
Maybe we could try that?
Brilliant! Lead the way!

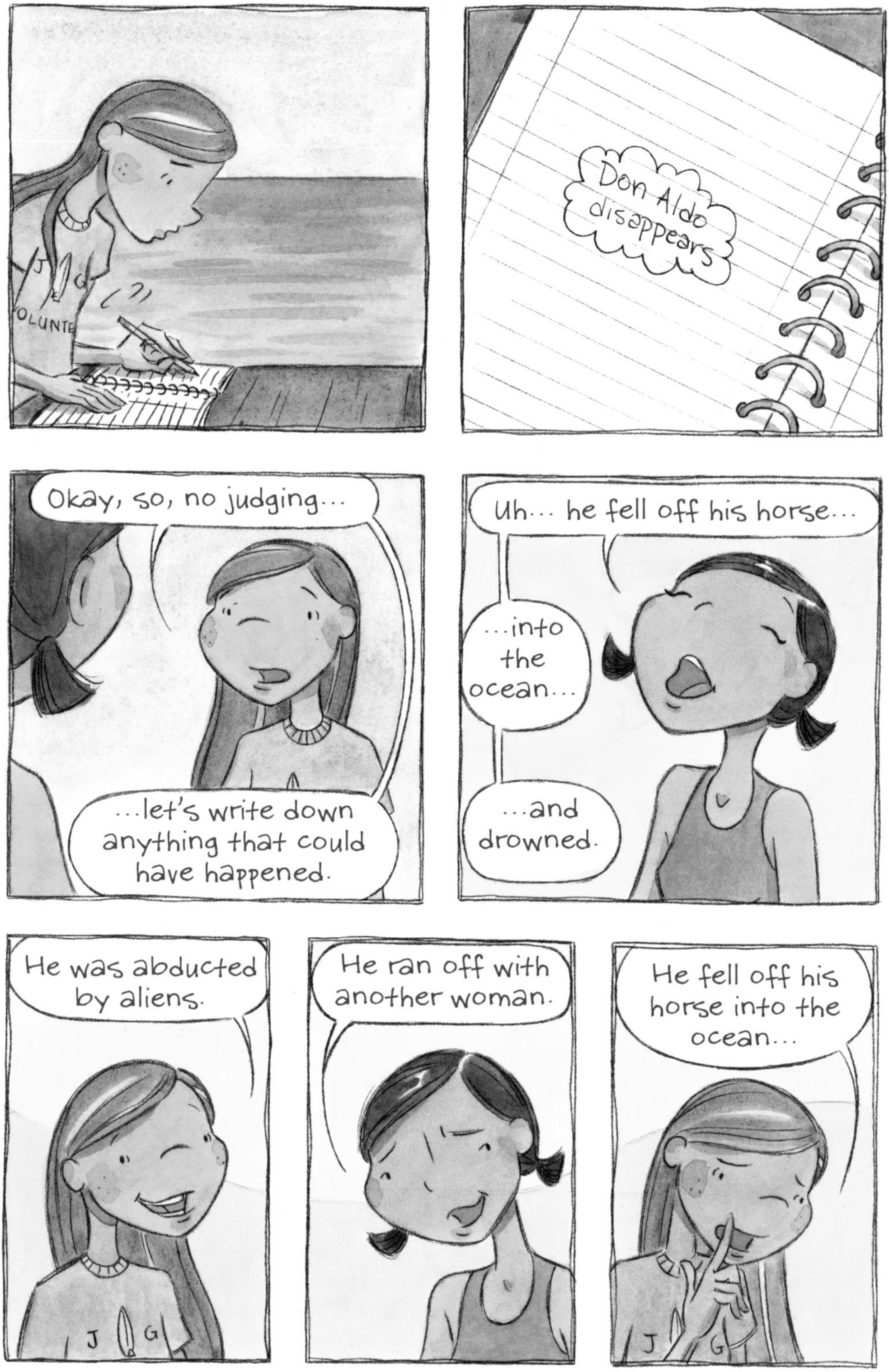
Don Aldo disappears
Okay, so, no judging...
...let's write down anything that could have happened.
Uh... he fell off his horse...
...into the ocean...
...and drowned.
He was abducted by aliens.
He ran off with another woman.
He fell off his horse into the ocean...

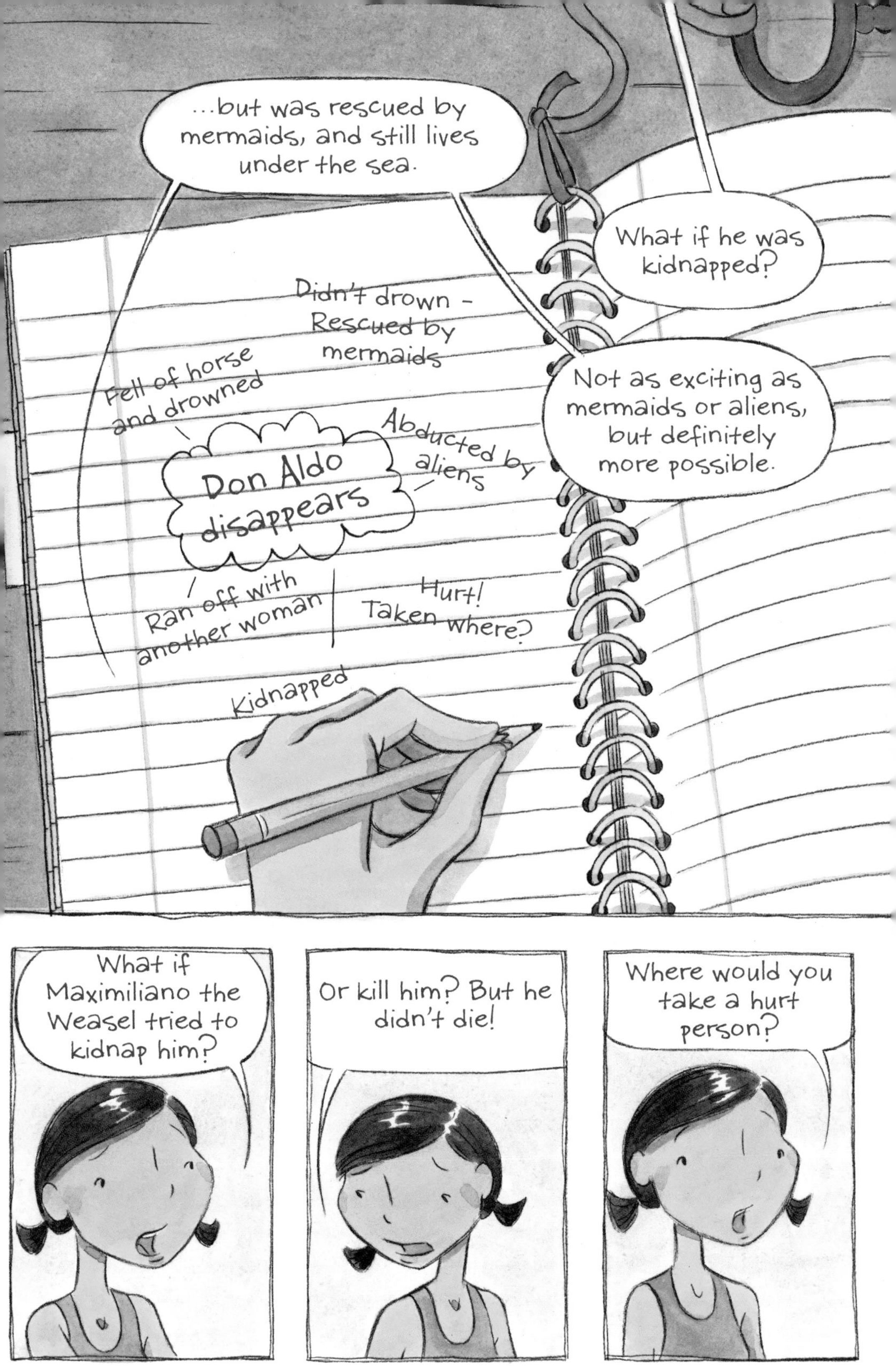
...but was rescued by mermaids, and still lives under the sea.
What if he was kidnapped?
Didn't drown - Rescued by mermaids
Fell of horse and drowned
Abducted by aliens
Don Aldo disappears
Ran off with another woman
Hurt! Taken where?
Kidnapped
Not as exciting as mermaids or aliens, but definitely more possible.
What if Maximiliano the Weasel tried to kidnap him?
Or kill him? But he didn't die!
Where would you take a hurt person?

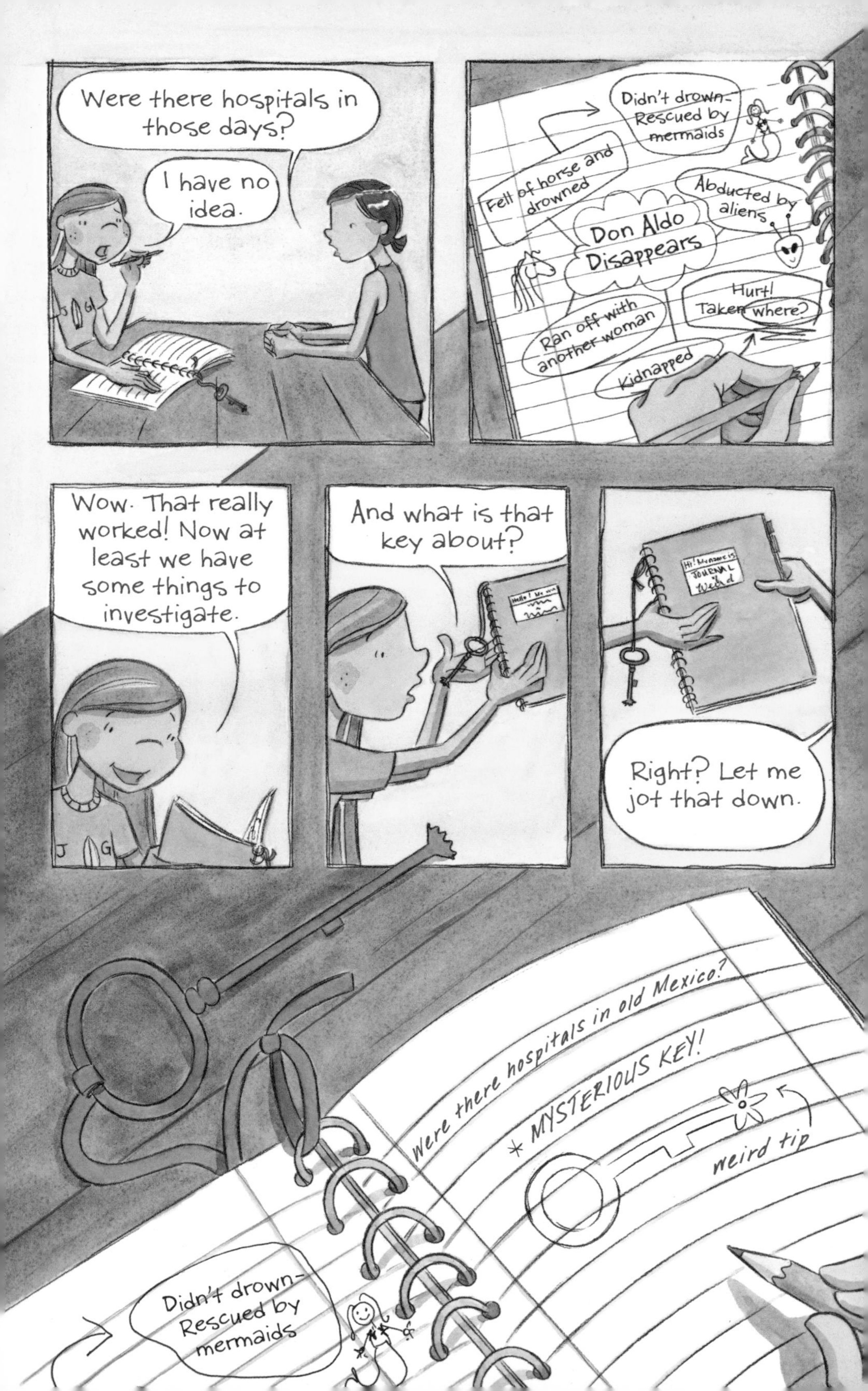

Were there hospitals in those days?
I have no idea.
Didn't drown- Rescued by mermaids
Fell of horse and drowned
Abducted by aliens
Don Aldo Disappears
Hurt! Taken where?
Ran off with another woman
Kidnapped
Wow. That really worked! Now at least we have some things to investigate.
And what is that key about?
Right? Let me jot that down.
Were there hospitals in old Mexico?
* MYSTERIOUS KEY!
weird tip
Didn't drown- Rescued by mermaids

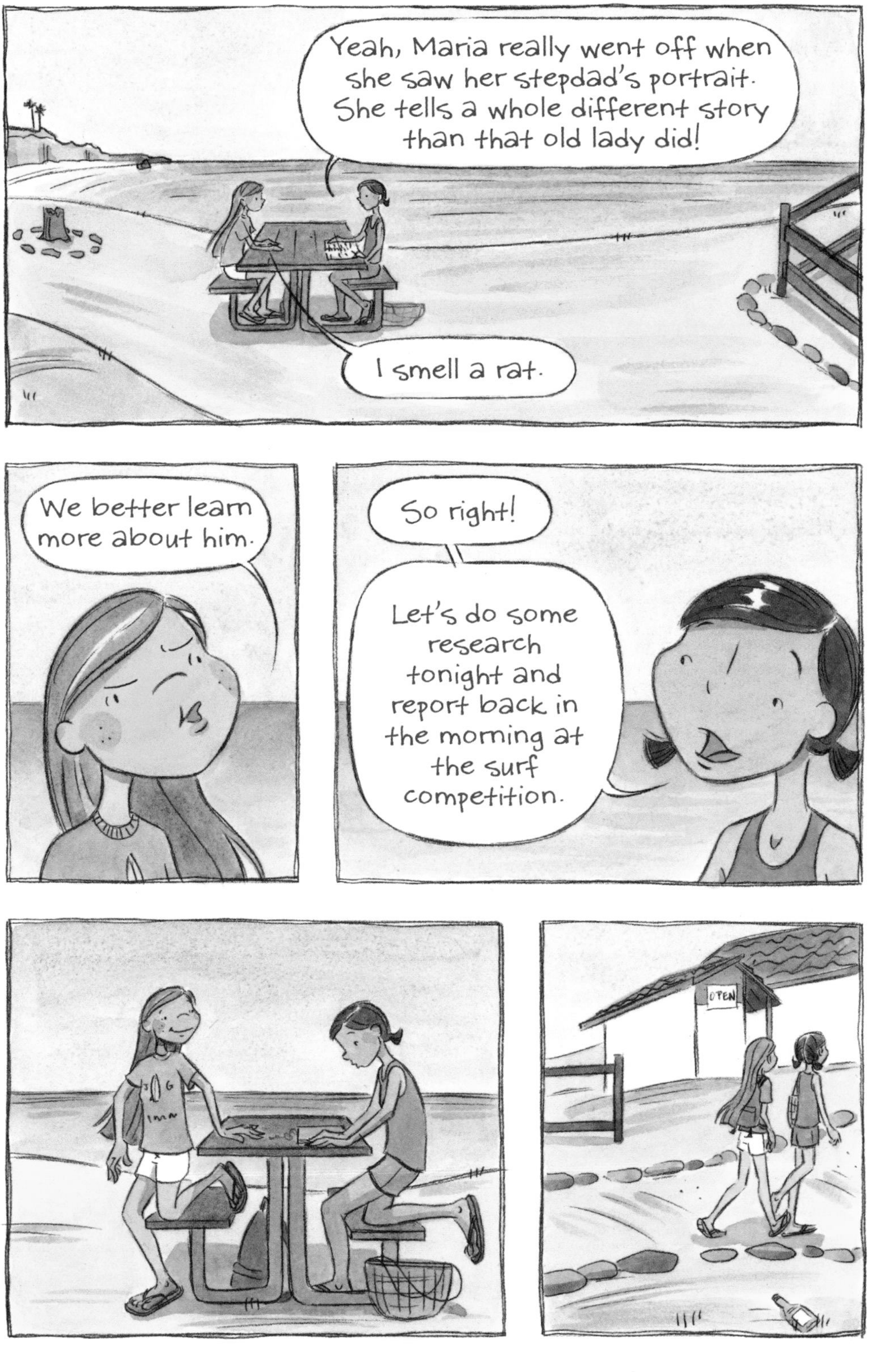
Yeah, Maria really went off when she saw her stepdad's portrait. She tells a whole different story than that old lady did!
I smell a rat.
We better learn more about him.
So right!
Let's do some research tonight and report back in the morning at the surf competition.
OPEN

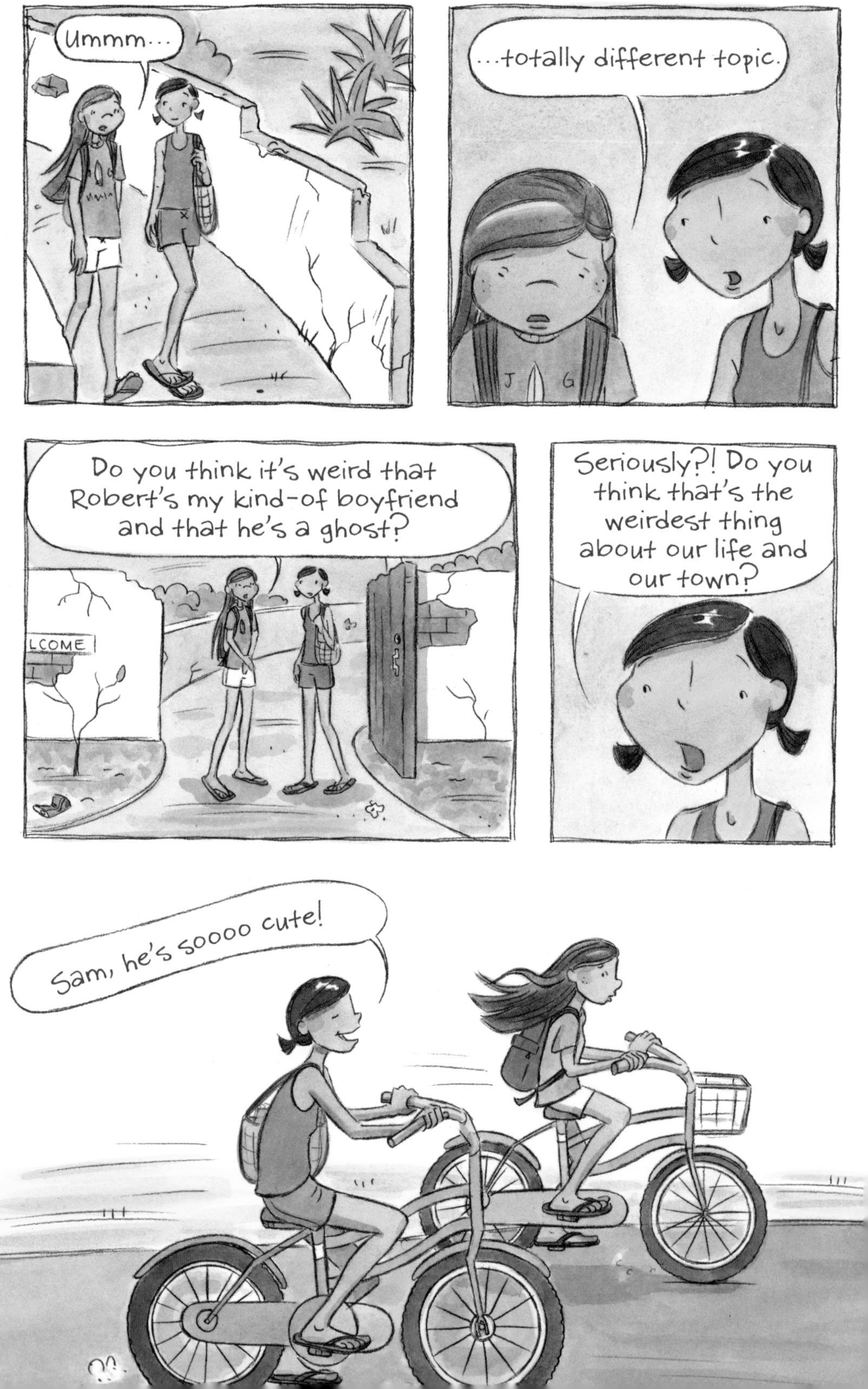
Ummm...
...totally different topic.
Do you think it's weird that Robert's my kind-of boyfriend and that he's a ghost?
LCOME
Seriously?! Do you think that's the weirdest thing about our life and our town?
Sam, he's soooo cute!

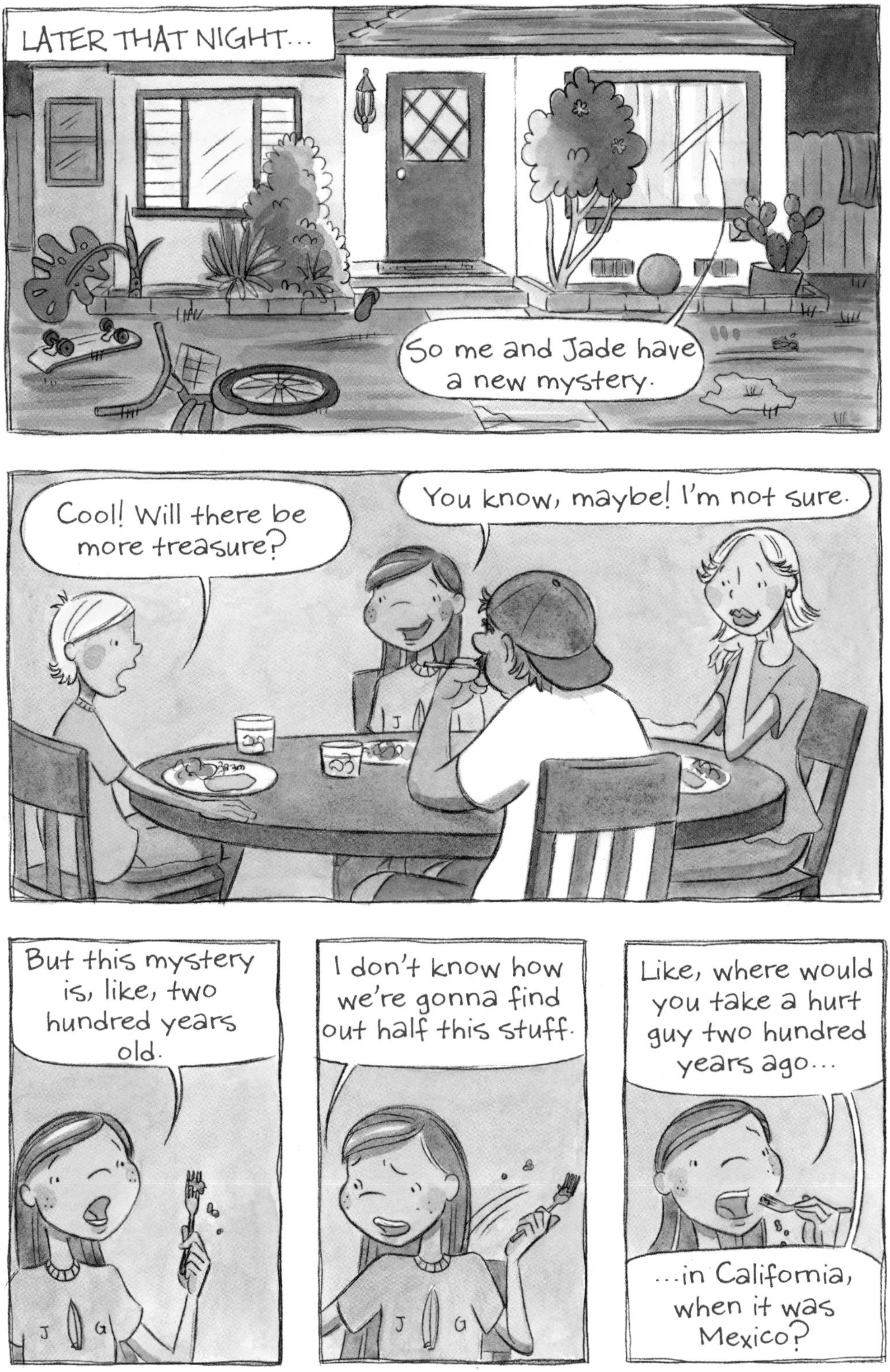
LATER THAT NIGHT...
So me and Jade have a new mystery.
Cool! Will there be more treasure?
You know, maybe! I'm not sure.
But this mystery is, like, two hundred years old.
I don't know how we're gonna find out half this stuff.
Like, where would you take a hurt guy two hundred years ago...
...in California, when it was Mexico?

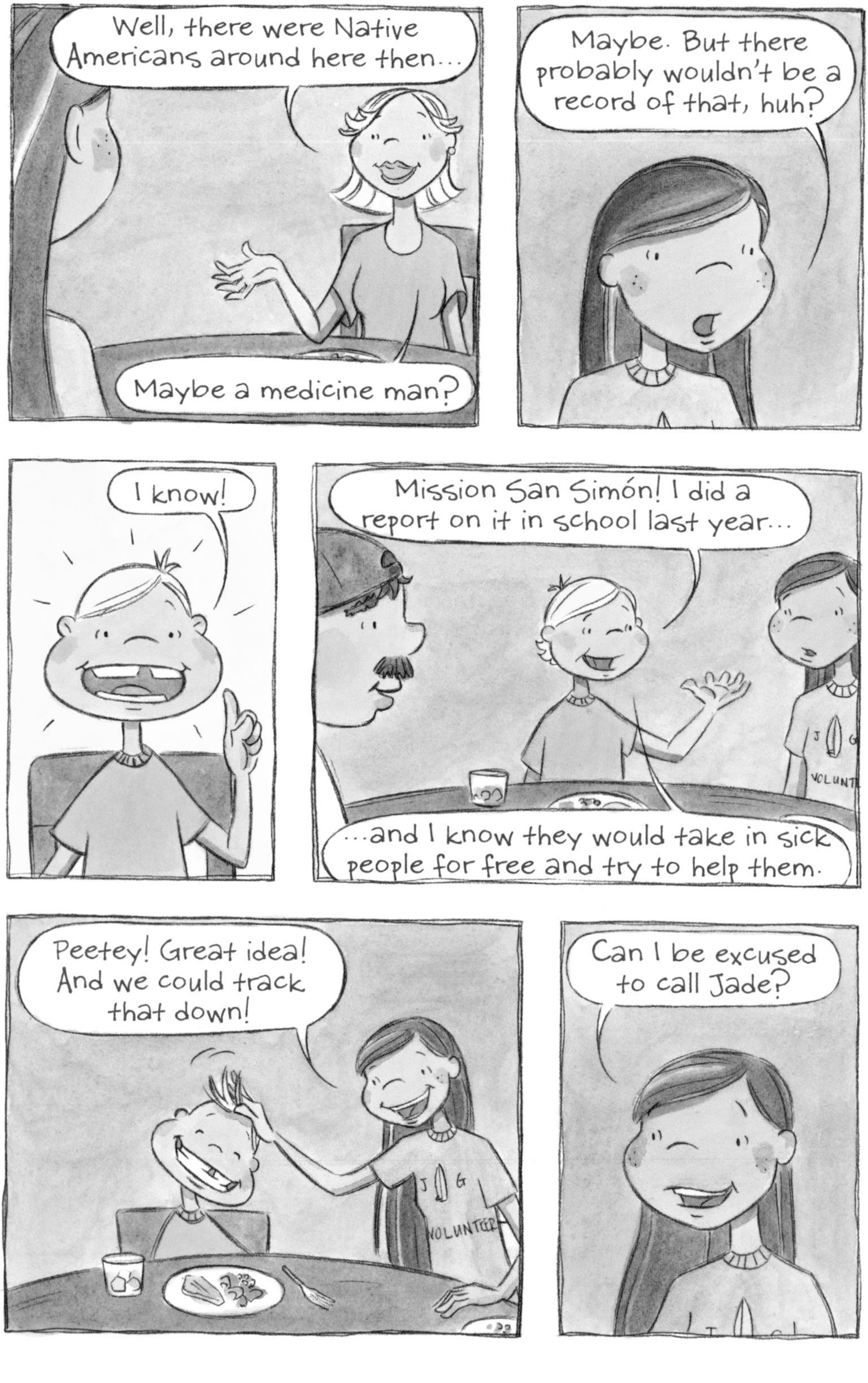
Well, there were Native Americans around here then...
Maybe a medicine man?
Maybe. But there probably wouldn't be a record of that, huh?
I know!
Mission San Simón! I did a report on it in school last year...
...and I know they would take in sick people for free and try to help them.
Peetey! Great idea! And we could track that down!
Can I be excused to call Jade?

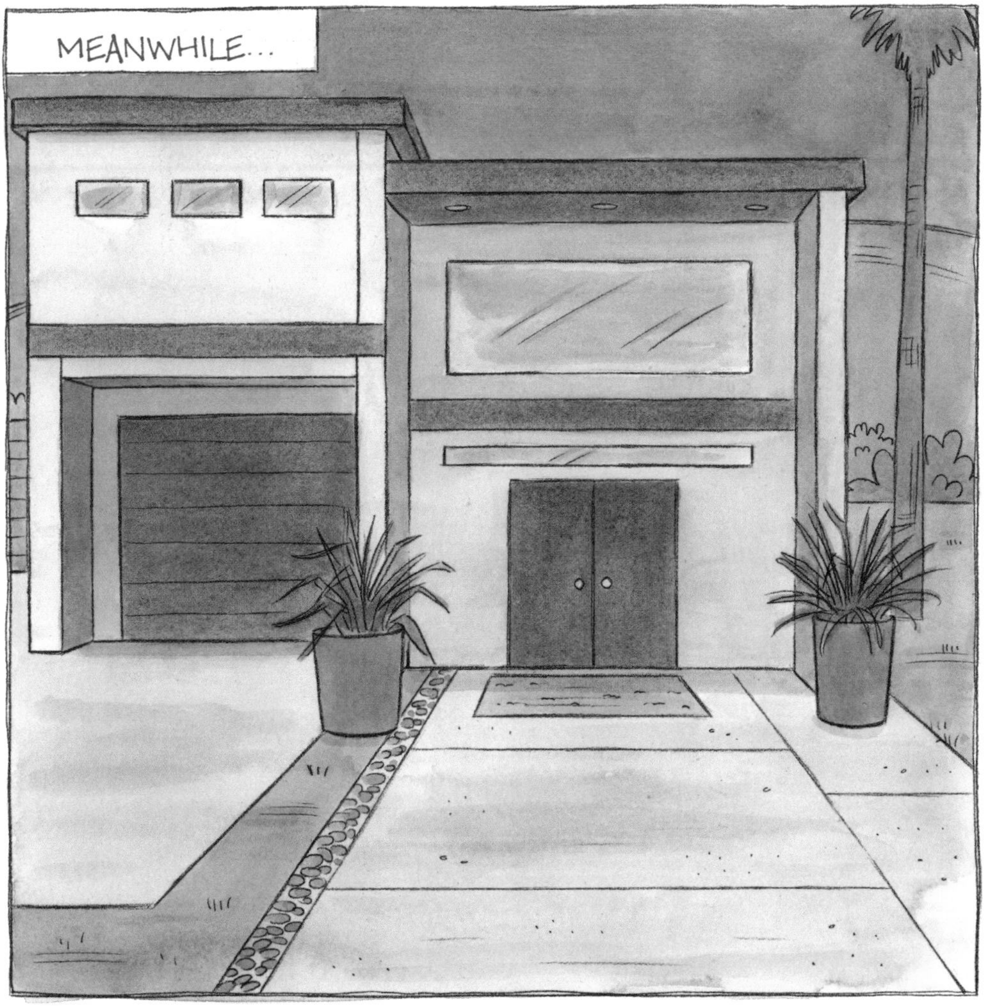
MEANWHILE...

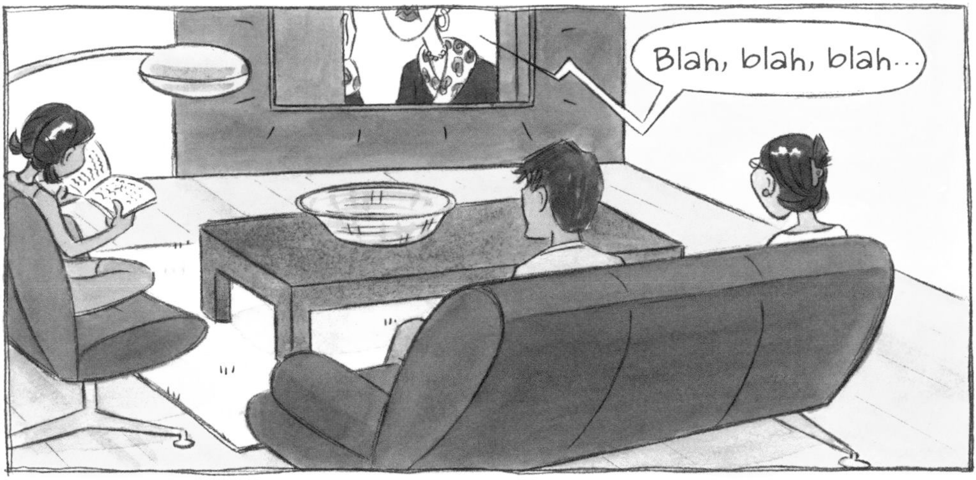
Blah, blah, blah...

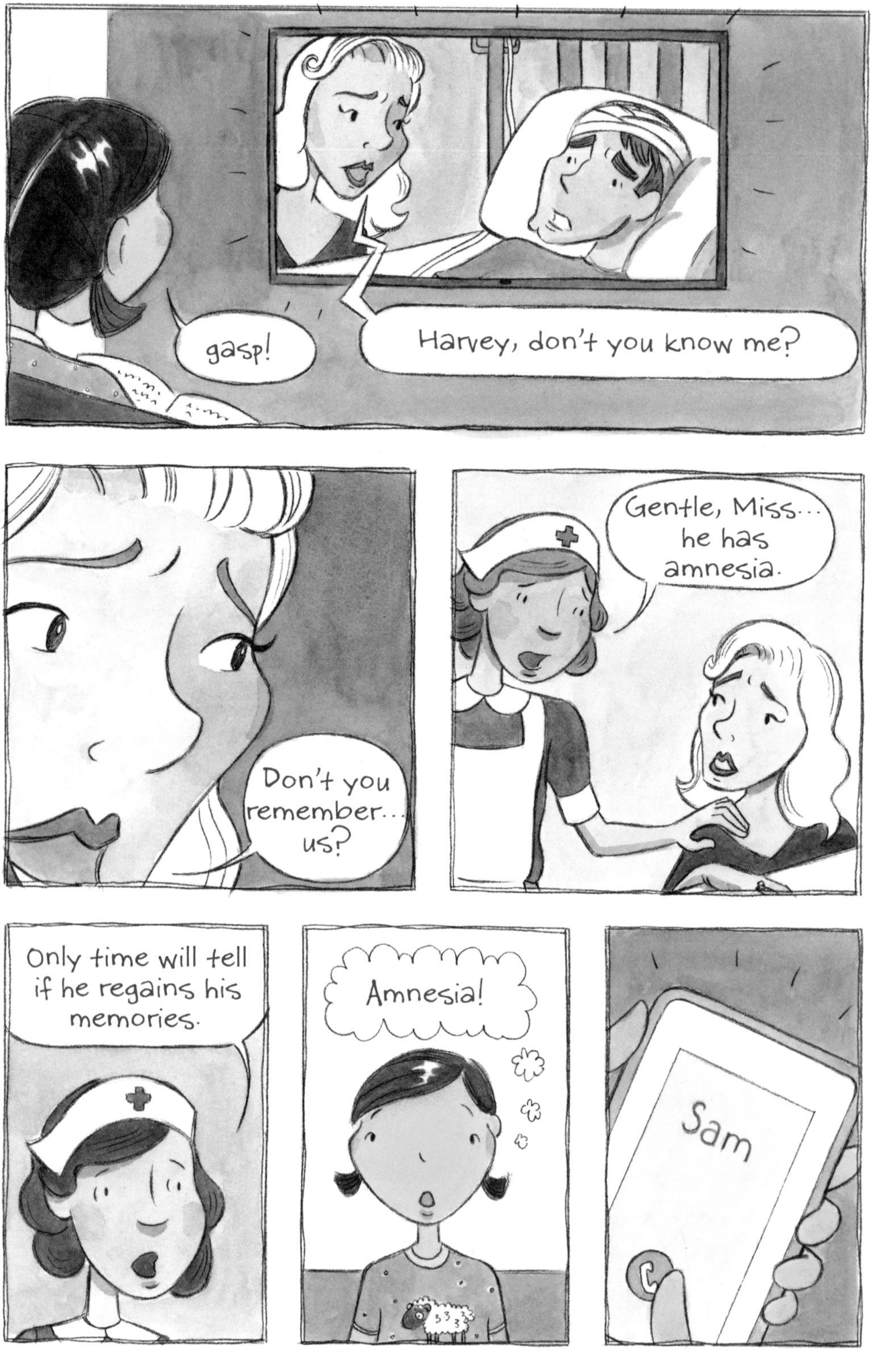
gasp!
Harvey, don't you know me?
Don't you remember... us?
Gentle, Miss... he has amnesia.
Only time will tell if he regains his memories.
Amnesia!
Sam

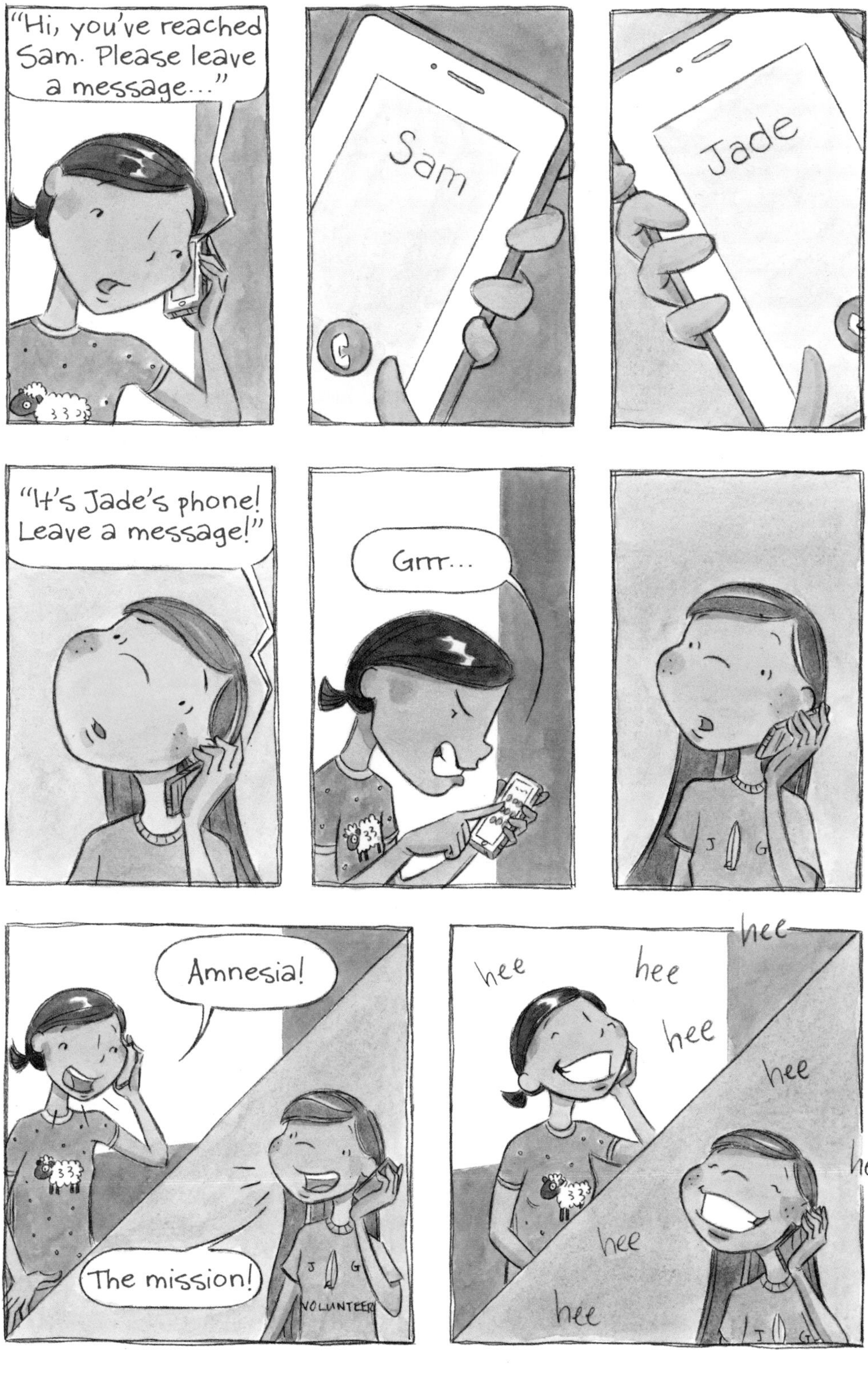
"Hi, you've reached Sam. Please leave a message..."
Sam
Jade
"It's Jade's phone! Leave a message!"
Grrr...
Amnesia!
The mission!
J G VOLUNTEER
hee hee hee hee hee hee hee hee

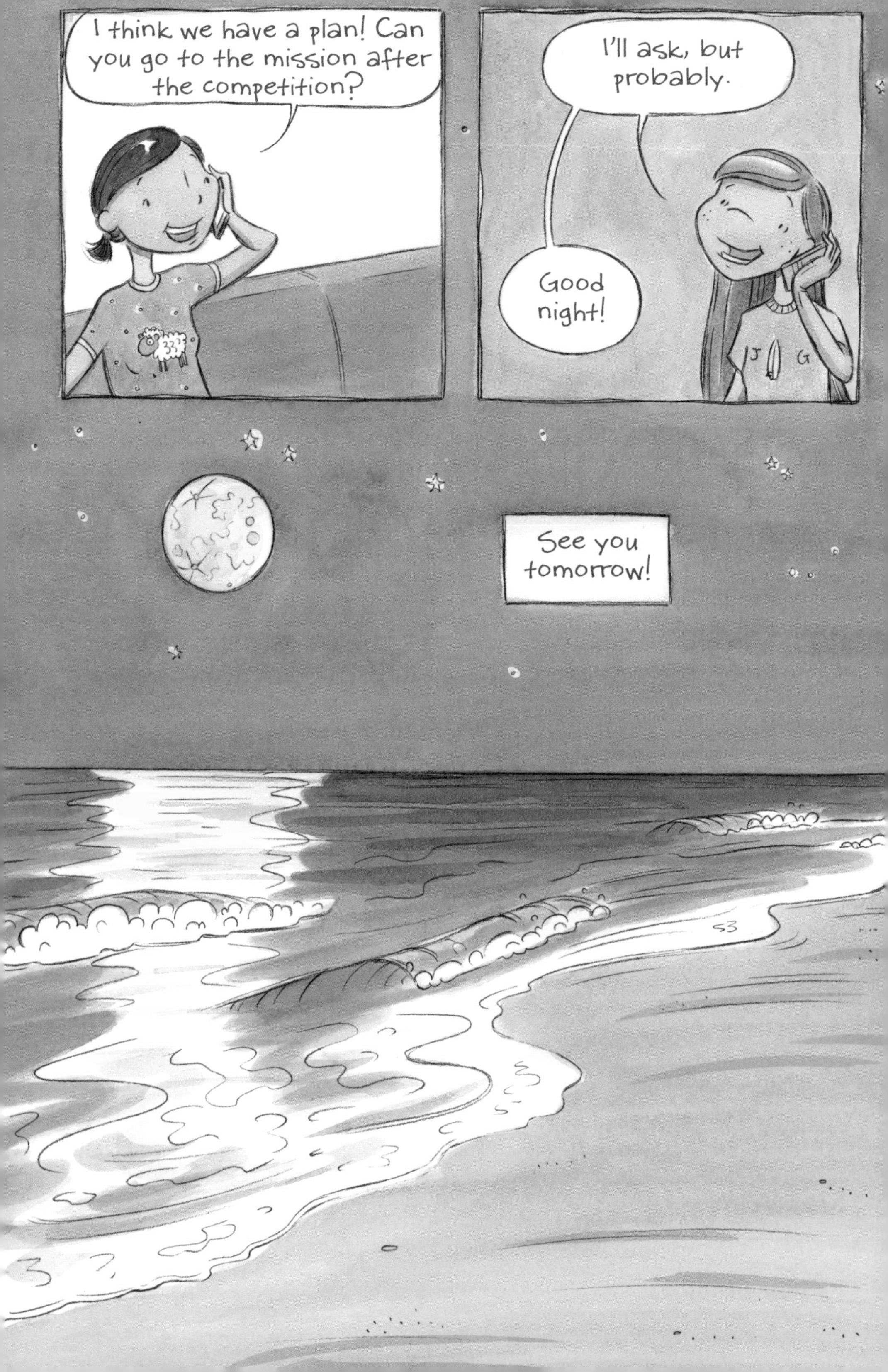
I think we have a plan! Can you go to the mission after the competition?
I'll ask, but probably.
Good night!
See you tomorrow!

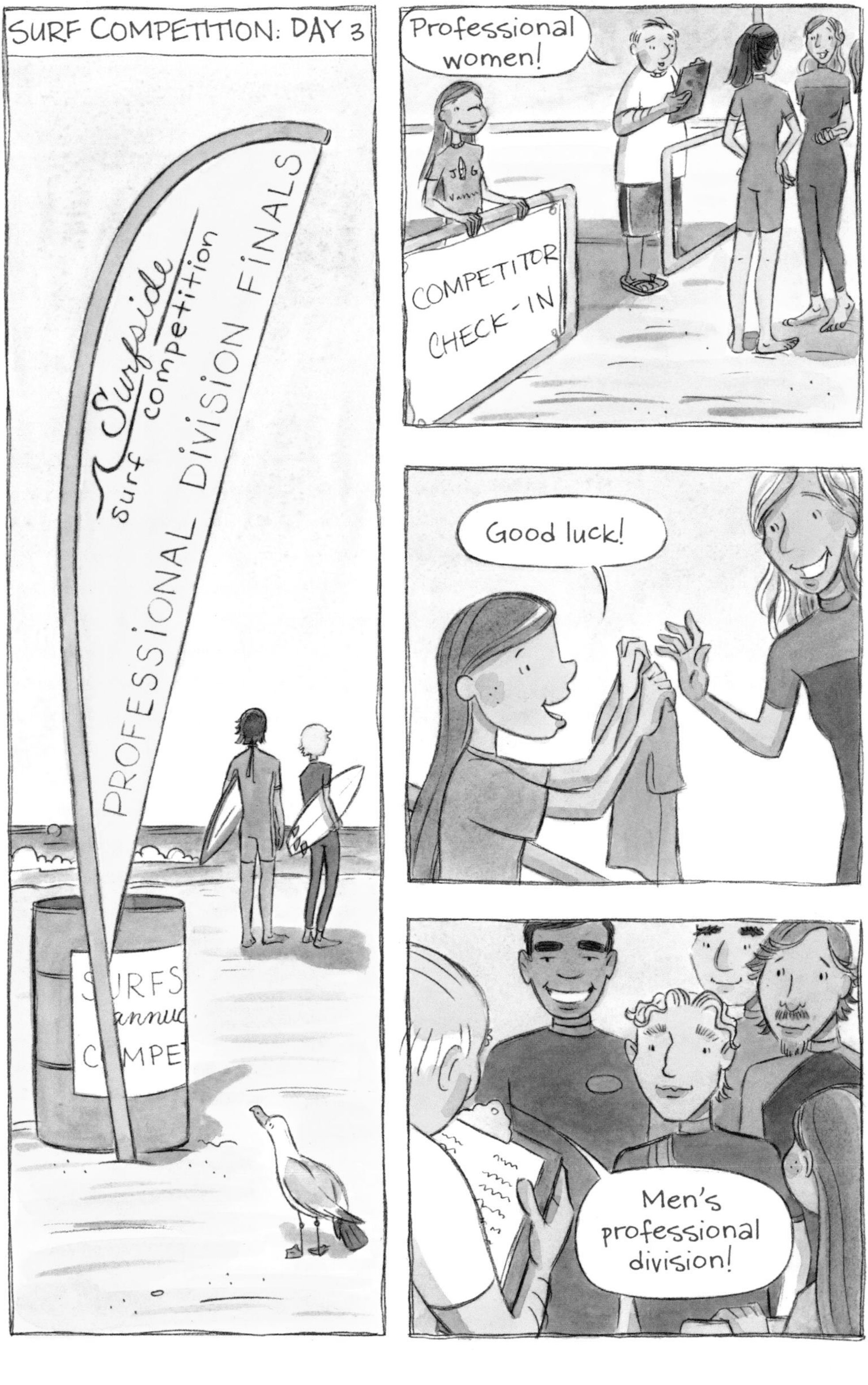
SURF COMPETITION: DAY 3
Surfside surf competition
PROFESSIONAL DIVISION FINALS
Professional women!
COMPETITOR CHECK-IN
Good luck!
Men's professional division!

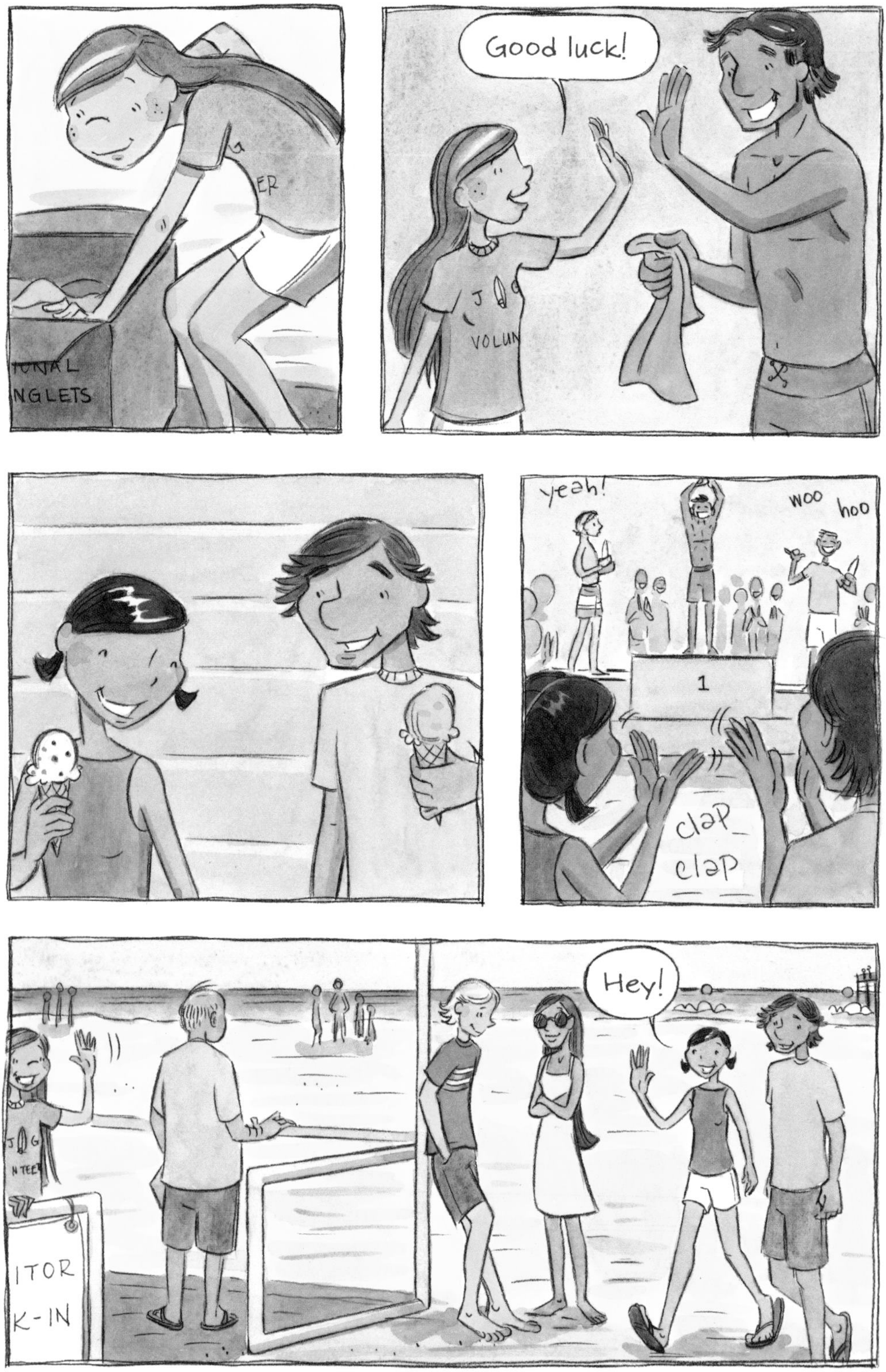

IONAL
NGLETS
Good luck!
VOLUN
yeah!
woo
hoo
1
clap
clap
Hey!
ITOR
K-IN

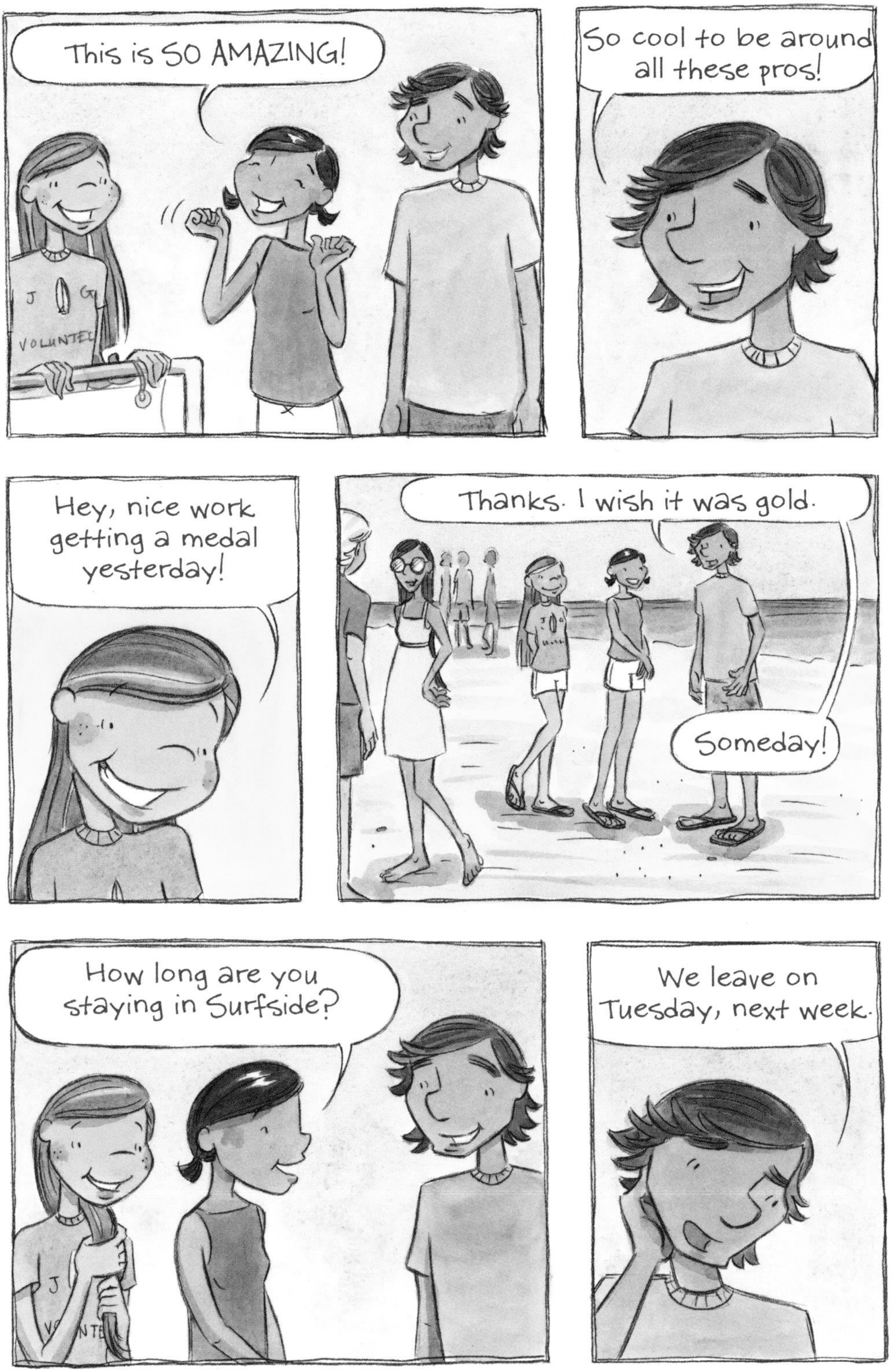
This is SO AMAZING!
J
VOLUNTE
So cool to be around all these pros!
Hey, nice work getting a medal yesterday!
Thanks. I wish it was gold.
Someday!
How long are you staying in Surfside?
We leave on Tuesday, next week.

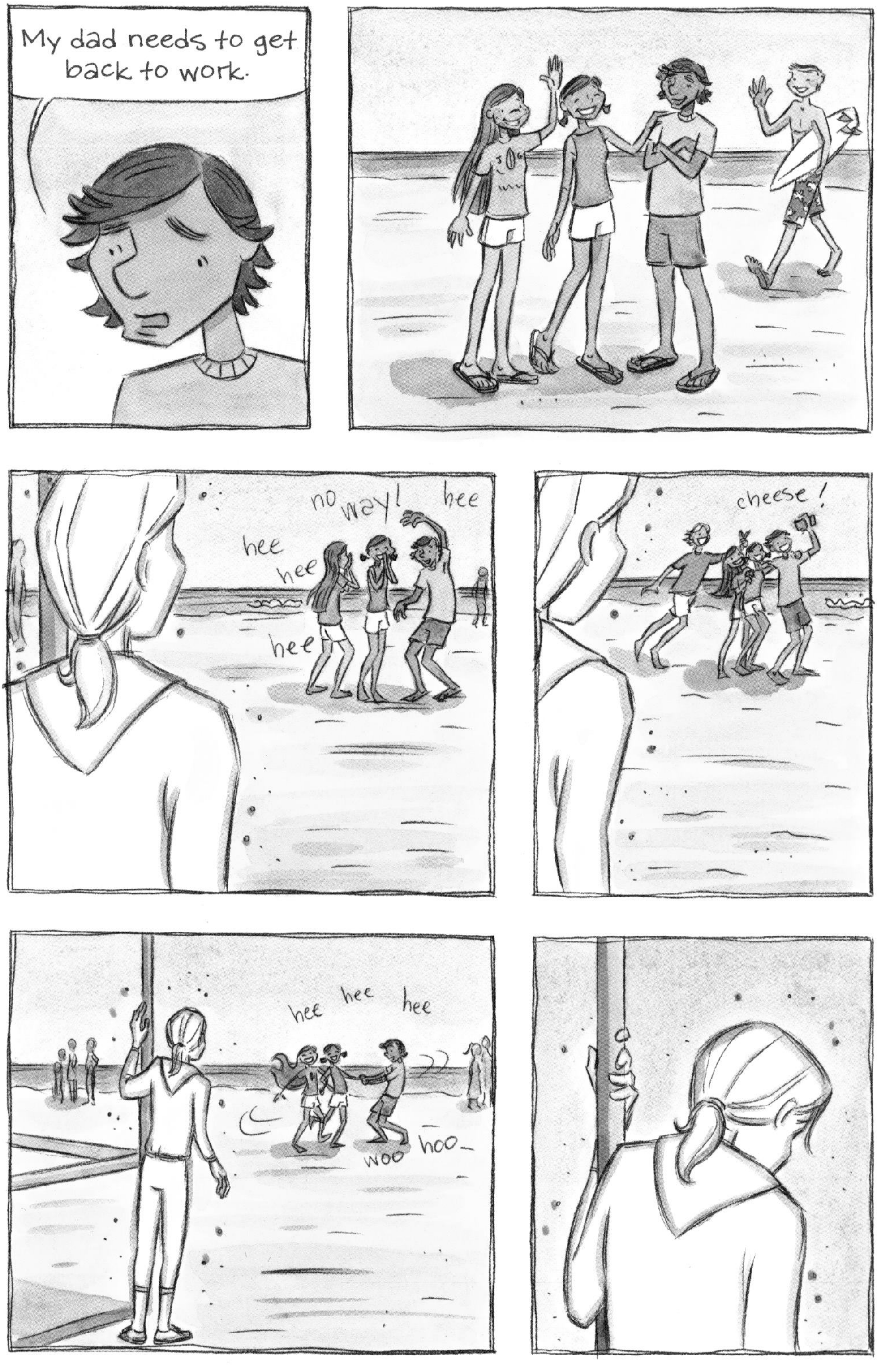
My dad needs to get back to work.
no way!
hee
hee
hee
hee
cheese!
hee
hee
hee
woo
hoo

SCHEDULE

Route	Time
181	12:35
182	12:55
183	1:15
184	1:30
185	1:40
186	1:55
187	2:10
188	2:20

It looks like...

...it will take us about an hour and a half to get to the mission. We're looking for bus 181, southbound.

It will say San Simón. Oh, and I did some digging on our Maximiliano. I found NOTHING on him. He is never mentioned before he marries Maria's mom.

Hmmm... suspicious!

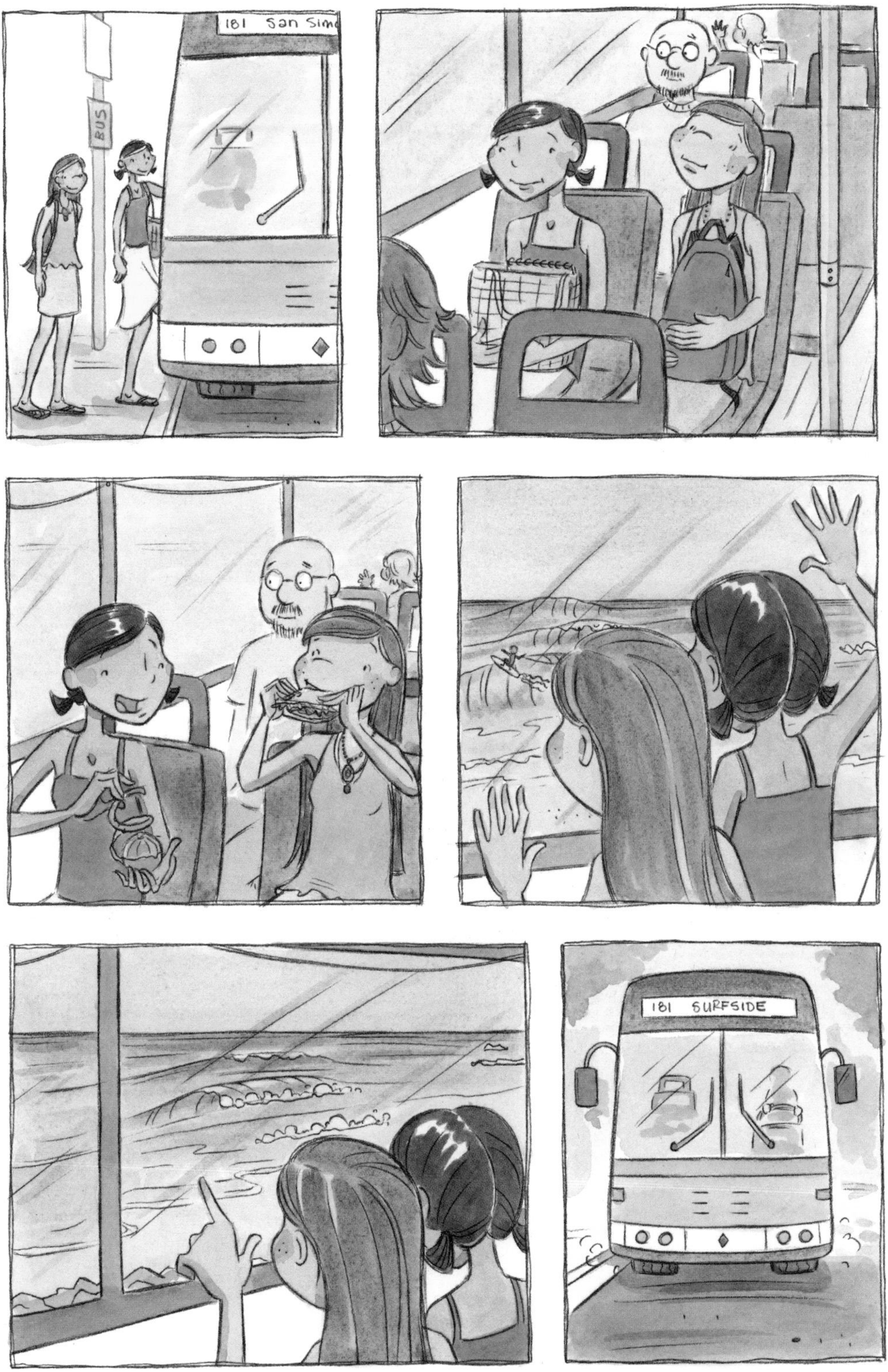
181 San Sim
BUS
181 SURFSIDE

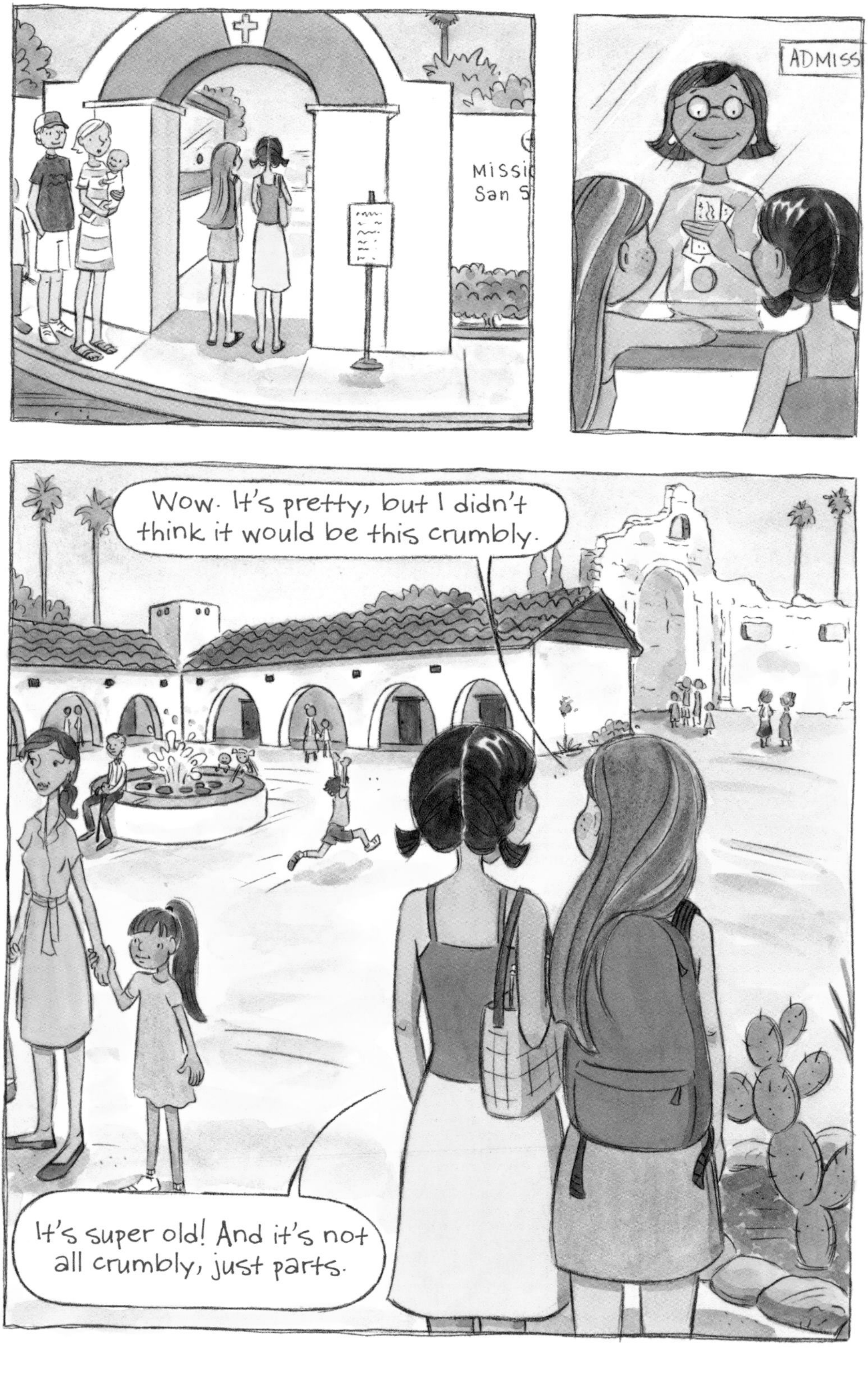
MISSI
San S
ADMISS
Wow. It's pretty, but I didn't think it would be this crumbly.
It's super old! And it's not all crumbly, just parts.

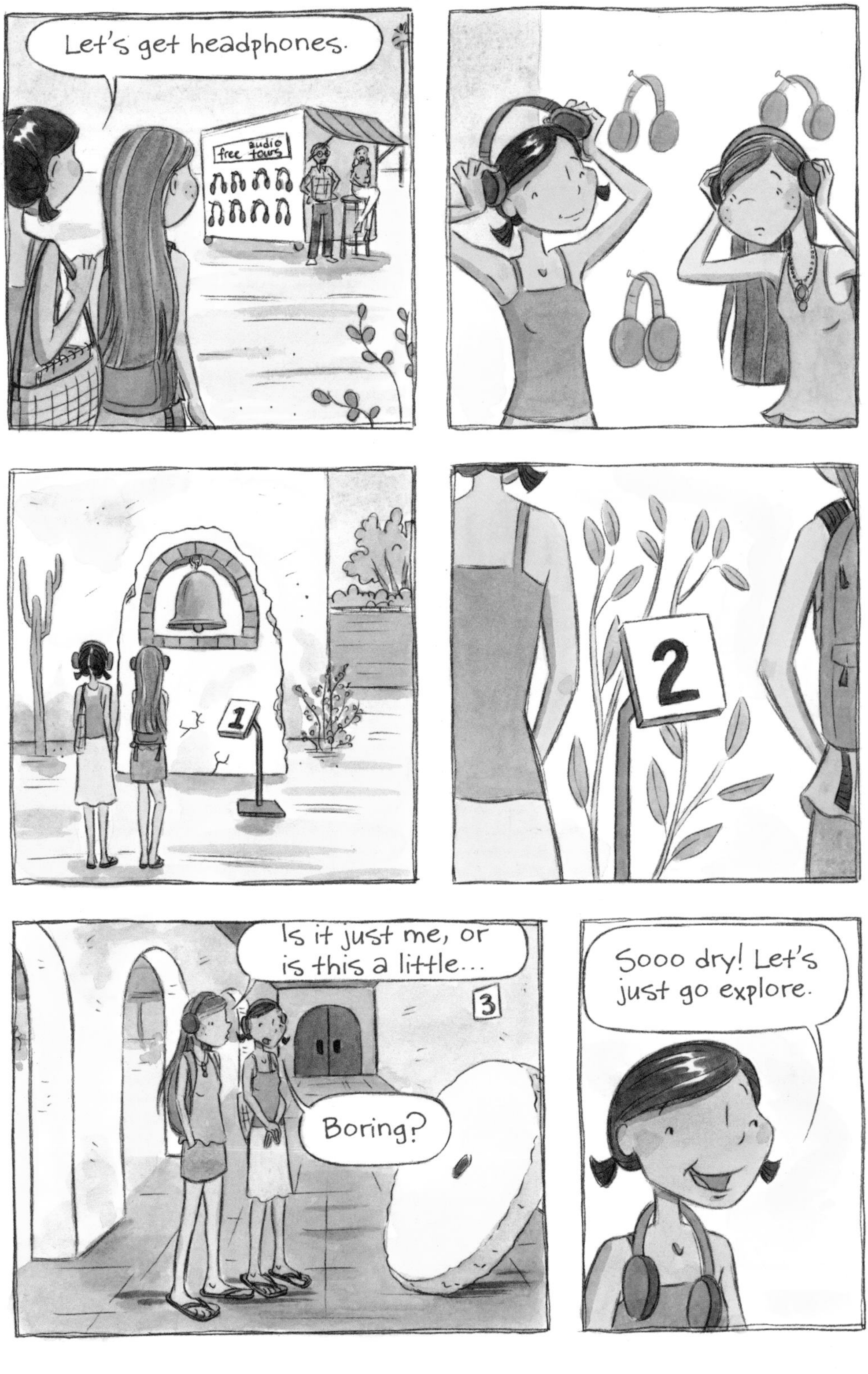
Let's get headphones.
free audio tours
1
2
Is it just me, or is this a little...
Boring?
3
Sooo dry! Let's just go explore.

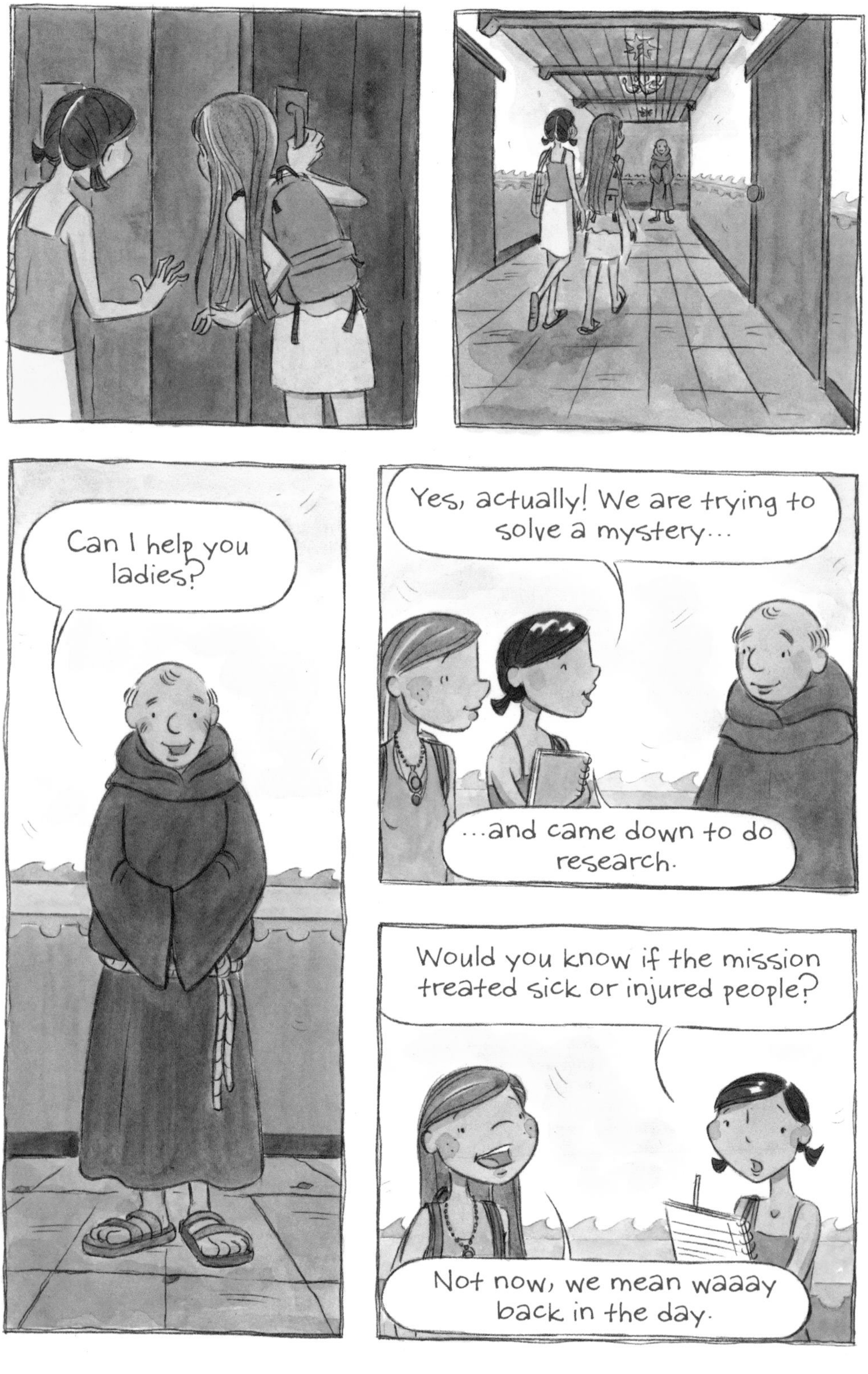
Can I help you ladies?
Yes, actually! We are trying to solve a mystery...
...and came down to do research.
Would you know if the mission treated sick or injured people?
Not now, we mean waaay back in the day.

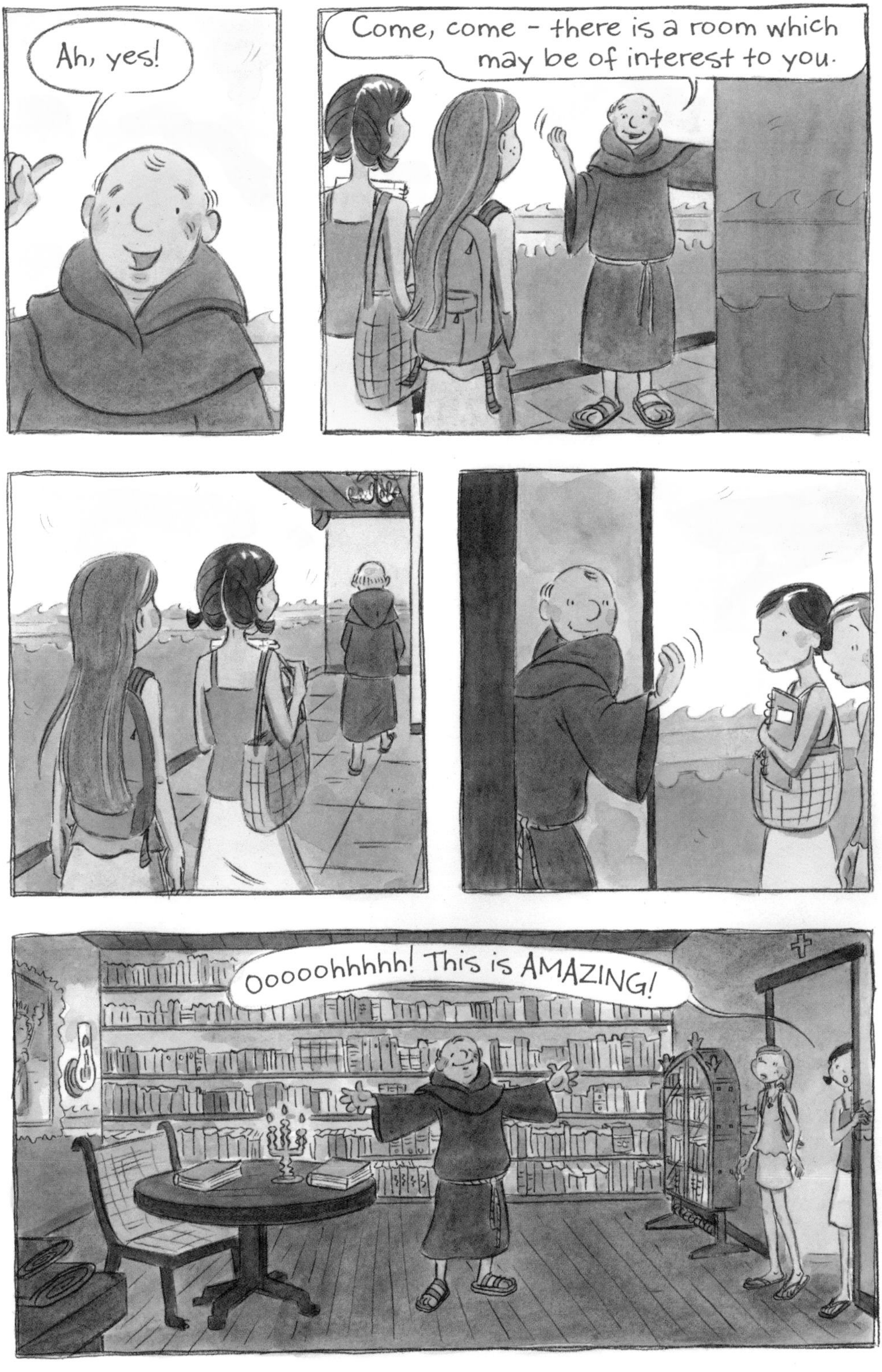
Ah, yes!
Come, come - there is a room which may be of interest to you.
Ooooohhhhh! This is AMAZING!

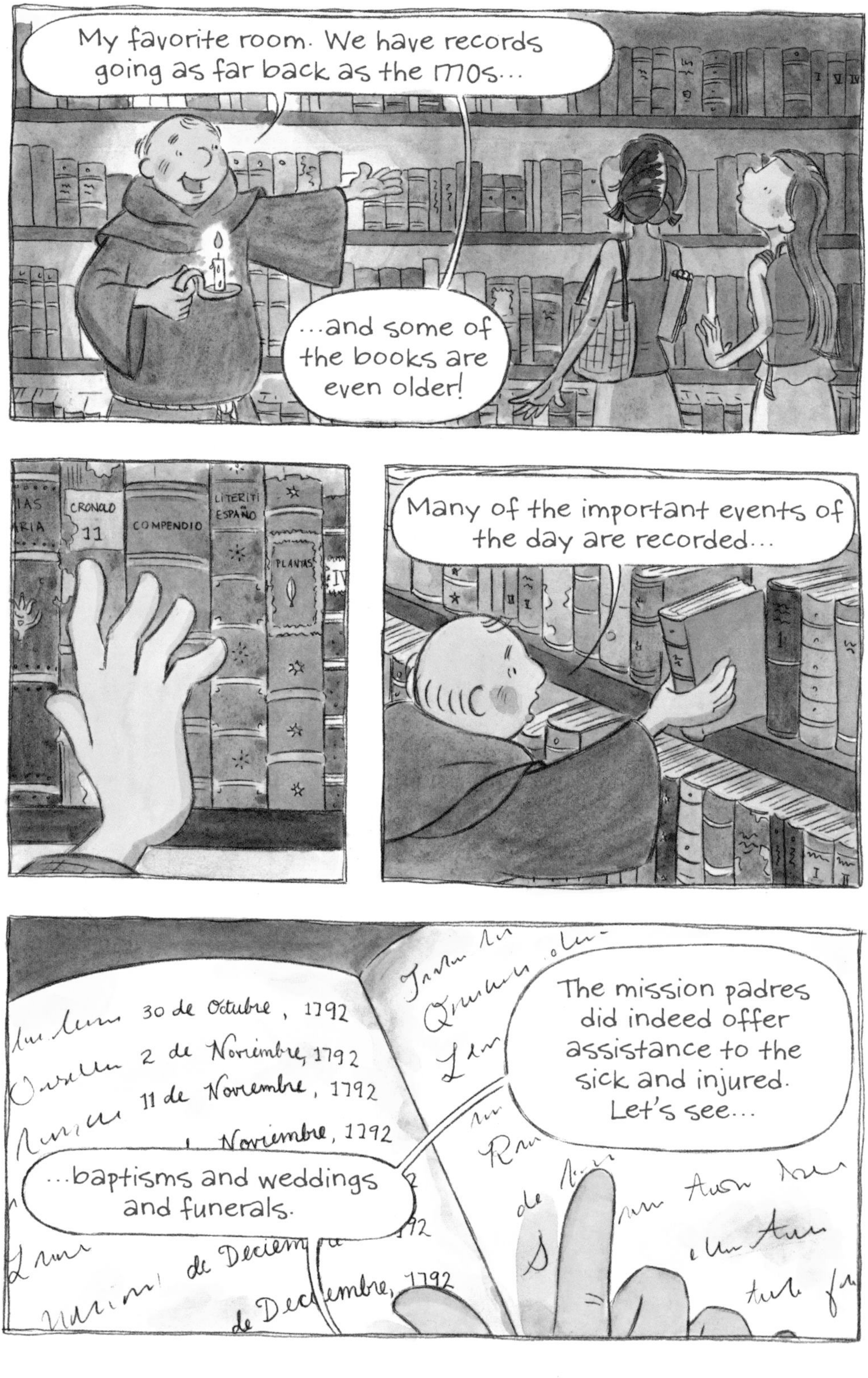
My favorite room. We have records going as far back as the 1770s...
...and some of the books are even older!
CRONOLO 11
COMPENDIO
LITERITI ESPAÑO
PLANTAS
Many of the important events of the day are recorded...
30 de Octubre, 1792
2 de Noviembre, 1792
11 de Noviembre, 1792
Noviembre, 1792
...baptisms and weddings and funerals.
The mission padres did indeed offer assistance to the sick and injured. Let's see...
de Decembre, 1792

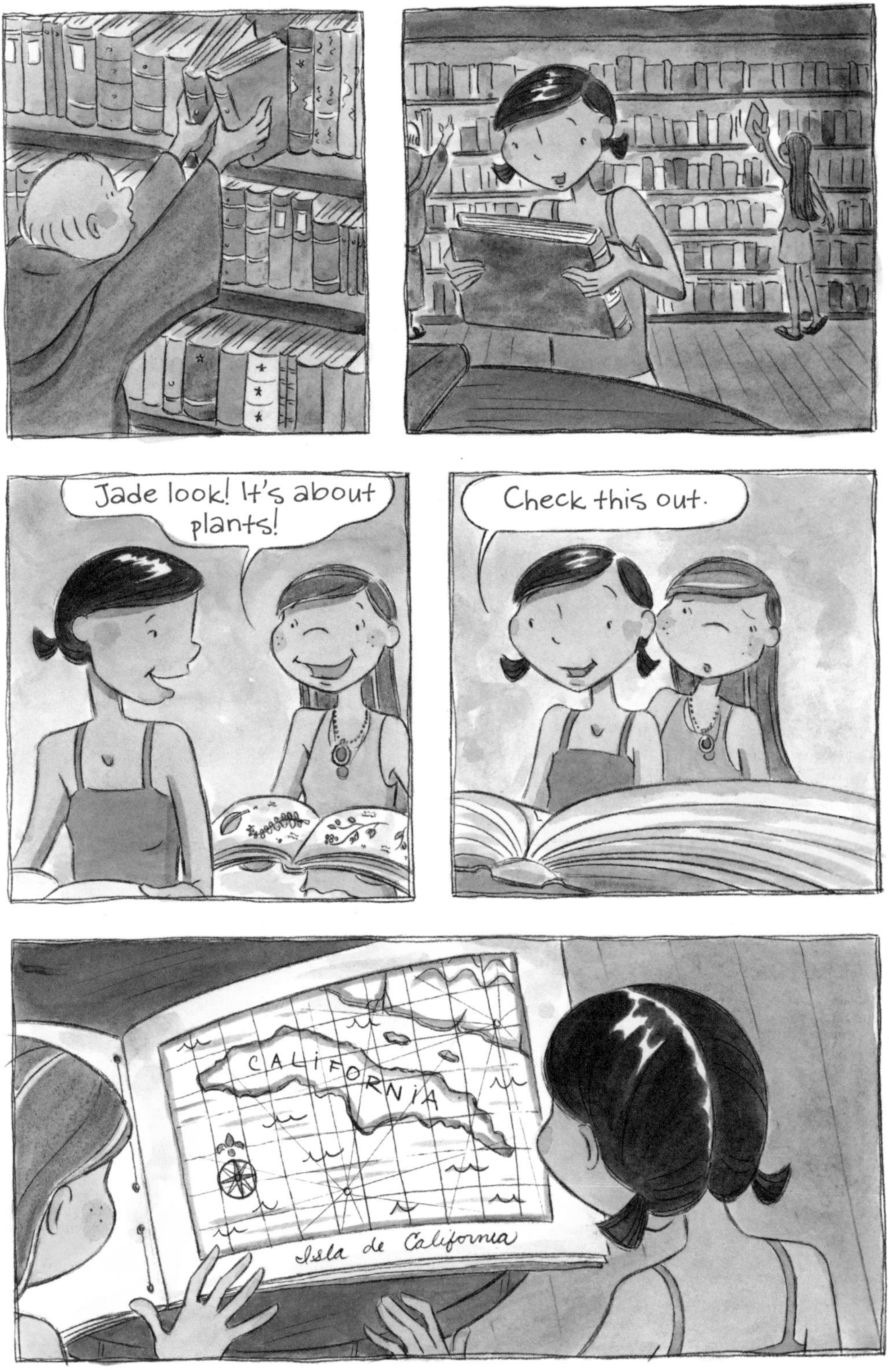
Jade look! It's about plants!
Check this out.
CALIFORNIA
Isla de California

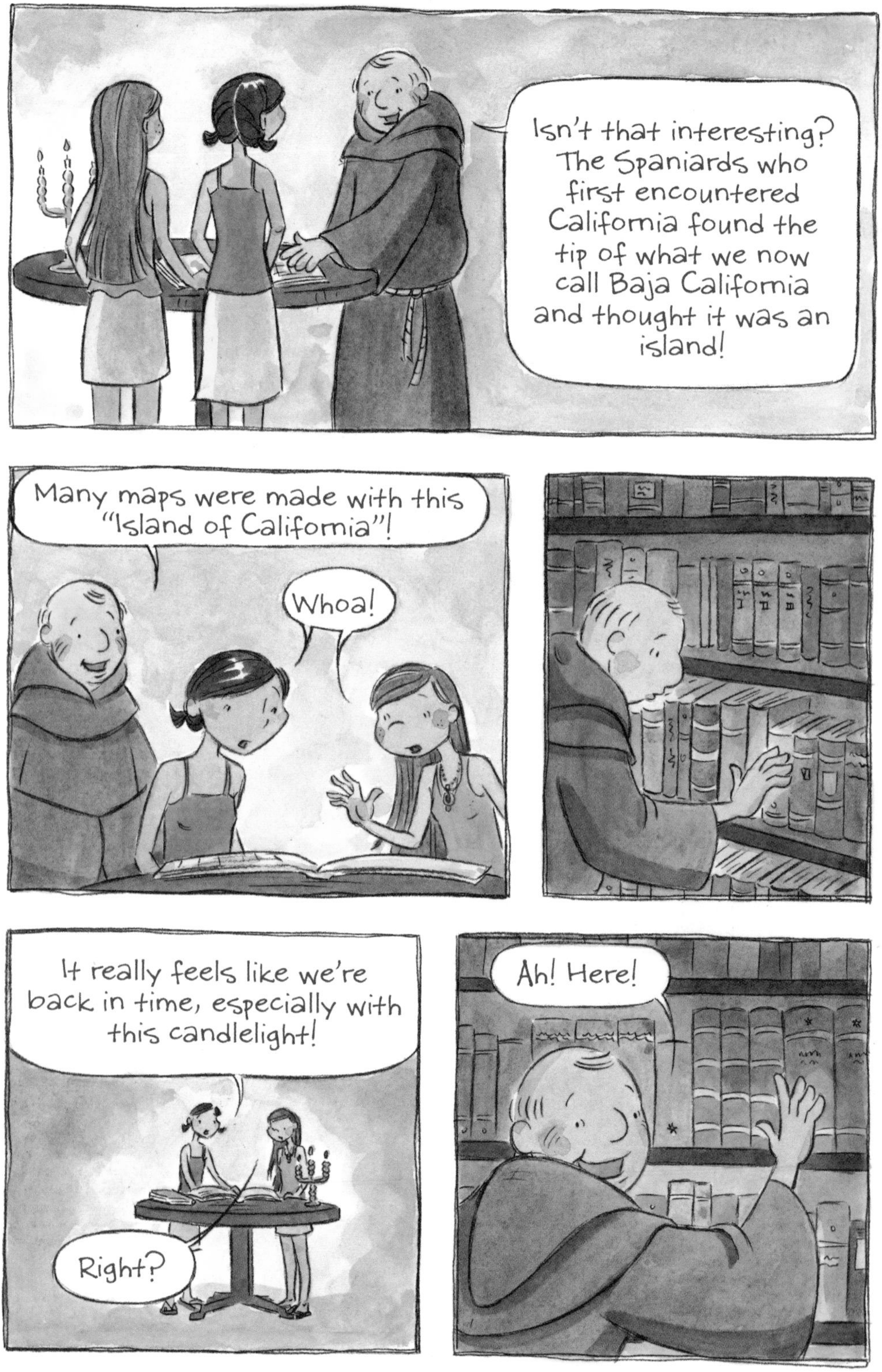
Isn't that interesting? The Spaniards who first encountered California found the tip of what we now call Baja California and thought it was an island!
Many maps were made with this "Island of California"!
Whoa!
It really feels like we're back in time, especially with this candlelight!
Right?
Ah! Here!

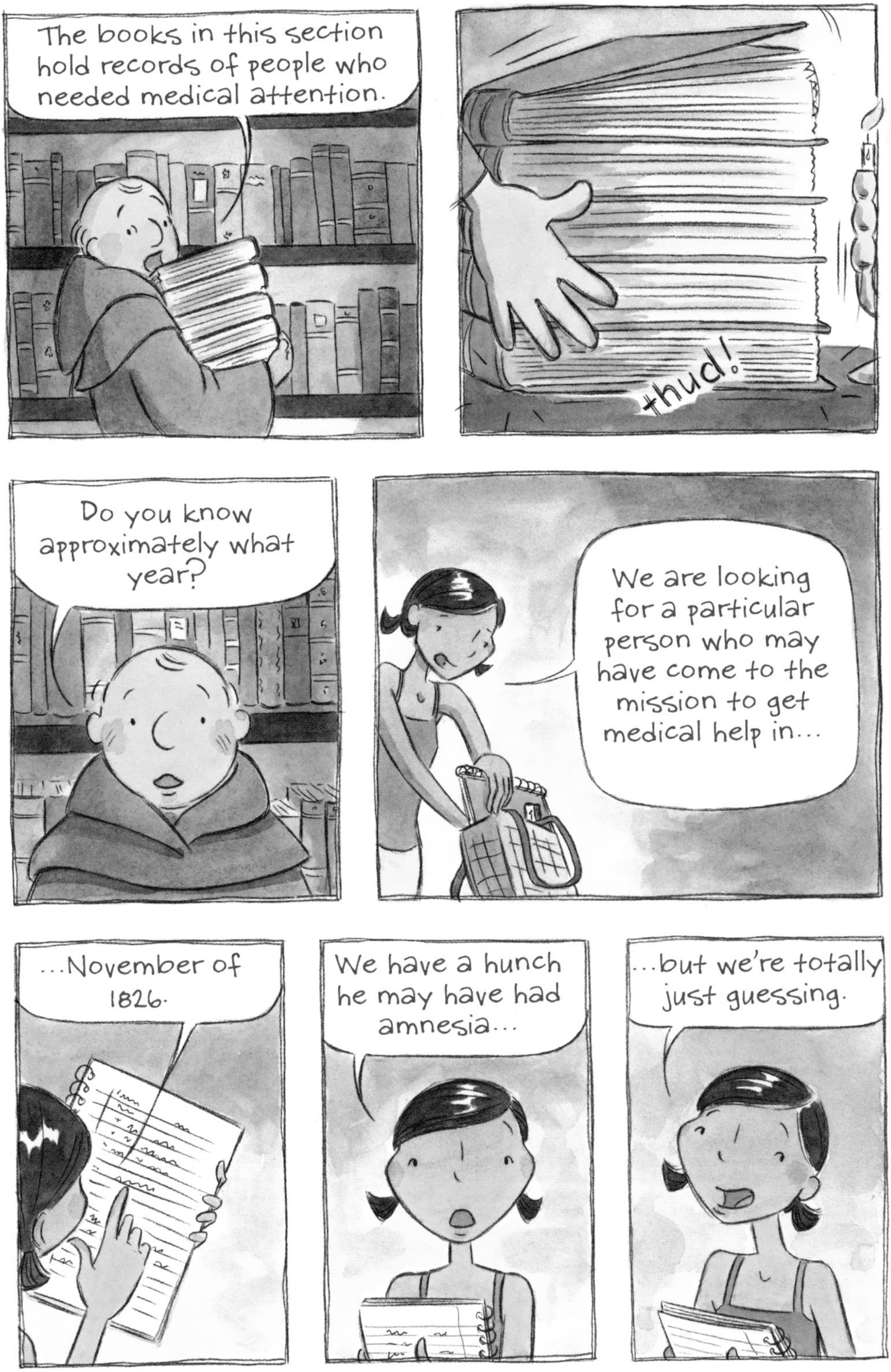
The books in this section hold records of people who needed medical attention.
thud!
Do you know approximately what year?
We are looking for a particular person who may have come to the mission to get medical help in...
...November of 1826.
We have a hunch he may have had amnesia...
...but we're totally just guessing.

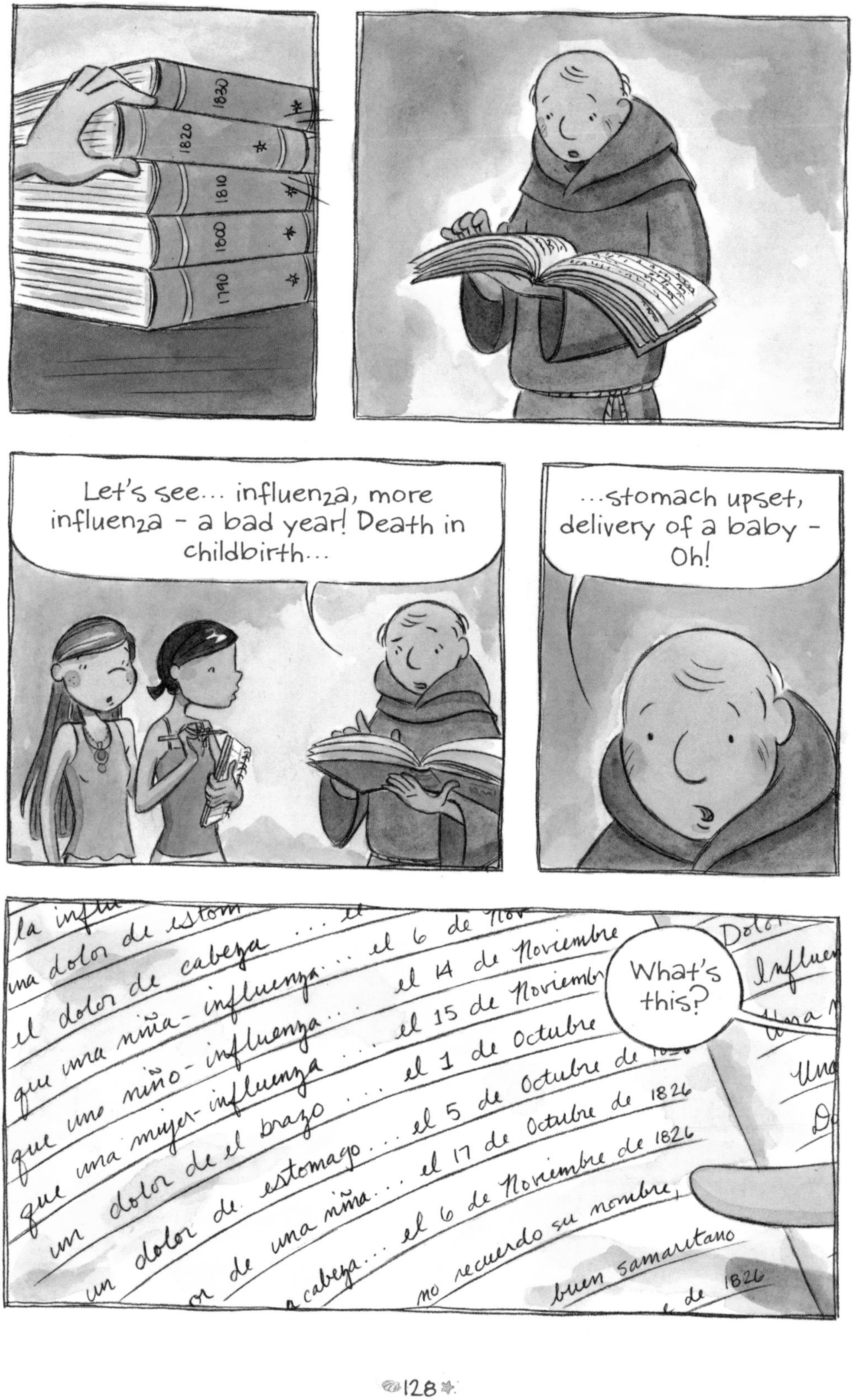
1830
1820
1810
1800
1790
Let's see... influenza, more influenza – a bad year! Death in childbirth...
...stomach upset, delivery of a baby – Oh!
el dolor de cabeza ... el 6 de Noviembre
que una niña- influenza ... el 14 de Noviembre
que uno niño- influenza ... el 15 de Octubre
que una mujer-influenza ... el 1 de Octubre
un dolor de el brazo ... el 5 de Octubre de 1826
un dolor de estomago ... el 17 de Octubre de 1826
de una niña ... el 6 de Noviembre de 1826
no recuerdo su nombre,
buen samaritano
What's this?

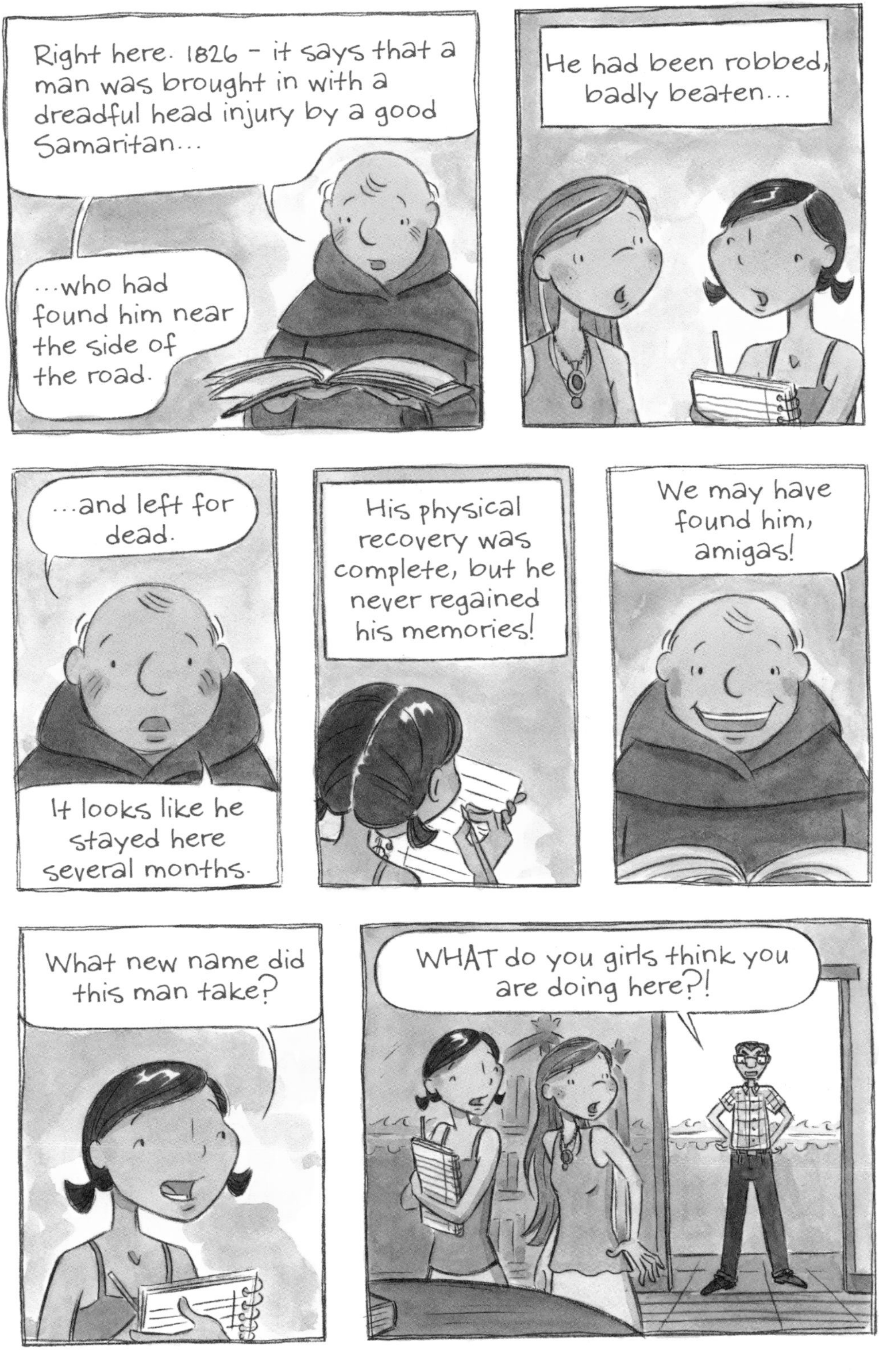
Right here. 1826 - it says that a man was brought in with a dreadful head injury by a good Samaritan...
...who had found him near the side of the road.
He had been robbed, badly beaten...
...and left for dead.
It looks like he stayed here several months.
His physical recovery was complete, but he never regained his memories!
We may have found him, amigas!
What new name did this man take?
WHAT do you girls think you are doing here?!

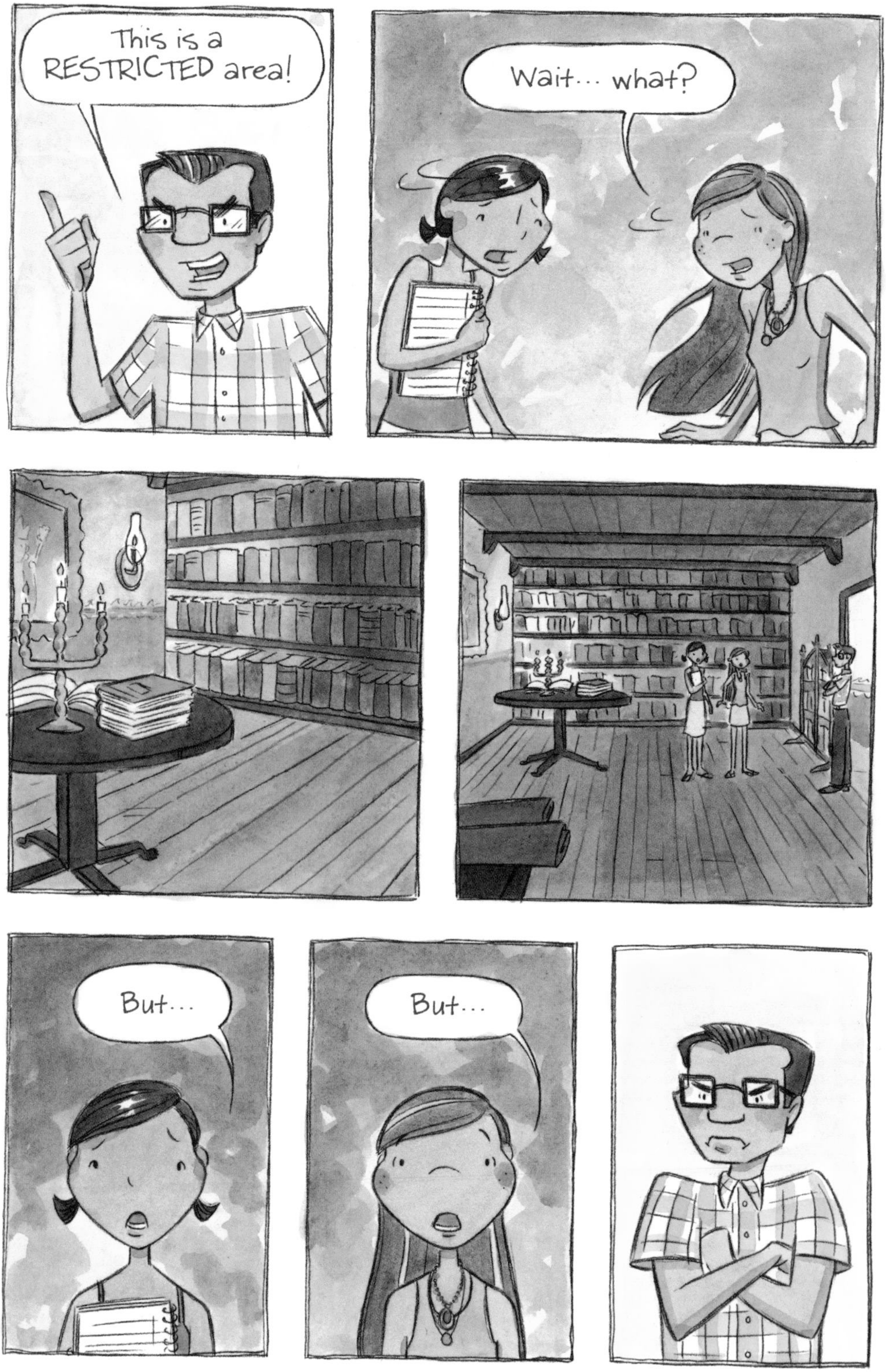
This is a RESTRICTED area!
Wait... what?
But...
But...

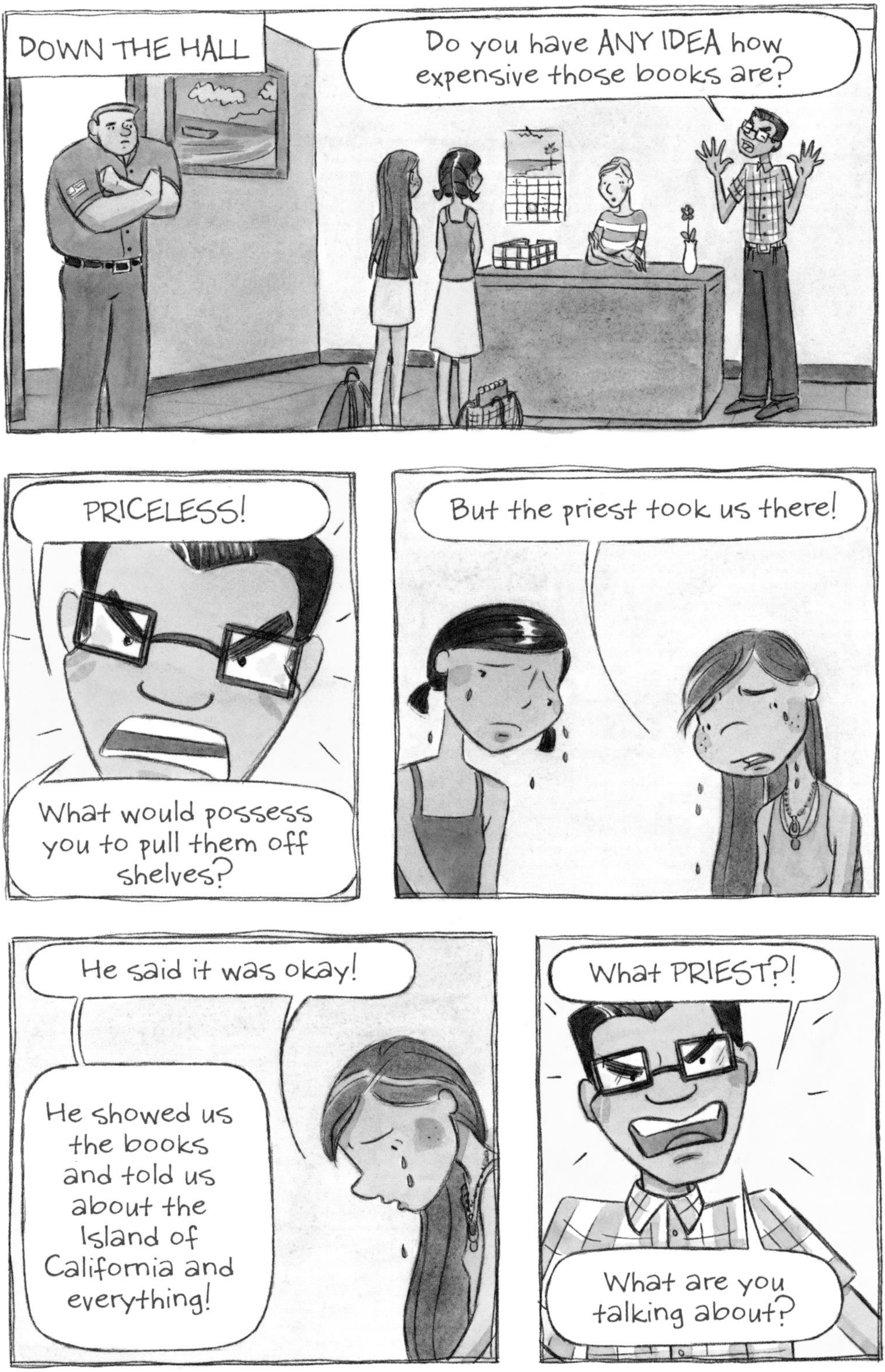
DOWN THE HALL
Do you have ANY IDEA how expensive those books are?
PRICELESS!
What would possess you to pull them off shelves?
But the priest took us there!
He said it was okay!
He showed us the books and told us about the Island of California and everything!
What PRIEST?!
What are you talking about?

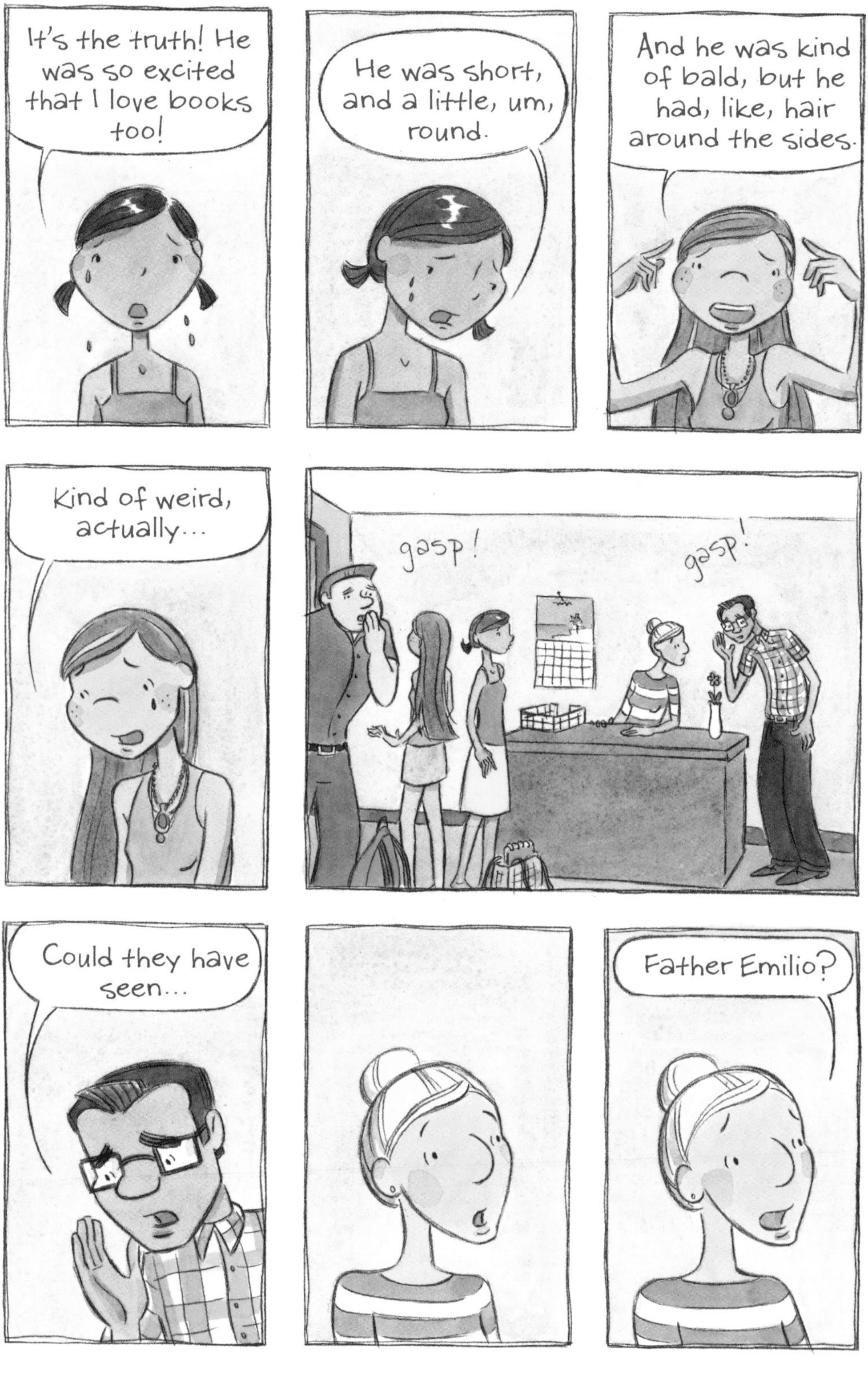
It's the truth! He was so excited that I love books too!
He was short, and a little, um, round.
And he was kind of bald, but he had, like, hair around the sides.
Kind of weird, actually...
gasp!
gasp!
Could they have seen...
Father Emilio?

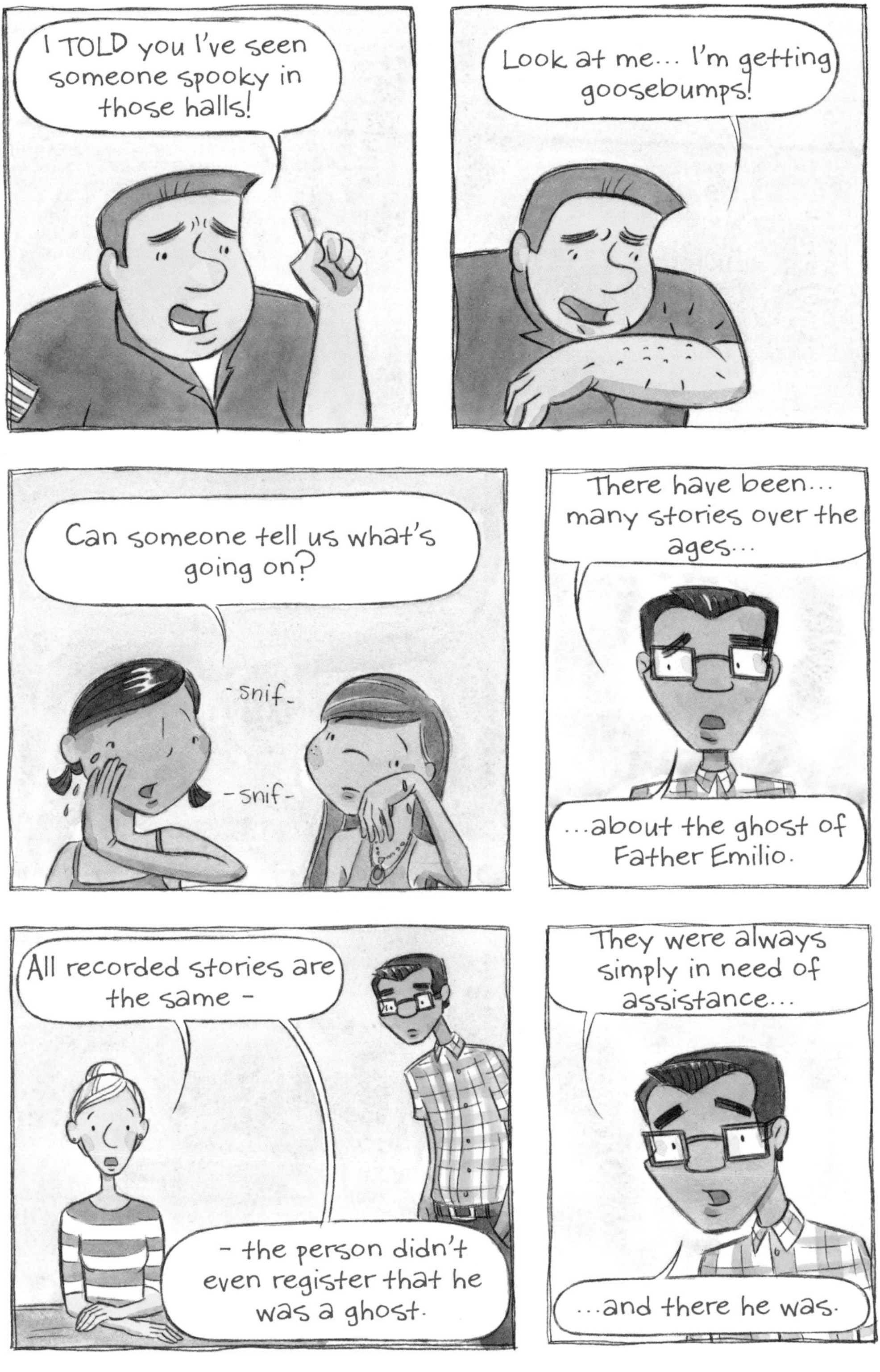
I TOLD you I've seen someone spooky in those halls!
Look at me... I'm getting goosebumps!
Can someone tell us what's going on?
-snif-
-snif-
There have been... many stories over the ages...
...about the ghost of Father Emilio.
All recorded stories are the same -
- the person didn't even register that he was a ghost.
They were always simply in need of assistance...
...and there he was.

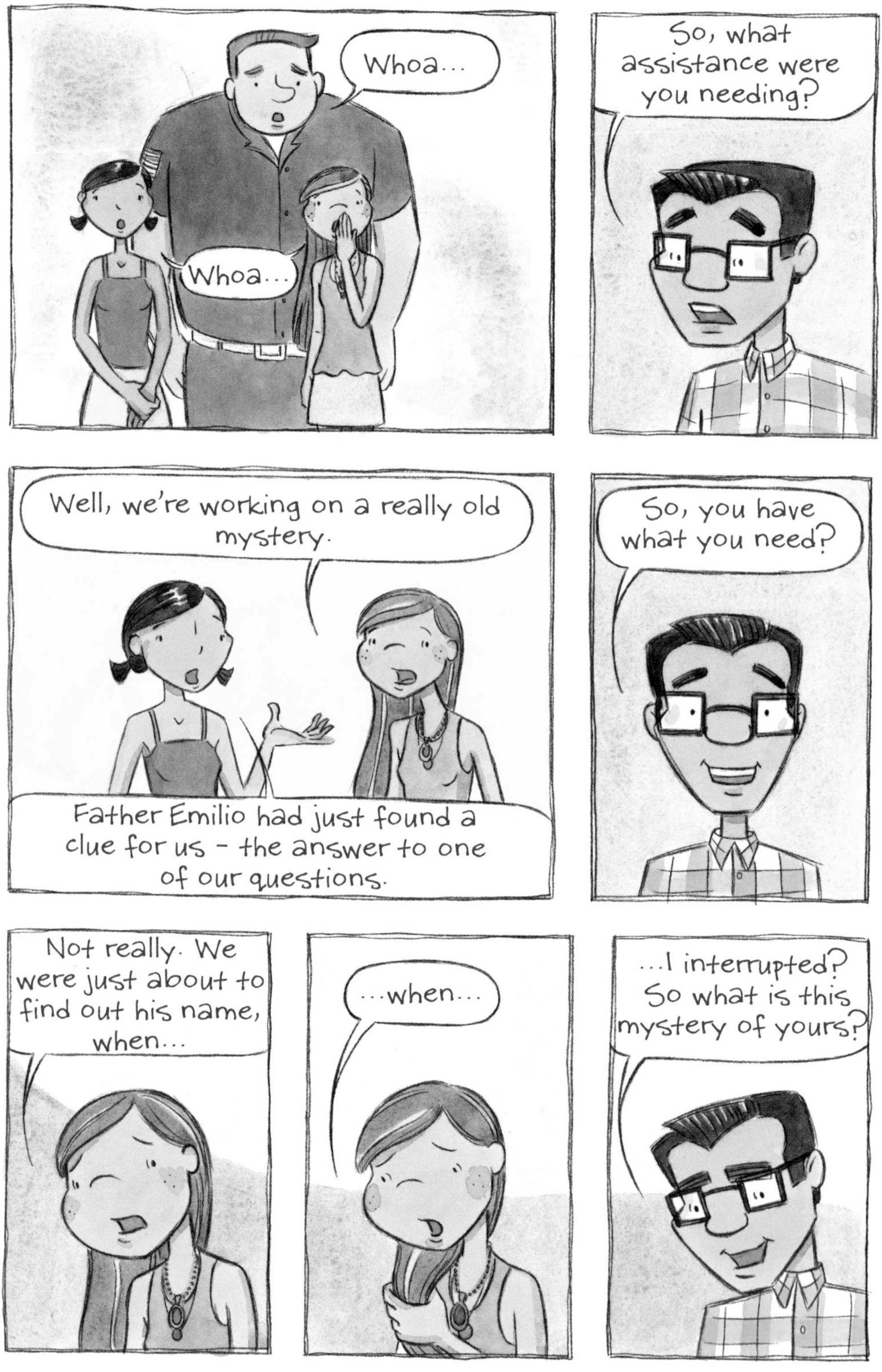

Whoa...
Whoa...
So, what assistance were you needing?
Well, we're working on a really old mystery.
Father Emilio had just found a clue for us - the answer to one of our questions.
So, you have what you need?
Not really. We were just about to find out his name, when...
...when...
...I interrupted? So what is this mystery of yours?

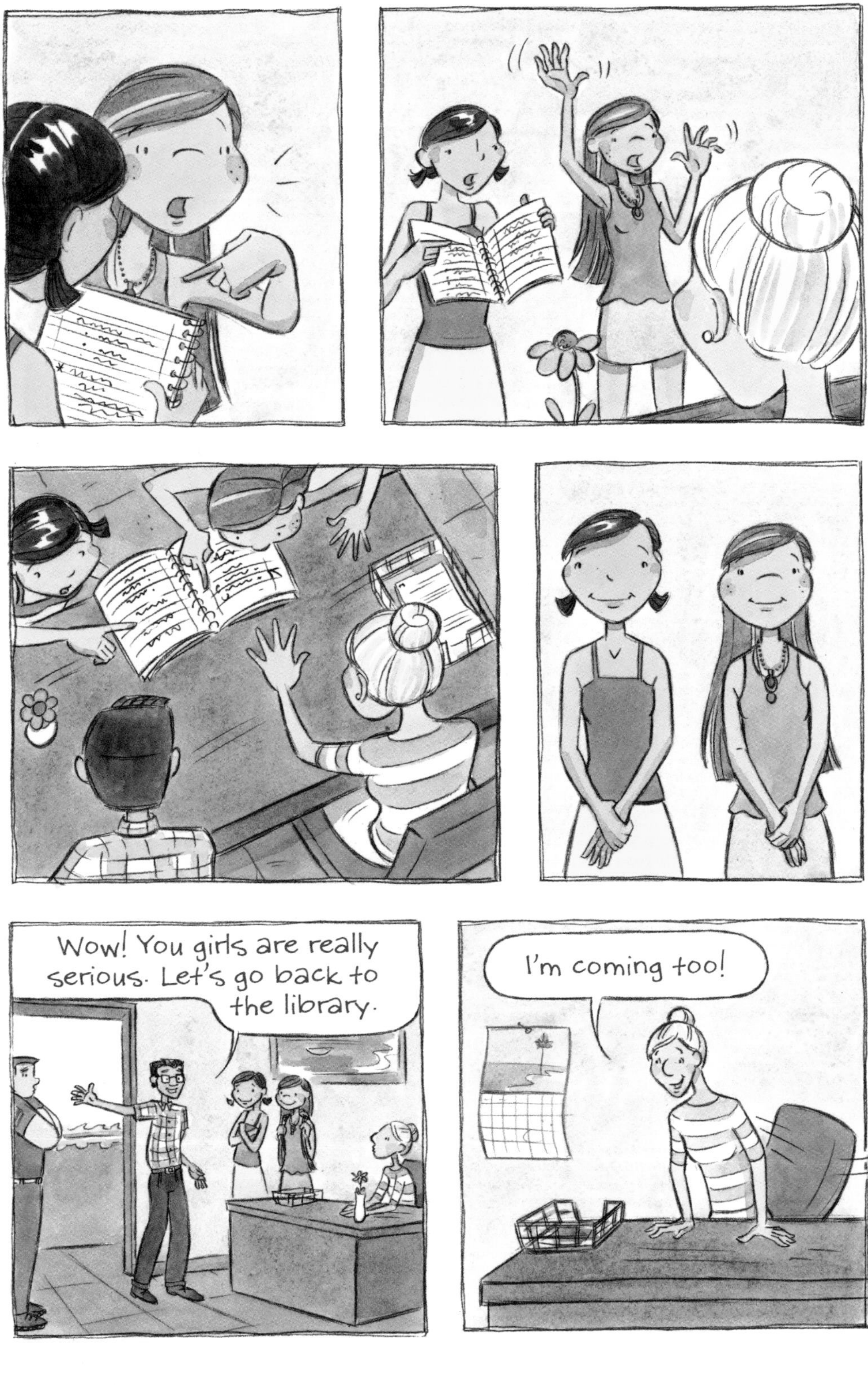
Wow! You girls are really serious. Let's go back to the library.
I'm coming too!

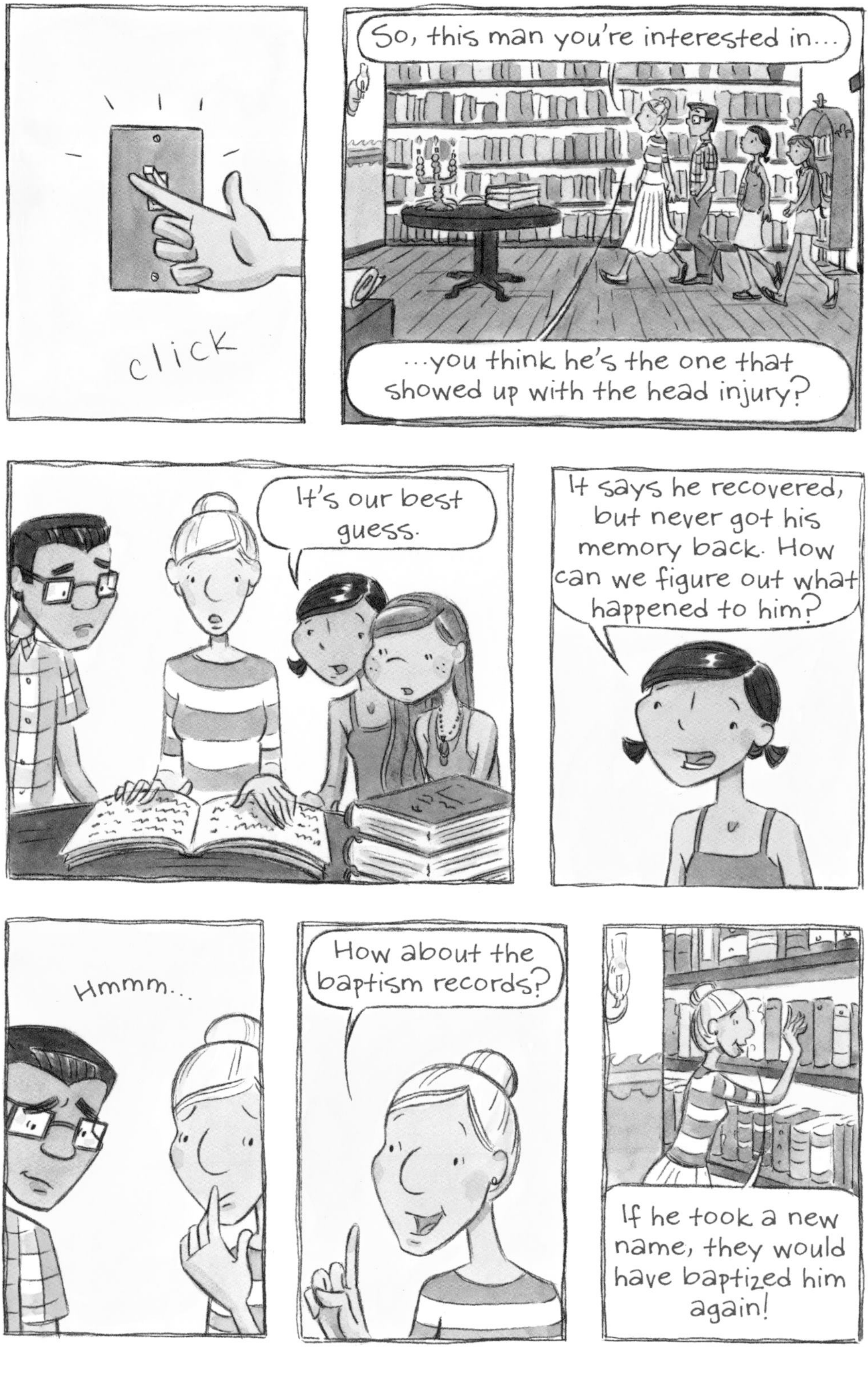
click
So, this man you're interested in...
...you think he's the one that showed up with the head injury?
It's our best guess.
It says he recovered, but never got his memory back. How can we figure out what happened to him?
Hmmm...
How about the baptism records?
If he took a new name, they would have baptized him again!

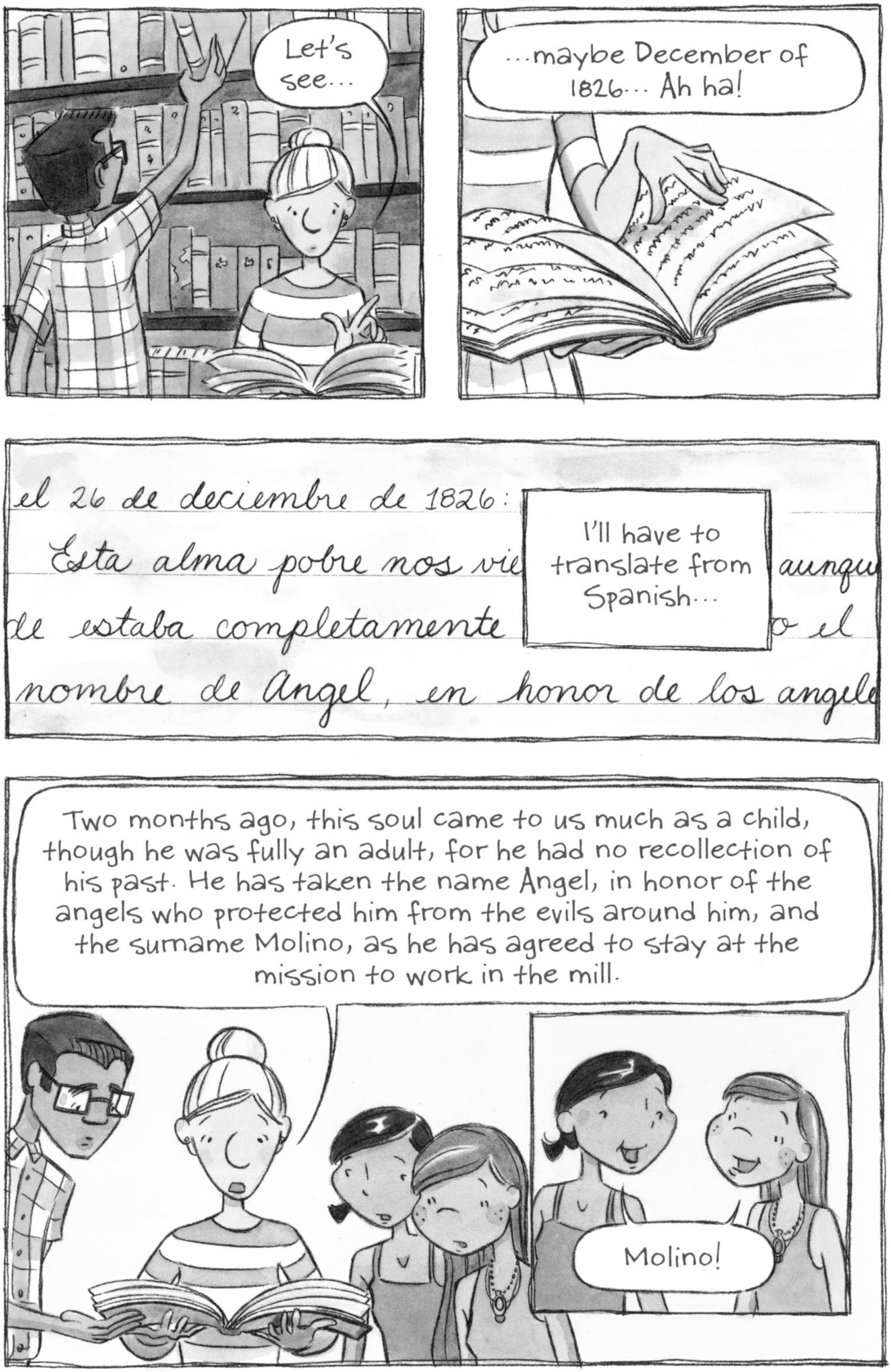
Let's see...
...maybe December of 1826... Ah ha!
el 26 de deciembre de 1826:
Esta alma pobre nos vie
aunqu
de estaba completamente
o el
nombre de Angel, en honor de los angele
I'll have to translate from Spanish...
Two months ago, this soul came to us much as a child, though he was fully an adult, for he had no recollection of his past. He has taken the name Angel, in honor of the angels who protected him from the evils around him, and the surname Molino, as he has agreed to stay at the mission to work in the mill.
Molino!

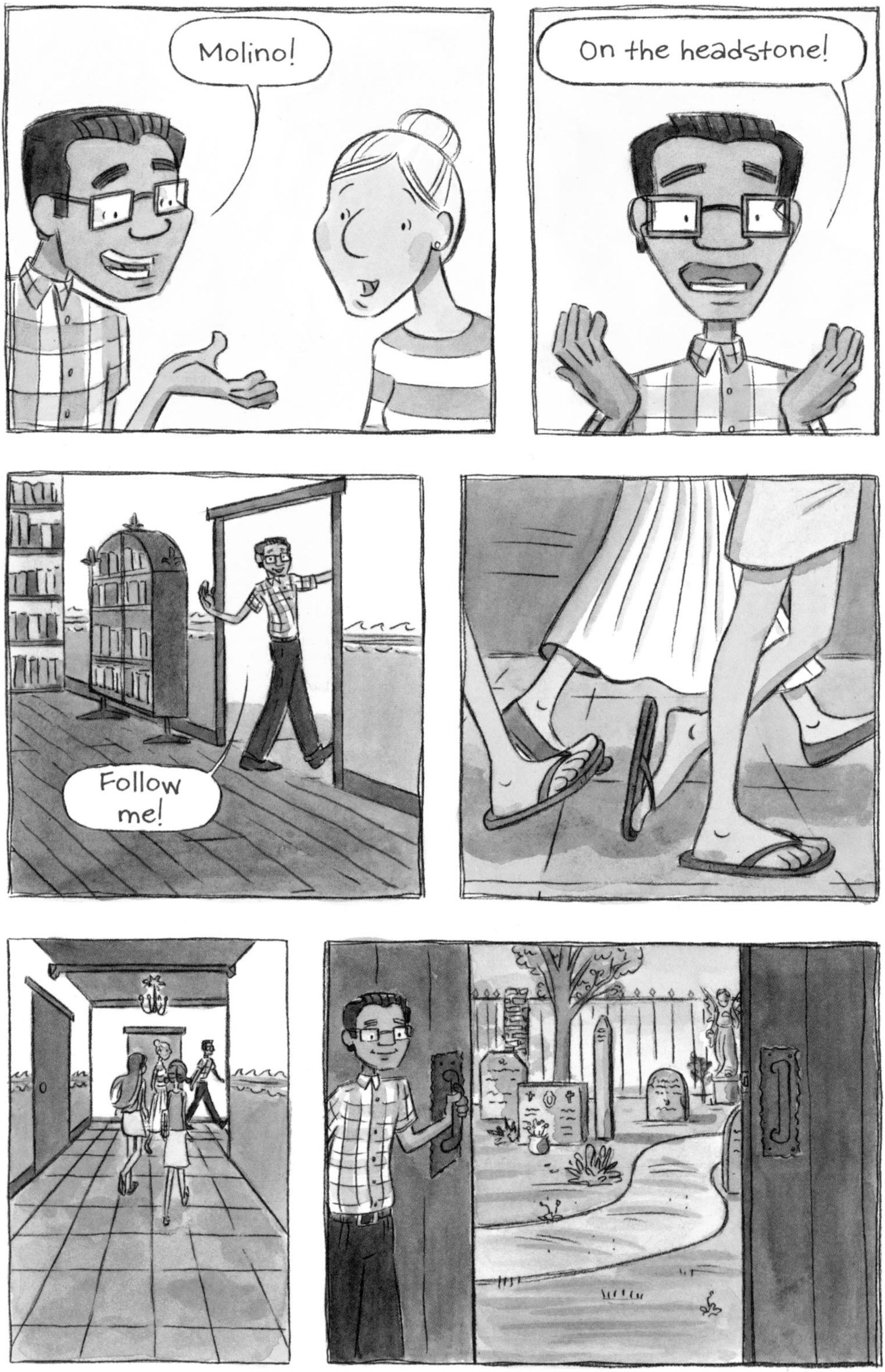
Molino!
On the headstone!
Follow me!

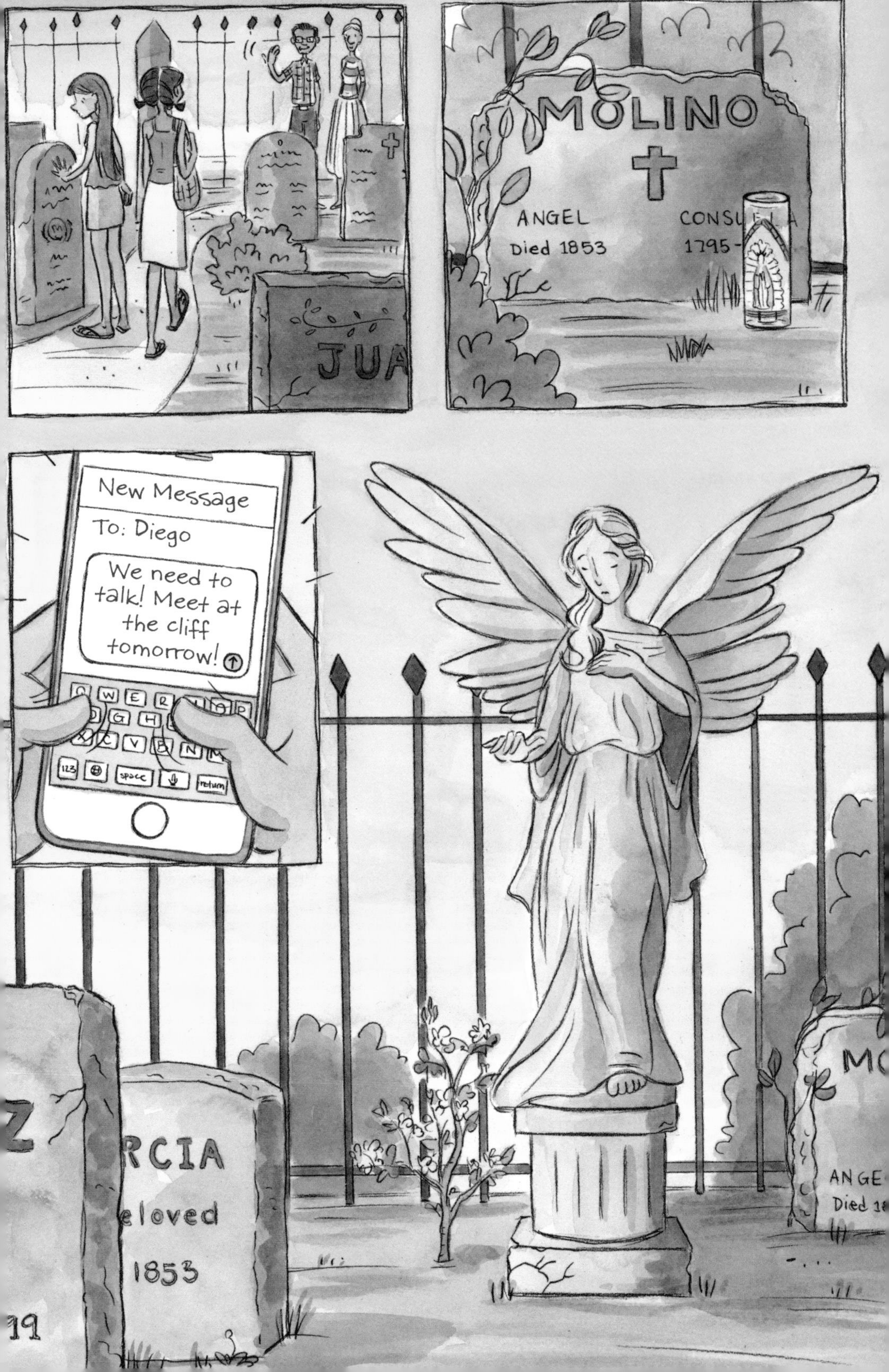
JUA
MOLINO
ANGEL
Died 1853
CONSU
1795-
New Message
To: Diego
We need to talk! Meet at the cliff tomorrow!
RCIA
eloved
1853
MO
ANGE

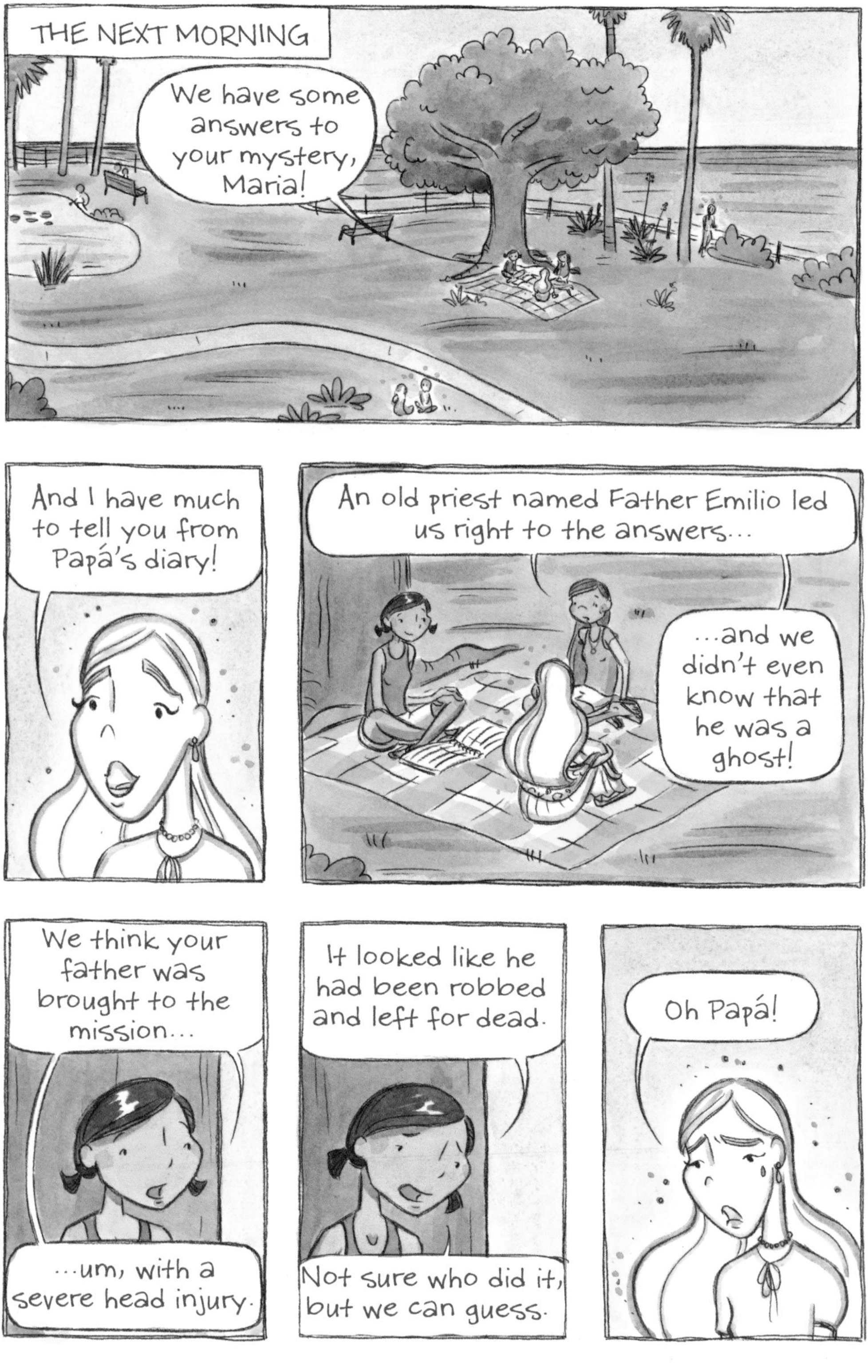
THE NEXT MORNING
We have some answers to your mystery, Maria!
And I have much to tell you from Papá's diary!
An old priest named Father Emilio led us right to the answers...
...and we didn't even know that he was a ghost!
We think your father was brought to the mission...
...um, with a severe head injury.
It looked like he had been robbed and left for dead.
Not sure who did it, but we can guess.
Oh Papá!

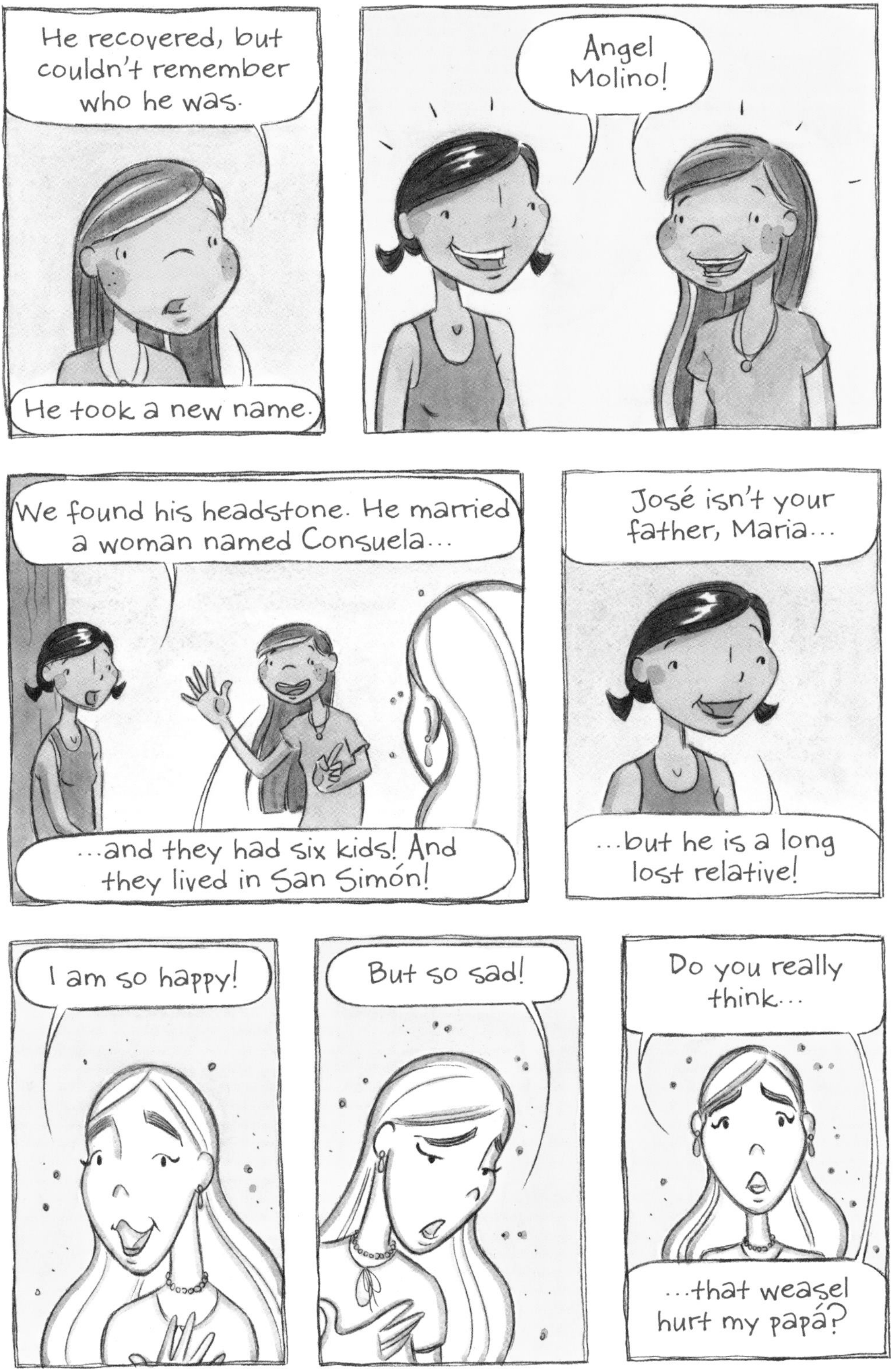
He recovered, but couldn't remember who he was.
He took a new name.
Angel Molino!
We found his headstone. He married a woman named Consuela...
...and they had six kids! And they lived in San Simón!
José isn't your father, Maria...
...but he is a long lost relative!
I am so happy!
But so sad!
Do you really think...
...that weasel hurt my papá?

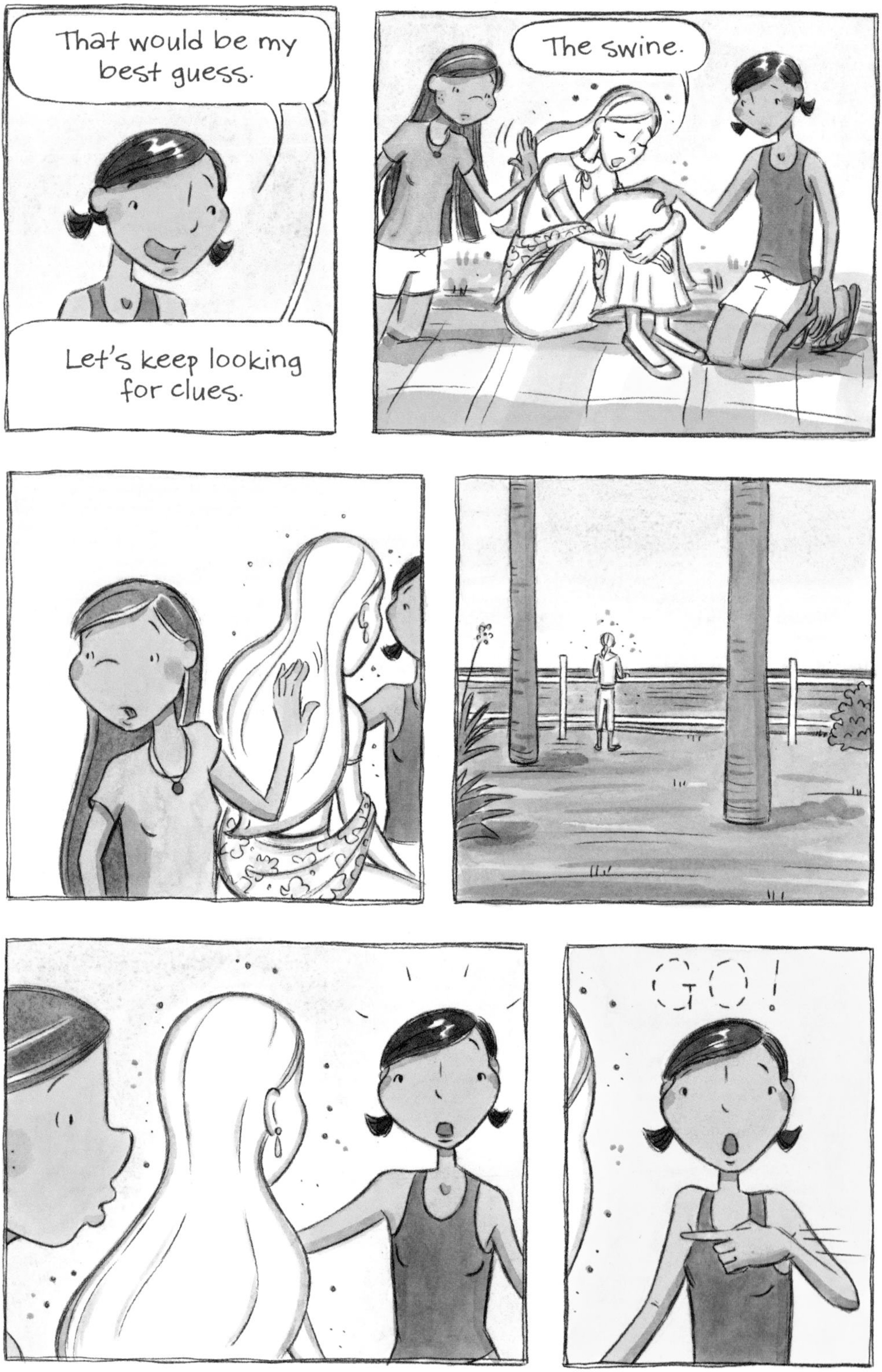
That would be my best guess.
Let's keep looking for clues.
The swine.
GO!

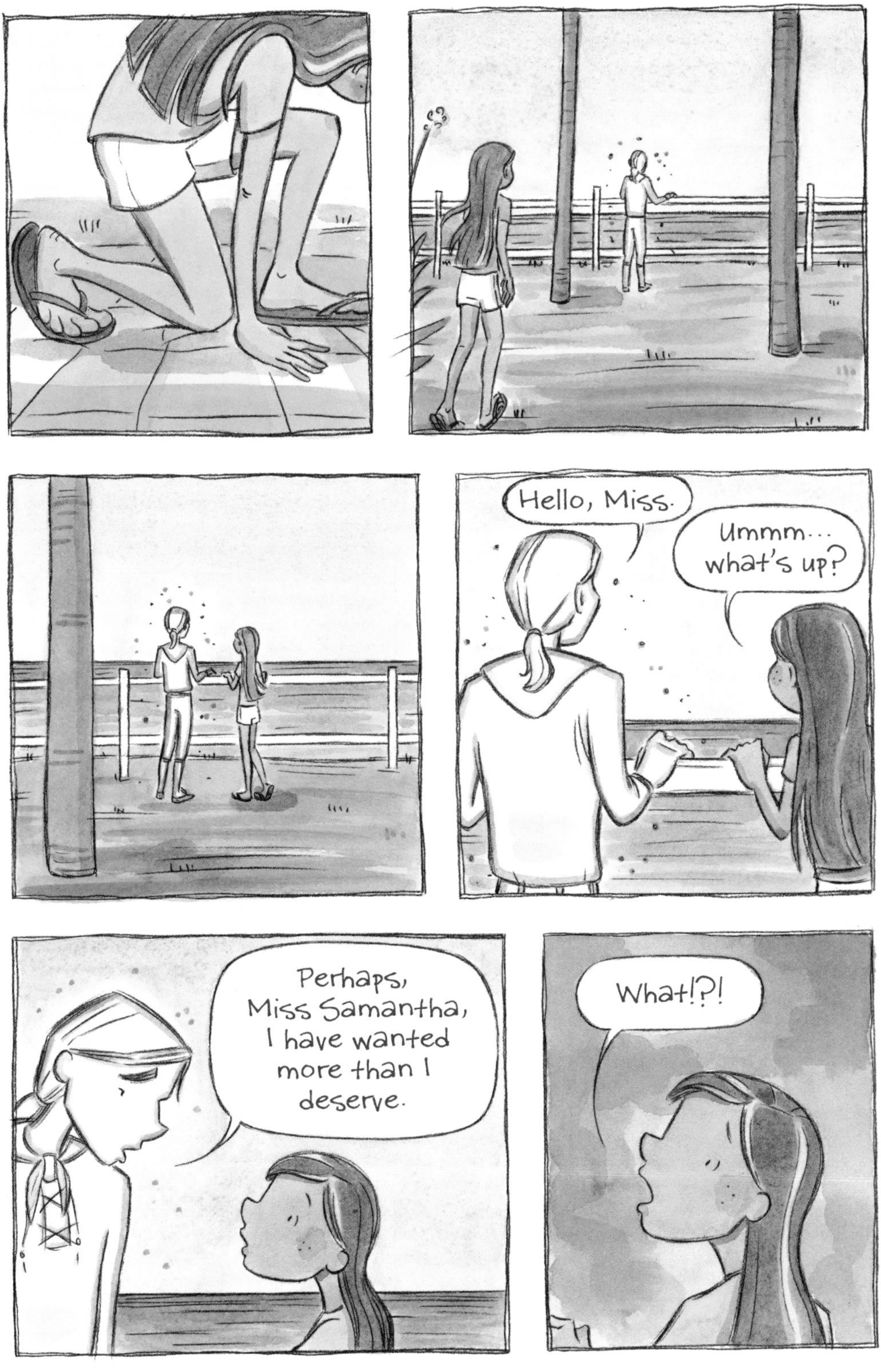
Hello, Miss.
Ummm... what's up?
Perhaps, Miss Samantha, I have wanted more than I deserve.
What!?!

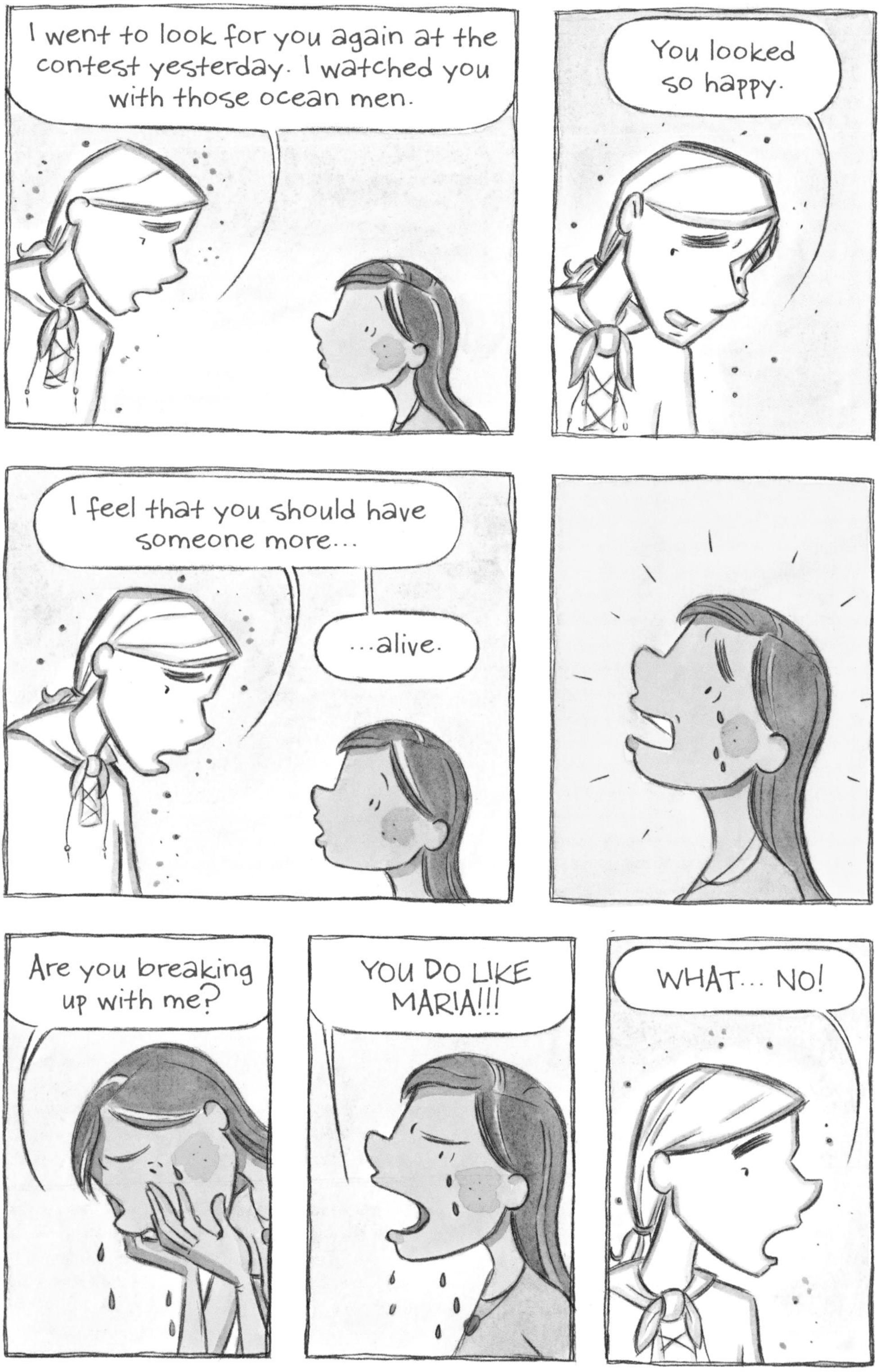
I went to look for you again at the contest yesterday. I watched you with those ocean men.
You looked so happy.
I feel that you should have someone more...
...alive.
Are you breaking up with me?
YOU DO LIKE MARIA!!!
WHAT... NO!

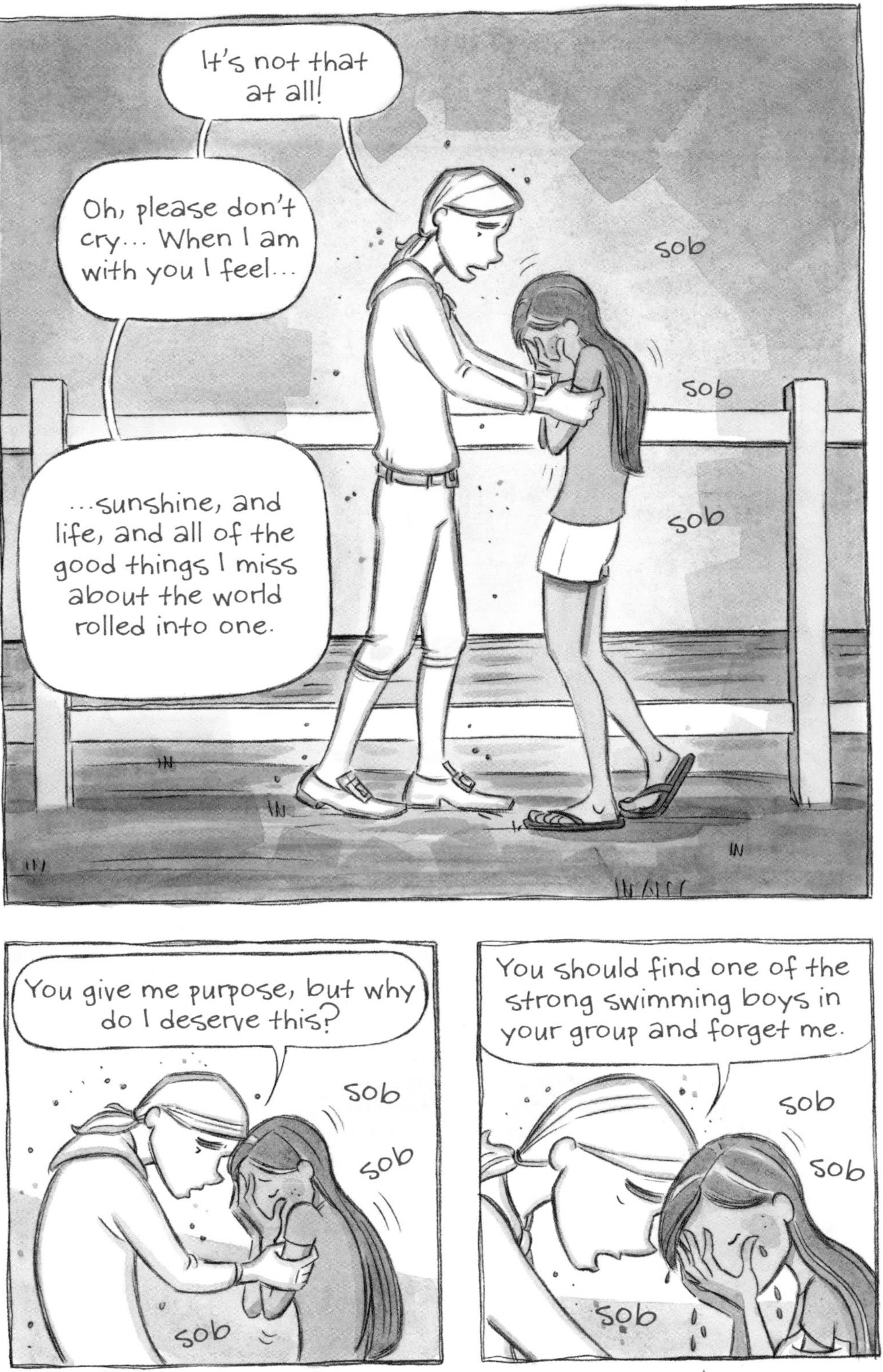
It's not that at all!
Oh, please don't cry... When I am with you I feel...
...sunshine, and life, and all of the good things I miss about the world rolled into one.
sob
sob
sob
You give me purpose, but why do I deserve this?
sob
sob
sob
You should find one of the strong swimming boys in your group and forget me.
sob
sob
sob

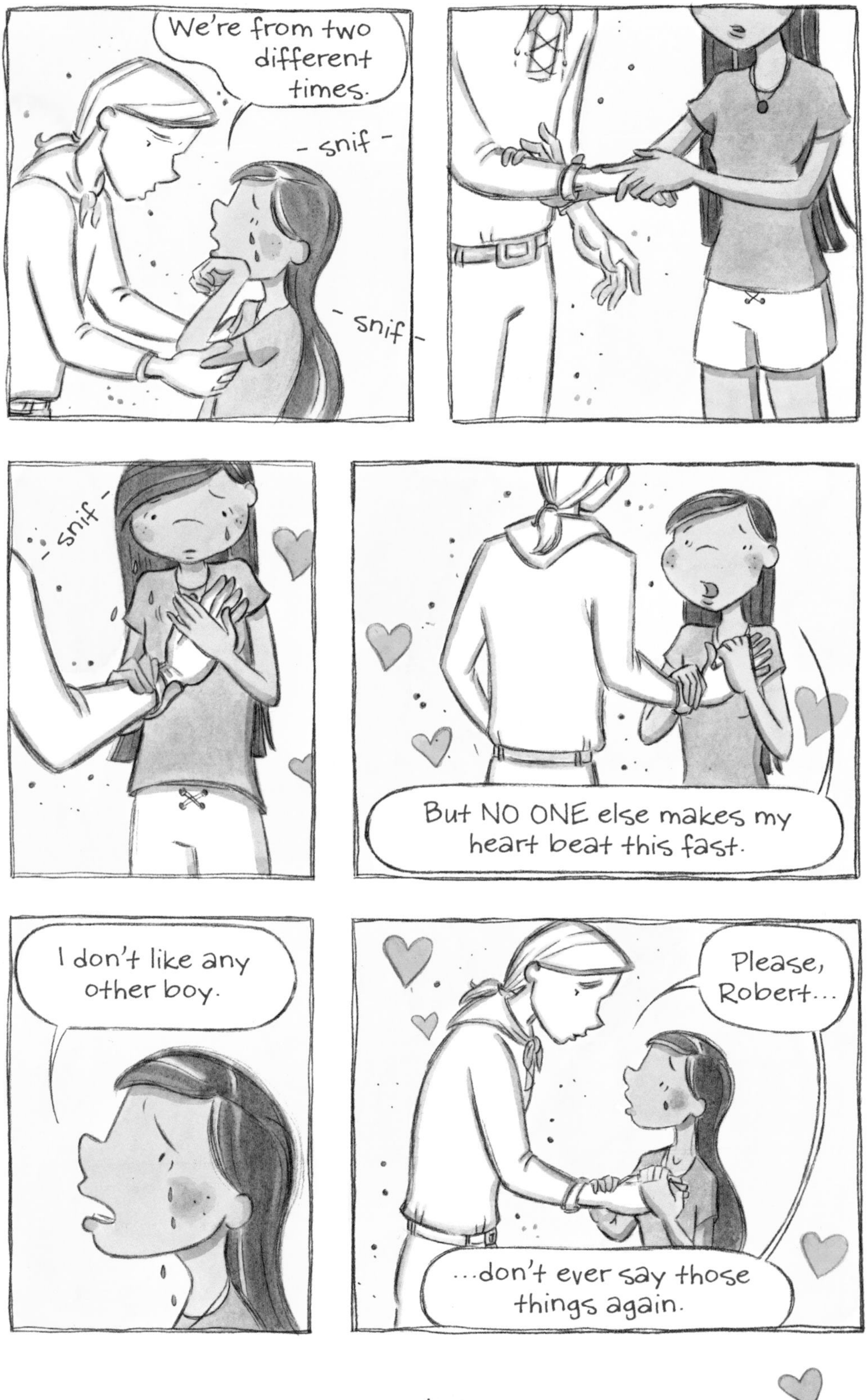
We're from two different times.
- snif -
- snif -
- snif -
But NO ONE else makes my heart beat this fast.
I don't like any other boy.
Please, Robert...
...don't ever say those things again.

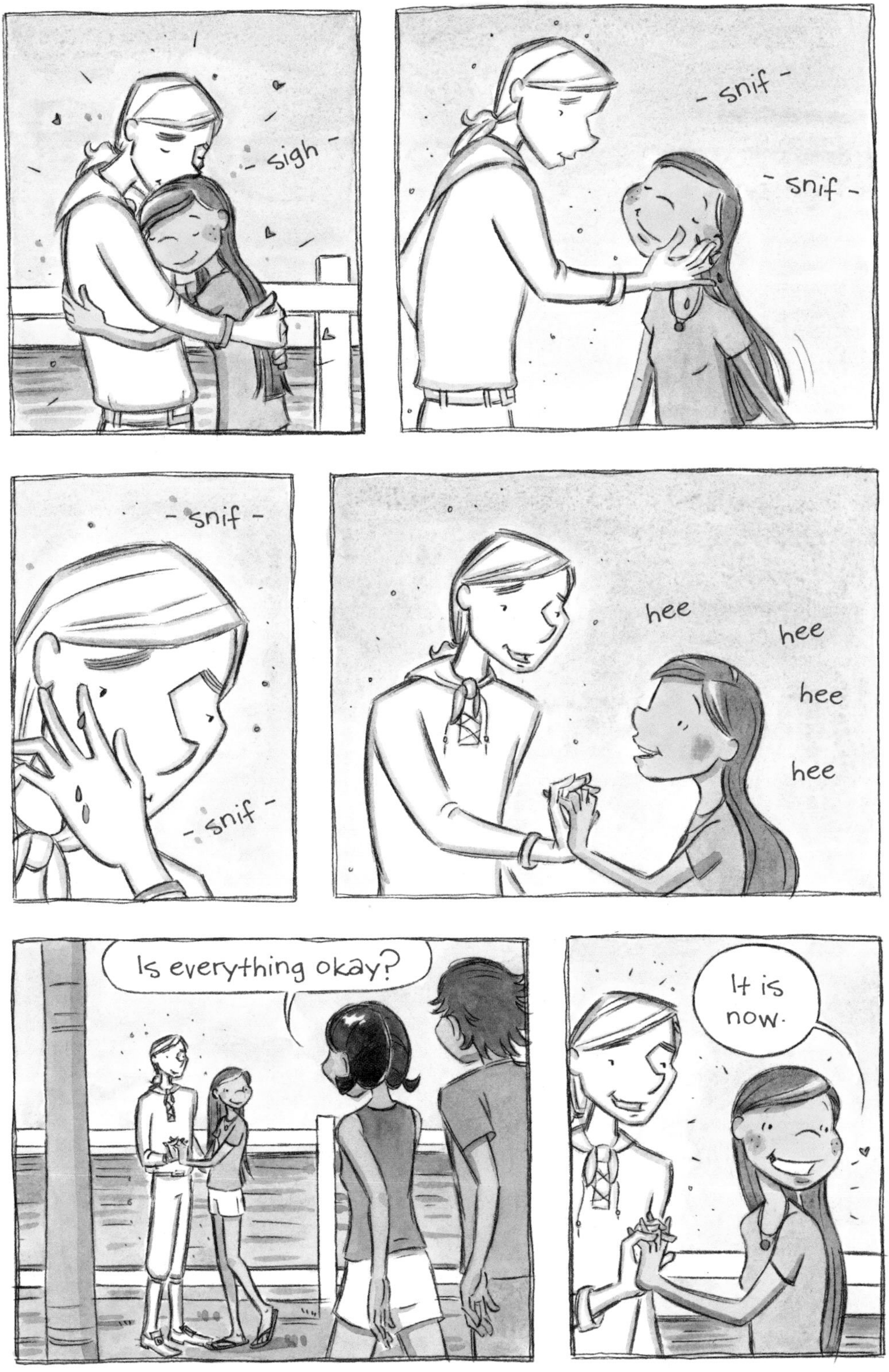
- sigh -
- snif -
- snif -
- snif -
- snif -
hee
hee
hee
hee
Is everything okay?
It is now.

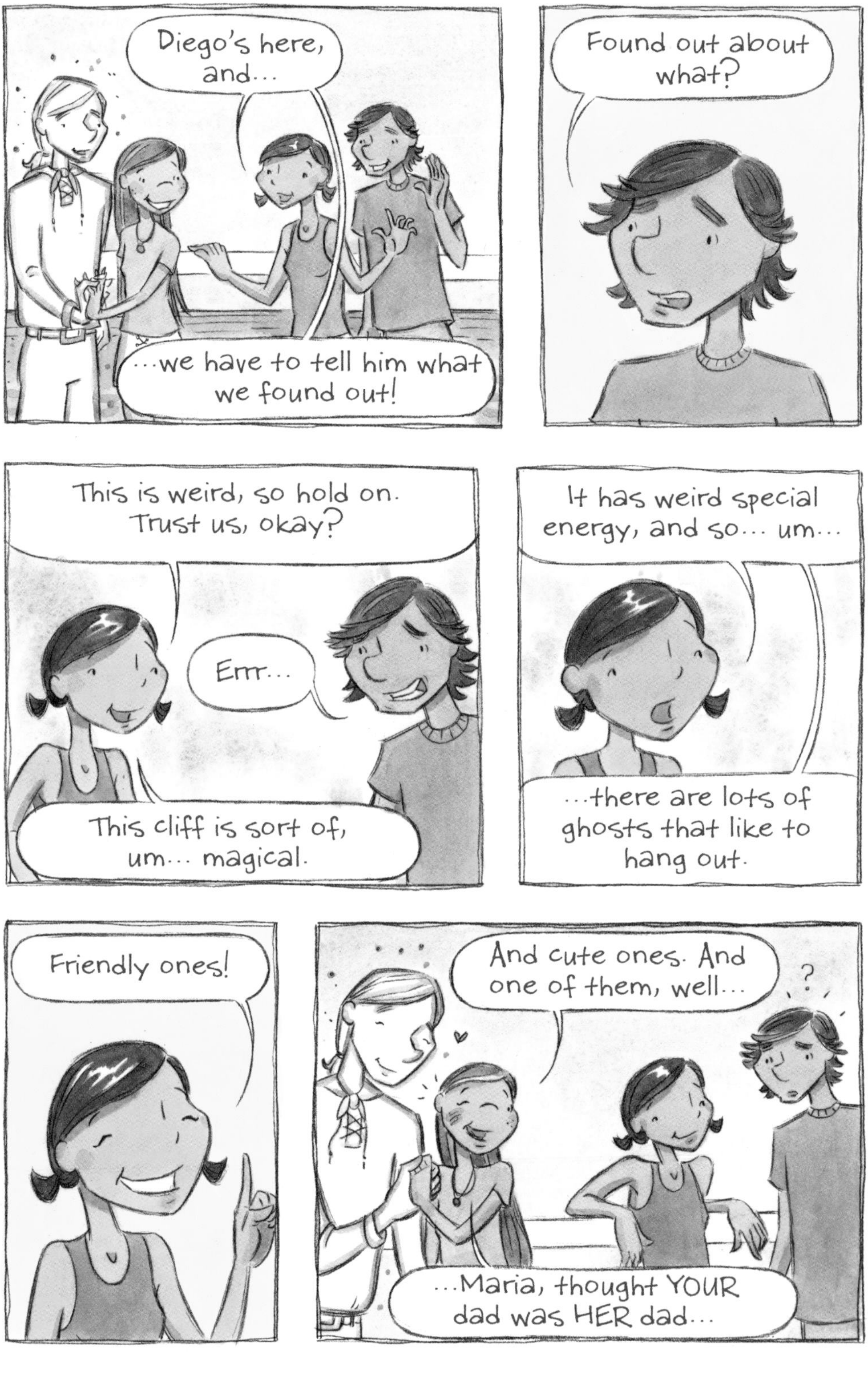
Diego's here, and...
...we have to tell him what we found out!
Found out about what?
This is weird, so hold on. Trust us, okay?
Errr...
This cliff is sort of, um... magical.
It has weird special energy, and so... um...
...there are lots of ghosts that like to hang out.
Friendly ones!
And cute ones. And one of them, well...
?
...Maria, thought YOUR dad was HER dad...

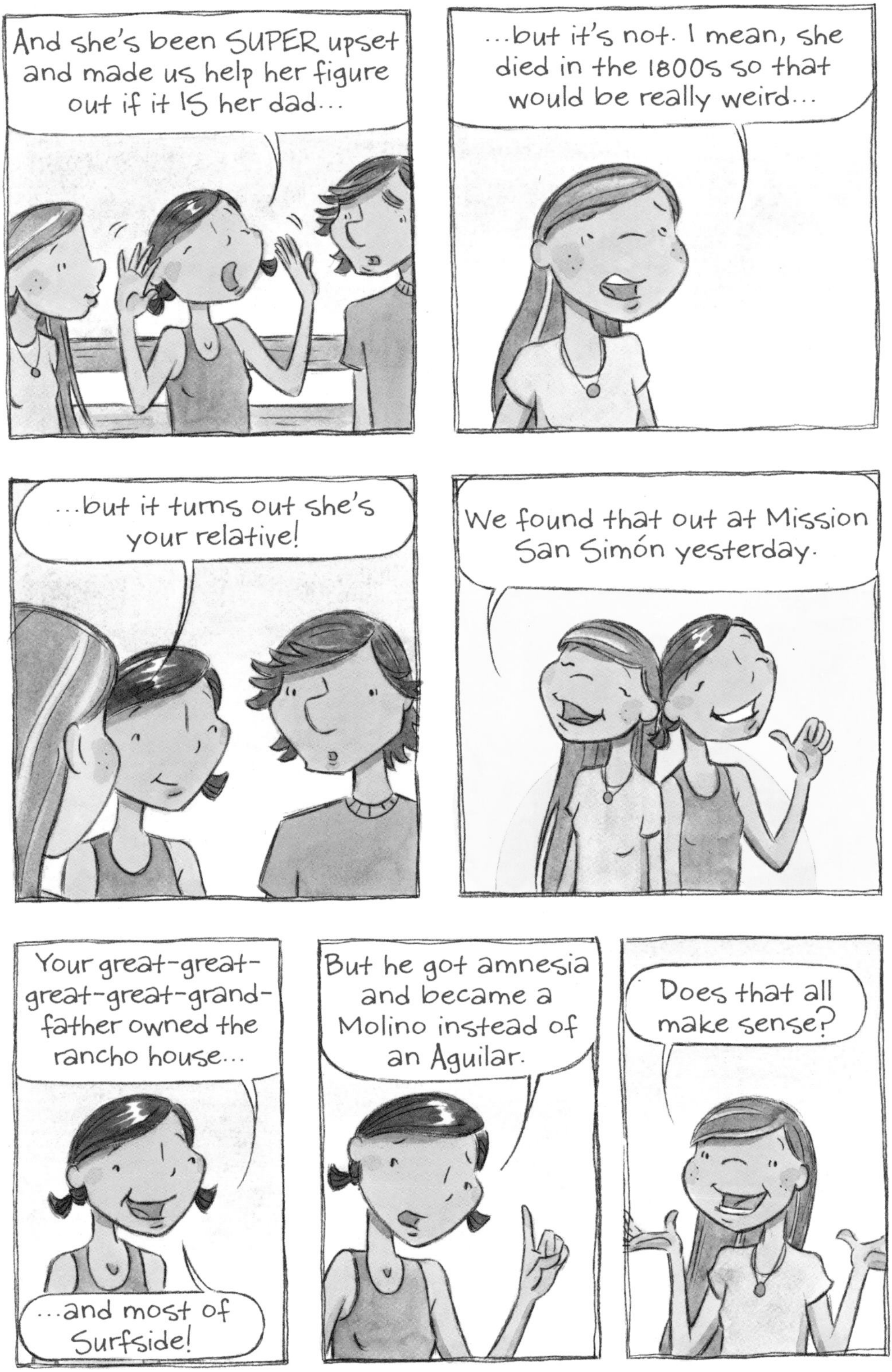
And she's been SUPER upset and made us help her figure out if it IS her dad...
...but it's not. I mean, she died in the 1800s so that would be really weird...
...but it turns out she's your relative!
We found that out at Mission San Simón yesterday.
Your great-great-great-great-grandfather owned the rancho house...
...and most of Surfside!
But he got amnesia and became a Molino instead of an Aguilar.
Does that all make sense?

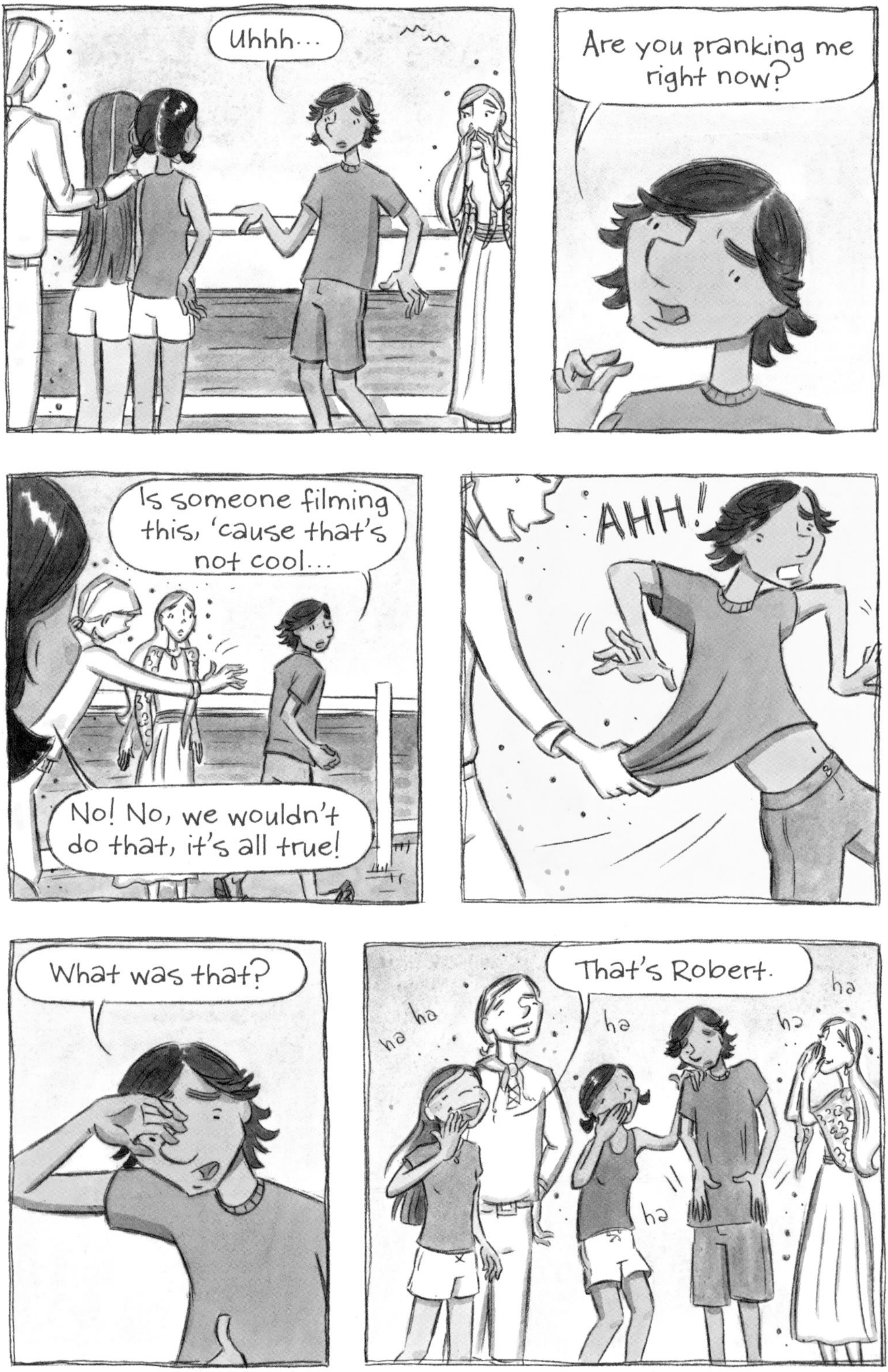
Uhhh...
Are you pranking me right now?
Is someone filming this, 'cause that's not cool...
No! No, we wouldn't do that, it's all true!
AHH!
What was that?
That's Robert.
ha
ha
ha
ha
ha
ha

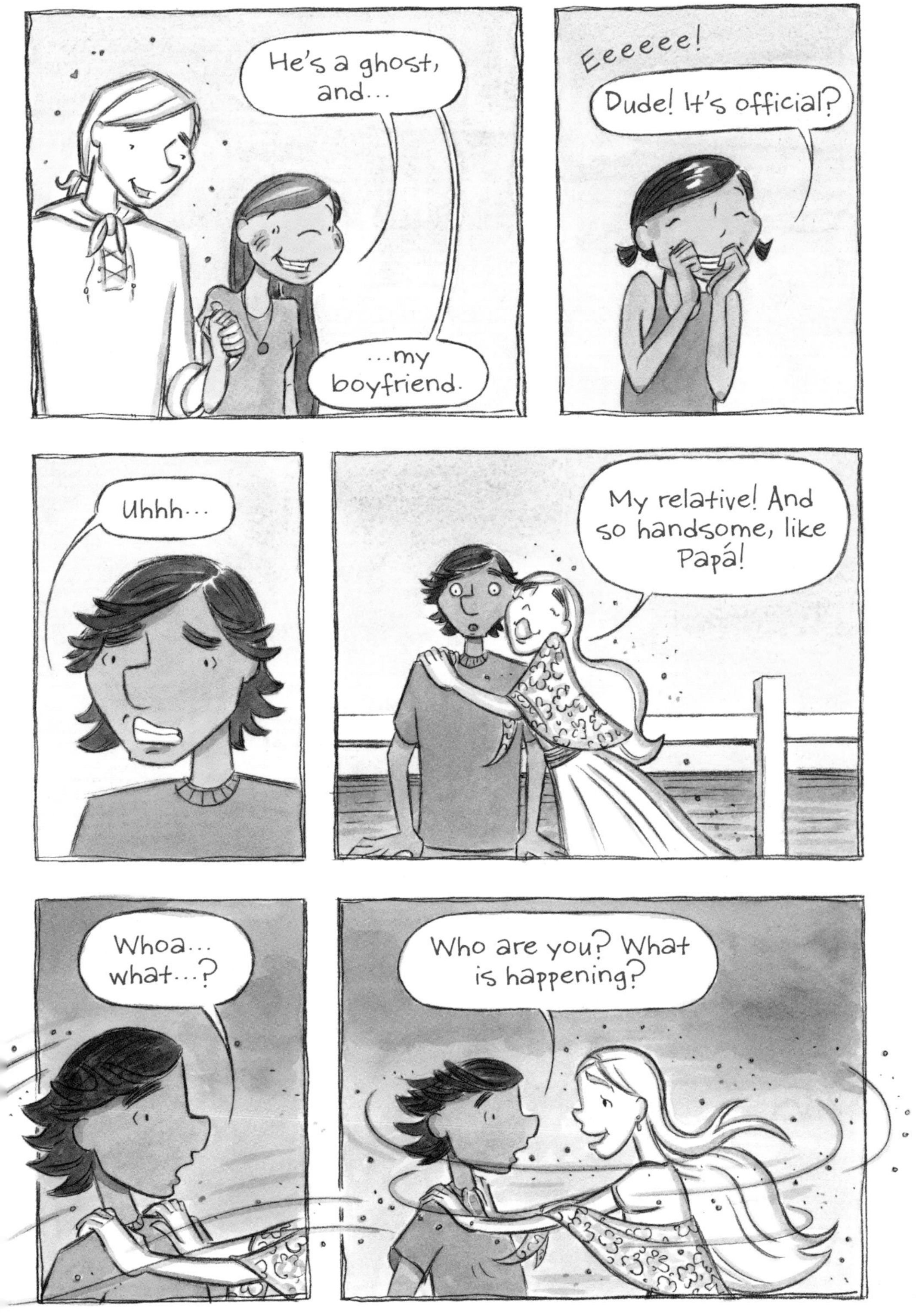
He's a ghost, and...
...my boyfriend.
Eeeeee!
Dude! It's official?
Uhhh...
My relative! And so handsome, like Papá!
Whoa... what...?
Who are you? What is happening?

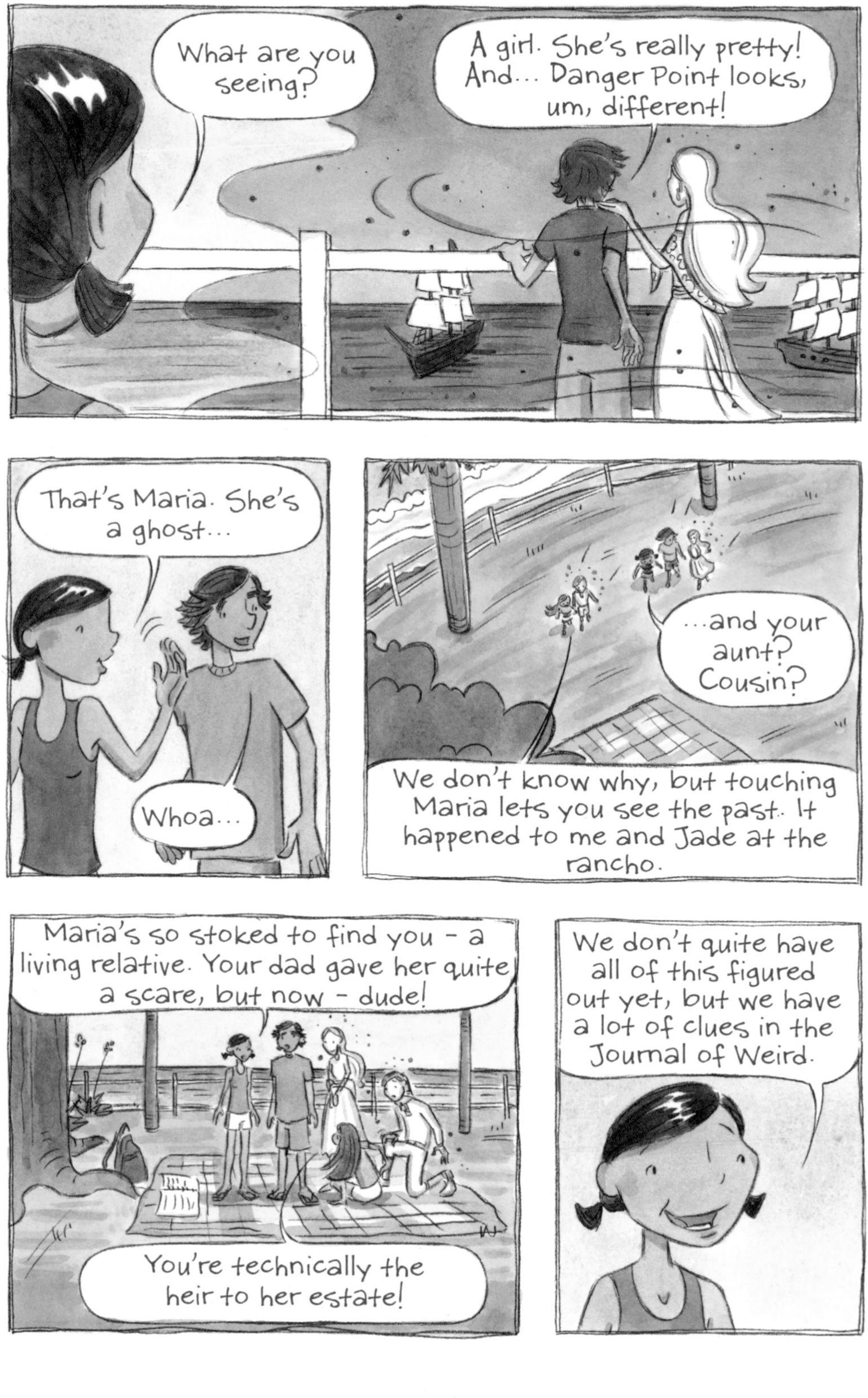
What are you seeing?
A girl. She's really pretty! And... Danger Point looks, um, different!
That's Maria. She's a ghost...
Whoa...
...and your aunt? Cousin?
We don't know why, but touching Maria lets you see the past. It happened to me and Jade at the rancho.
Maria's so stoked to find you - a living relative. Your dad gave her quite a scare, but now - dude!
You're technically the heir to her estate!
We don't quite have all of this figured out yet, but we have a lot of clues in the Journal of Weird.

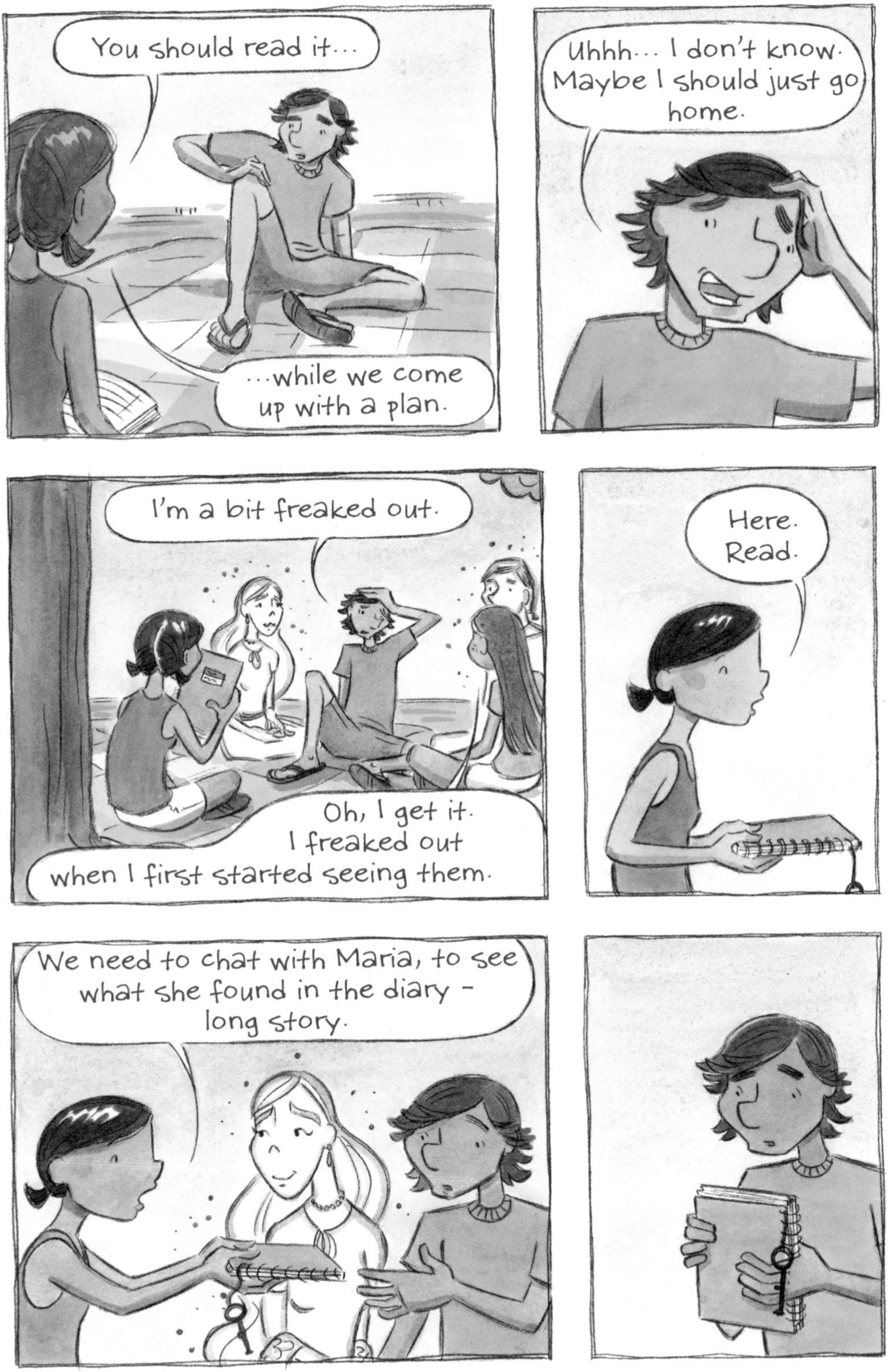
You should read it...
...while we come up with a plan.
Uhhh... I don't know. Maybe I should just go home.
I'm a bit freaked out.
Oh, I get it. I freaked out when I first started seeing them.
Here. Read.
We need to chat with Maria, to see what she found in the diary - long story.

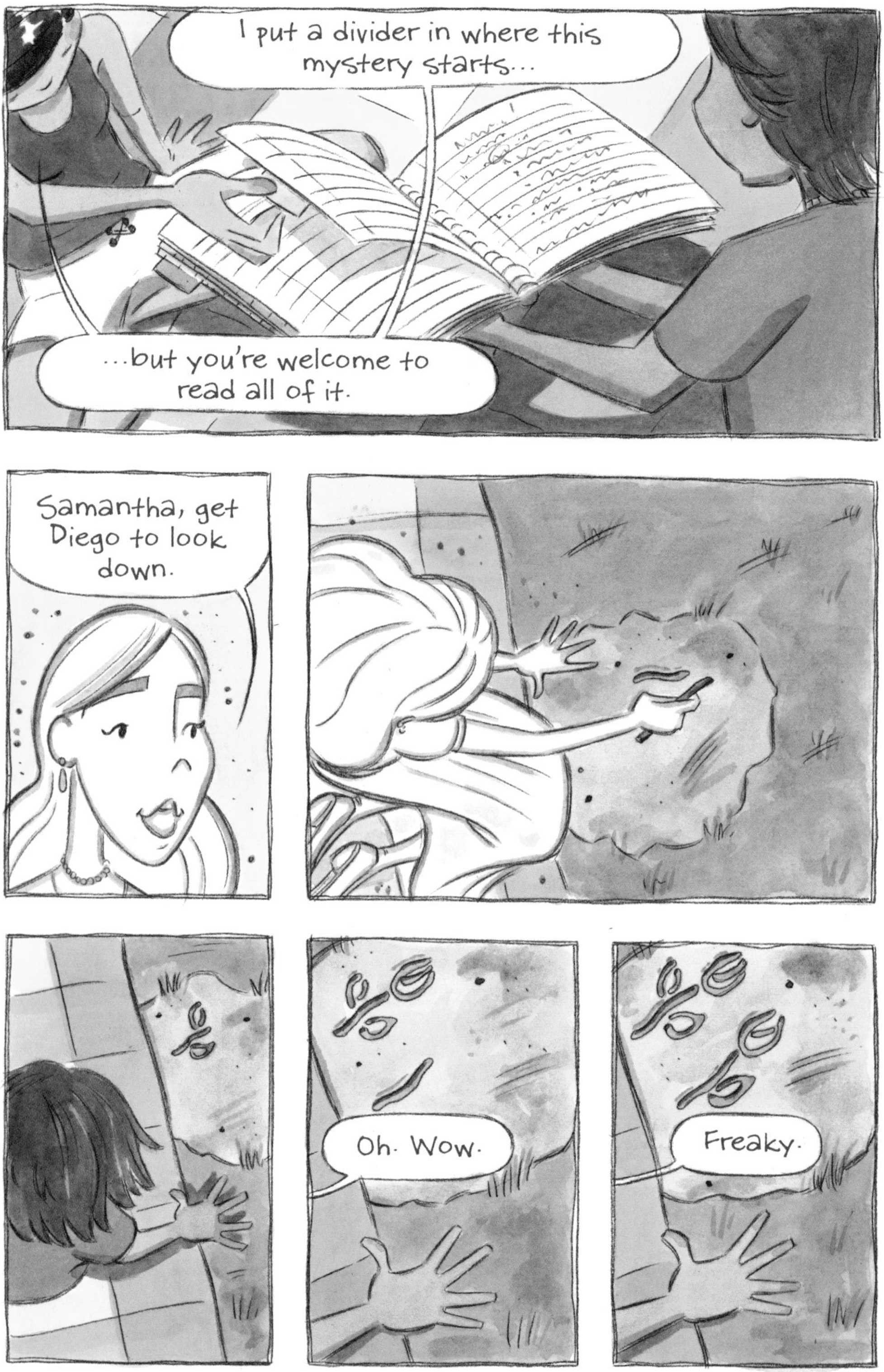
I put a divider in where this mystery starts...
...but you're welcome to read all of it.
Samantha, get Diego to look down.
Oh. Wow.
Freaky.

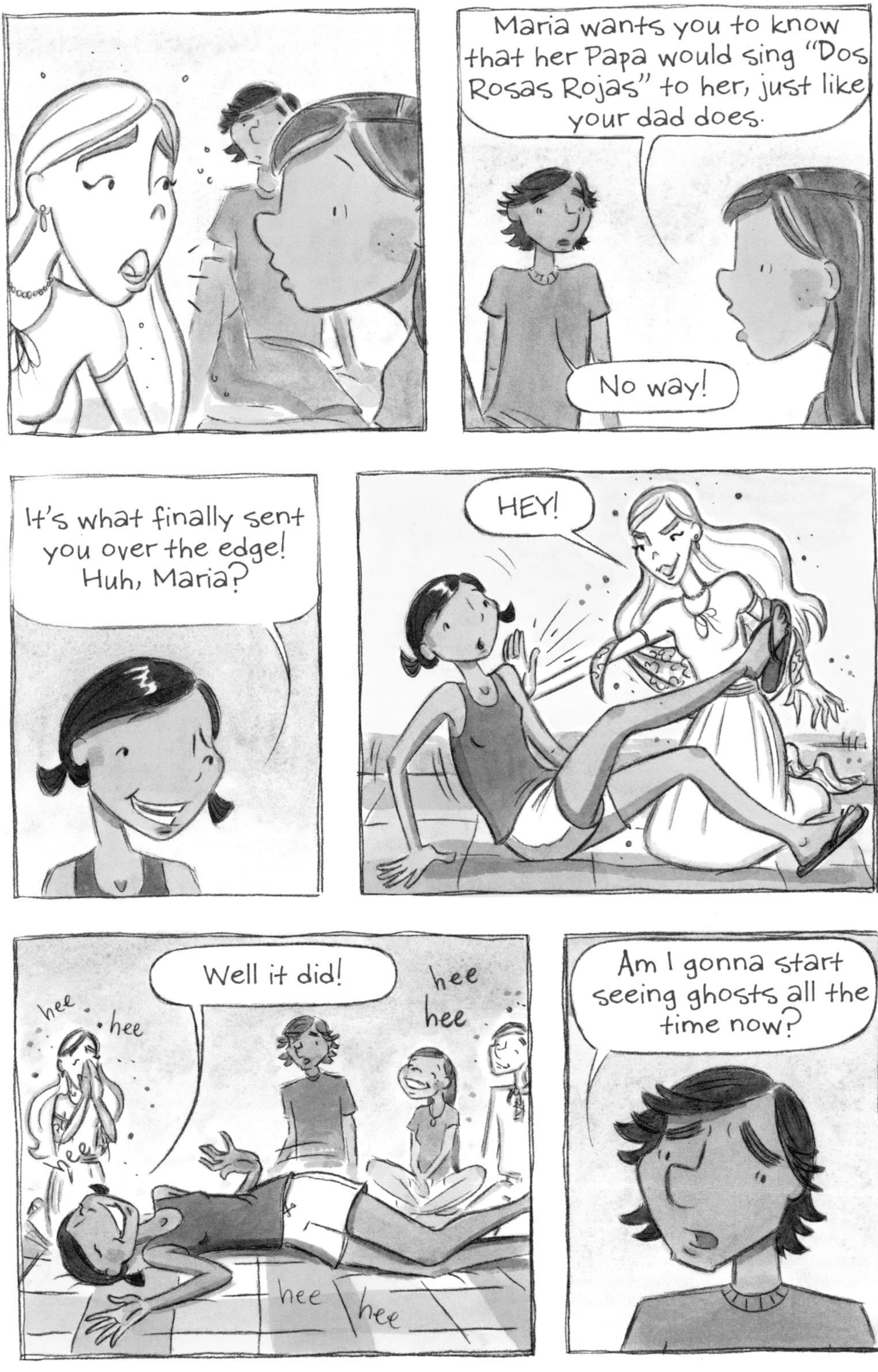
Maria wants you to know that her Papa would sing "Dos Rosas Rojas" to her, just like your dad does.
No way!
It's what finally sent you over the edge! Huh, Maria?
HEY!
Well it did!
hee hee
hee hee
hee
hee hee
Am I gonna start seeing ghosts all the time now?

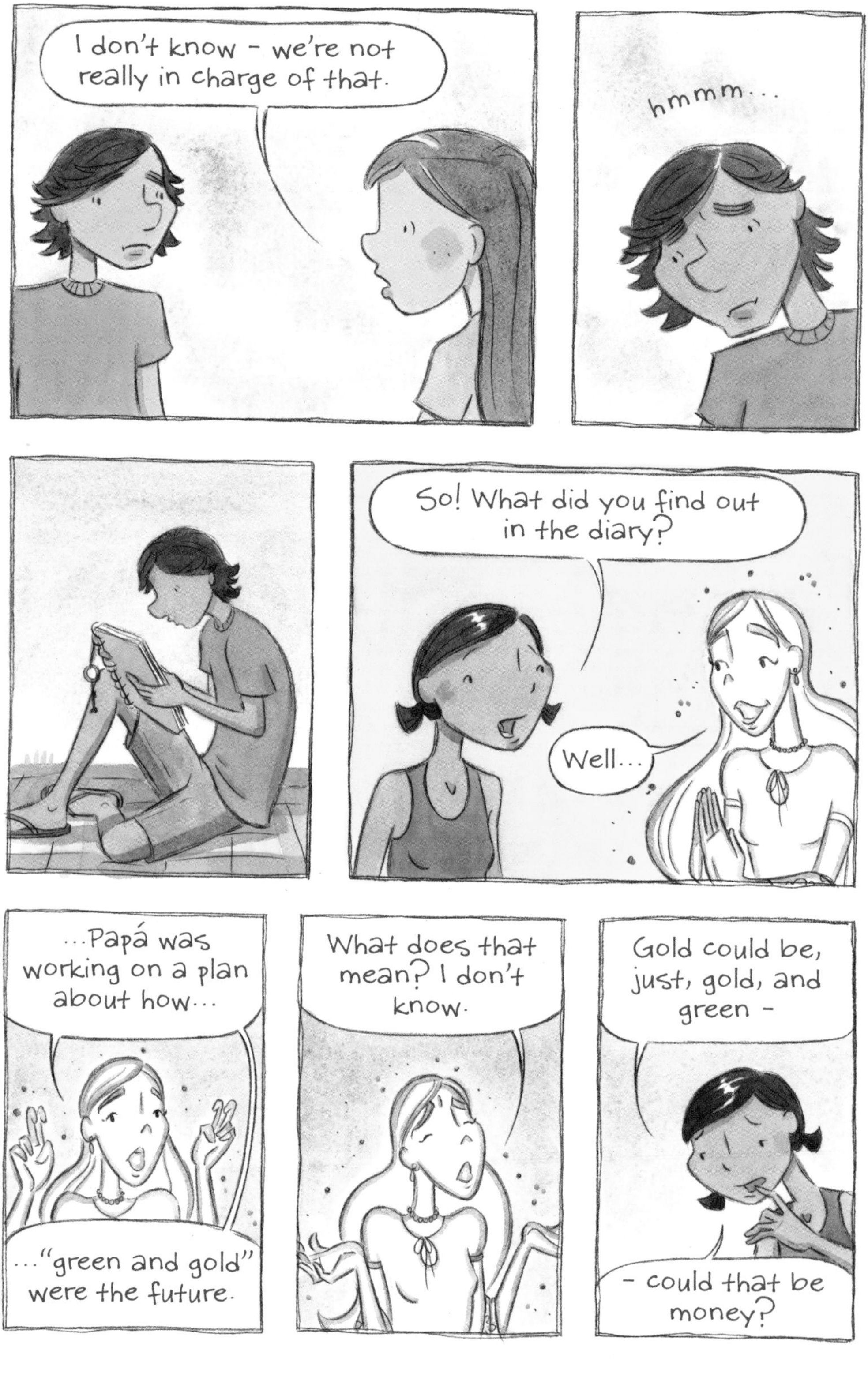
I don't know - we're not really in charge of that.
hmmm...
So! What did you find out in the diary?
Well...
...Papá was working on a plan about how...
..."green and gold" were the future.
What does that mean? I don't know.
Gold could be, just, gold, and green -
- could that be money?

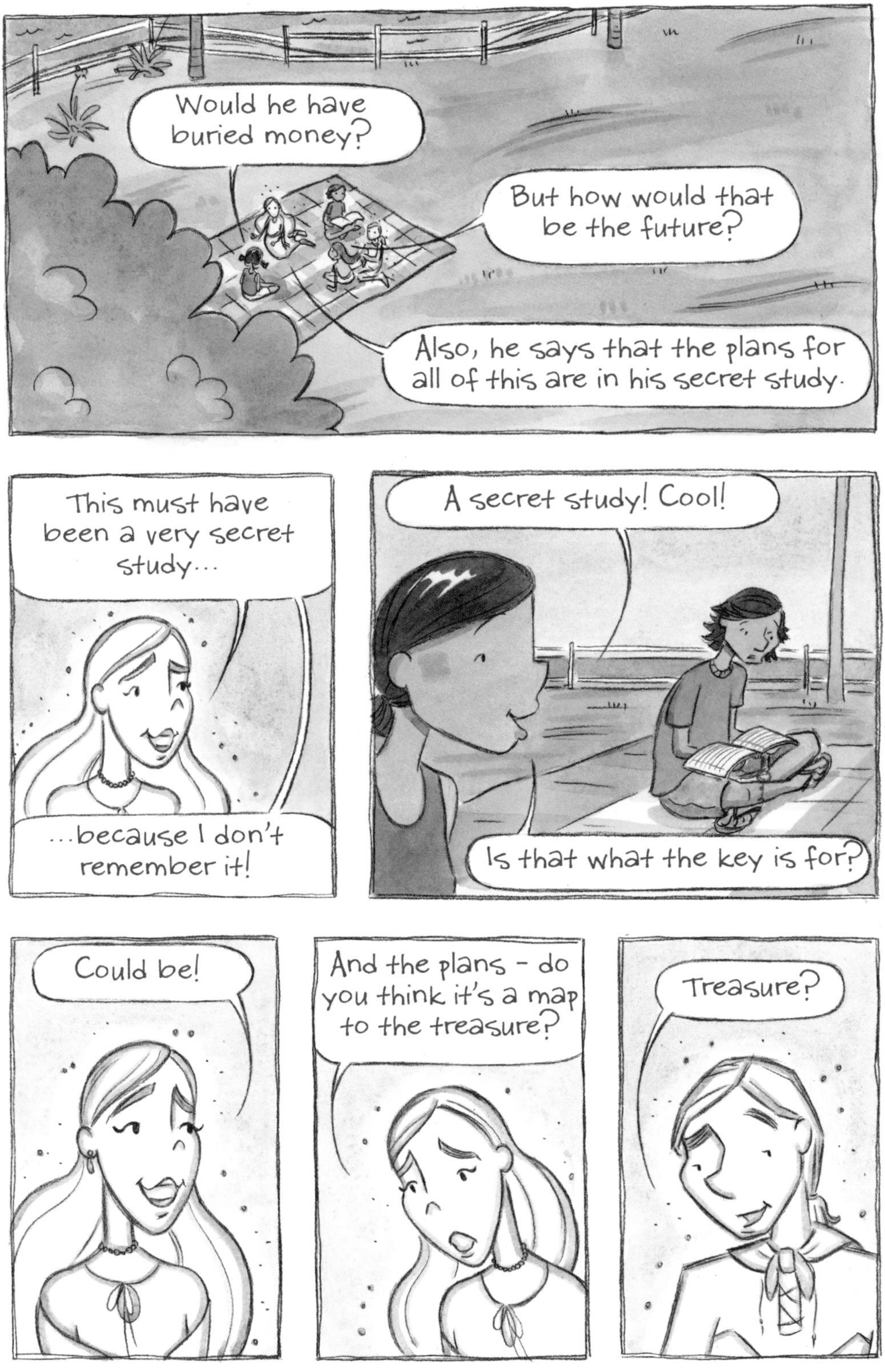

Would he have buried money?
But how would that be the future?
Also, he says that the plans for all of this are in his secret study.
This must have been a very secret study...
...because I don't remember it!
A secret study! Cool!
Is that what the key is for?
Could be!
And the plans - do you think it's a map to the treasure?
Treasure?

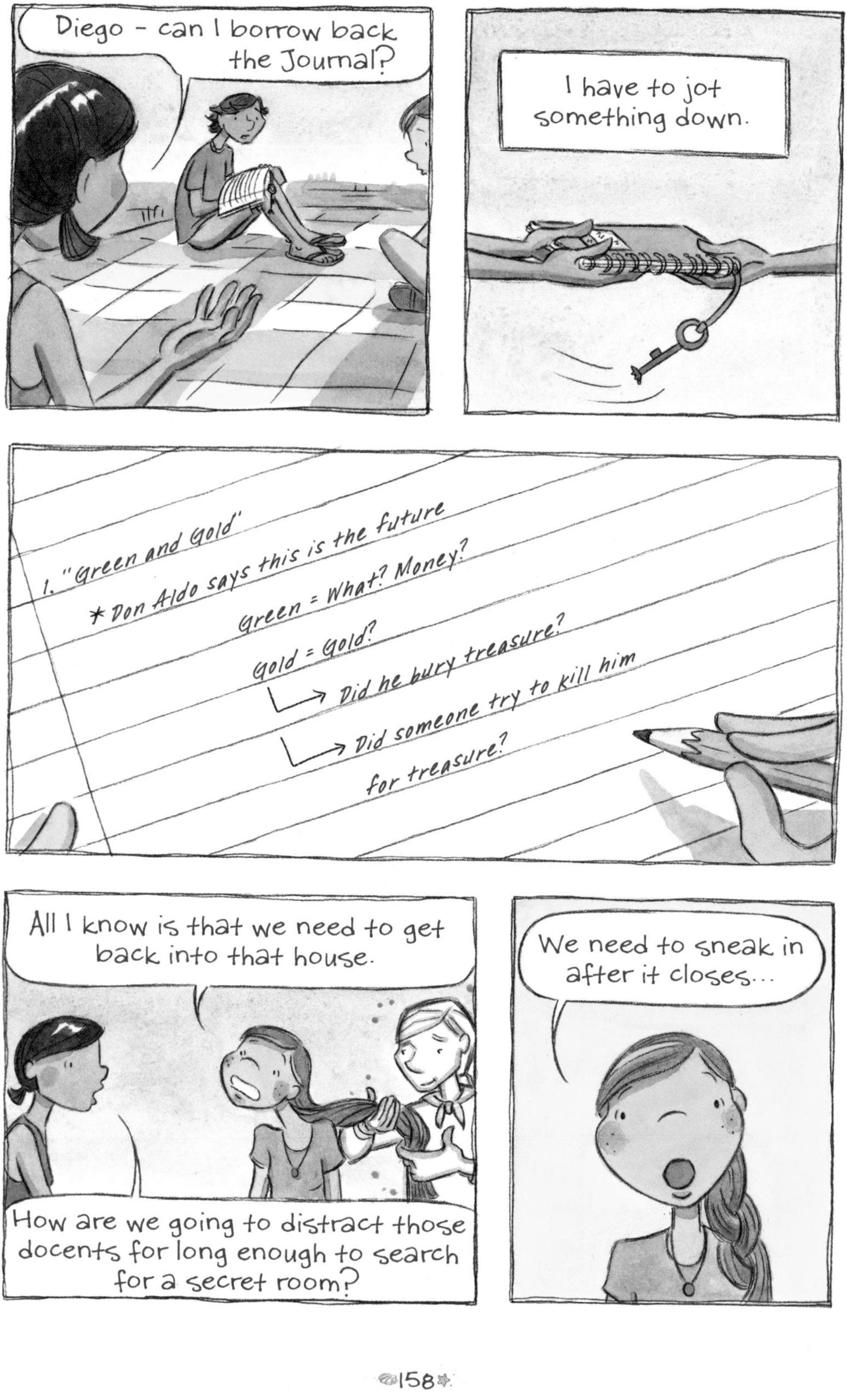
Diego - can I borrow back the Journal?
I have to jot something down.
1. "Green and Gold"
* Don Aldo says this is the future
Green = What? Money?
Gold = Gold?
→ Did he bury treasure?
→ Did someone try to kill him for treasure?
All I know is that we need to get back into that house.
How are we going to distract those docents for long enough to search for a secret room?
We need to sneak in after it closes...

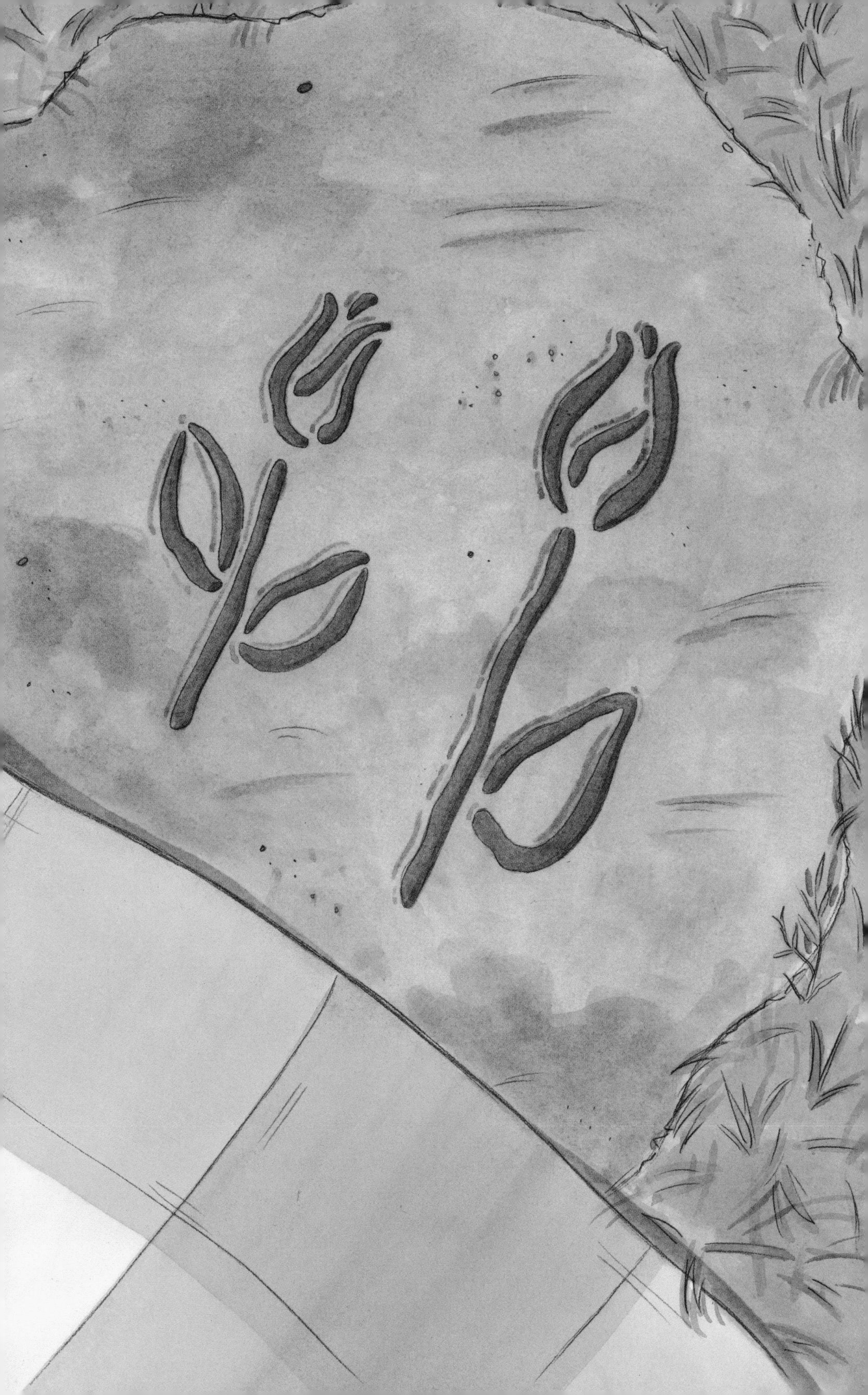

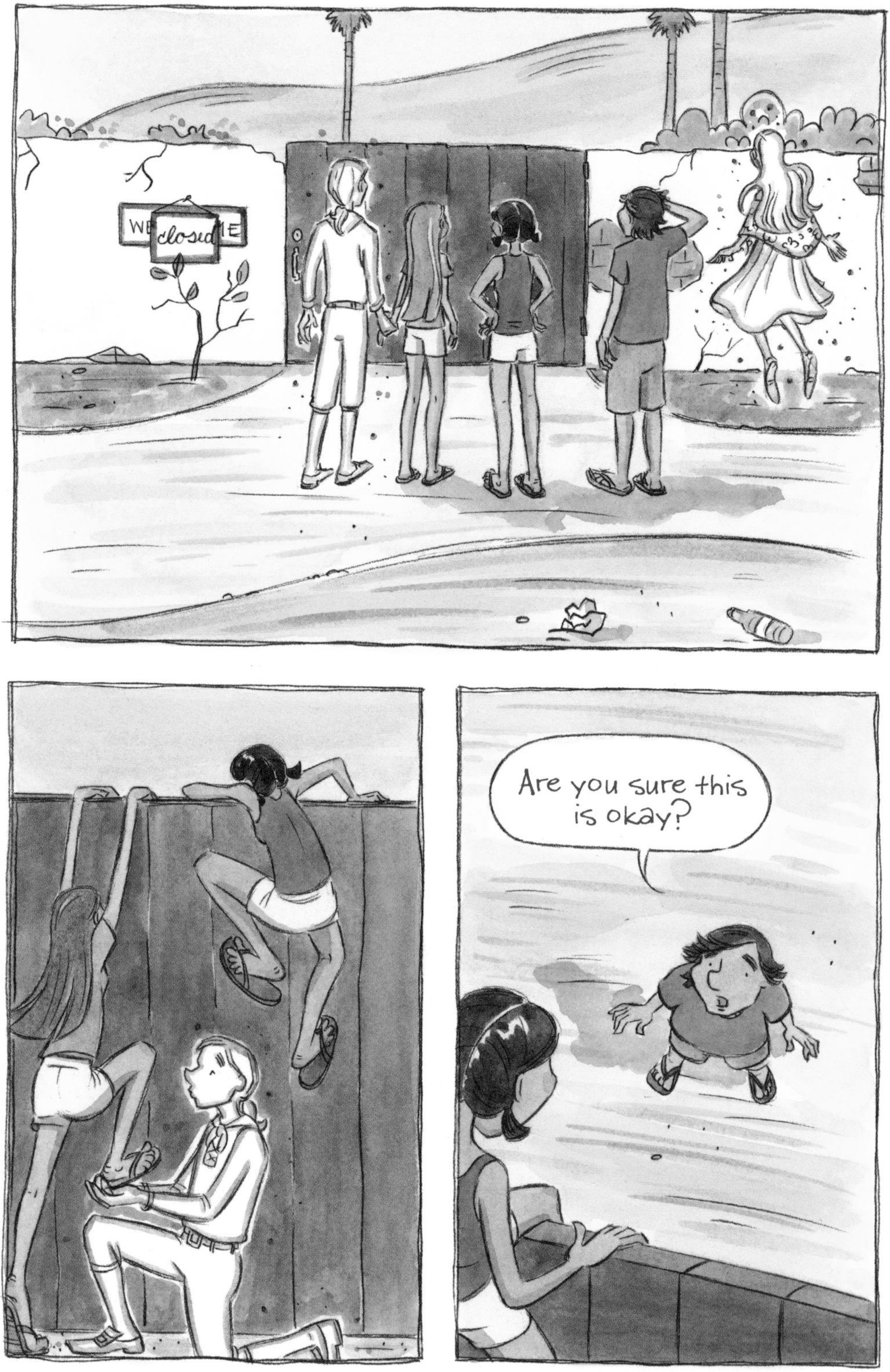
WE
closed
ME
Are you sure this is okay?

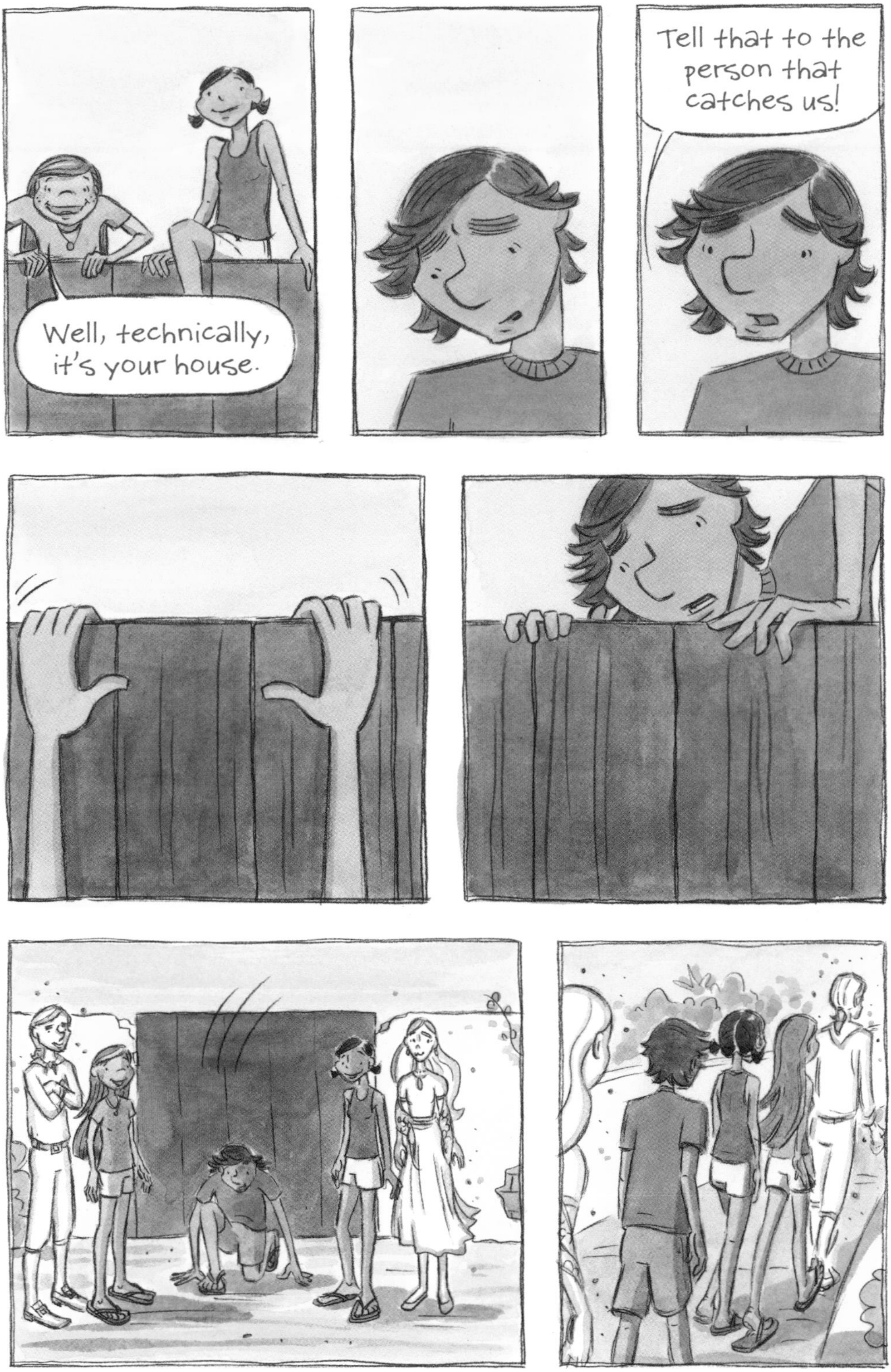
Well, technically, it's your house.
Tell that to the person that catches us!

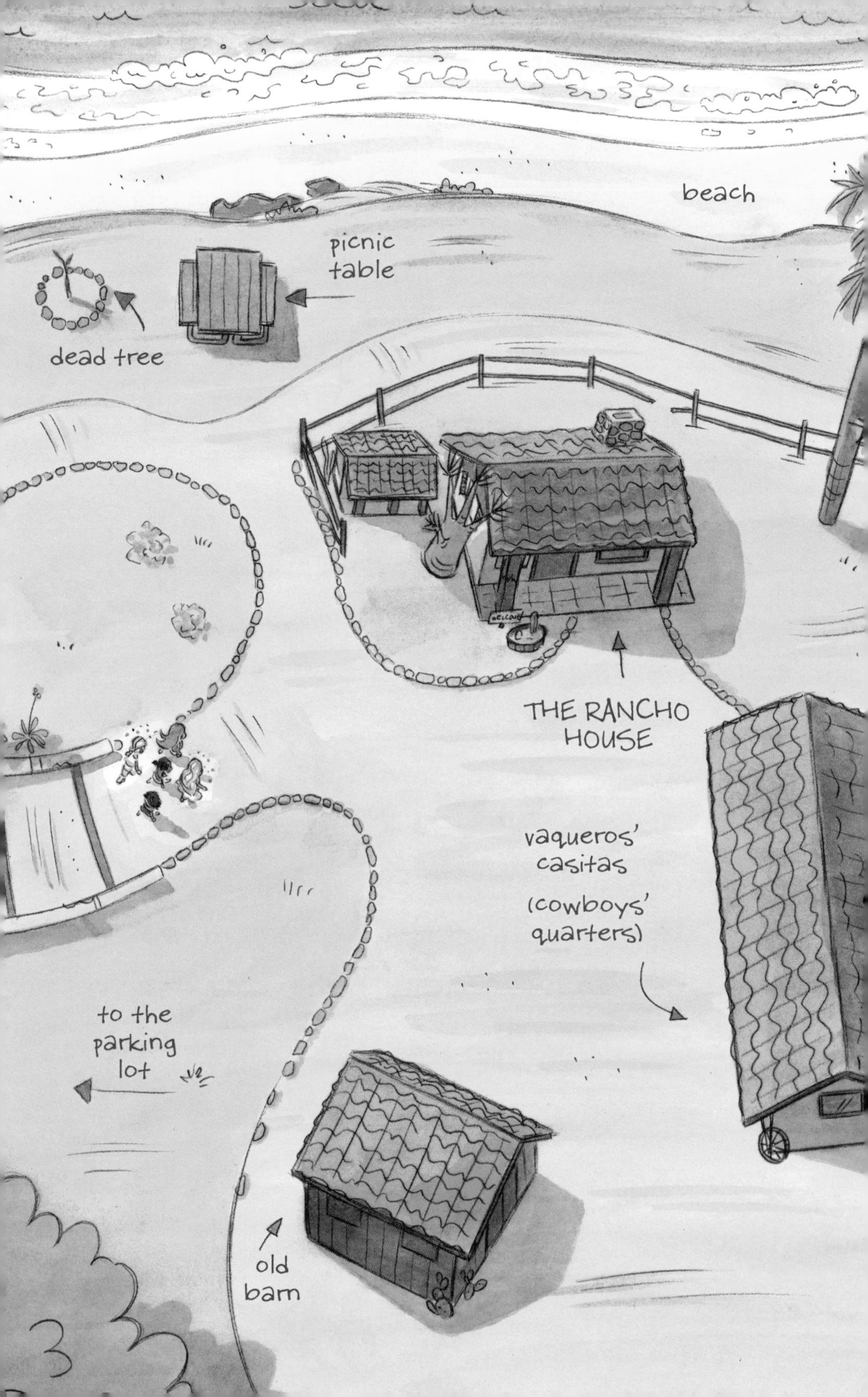
beach
picnic table
dead tree
THE RANCHO HOUSE
vaqueros' casitas
(cowboys' quarters)
to the parking lot
old barn

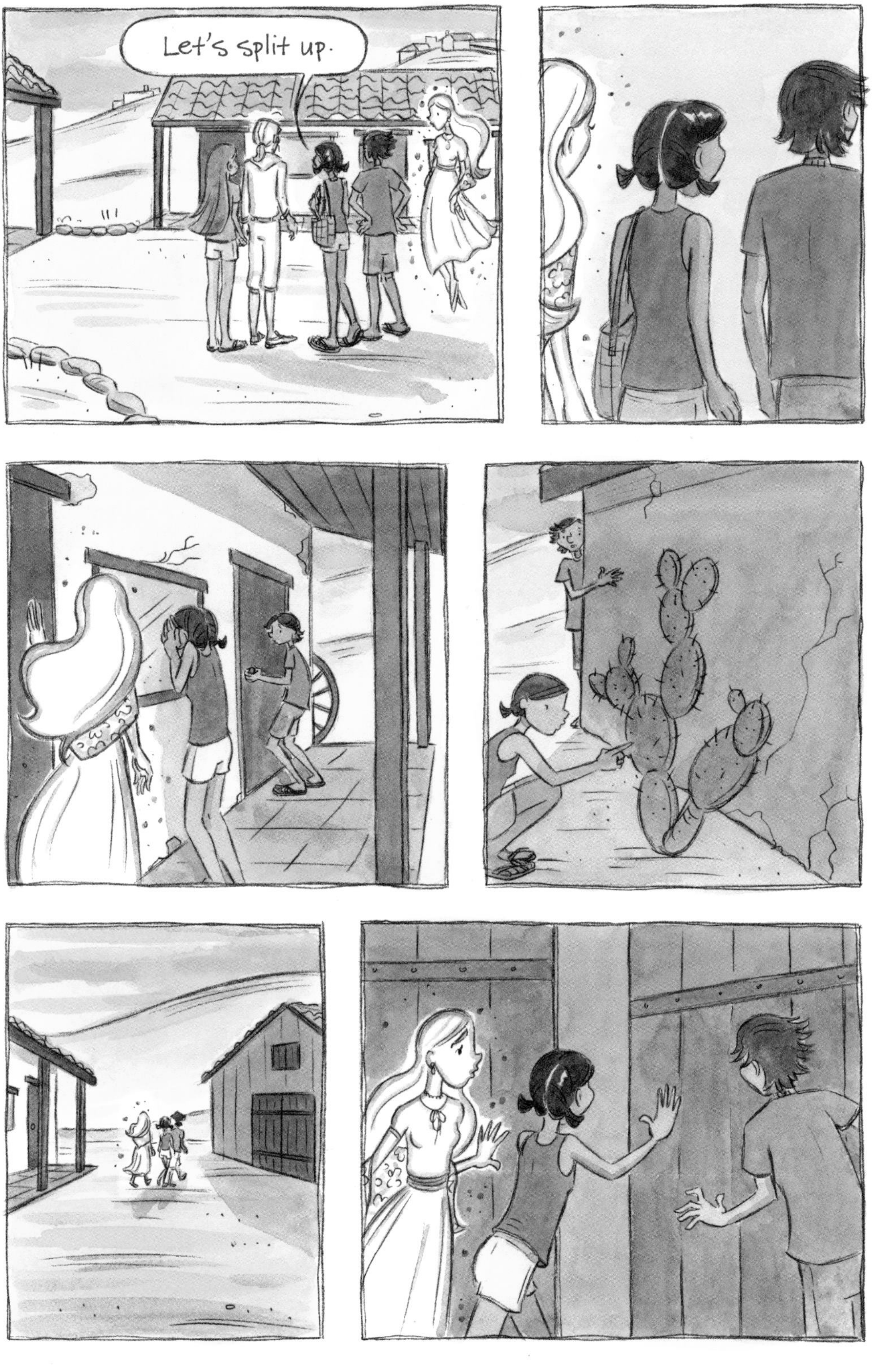
Let's split up.

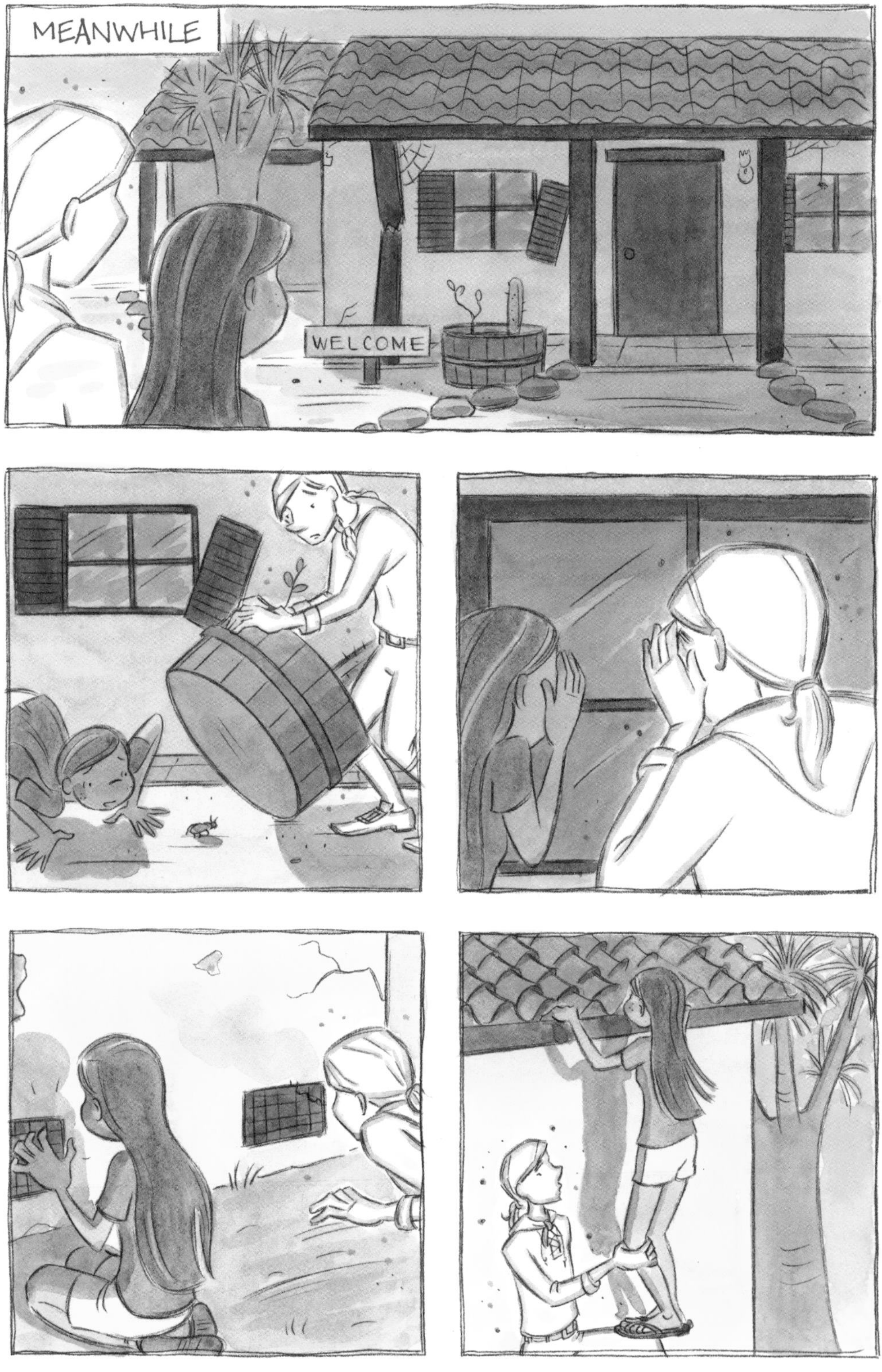
MEANWHILE
WELCOME

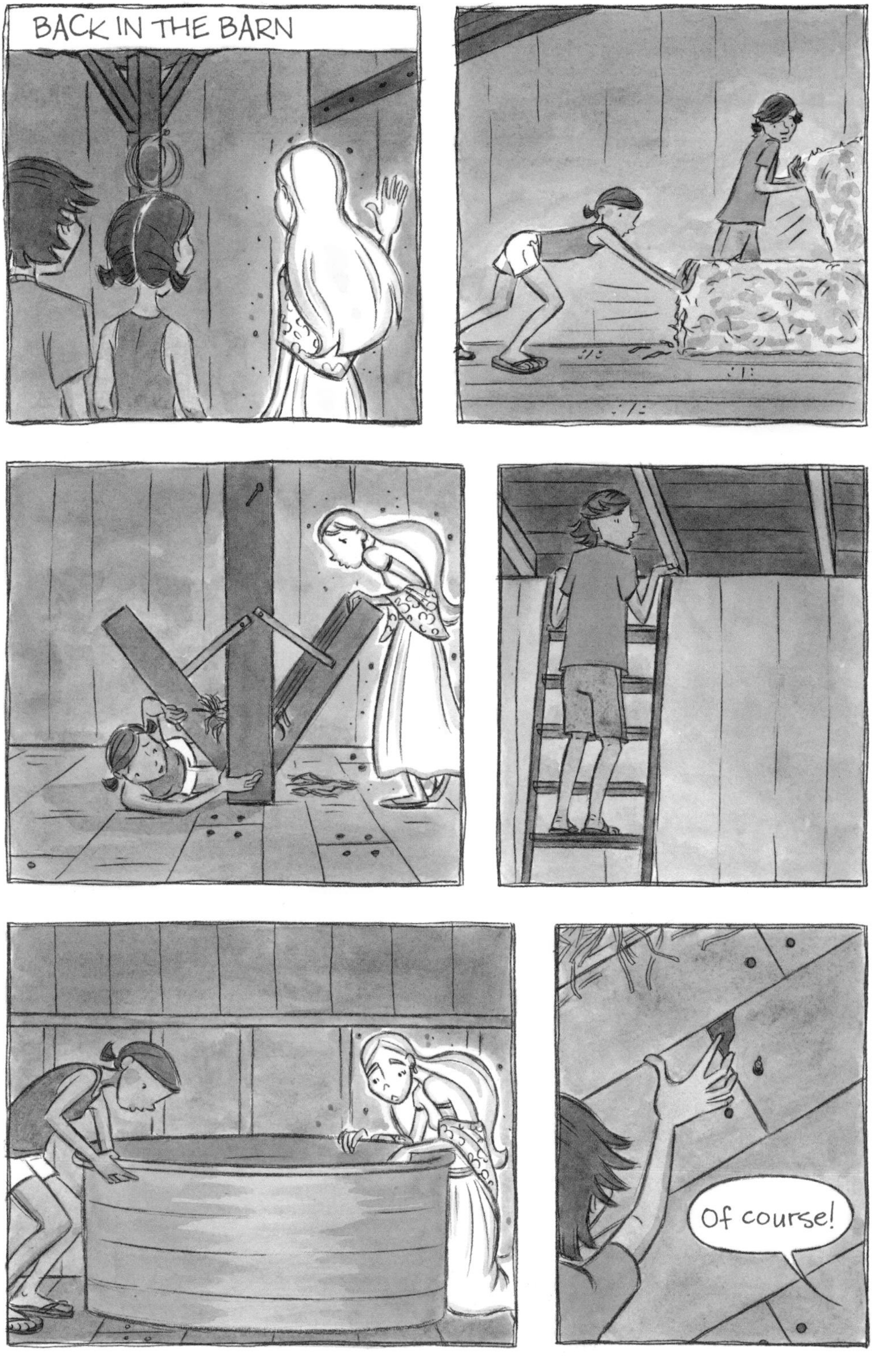
BACK IN THE BARN
Of course!

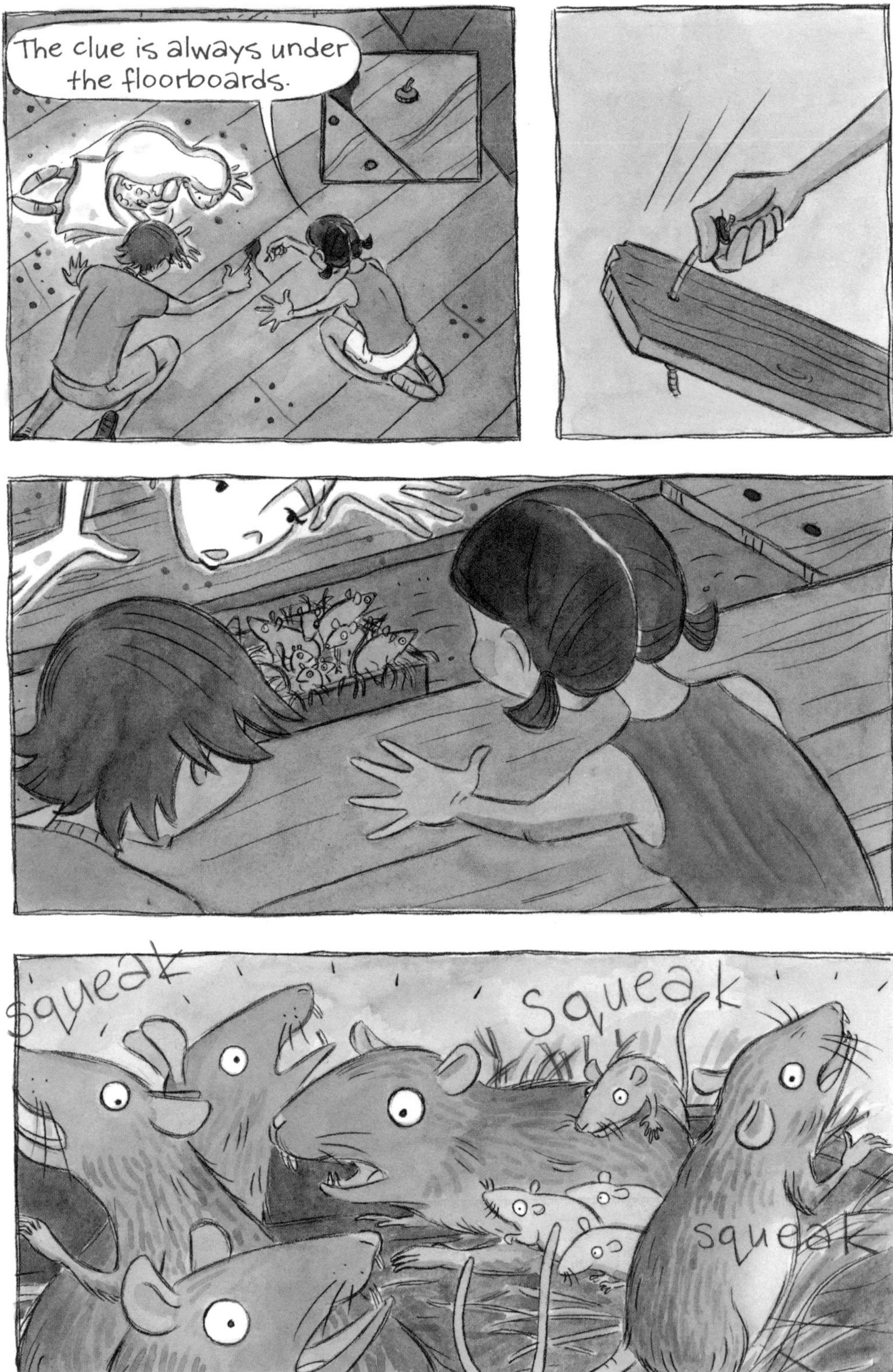
The clue is always under the floorboards.
squeak
squeak
squeak

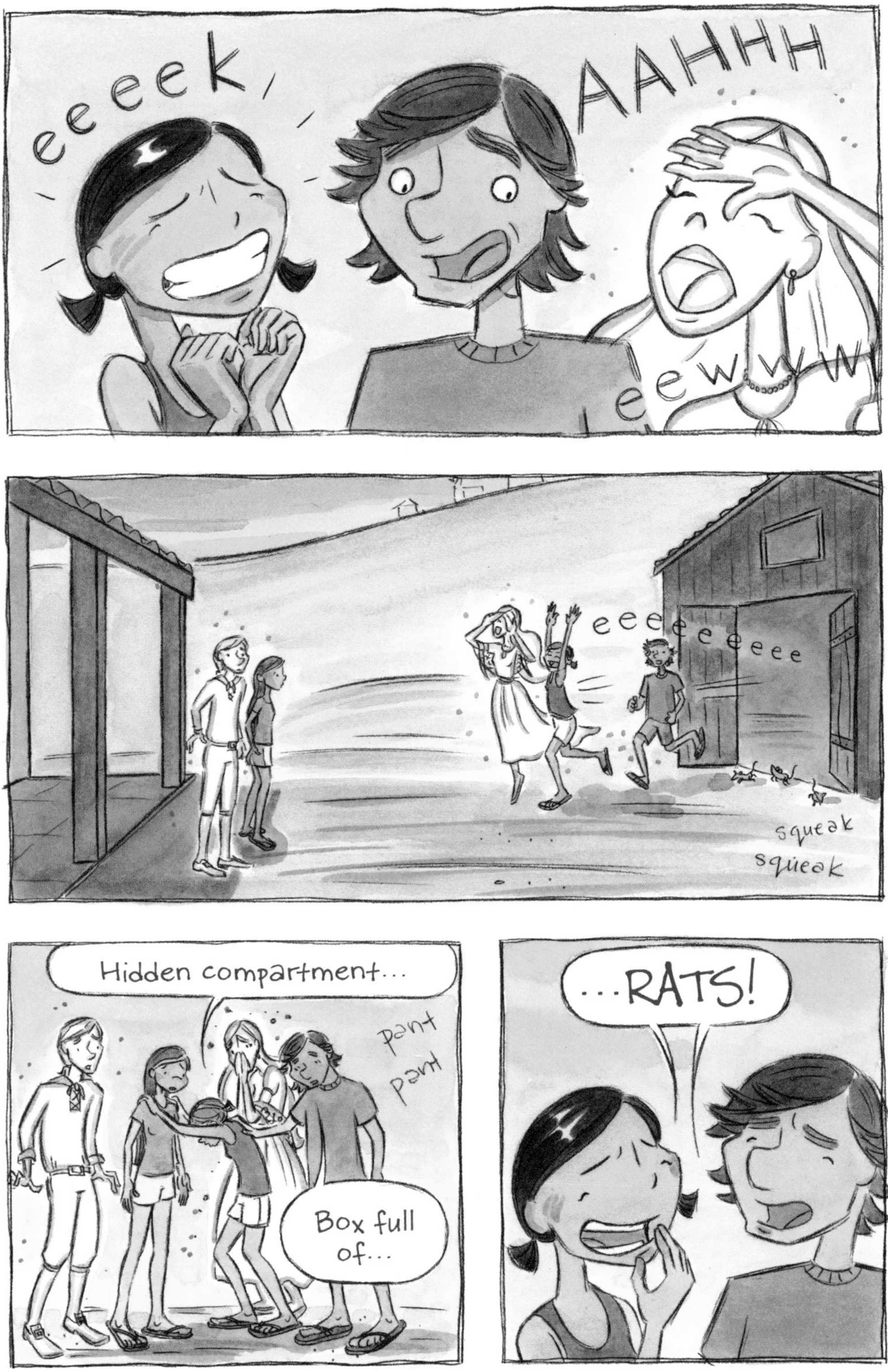
eeeek
AAHHH
eewww
eeeeeeeeee
squeak
squeak
Hidden compartment...
pant
pant
Box full of...
...RATS!

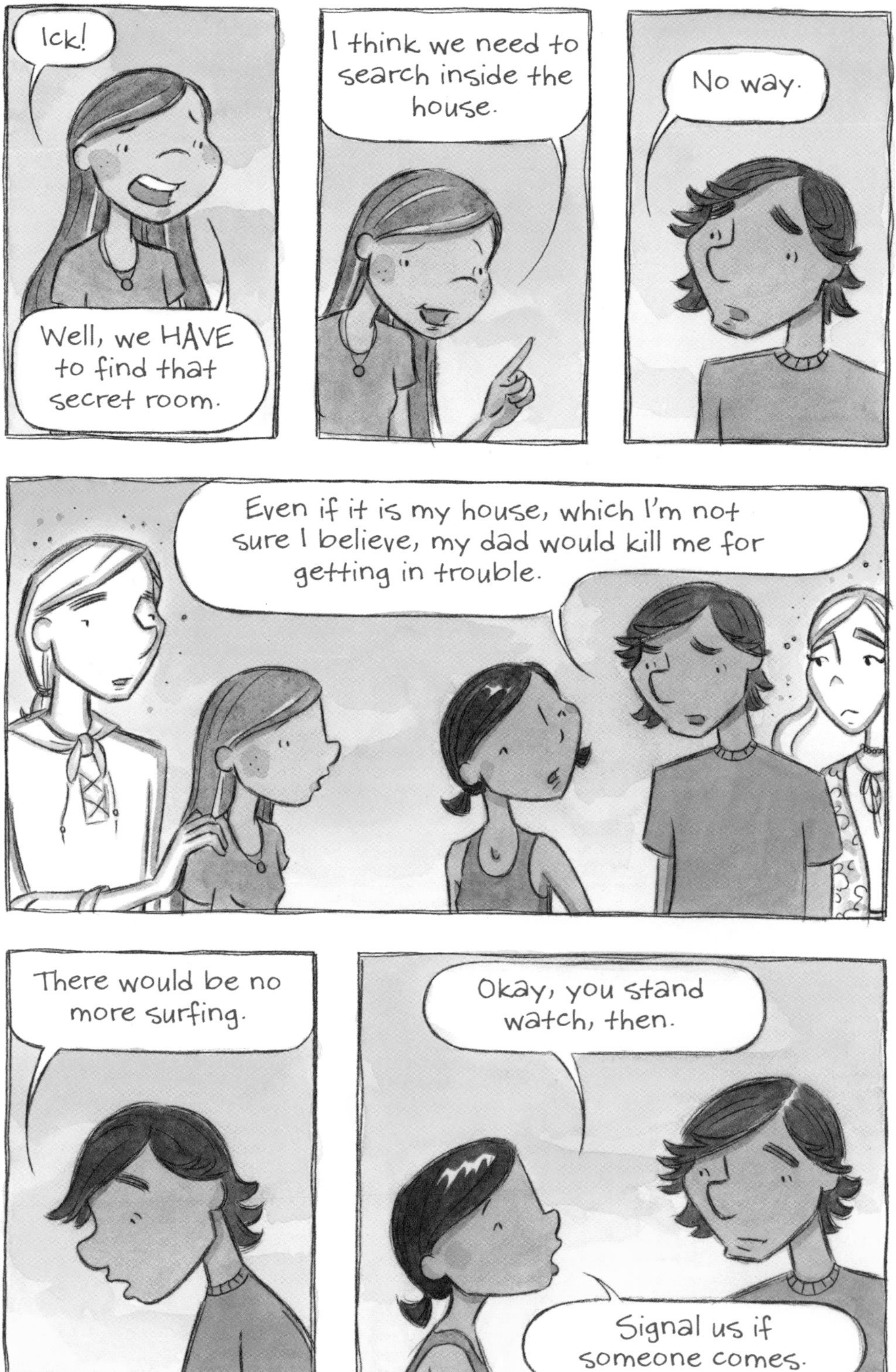
Ick!
Well, we HAVE to find that secret room.
I think we need to search inside the house.
No way.
Even if it is my house, which I'm not sure I believe, my dad would kill me for getting in trouble.
There would be no more surfing.
Okay, you stand watch, then.
Signal us if someone comes.

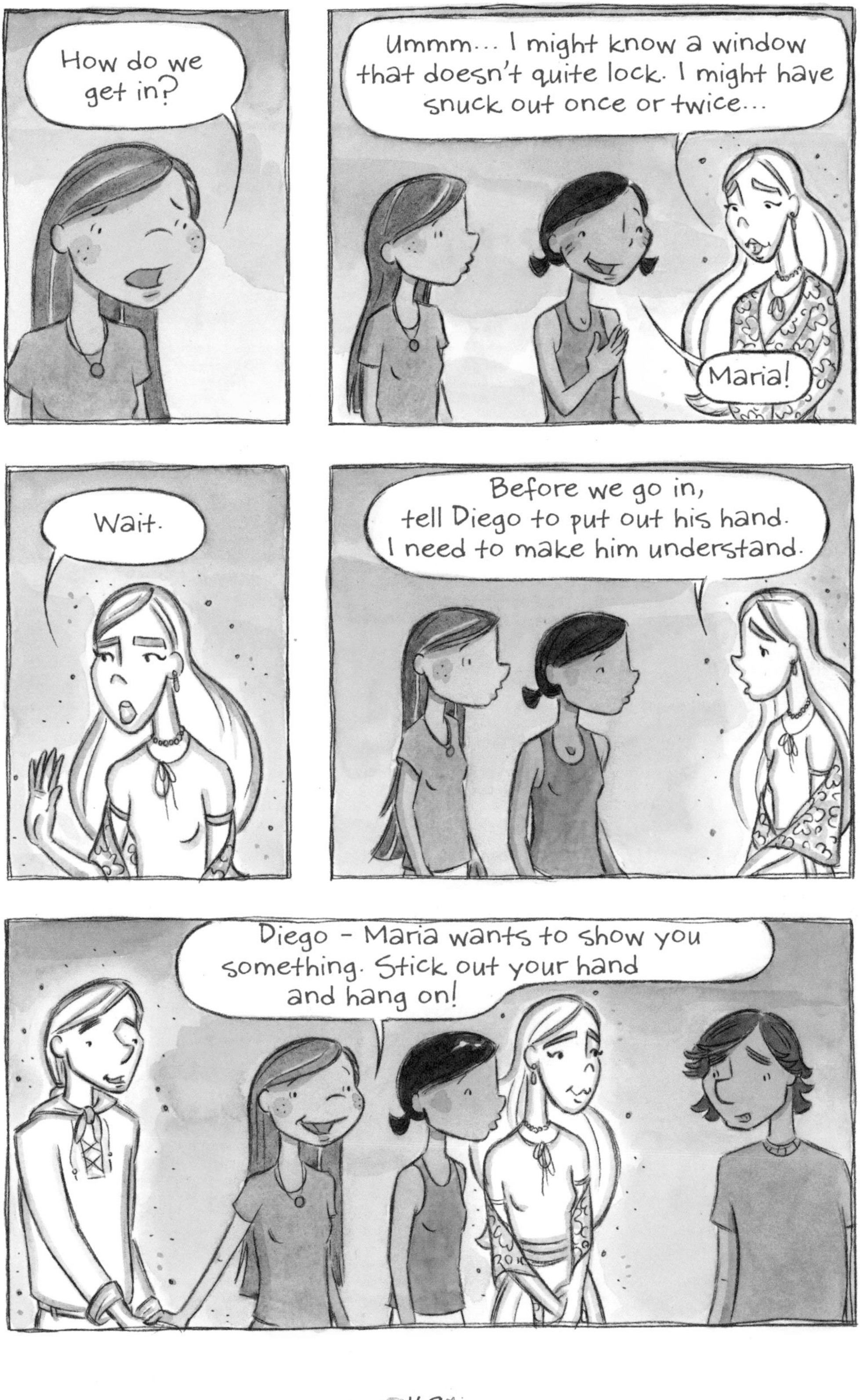
How do we get in?
Ummm... I might know a window that doesn't quite lock. I might have snuck out once or twice...
Maria!
Wait.
Before we go in, tell Diego to put out his hand. I need to make him understand.
Diego - Maria wants to show you something. Stick out your hand and hang on!

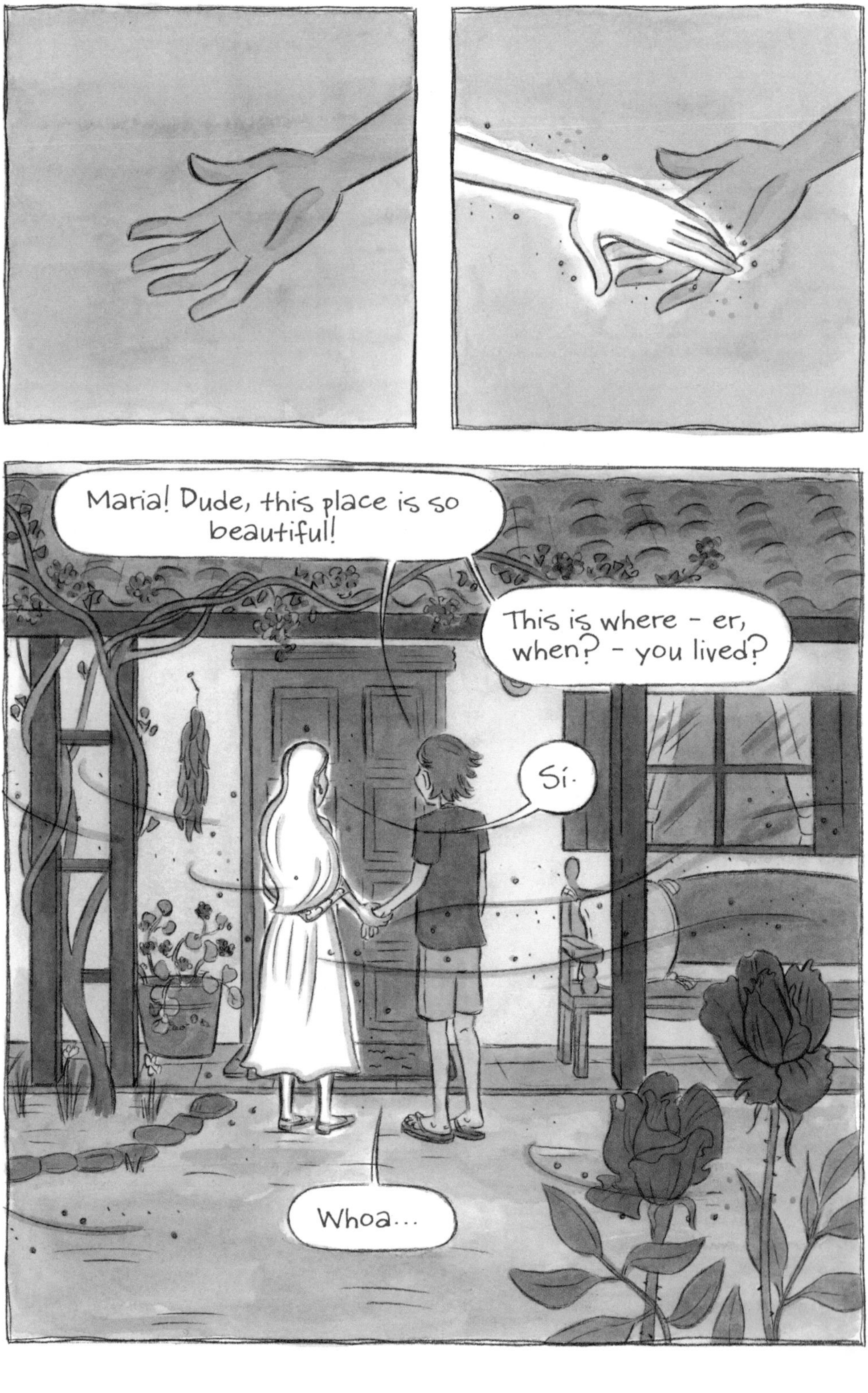
Maria! Dude, this place is so beautiful!
This is where - er, when? - you lived?
Sí.
Whoa...

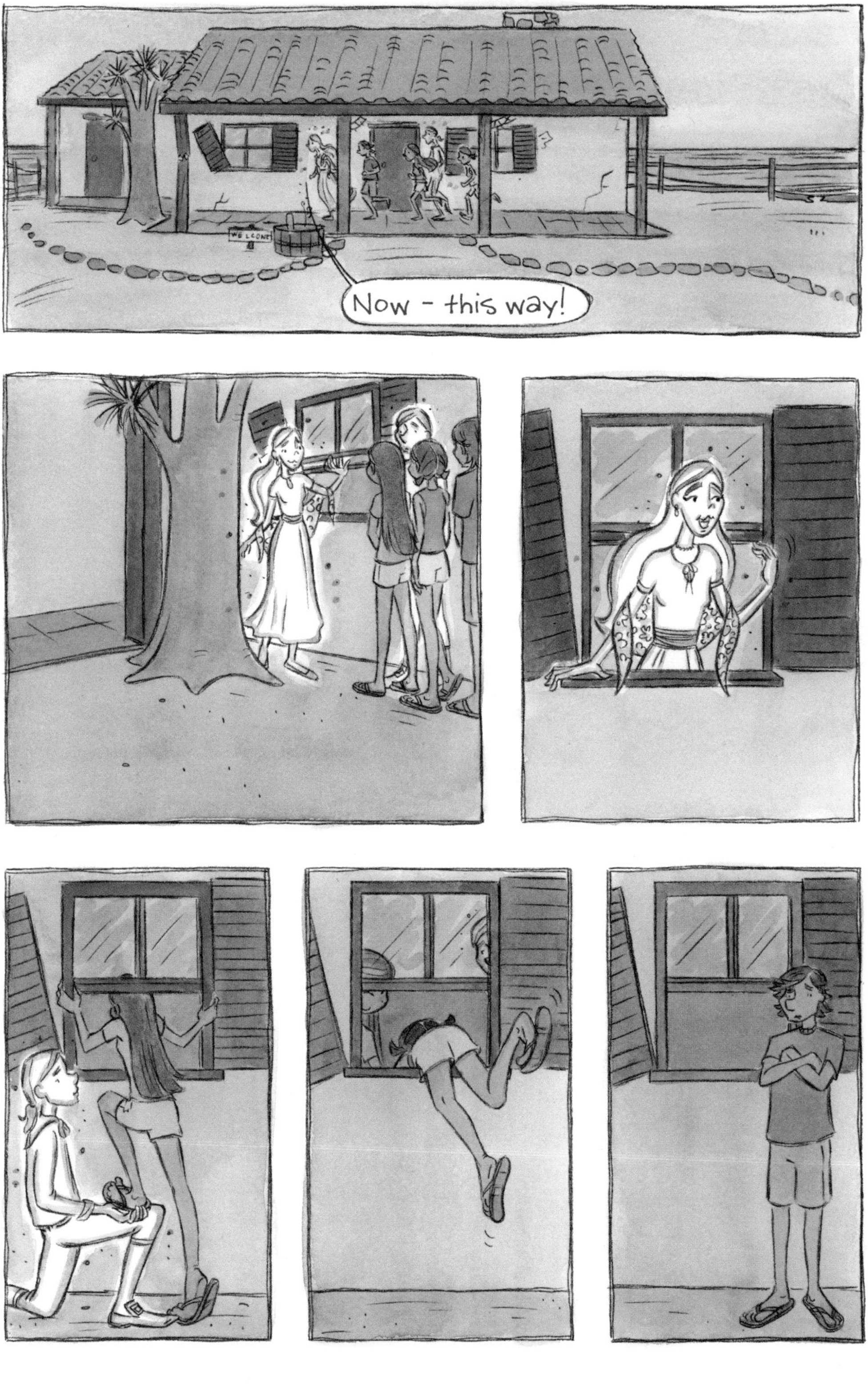
WELCOME
Now - this way!

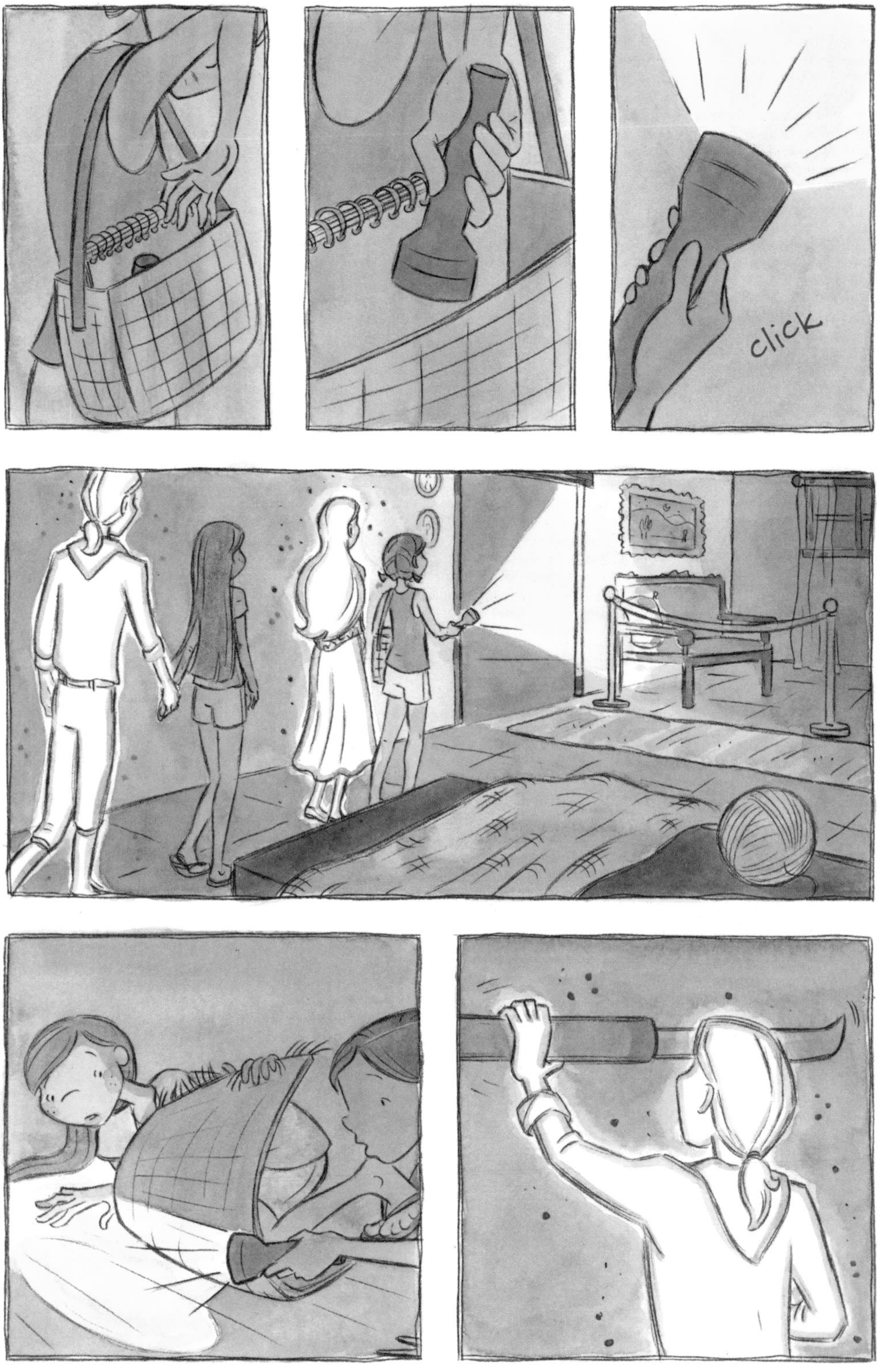
click

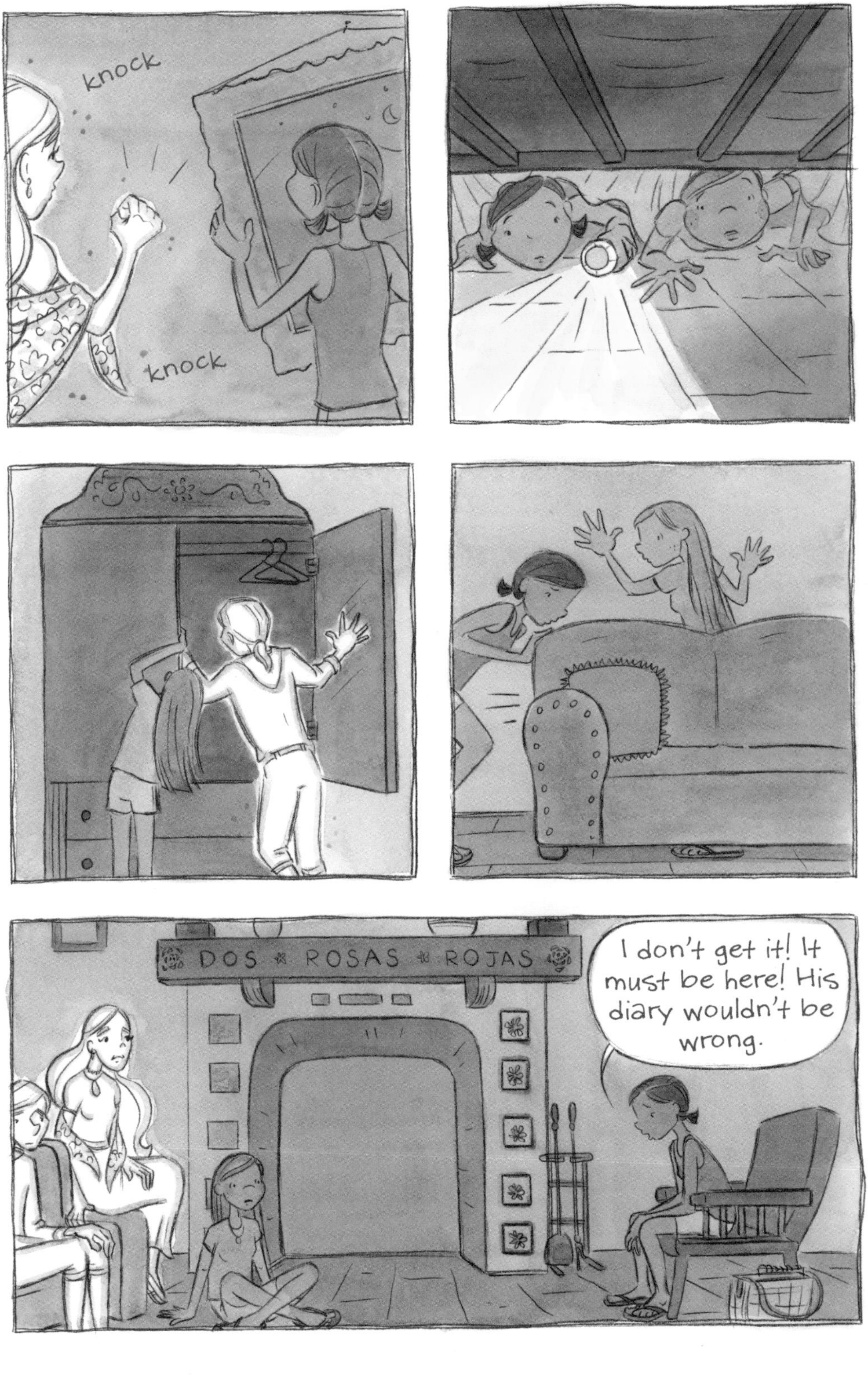
knock
knock
DOS ROSAS ROJAS
I don't get it! It must be here! His diary wouldn't be wrong.

DOS
Dos... rosas... rojas...
gasp!
Hello!

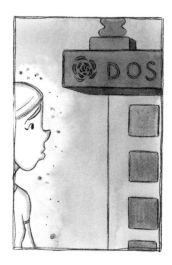

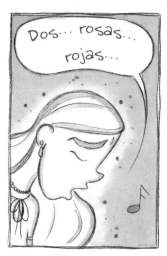

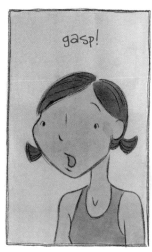

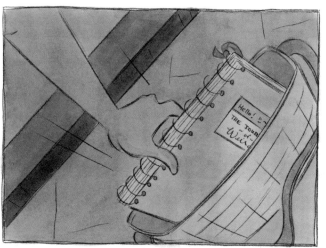

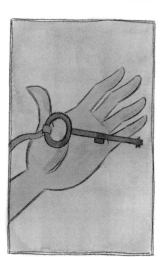

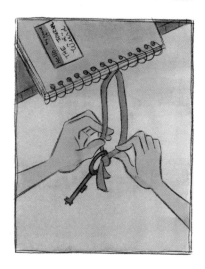

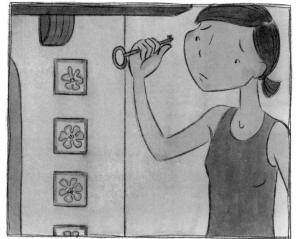

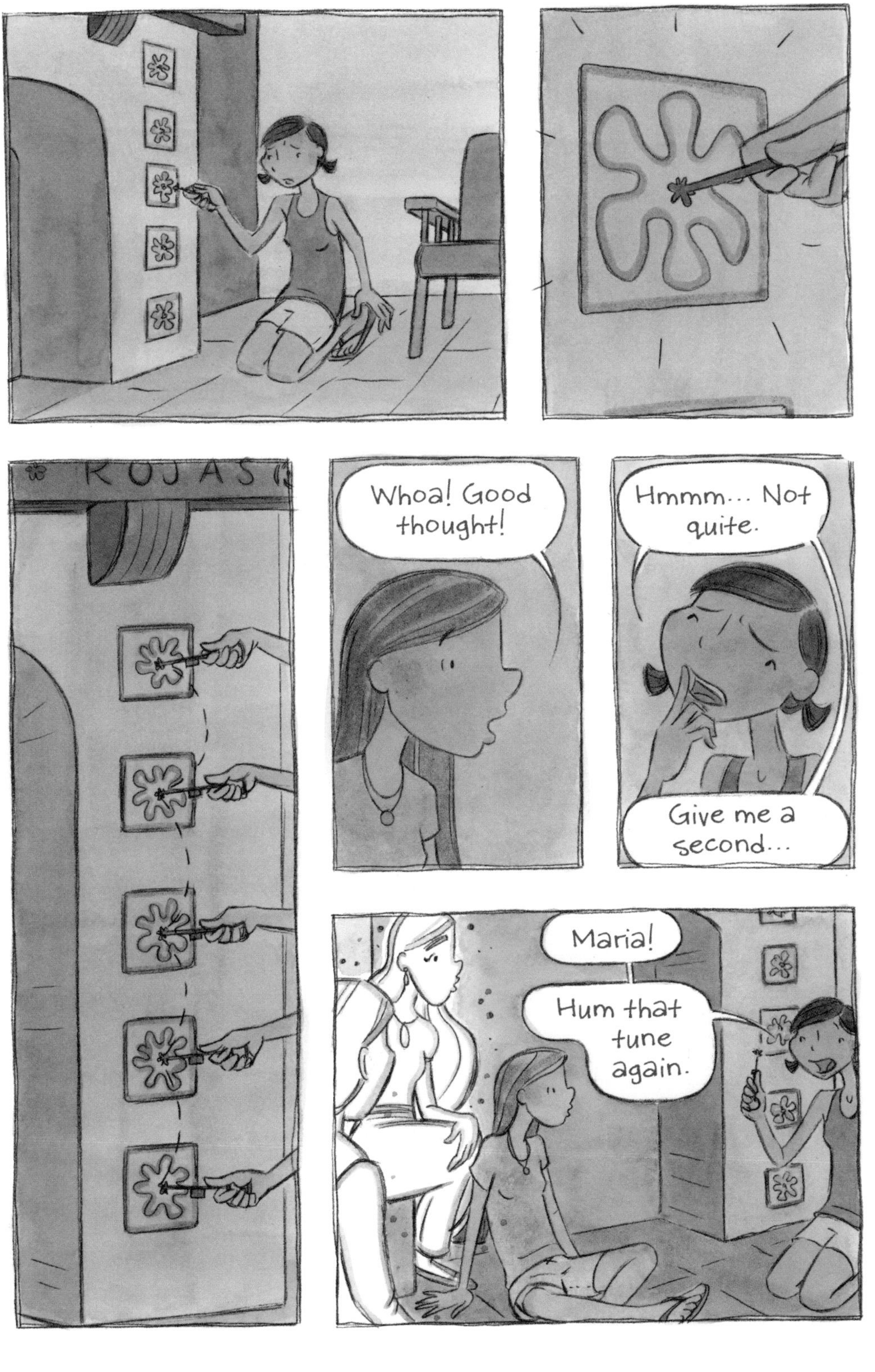
ROJAS
Whoa! Good thought!
Hmmm... Not quite.
Give me a second...
Maria!
Hum that tune again.

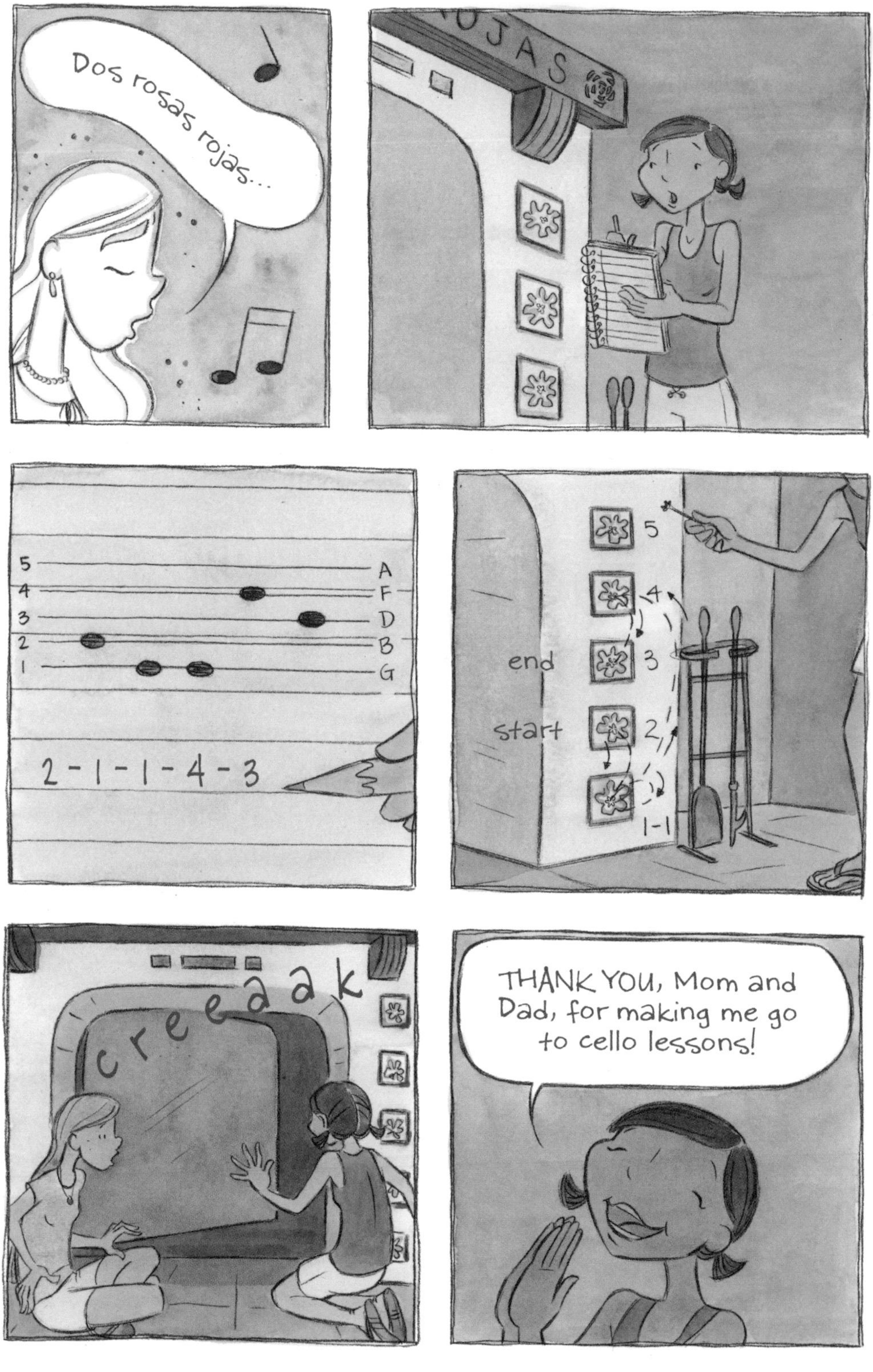
Dos rosas rojas...
OJAS
5
4
3
2
1
A
F
D
B
G
2-1-1-4-3
5
4
end
3
start
2
1-1
creeeaak
THANK YOU, Mom and Dad, for making me go to cello lessons!

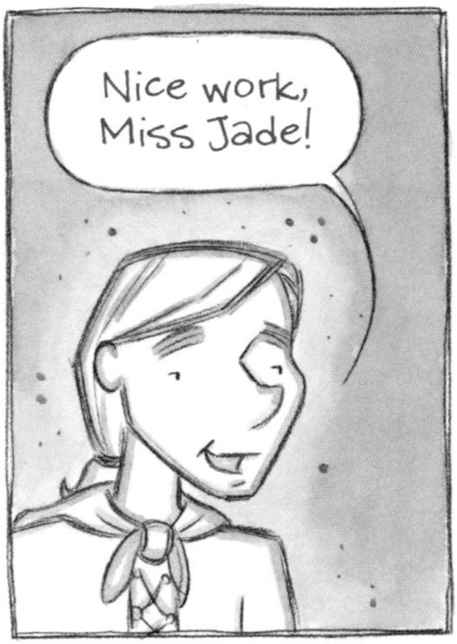
Nice work, Miss Jade!

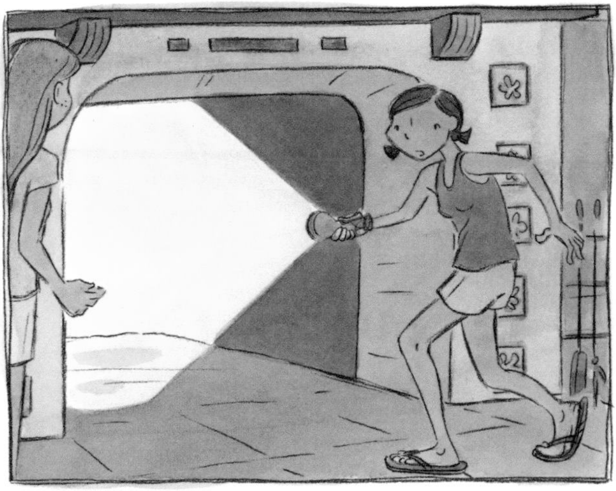

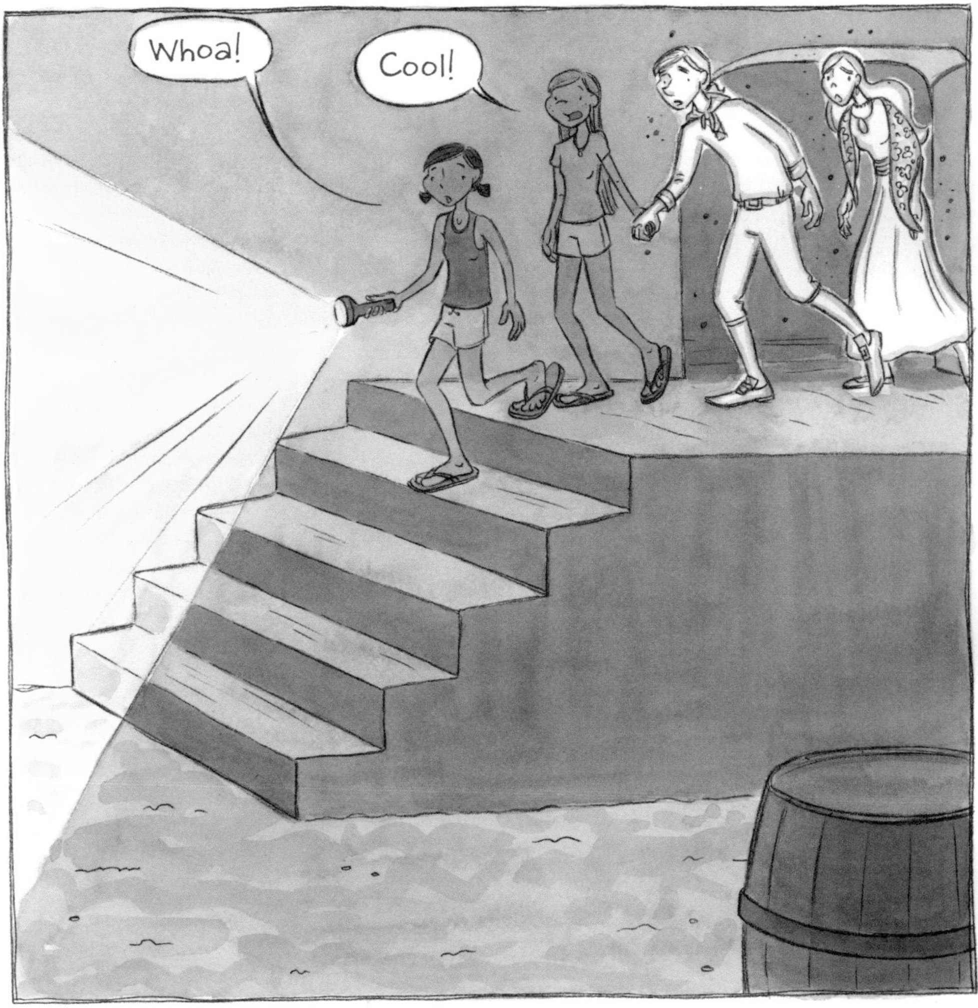
Whoa!
Cool!

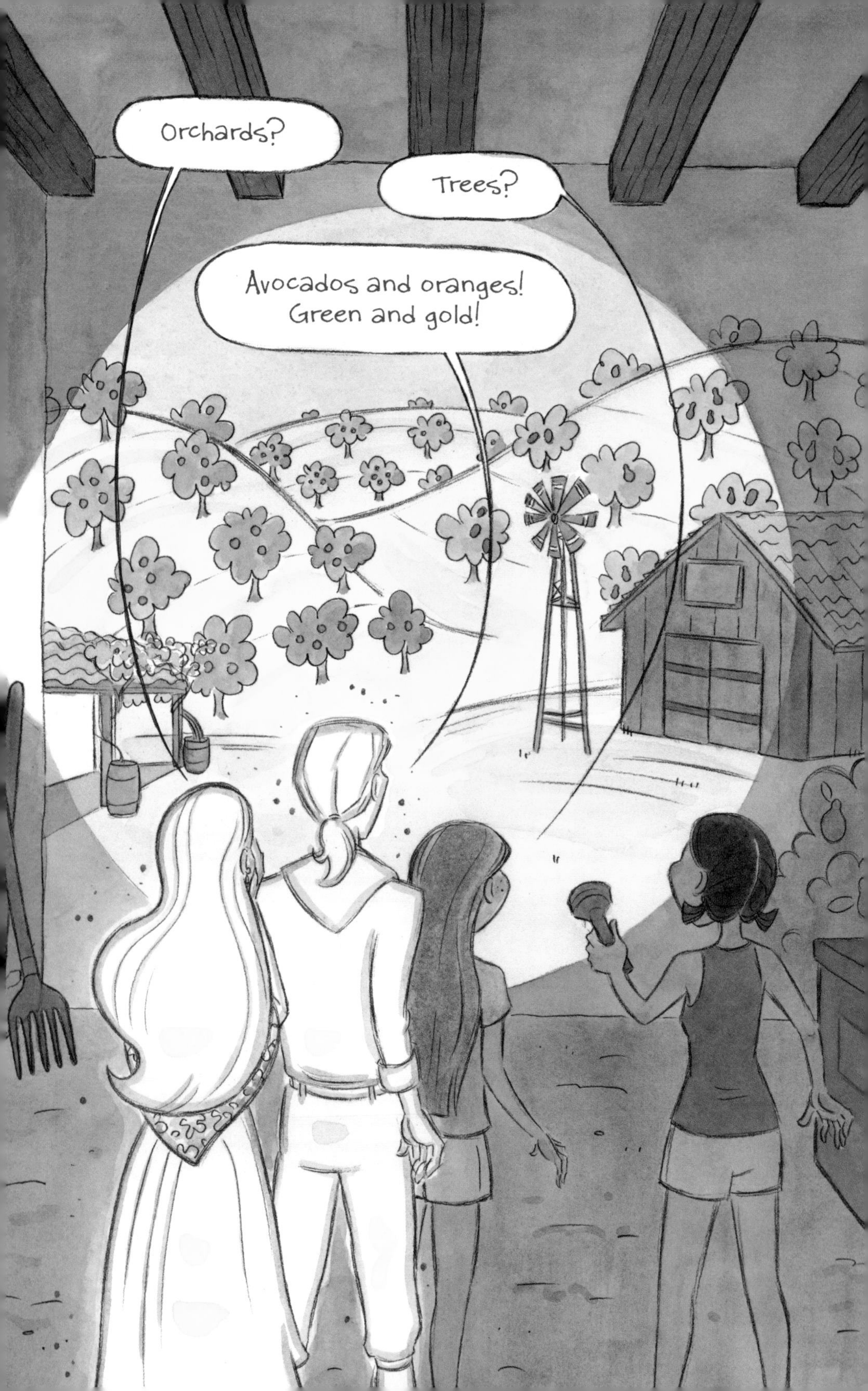
Orchards?
Trees?
Avocados and oranges! Green and gold!

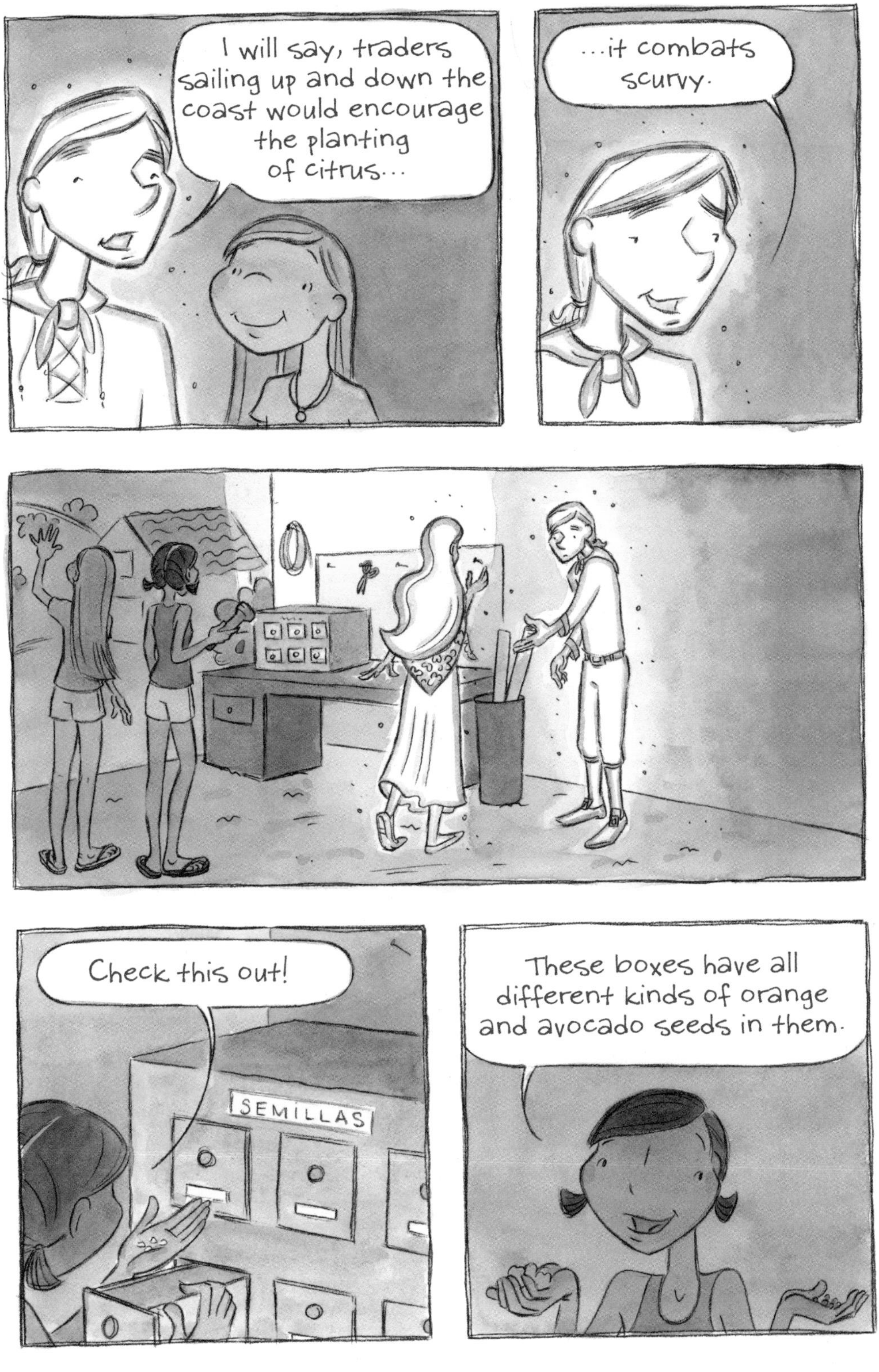
I will say, traders sailing up and down the coast would encourage the planting of citrus...
...it combats scurvy.
Check this out!
SEMILLAS
These boxes have all different kinds of orange and avocado seeds in them.

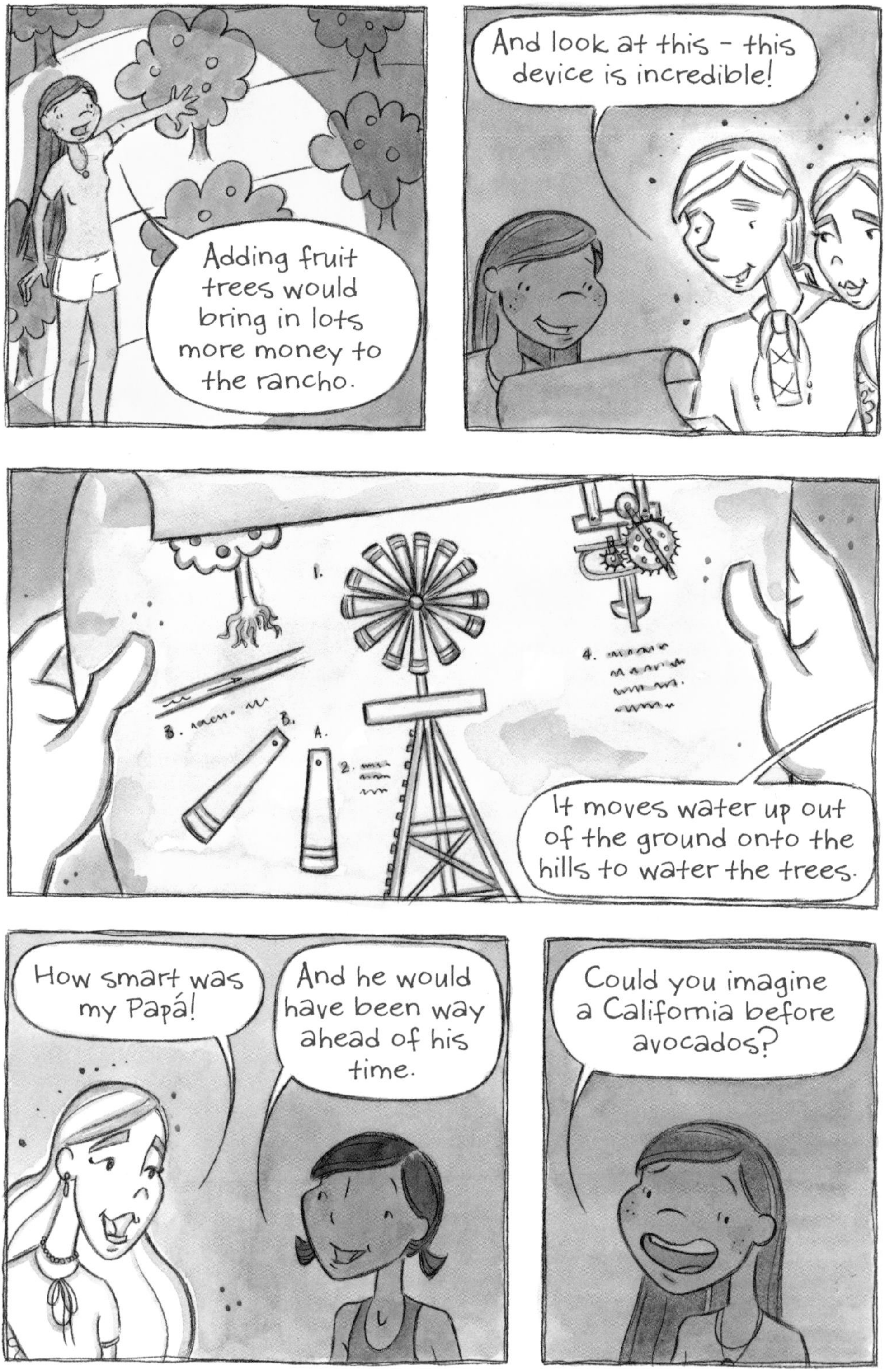
Adding fruit trees would bring in lots more money to the rancho.
And look at this - this device is incredible!
1.
4.
3.
B.
A.
2.
It moves water up out of the ground onto the hills to water the trees.
How smart was my Papá!
And he would have been way ahead of his time.
Could you imagine a California before avocados?

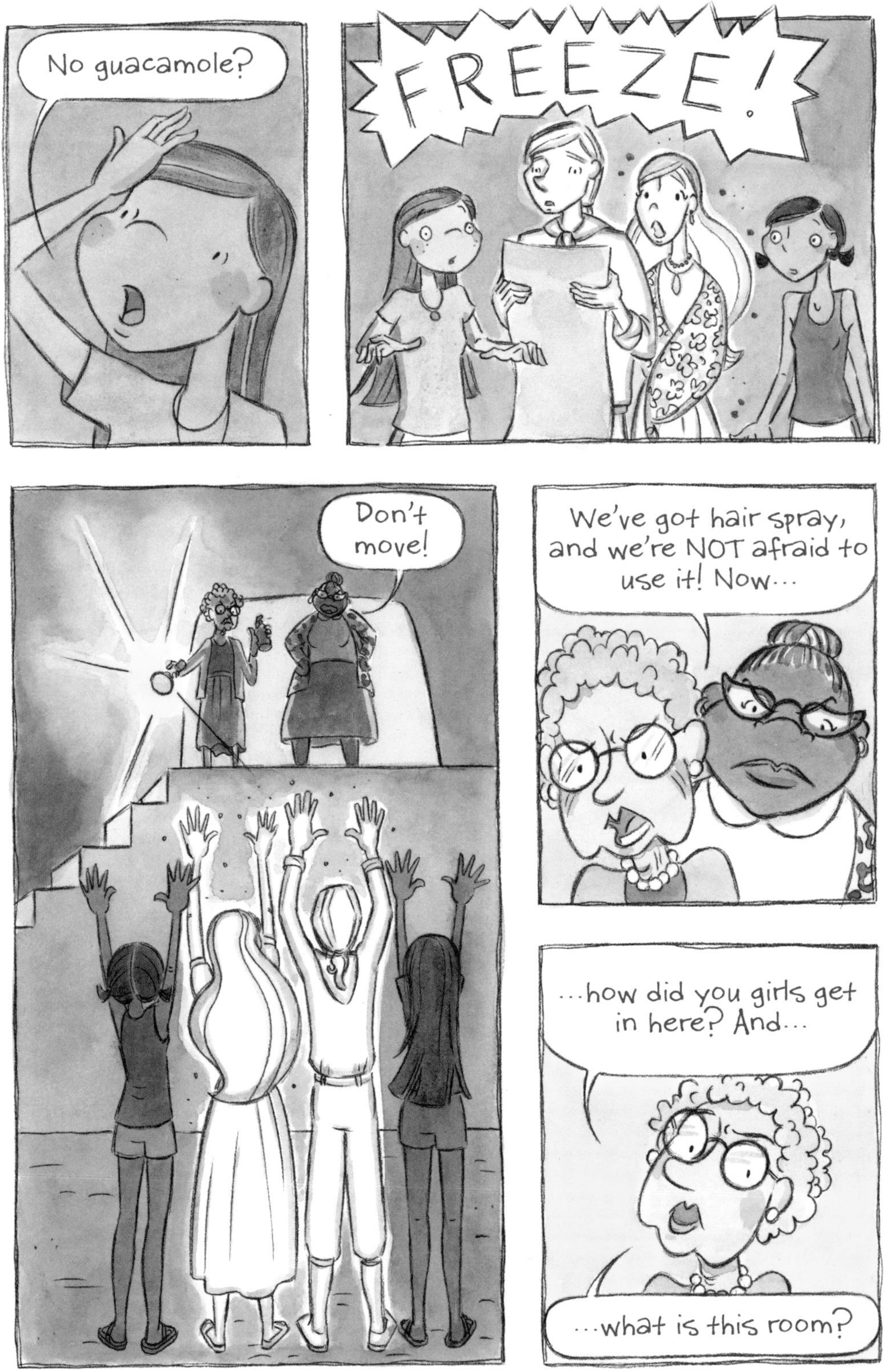
No guacamole?
FREEZE!
Don't move!
We've got hair spray, and we're NOT afraid to use it! Now...
...how did you girls get in here? And...
...what is this room?

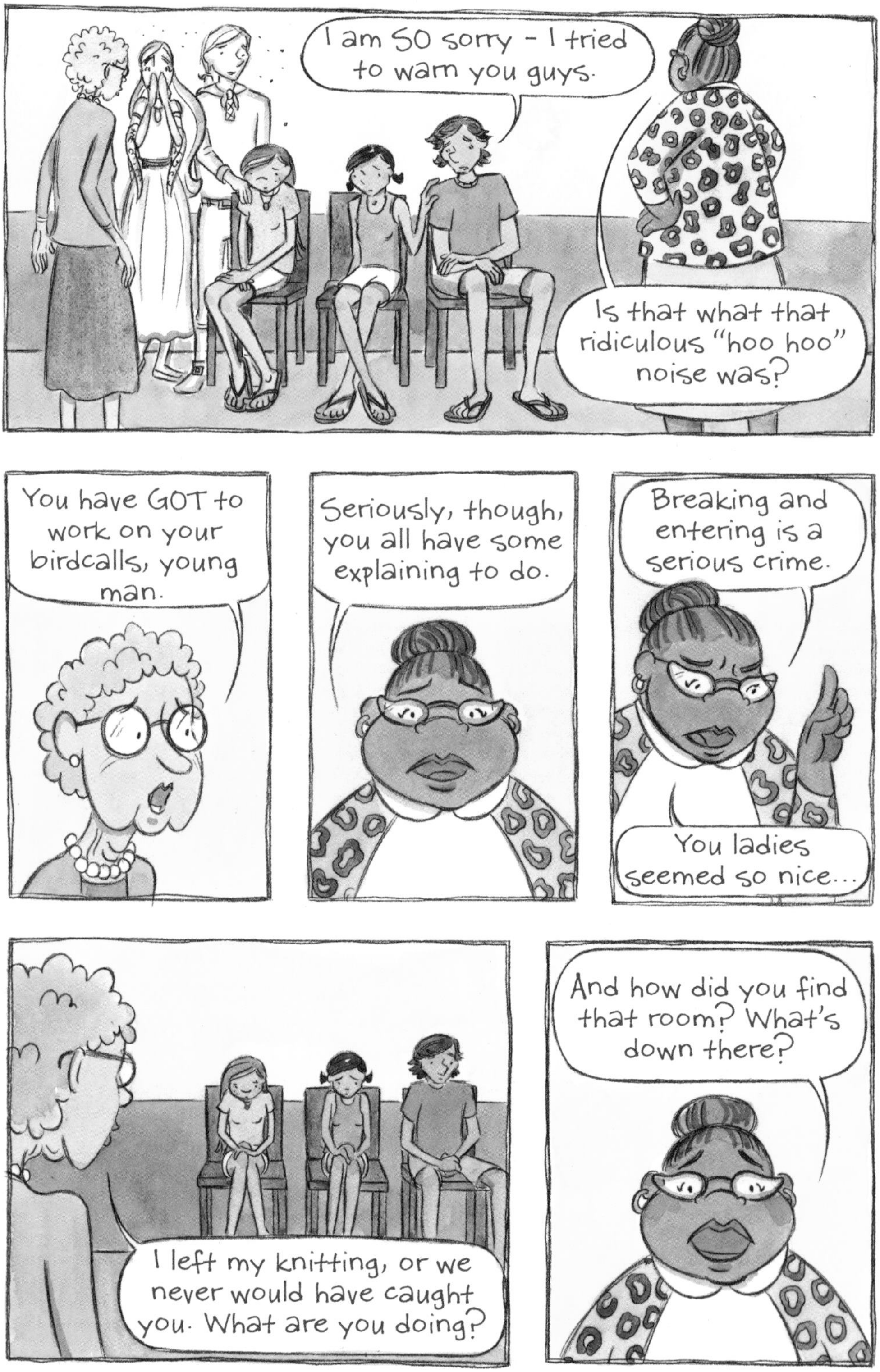
I am SO sorry - I tried to warn you guys.
Is that what that ridiculous "hoo hoo" noise was?
You have GOT to work on your birdcalls, young man.
Seriously, though, you all have some explaining to do.
Breaking and entering is a serious crime.
You ladies seemed so nice...
I left my knitting, or we never would have caught you. What are you doing?
And how did you find that room? What's down there?

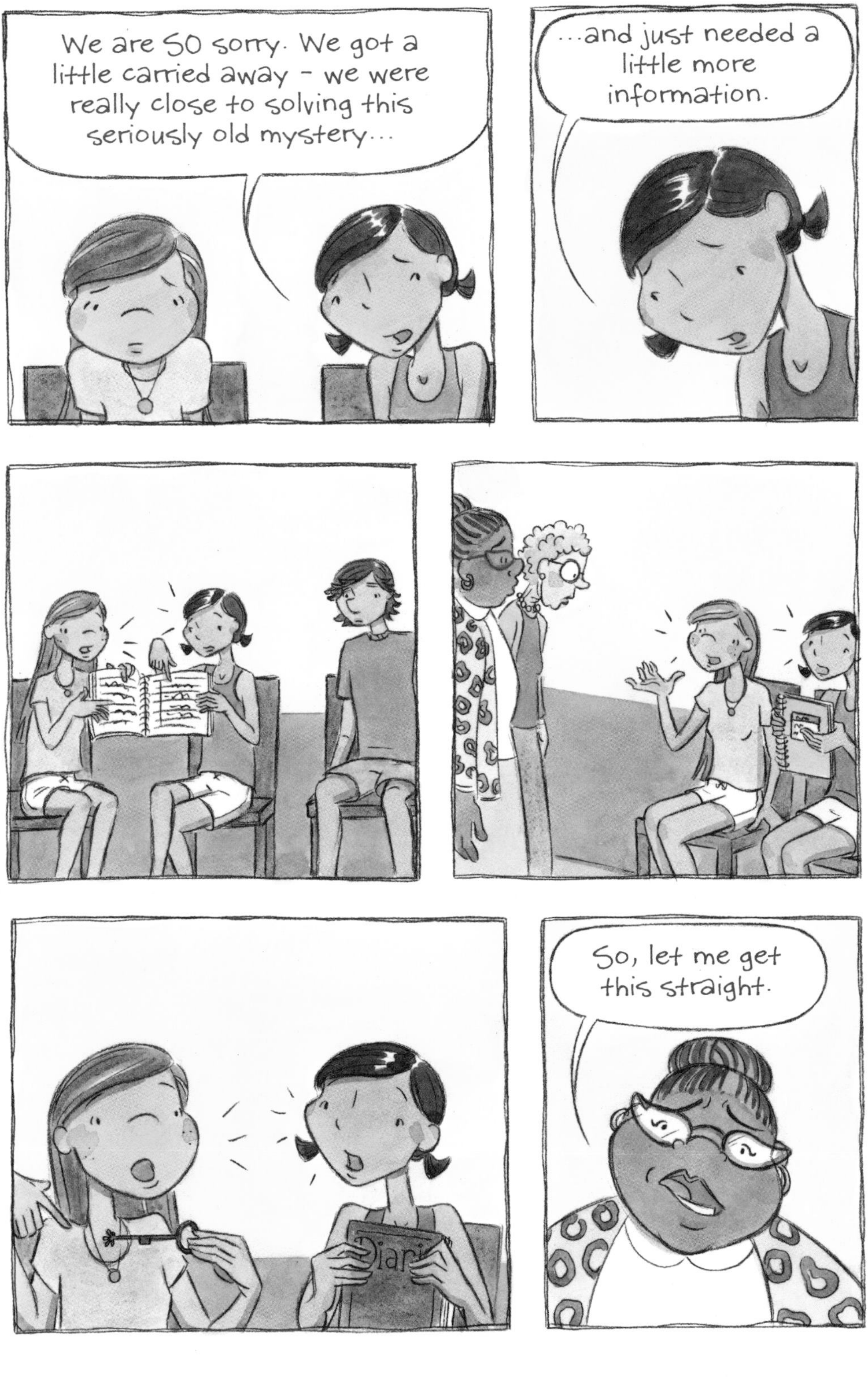
We are SO sorry. We got a little carried away - we were really close to solving this seriously old mystery...
...and just needed a little more information.
So, let me get this straight.

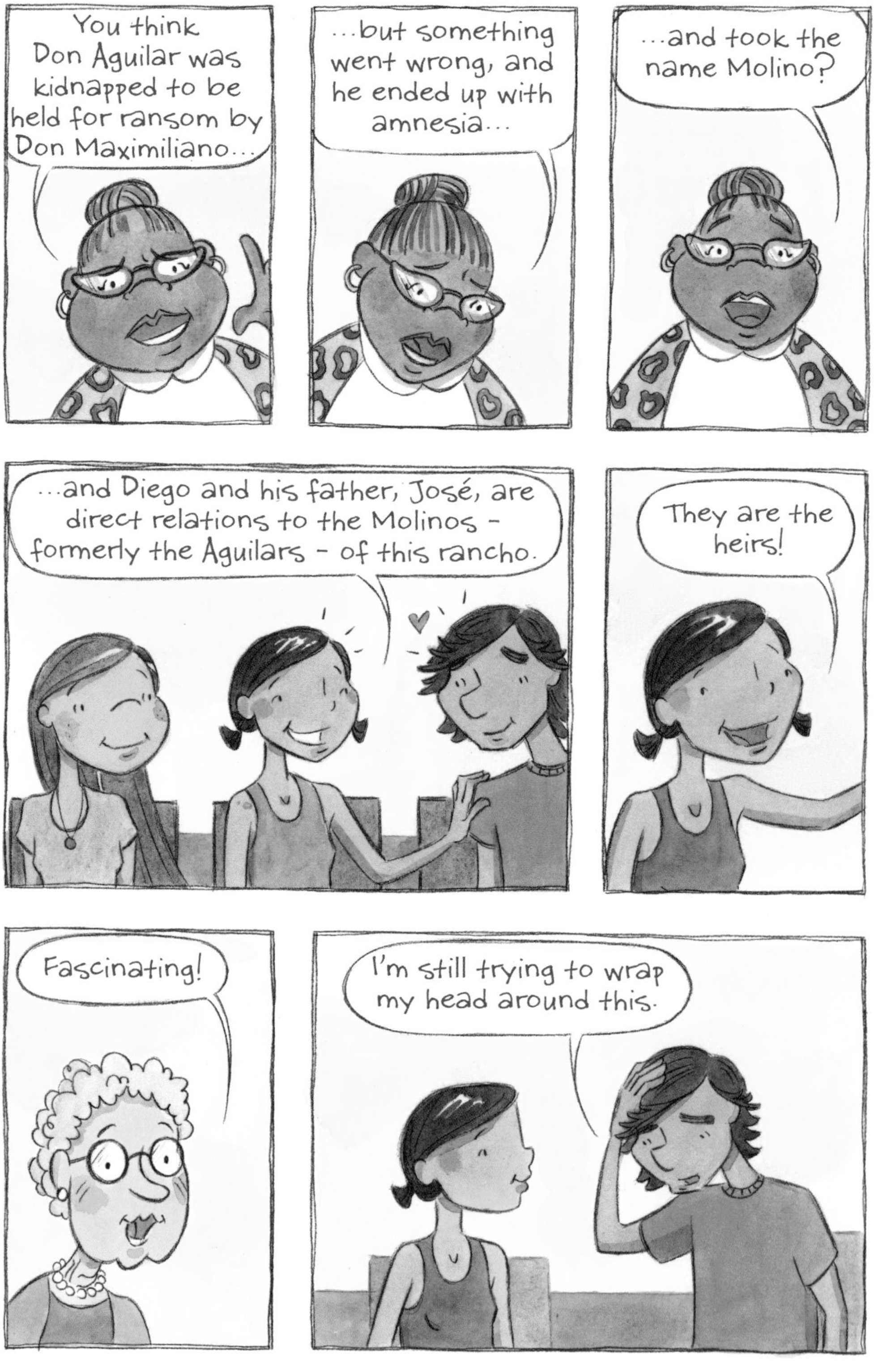
You think Don Aguilar was kidnapped to be held for ransom by Don Maximiliano...
...but something went wrong, and he ended up with amnesia...
...and took the name Molino?
...and Diego and his father, José, are direct relations to the Molinos - formerly the Aguilars - of this rancho.
They are the heirs!
Fascinating!
I'm still trying to wrap my head around this.

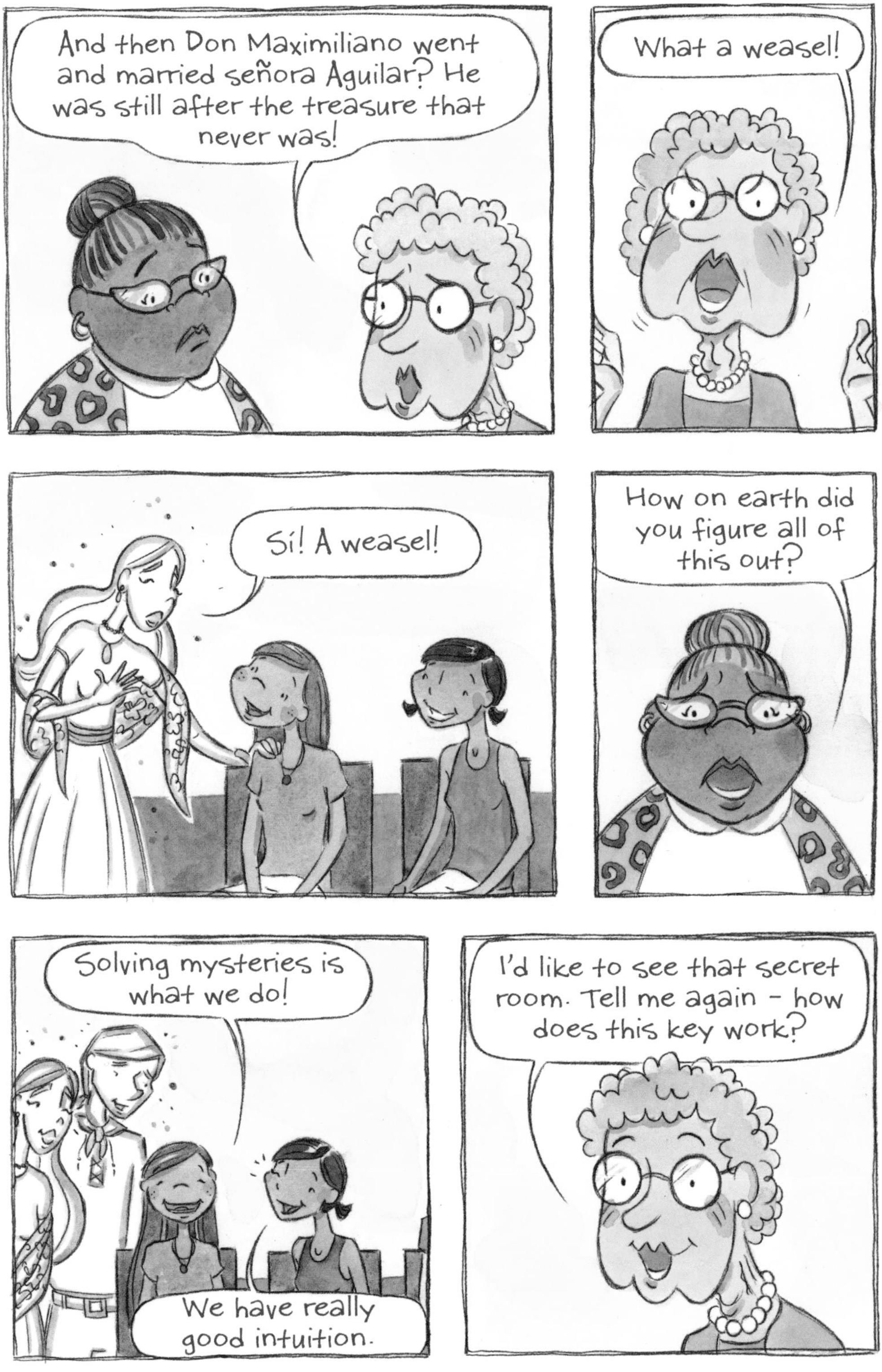
And then Don Maximiliano went and married señora Aguilar? He was still after the treasure that never was!
What a weasel!
Sí! A weasel!
How on earth did you figure all of this out?
Solving mysteries is what we do!
We have really good intuition.
I'd like to see that secret room. Tell me again - how does this key work?

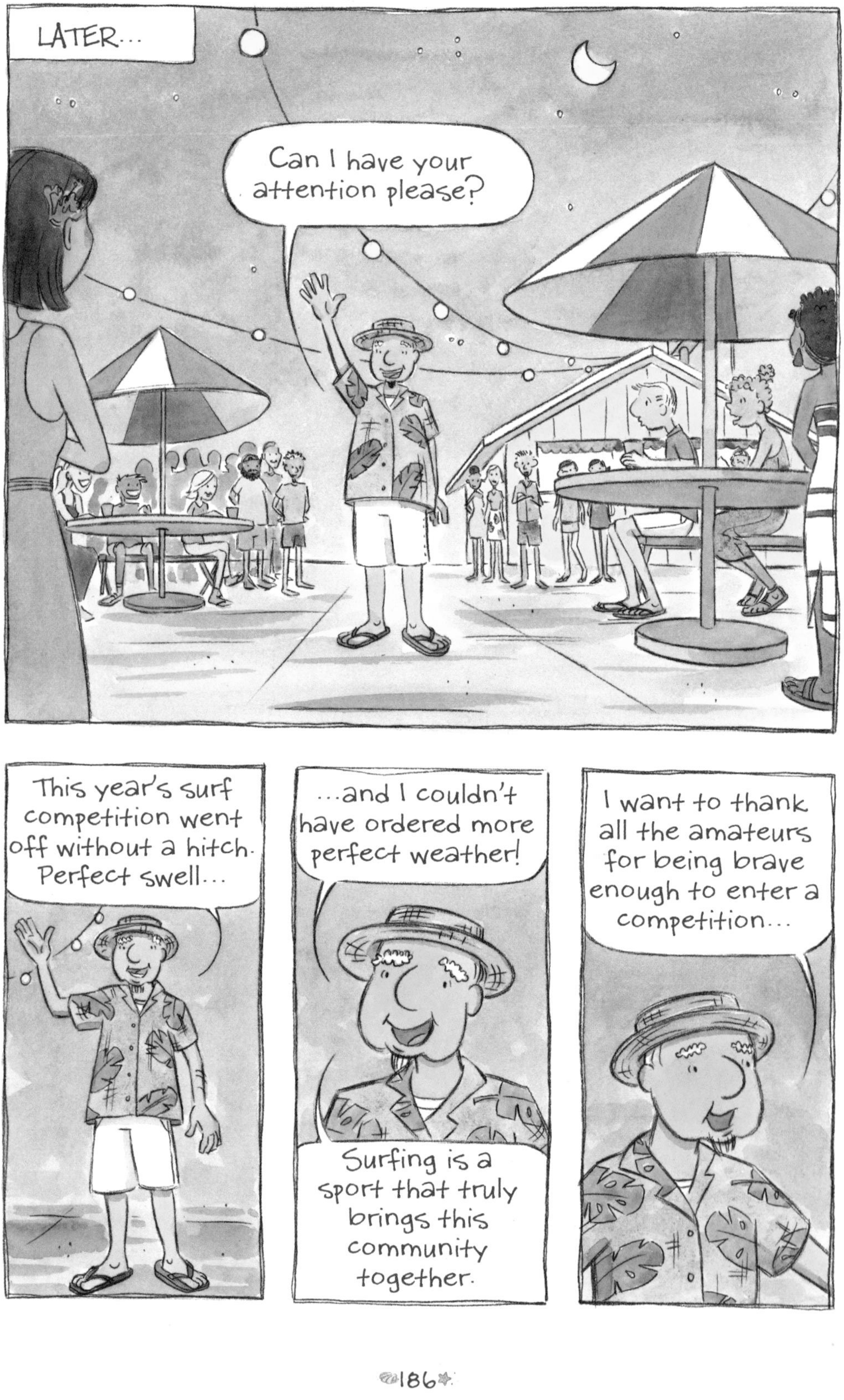
LATER...
Can I have your attention please?
This year's surf competition went off without a hitch. Perfect swell...
...and I couldn't have ordered more perfect weather!
Surfing is a sport that truly brings this community together.
I want to thank all the amateurs for being brave enough to enter a competition...

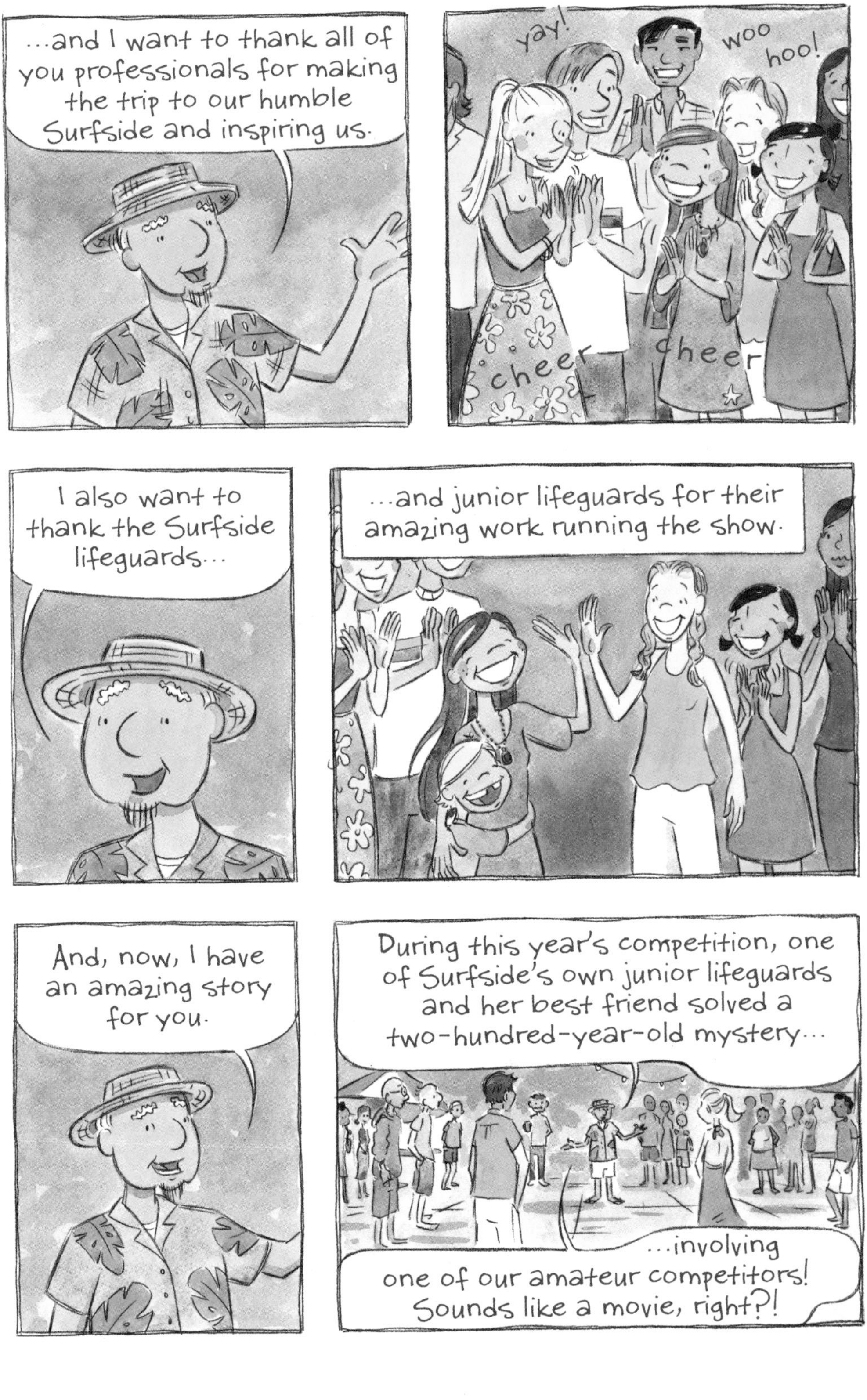
...and I want to thank all of you professionals for making the trip to our humble Surfside and inspiring us.
yay!
woo hoo!
cheer
cheer
I also want to thank the Surfside lifeguards...
...and junior lifeguards for their amazing work running the show.
And, now, I have an amazing story for you.
During this year's competition, one of Surfside's own junior lifeguards and her best friend solved a two-hundred-year-old mystery...
...involving one of our amateur competitors! Sounds like a movie, right?!

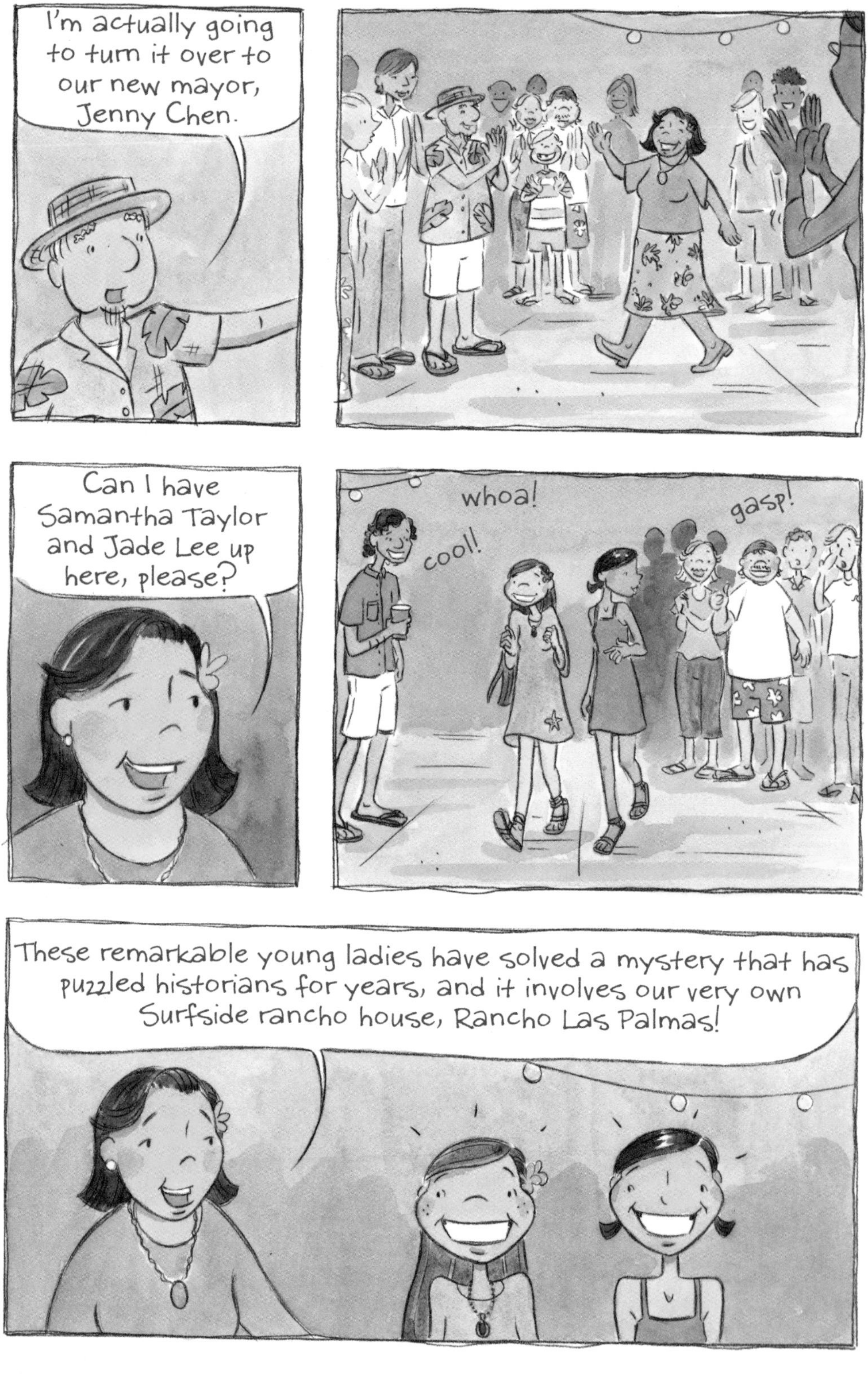
I'm actually going to turn it over to our new mayor, Jenny Chen.
Can I have Samantha Taylor and Jade Lee up here, please?
whoa!
cool!
gasp!
These remarkable young ladies have solved a mystery that has puzzled historians for years, and it involves our very own Surfside rancho house, Rancho Las Palmas!

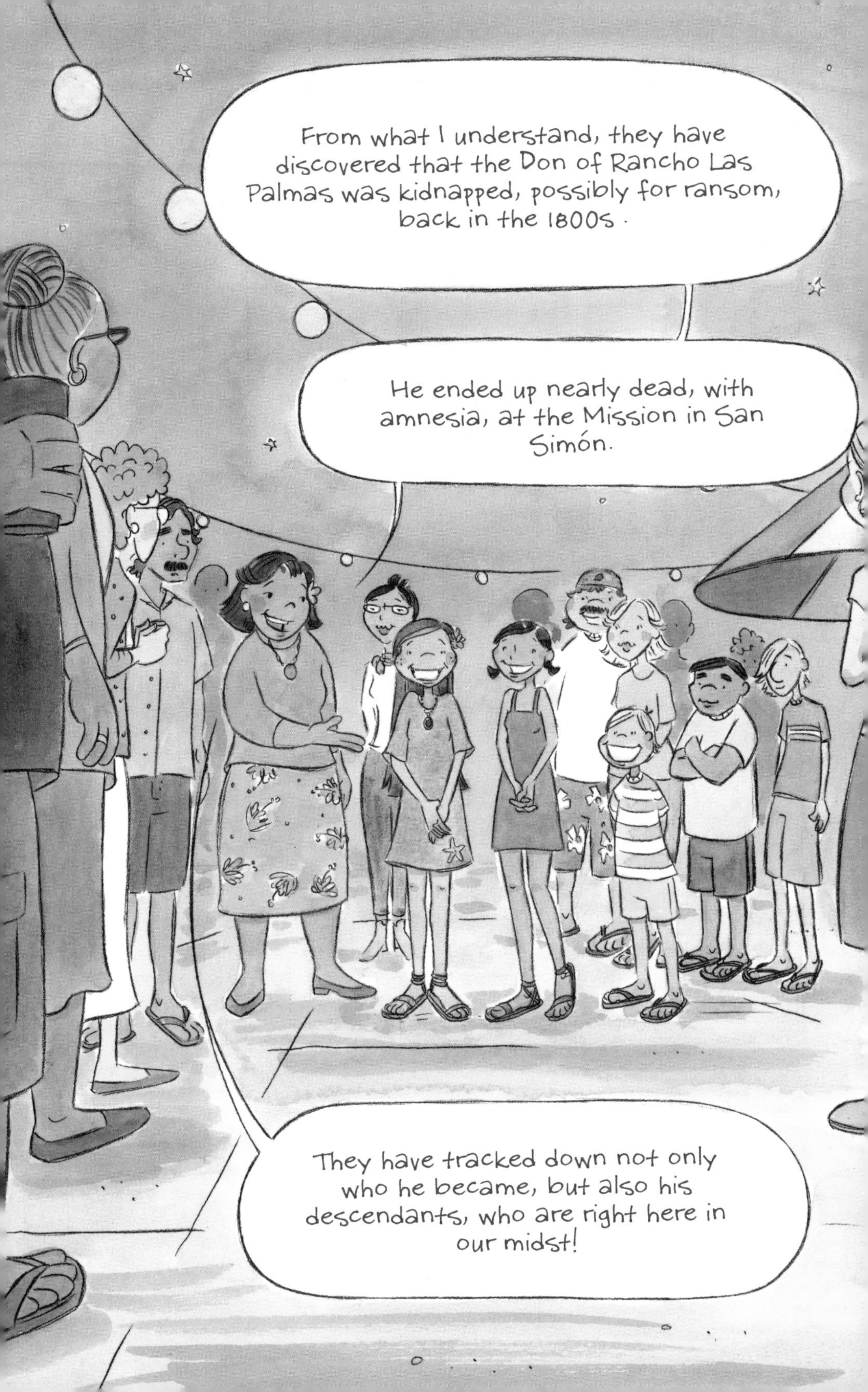
From what I understand, they have discovered that the Don of Rancho Las Palmas was kidnapped, possibly for ransom, back in the 1800s.
He ended up nearly dead, with amnesia, at the Mission in San Simón.
They have tracked down not only who he became, but also his descendants, who are right here in our midst!

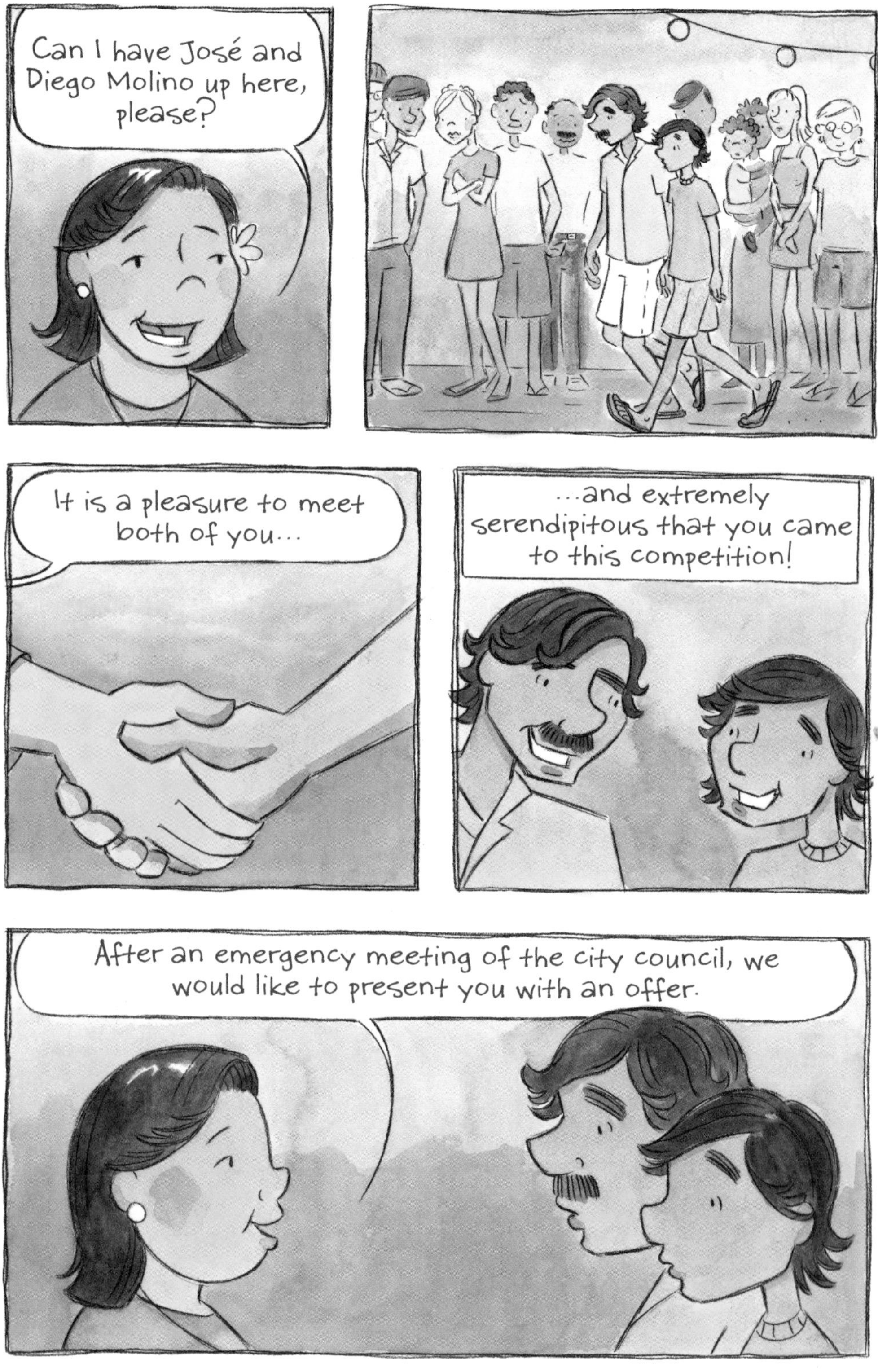
Can I have José and Diego Molino up here, please?
It is a pleasure to meet both of you...
...and extremely serendipitous that you came to this competition!
After an emergency meeting of the city council, we would like to present you with an offer.

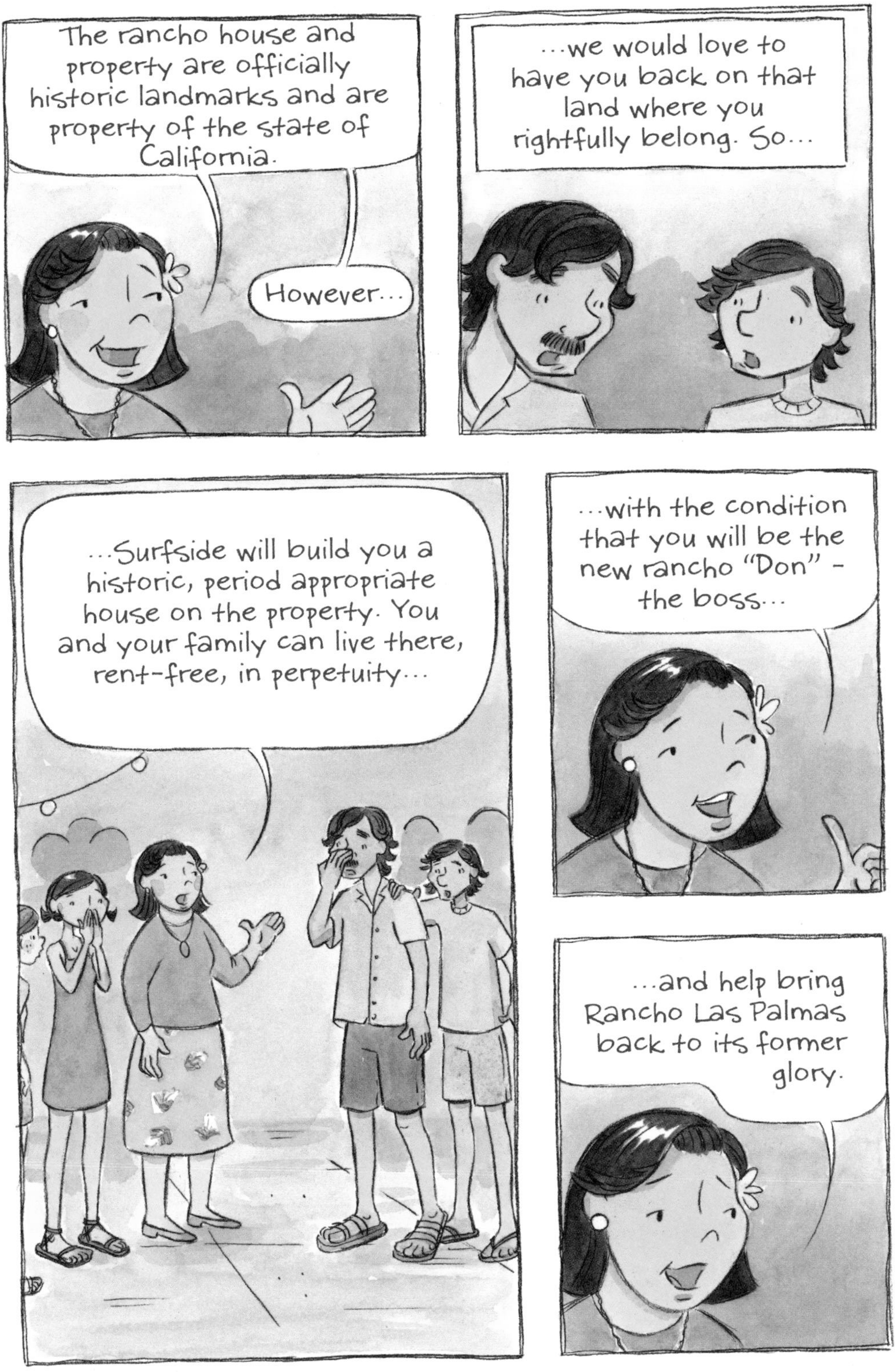
The rancho house and property are officially historic landmarks and are property of the state of California.
However...
...we would love to have you back on that land where you rightfully belong. So...
...Surfside will build you a historic, period appropriate house on the property. You and your family can live there, rent-free, in perpetuity...
...with the condition that you will be the new rancho "Don" - the boss...
...and help bring Rancho Las Palmas back to its former glory.

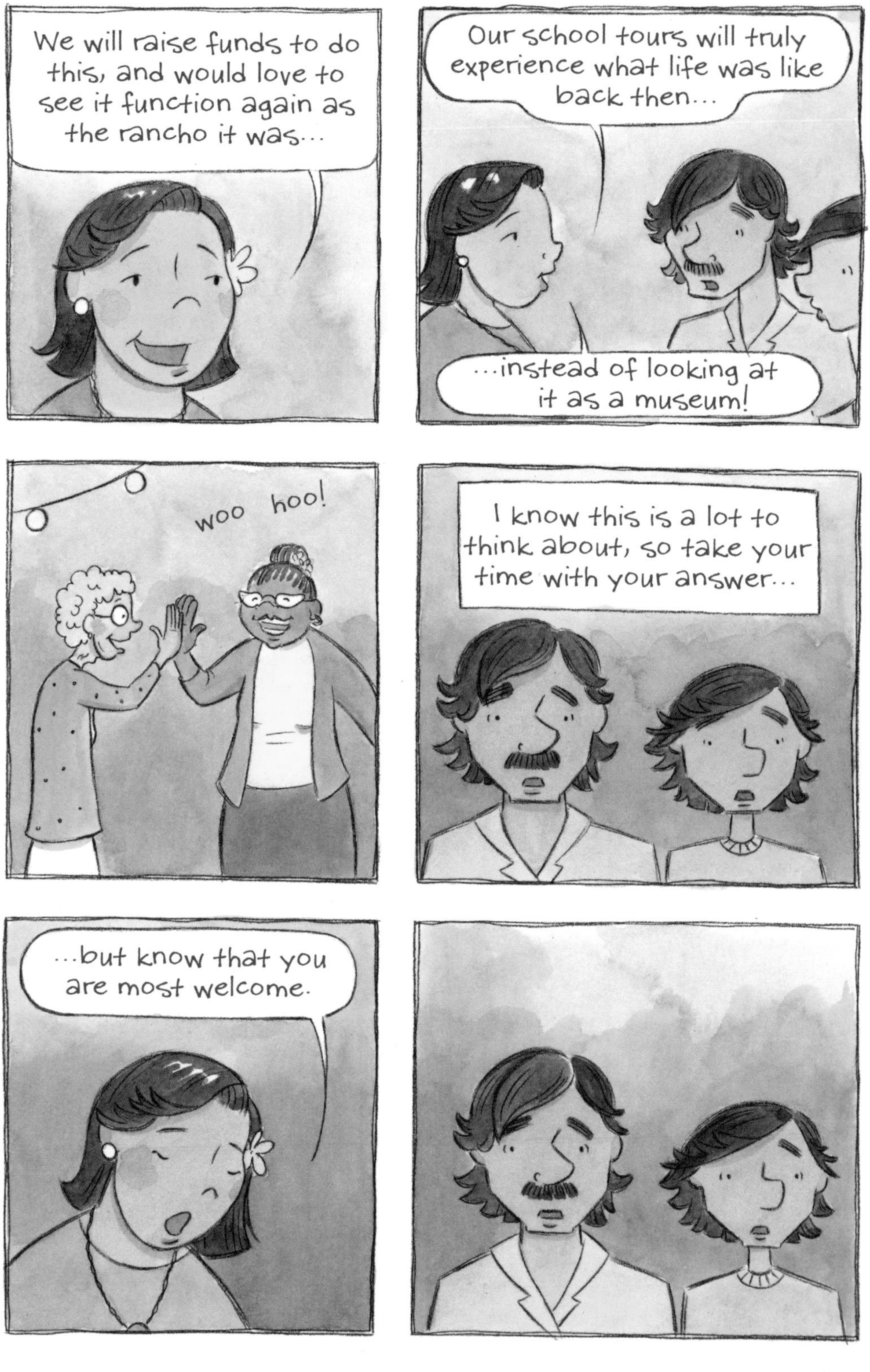
We will raise funds to do this, and would love to see it function again as the rancho it was...
Our school tours will truly experience what life was like back then...
...instead of looking at it as a museum!
woo hoo!
I know this is a lot to think about, so take your time with your answer...
...but know that you are most welcome.

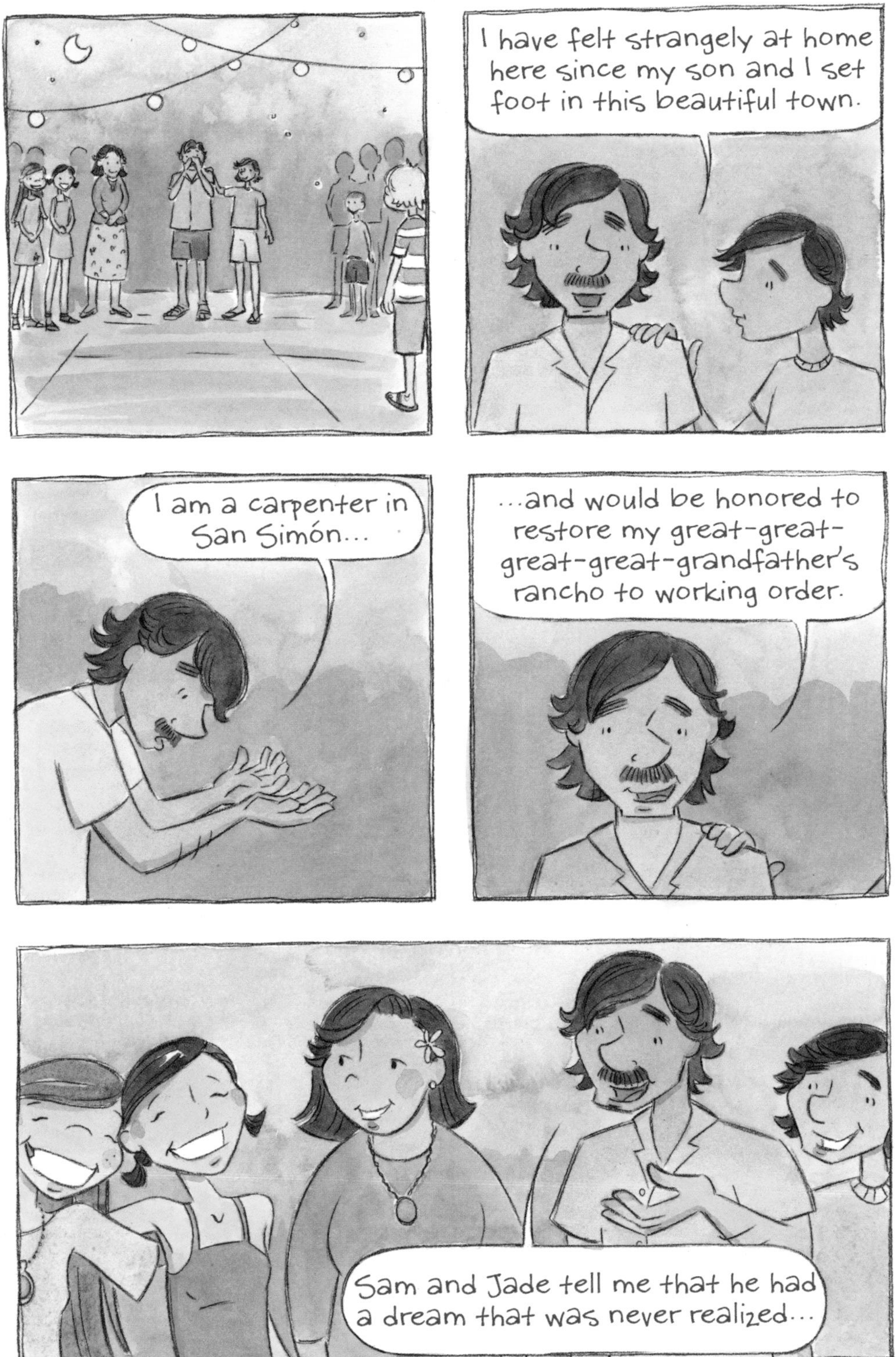
I have felt strangely at home here since my son and I set foot in this beautiful town.
I am a carpenter in San Simón...
...and would be honored to restore my great-great-great-great-grandfather's rancho to working order.
Sam and Jade tell me that he had a dream that was never realized...

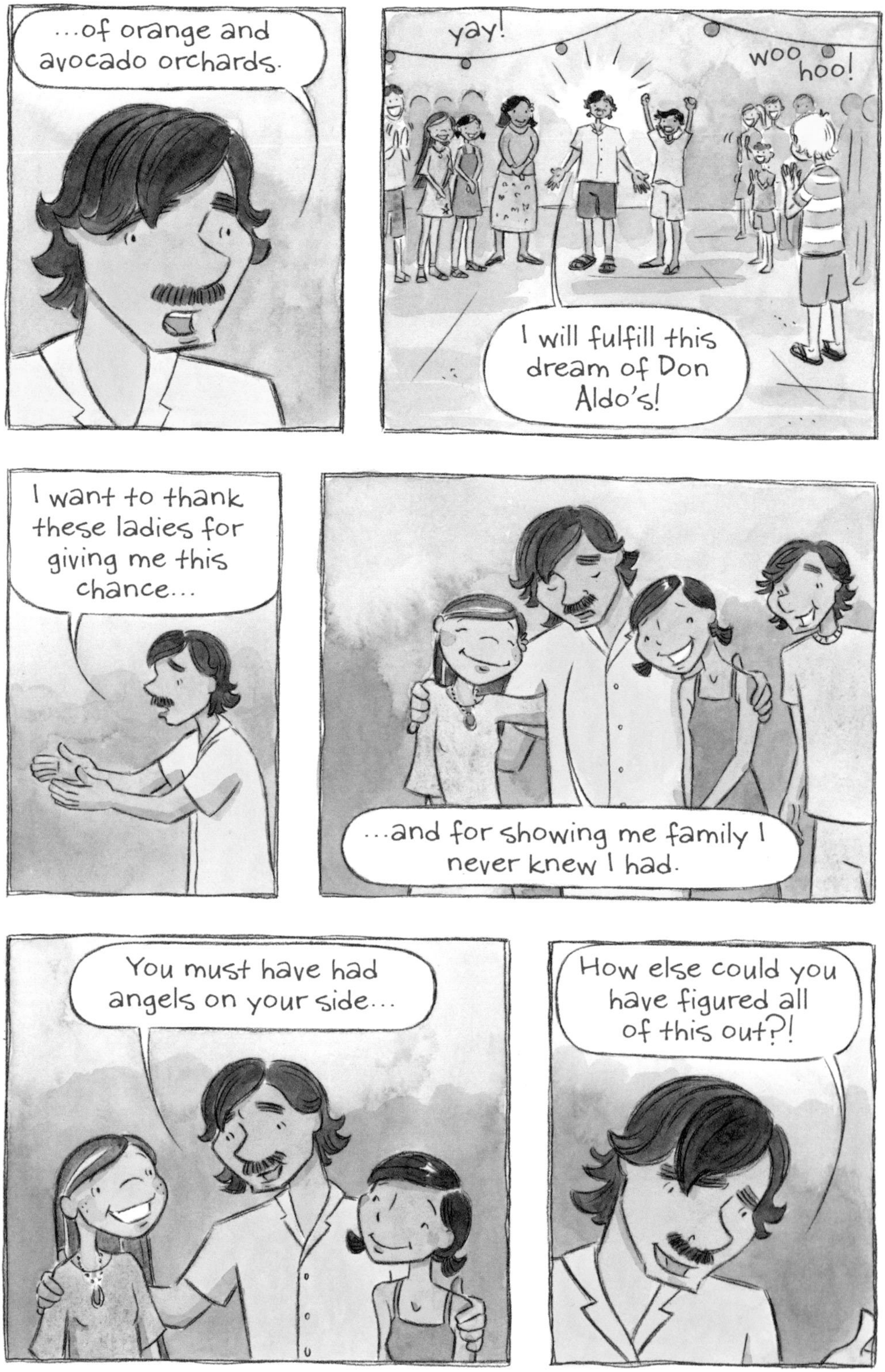
...of orange and avocado orchards.
yay!
woo hoo!
I will fulfill this dream of Don Aldo's!
I want to thank these ladies for giving me this chance...
...and for showing me family I never knew I had.
You must have had angels on your side...
How else could you have figured all of this out?!

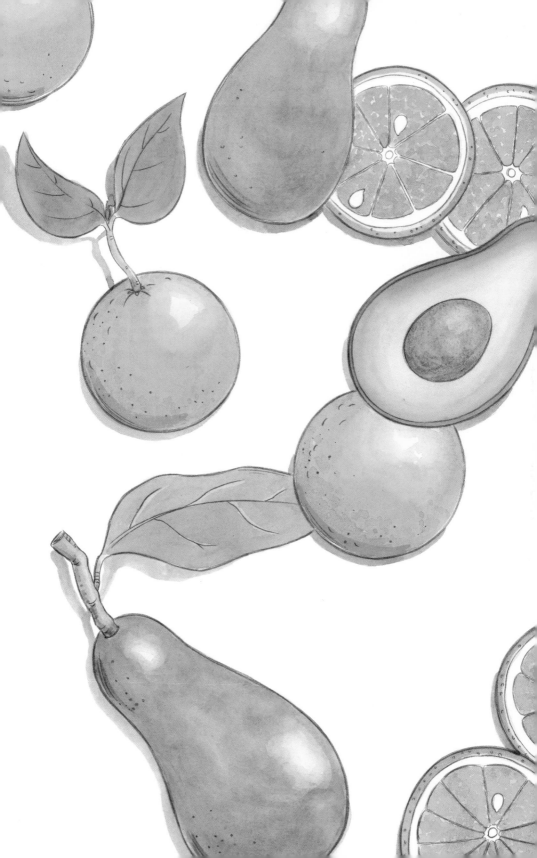

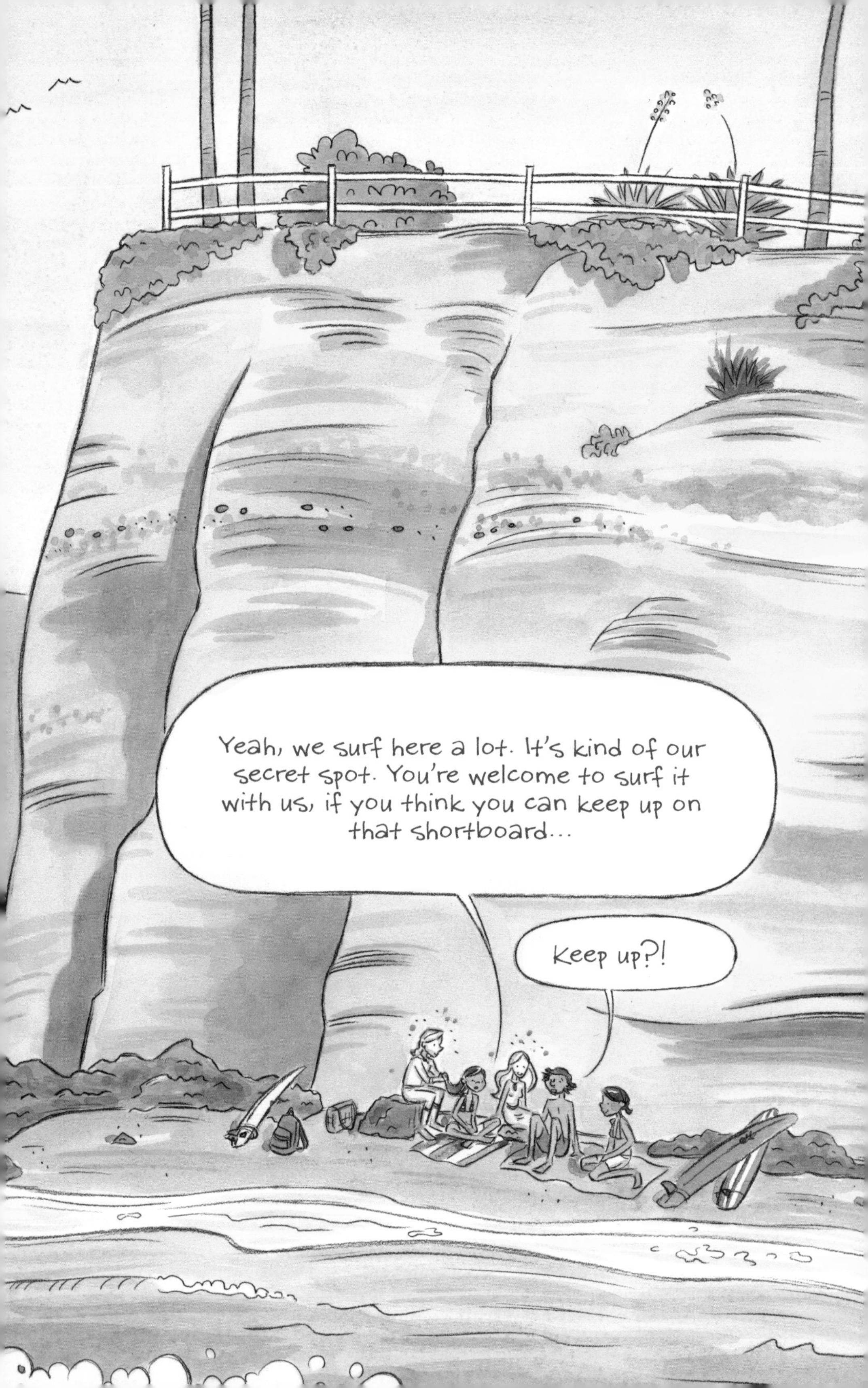
Yeah, we surf here a lot. It's kind of our secret spot. You're welcome to surf it with us, if you think you can keep up on that shortboard...
Keep up?!

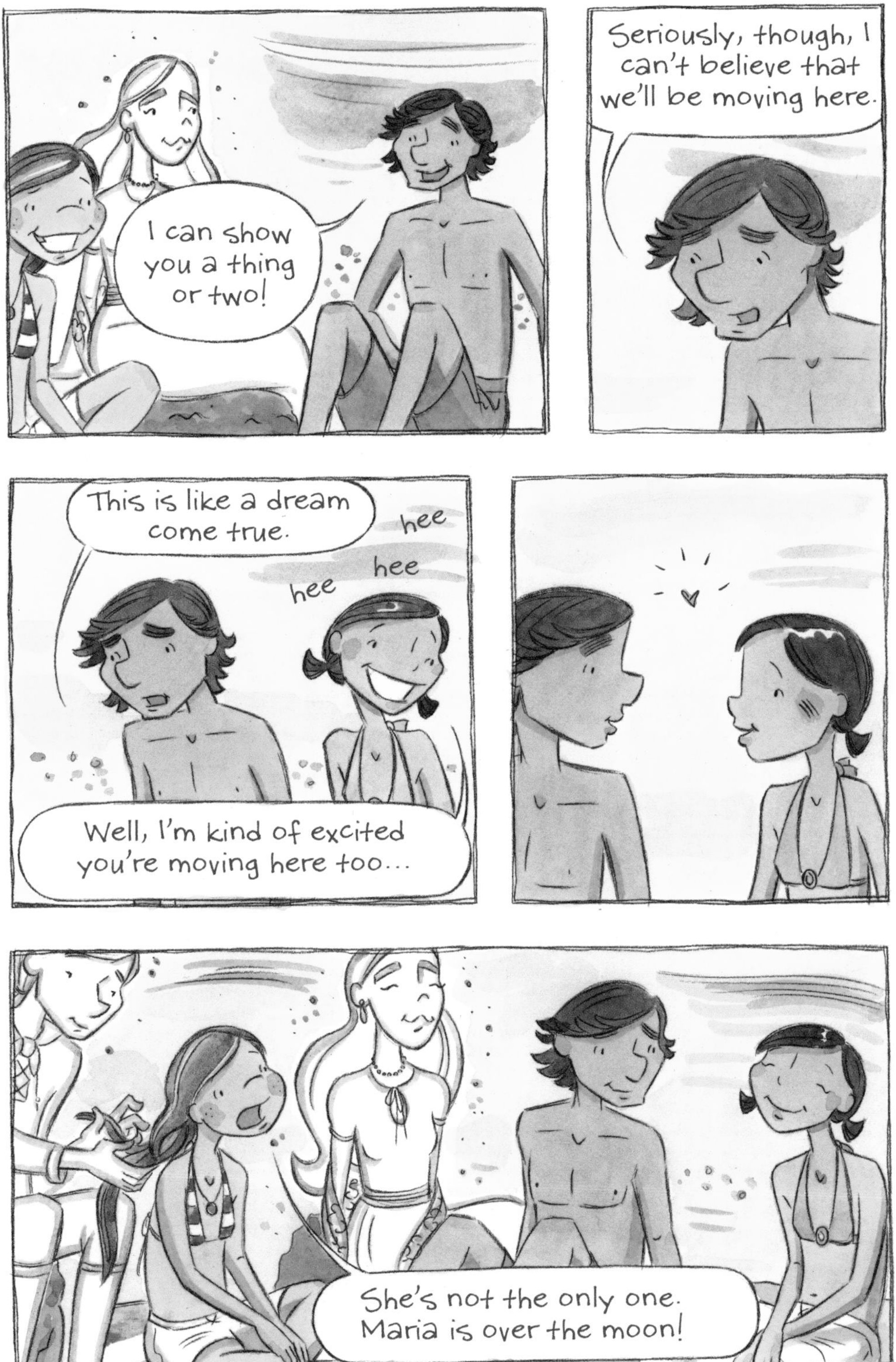
I can show you a thing or two!
Seriously, though, I can't believe that we'll be moving here.
This is like a dream come true.
hee
hee
hee
Well, I'm kind of excited you're moving here too...
She's not the only one. Maria is over the moon!

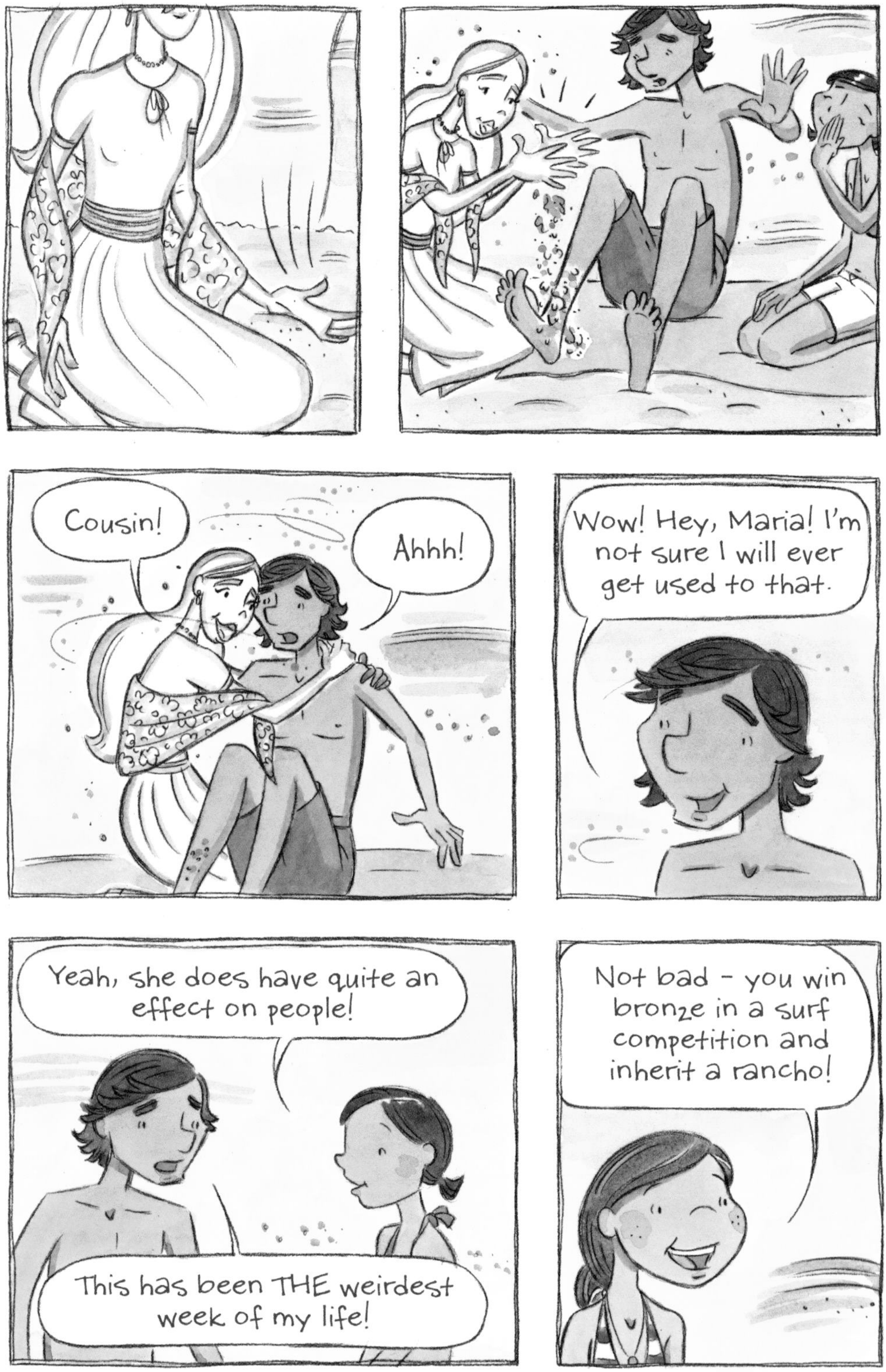
Cousin!
Ahhh!
Wow! Hey, Maria! I'm not sure I will ever get used to that.
Yeah, she does have quite an effect on people!
This has been THE weirdest week of my life!
Not bad - you win bronze in a surf competition and inherit a rancho!

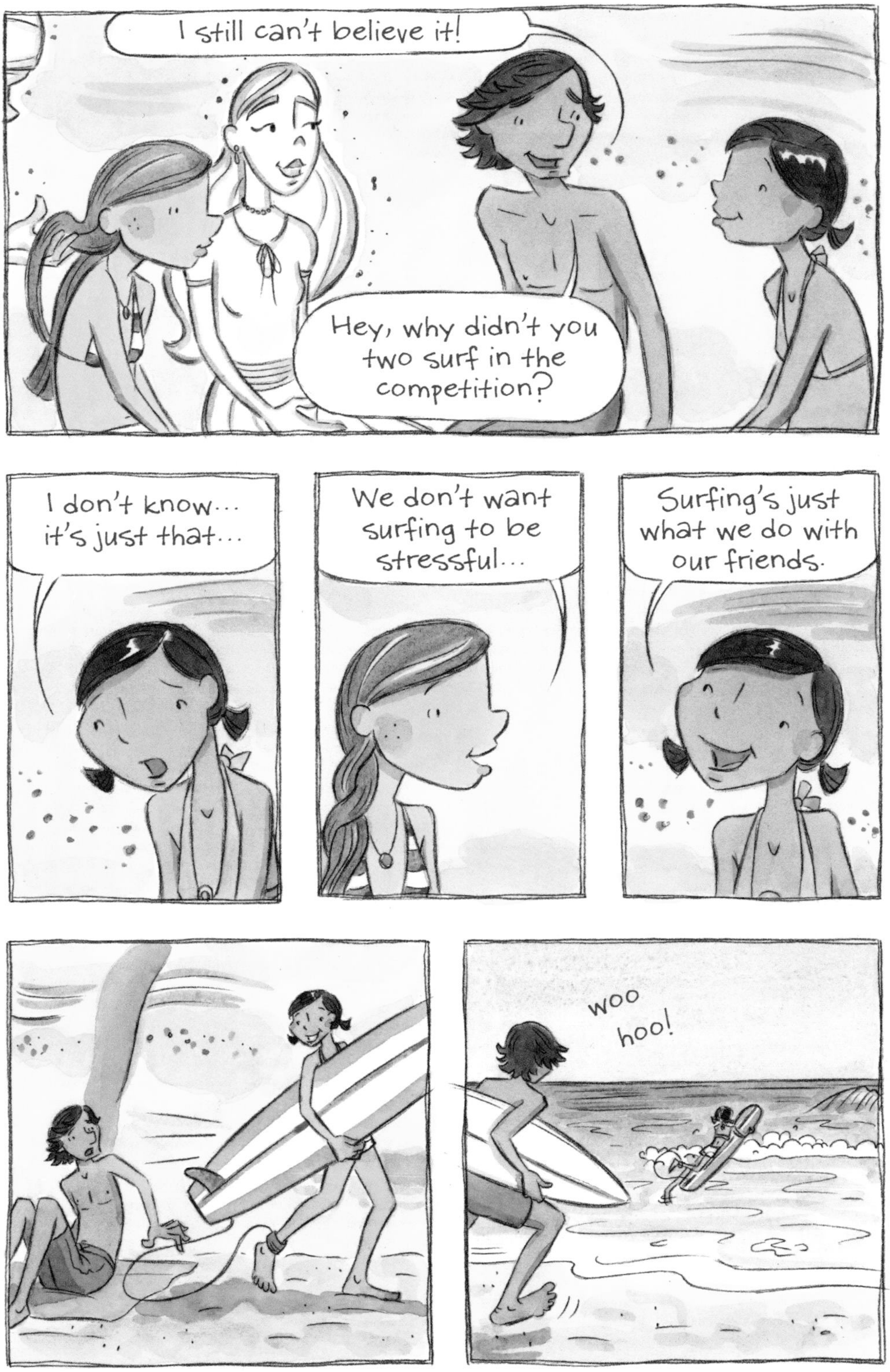
I still can't believe it!
Hey, why didn't you two surf in the competition?
I don't know... it's just that...
We don't want surfing to be stressful...
Surfing's just what we do with our friends.
woo hoo!

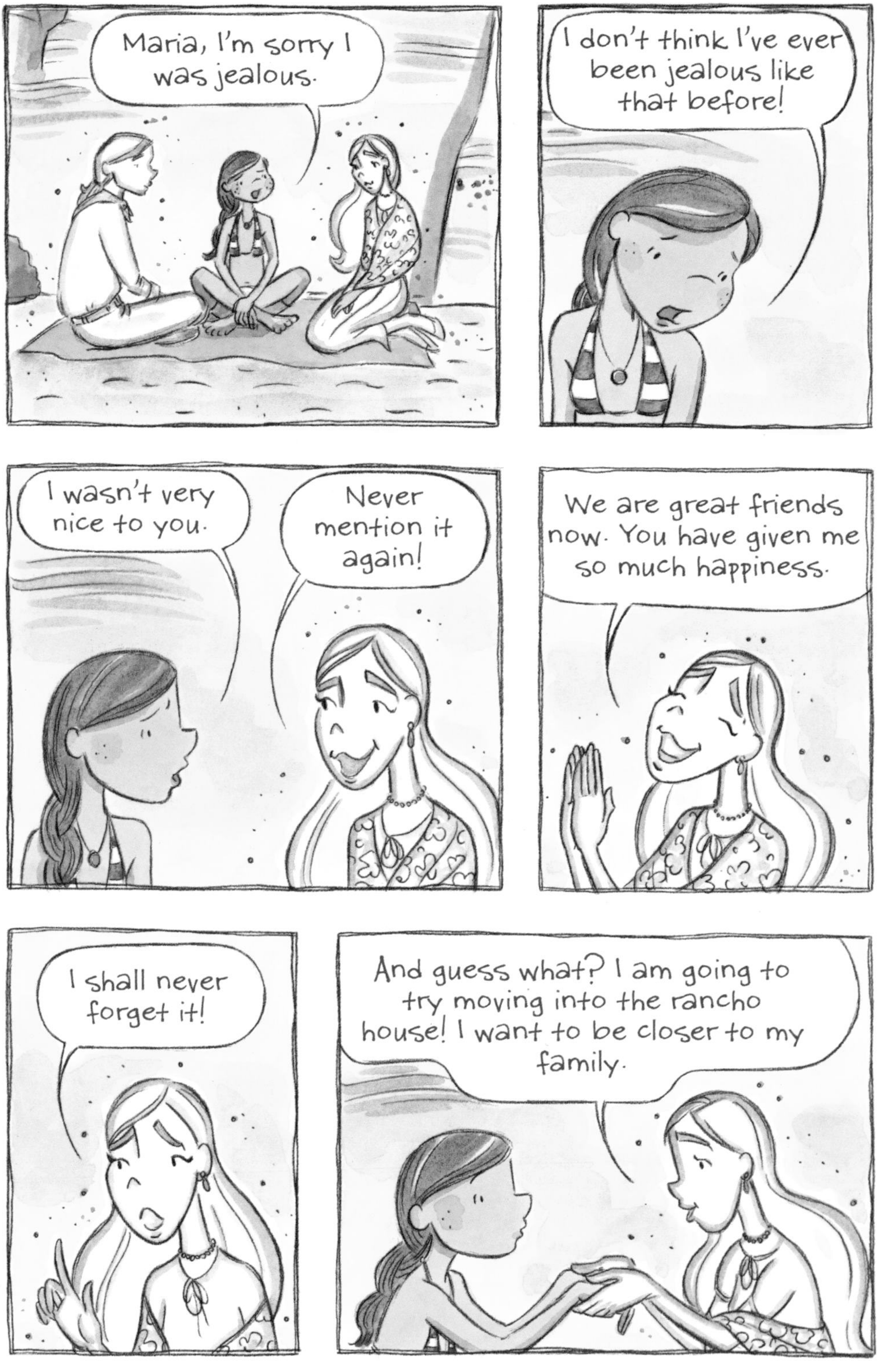
Maria, I'm sorry I was jealous.
I don't think I've ever been jealous like that before!
I wasn't very nice to you.
Never mention it again!
We are great friends now. You have given me so much happiness.
I shall never forget it!
And guess what? I am going to try moving into the rancho house! I want to be closer to my family.

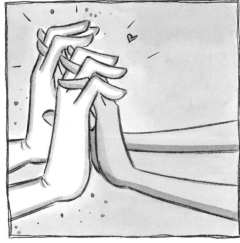

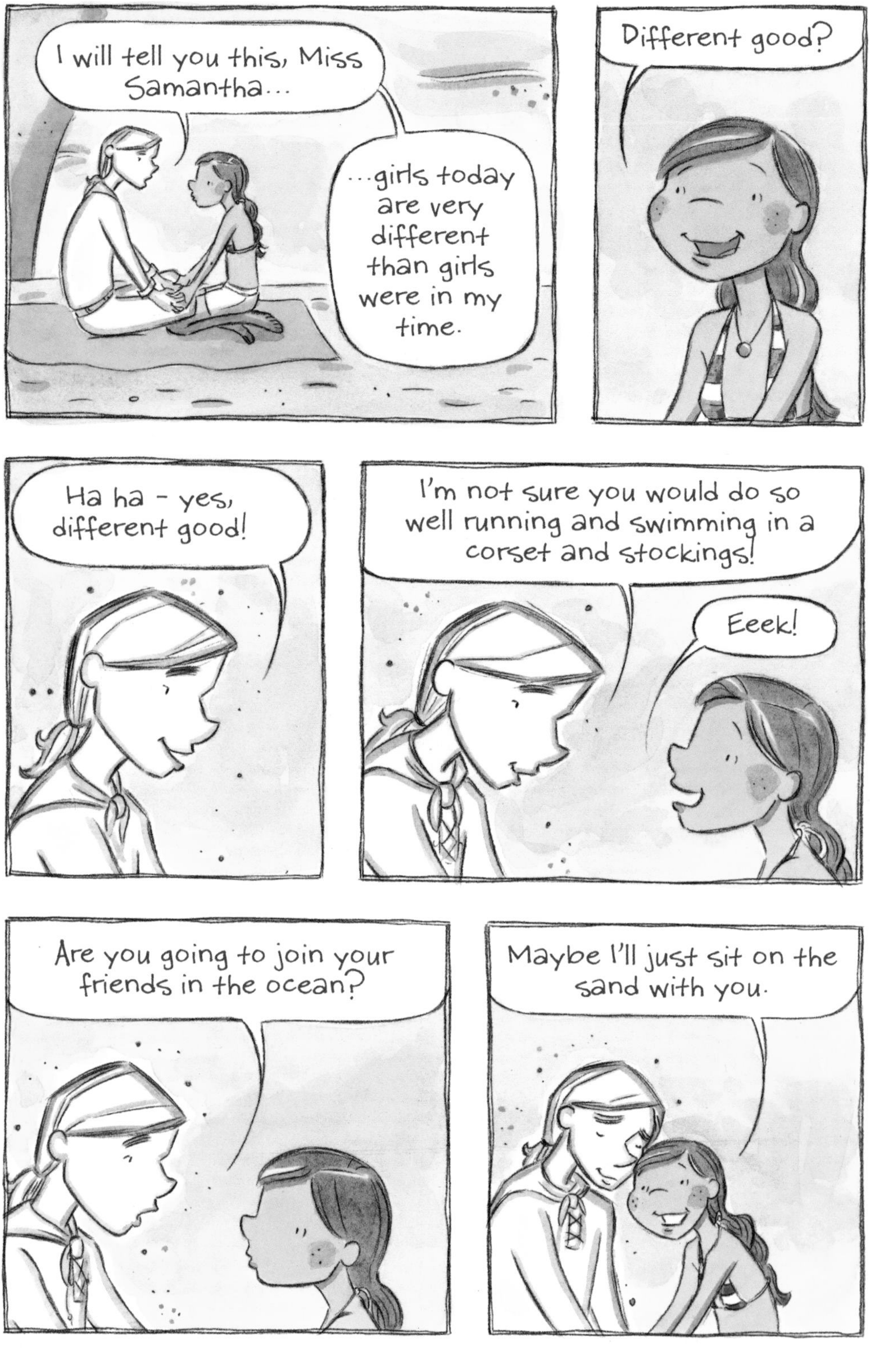
I will tell you this, Miss Samantha...
...girls today are very different than girls were in my time.
Different good?
Ha ha - yes, different good!
I'm not sure you would do so well running and swimming in a corset and stockings!
Eeek!
Are you going to join your friends in the ocean?
Maybe I'll just sit on the sand with you.

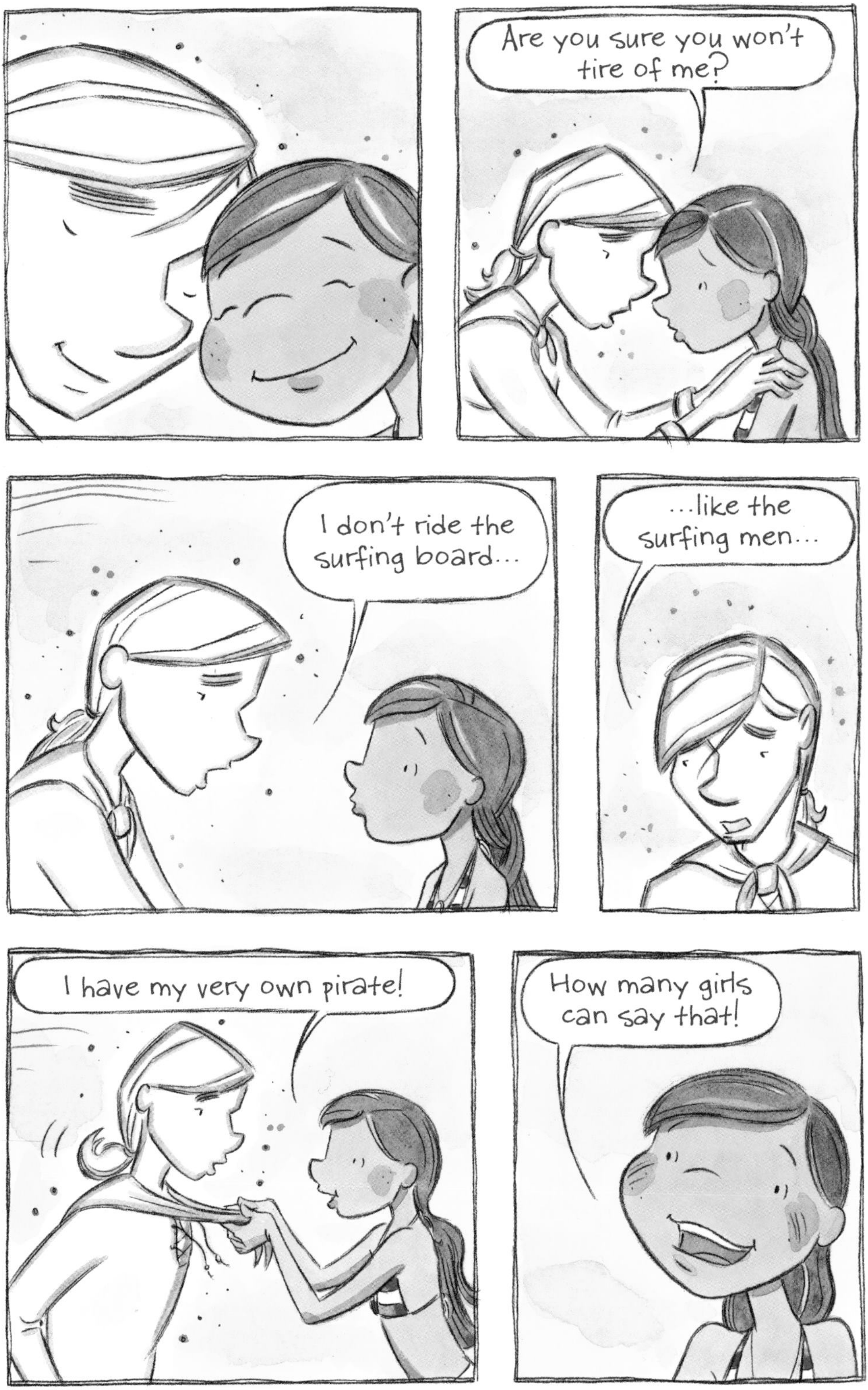
Are you sure you won't tire of me?
I don't ride the surfing board...
...like the surfing men...
I have my very own pirate!
How many girls can say that!

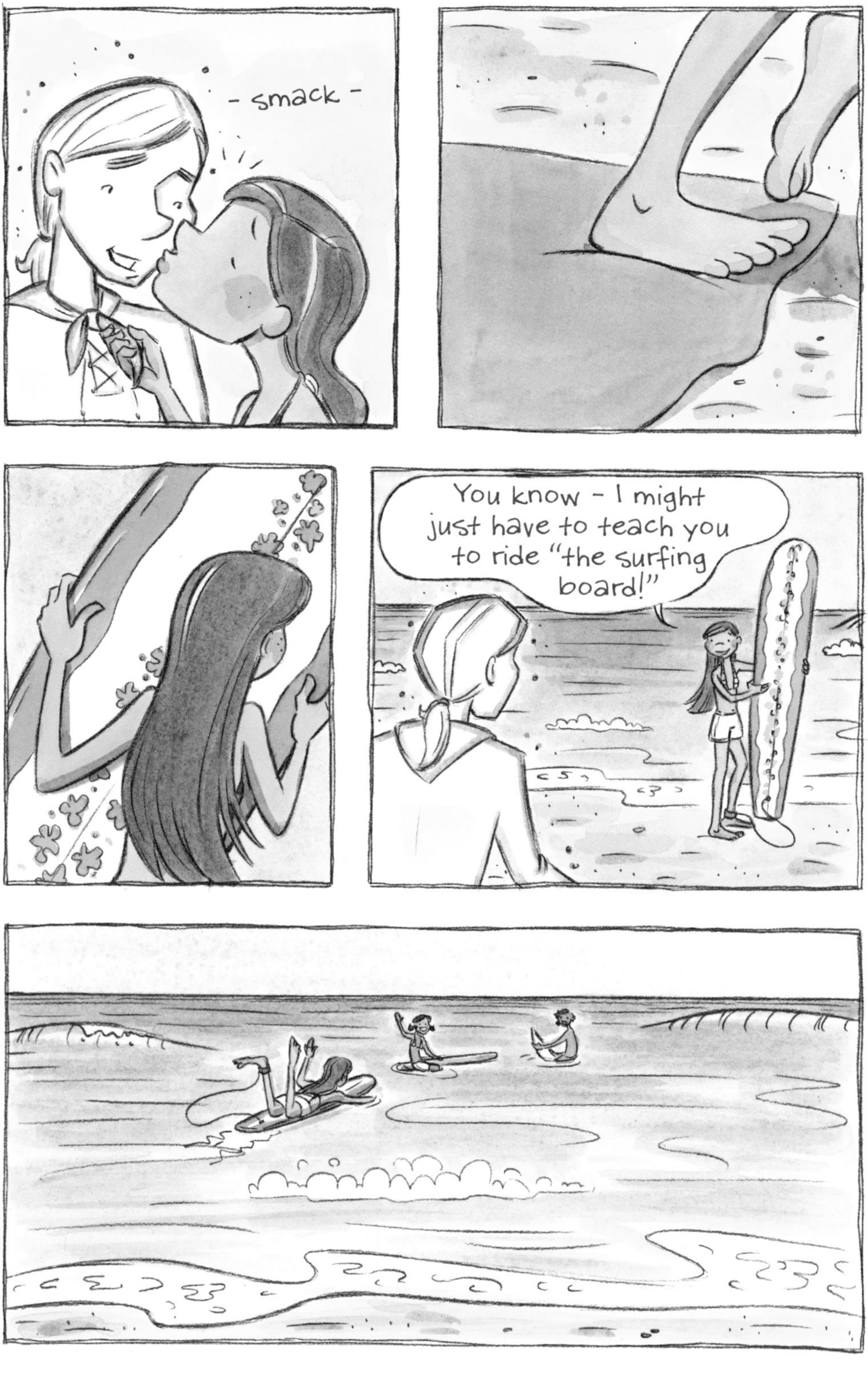
- smack -
You know - I might just have to teach you to ride "the surfing board!"

the
end

Dedicated to the beach. You are always there for me when I need you.

Oh – and to M and E, who are too.

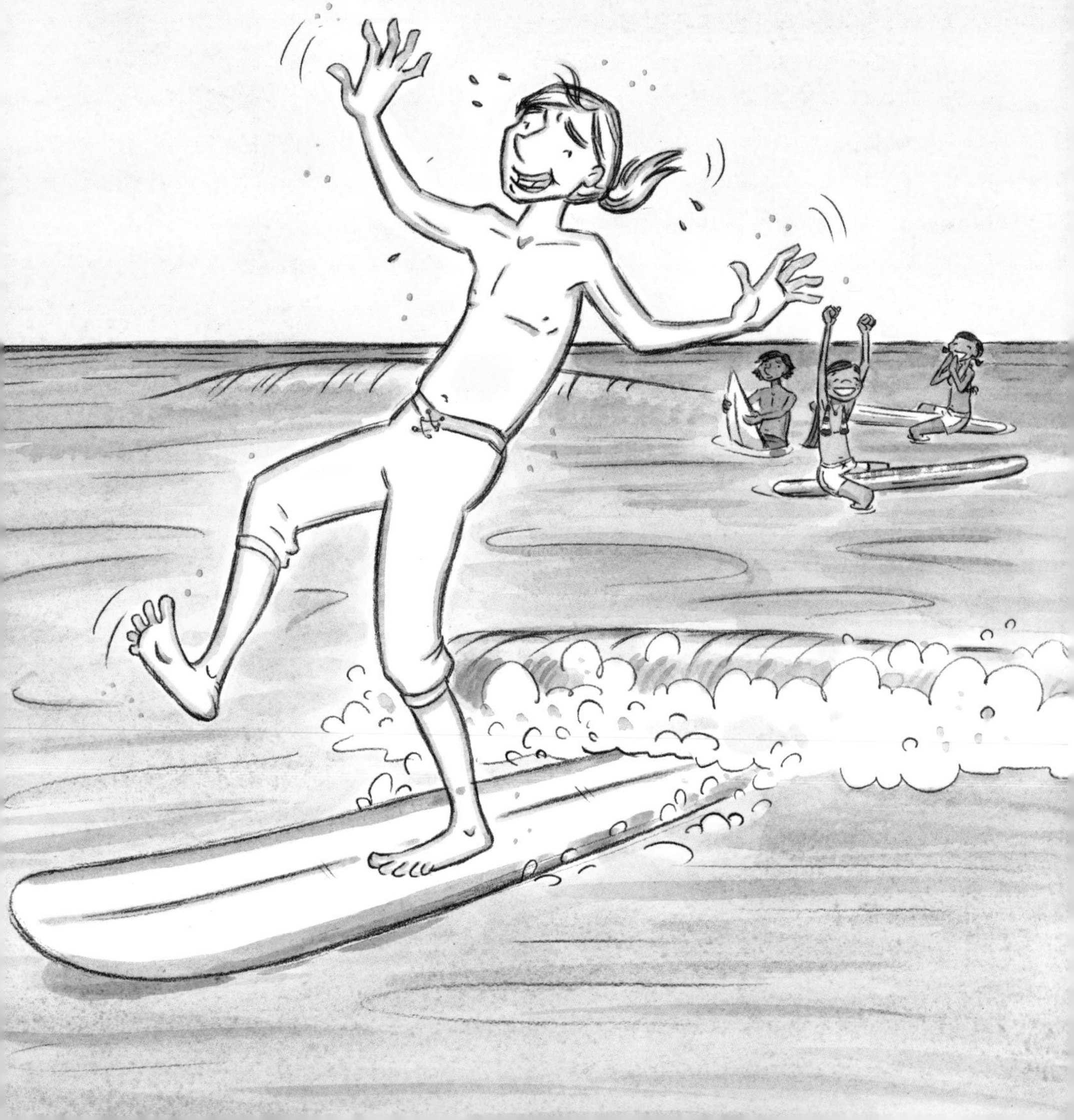

Also available from
KIM DWINELL:

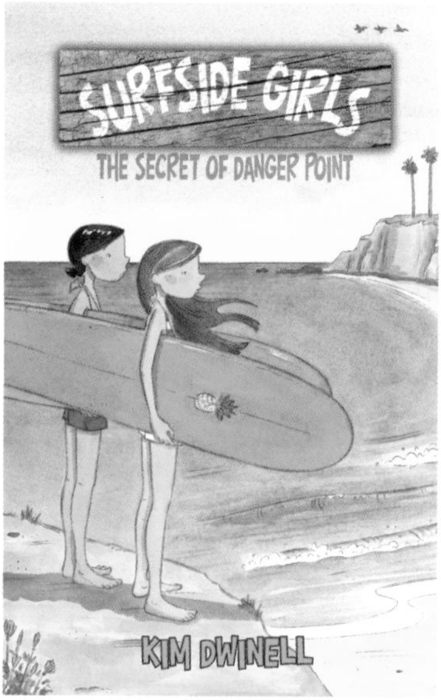
SURFSIDE GIRLS
THE SECRET OF DANGER POINT
KIM DWINELL

SURFSIDE GIRLS (Book One):
The Secret of Danger Point
ISBN 978-1-60309-411-5